BLURRED
FATES

PRAISE FOR *BLURRED FATES*

"A woman's seemingly perfect life unravels in this debut novel that explores what happens when past traumas resurface. . . . will keep readers glued to the page. . . . The author's tale is as chilling as it is affecting. . . . A hypnotic page-turner . . ."

—KIRKUS REVIEWS

"*Blurred Fates* is an unerring portrayal of the realities of trauma survival in an enthralling tale of tragedy, love, and betrayal. Broken family, sexual assault, infidelity, and ulterior motives—turning each page makes you cringe, gasp, then breathe and repeat. Zadeik's elegance on the page is captivating from start to finish."

—AMELIA ZACHRY, author of *Enough: A Memoir of Mistakes, Mania, and Motherhood*

"*Blurred Fates* is a beautifully written debut novel about love, betrayal, secrets, and the courage to speak the truth . . . whatever the consequences."

—SONDRA HELENE, author of *Appearances*

"In the haunting and finely written *Blurred Fates*, Anastasia Zadeik unravels themes of adultery, jealousy, crimes of passion, betrayal, loss, and guilt. It's impossible to not keep turning the pages, as Zadeik's voice leads us deeper and deeper into a compulsively readable plot that takes the reader from a place of shock and horror to understanding and clarity. Zadeik has written a psychological thriller that is touching, troubling, and ultimately a story of redemption."

—DONNA BROWN AGINS, author of NAACP Image Award–nominated *Maya Angelou: Diversity Makes for a Rich Tapestry*

BLURRED FATES

A Novel

ANASTASIA ZADEIK

SHE WRITES PRESS

Published 2022
Printed in the United States of America
Print ISBN: 978-1-64742-379-7
E-ISBN: 978-1-64742-380-3
Library of Congress Control Number: 2022900537

For information, address:
She Writes Press
1569 Solano Ave #546
Berkeley, CA 94707

Interior design by Mimi Bark

She Writes Press is a division of SparkPoint Studio, LLC.

All company and/or product names may be trade names, logos, trademarks, and/or registered trademarks and are the property of their respective owners.

This is a work of fiction. Names, characters, places, and incidents either are the product of the author's imagination or are used fictitiously. Any resemblance to actual persons, living or dead, is entirely coincidental.

PROLOGUE

I HAVE NO CHILDHOOD SNAPSHOTS. No picture of an infant Kathryn swathed in a pink hospital blanket, head still misshapen from her descent down the birth canal. No picture of one-year-old Katie clutching her favorite stuffed animal. No awkward school photos with Peter Pan collars, pigtails, or braces. No baby books, scrapbooks, or yearbooks. Other than a slightly worn copy of Beatrix Potter's *The Tale of Peter Rabbit*, acquired at age seventeen, and a dog-eared copy of William Faulkner's *The Sound and the Fury*, acquired at age nine, I have nothing tangible from my childhood.

The remarkable thing is that, while I have no pictures of my brother, Daniel, and I never see his face in my dreams, I can easily recall his features: stormy slate-blue eyes that remind me of the sky before it opens with rain; curly dirty-blond hair framing a chiseled face; the perpetual shadow of a beard; his broad mouth, lips taut in a permanent sneer. He is frozen for me at age nineteen—cynicism and evil wrapped in shorts and a Grateful Dead T-shirt.

It is this version of him that randomly appears across the street at a busy intersection, in the window of a passing car as I park at the grocery store, or in my rearview mirror as I drive home or to the kids' school for pickup. Rationally, I know it cannot be him—he would be nearly forty by now, his appearance dulled by age and ravaged by

1

his life choices. Yet when I see, or imagine I see, his nineteen-year-old face, my heart races, sweat forms, my foot presses on the gas, my vision blurs, and I forget for a moment where I am. I drive past my destination, hoping to lose him.

Then, as quickly as he appeared, he is gone.

I focus on breathing, in and out, cycling the mantra *Be here, not there.* I tell myself that a mentally unstable, drug-abusing drifter is unlikely to persist in efforts to find me. Nevertheless, Daniel holds the power of the past, and over the years, with an intuitive sense of terrifying unpredictability, he has reminded me to be afraid—of him, of what he knows, of who I might become.

A call. A letter. A message.

The first one—sixteen years ago, less than a month after I married Jacob—a late-afternoon shower interrupted by the sound of the phone. Thinking it would be my new husband calling, I reached for the nearest towel—meant for hands, not bodies—and grabbed the handset. Post-honeymoon bliss shattered as I stood dripping onto the hardwood floor.

"Well, I'll be damned."

Not Jacob.

"My little sister struck it rich."

Daniel.

I can recall it as if it happened yesterday. Chest-crushing, breath-taking, visceral fear slammed into me like a truck, jostling my brain, making coherent thought nearly impossible. *How did he find me?*

"Old lady down the street saw your picture in *The New York Times.* Told Dad you married some high-class dude. Whitman, Whittier, something like that. John, no, Jacob. Yeah, that was it. Jacob Whittier."

Shit. The wedding announcement.

"Look at you. Doing the family proud."

The whip of sarcasm caught me around the ribcage, making me immediately aware of my vulnerability—how hope had placed me at a disadvantage.

Daniel's raspy voice coiled to strike again. "Lady said she couldn't help but notice"—he gave a short laugh—"there wasn't much about the bride."

"Why are you calling?" I wanted to sound strong. What I heard was pathetic. "What do you want?"

"Since you ask, I'd have liked to meet the guy. Bond. You know... share stories."

I said nothing.

"Dad was crestfallen he didn't get an invite. Said he thinks about *you* all the time. I didn't want to burst his bubble, but I'm guessing Mr. Whittier doesn't know about us—me or dear old Dad."

You're wrong, I thought but didn't say. Jacob did know, and he hadn't argued to include my family in the wedding celebrations. Despite prodigious editing and edge-softening, the life story I'd provided had been barely palatable to him, let alone to his parents: motherless since age eleven; estranged from a neglectful father and troubled older brother; determined to escape and put the past behind me, whatever the cost.

"Do you want money?" I asked.

"Money?" Daniel snorted. "Sorry to disappoint, little bitch, it won't be that easy. I don't need your fucking money, or should I say your husband's fucking money. Got an enterprise of my own. No, I'm just calling to remind you, I know what you've done, and as the saying goes..." His voice slowed to a crawl, each word enunciated: "You can run, but you can't—"

I yanked the phone from my ear, let "hide" drop away into silence.

Shivering, staring at my bedraggled image in the mirror, I weighed the risks and merits of coming clean to Jacob—for all of about thirty seconds. Not for the first time, I realized the truth would not set me free.

Phone numbers could be changed. Unlisted.

Secrets buried.

Family legacy suppressed.

For a while, it appeared my reasoning was sound. Six years went by without a word from my brother. But then a letter arrived. My name in block letters. The upper left corner complete with "D Barton" over a return address for the Federal Correctional Institute at Mendota. Inside, a simple message: "Out in four. I'll be in touch."

I took more precautions: a post-office box, new phone numbers, aliases on social media.

Four years went by—then another, and another—with no contact from Daniel.

Hope bubbled up again.

Until six months ago. An Unknown message in my voicemail box. A dry cough. That voice.

"My, my, little sister, actually took some work to track you down." The raspy short laugh. "Looks like things are going real well. Shame. All that running, for nothing." And then, the slow enunciation: "You can't hide. Remember this: I'll always find you."

I am propelled back to seventeen. Daniel standing over me, his hands clenching and unclenching with rage. The taste of iron in my mouth. "I'll always find you." Words like blows, punctuated with solid kicks. Curling inward, I wrap my arms around my head. Burning pain radiates from my cheekbone, jaw, and lower back.

I hear the door slam, shaking it in its frame, a cracking sound like glass breaking, and my father's slurred "What the hell's going on?"

And I hear Daniel's clear reply: "She's fucking crazy."

Here and now, miles and years away, I pray Daniel is wrong. But I fear he may be very, very right. His words ring in my head, reverberating through the darkness of memories, faulty synapses, and uneven neurotransmitters. Like magma stored in the core of the earth—pressurized, roiling, looking for an opening, waiting to scorch and destroy.

I change my number, again. I watch for him. I wait.

And I learn that, in the end, anticipating disaster does not prepare you for it. Life can change in the space of a heartbeat: tectonic plates shift, a violent squall strikes, a weakened vessel breaks, the phone rings, a lie is told.

Quite suddenly, an ordinary day becomes the last ordinary day.

ONE

HOMEMADE TOMATO SAUCE is simmering, the salad is tossed, and the pasta is just about al dente. I turn to call out to the kids that dinner is ready, and I'm startled to see Jacob standing next to the island, watching me. I wonder how it is I didn't hear him come in or feel his presence in the room.

"Hey, I didn't know you were there," I say before returning my attention to the stovetop. "Can you get the kids?"

He doesn't answer, so I turn my head again. "Honey?"

And then I notice—his expression is strange, indecipherable.

I feel an immediate sense of disorientation, the feeling that what is about to transpire will be life-altering, though I have no idea how or why. My hand stops mid-stir as my breath catches. I stand there, silently acknowledging the randomness of the moment. Of all things. For here I am, simply making dinner like I always do, day after day, in this *Architectural Digest*–worthy kitchen I don't need and certainly don't deserve, and I know my world is about to go haywire and there is nothing I can do to stop it.

All this from my husband's expression.

Jacob is an open book of limited pages: happiness, concern, mild disappointment, pride, and, most often, equable contentment. An old-money upbringing combined with a natural tendency toward restraint has produced a man devoted to subdued appropriateness. Allowed emotions are kept on a short lead. Disallowed emotions are bottled up tight and cellared. After nearly two decades together, I've rarely seen him head down the cellar stairs.

Reading the open book is easy. Happy is, well, happy—a genuine, though muted, smile and lightly crinkled eyes. Disappointment presents with a slight downward, diagonal tilt of his head, a firm jaw, lips sealed in a line. Contentment, his go-to expression, would best be described as pleasantly neutral everything.

Indecipherable is instantly, deeply troubling.

"Are you okay?" I ask, hoping he will answer with his standard, "All good, babe," and his face will revert to recognizable, neutral content.

Instead, I'm met with more silence and a pleading glance. No, not quite pleading—more like reluctance and a bit of frustration.

"Kathryn," he says.

And I know, it's real. Jacob does not call me by my given name. It's always "Kate," "babe," "honey." His face clouds over again, but I know whatever this is—it is significant. I recall hearing him on the phone earlier, the cadence of his voice strained. Long silences. I thought it was a business call, a dissatisfied client. Now I consider other possibilities. His mother is ill. The doctor's office called about the tests I had done a week ago.

Or, *oh my God, Daniel.*

A bubble of fear forms inside me.

"That call," I say.

Jacob's nod is barely perceptible. "There's something I need to tell you, about those tests . . ."

It was the doctor's office. Not Daniel. But Jacob's face says it all. Something's wrong, something serious. Cancer. The kids are so little. I look down, see red, and realize I've dropped the wooden spoon on the counter, splattering sauce.

"They called with the results?" I ask, but as soon as the words leave my mouth, I'm confused. Jacob couldn't have received the results because our concierge doctor uses this recorded system that requires typing in a personalized code, and Jacob doesn't know my code, so how could he know the results? My thoughts tumble one on top of the other, so many that I wonder how they fit into the space between my question and his reply.

"No, no. It wasn't the doctor. I shouldn't have said that." His expression is now clearly one of frustration. "I mean, it isn't about you or the tests."

I'm relieved for a split second, until Jacob's face contorts into a grimace. "Well, not really."

Jacob does not grimace, ever. My hand moves to my throat.

"What do you mean, not really?" I ask.

"I mean . . ." He shakes his head, sighs audibly. "I don't know how to tell you this."

"Whatever it is, Jacob, just tell me."

"Okay," he says—then repeats himself, "Okay," looking at me as he nods, like we've agreed to something. "Remember when I was in the city a couple of months ago and I extended the trip so the guys could take me out for my birthday?"

Though he ends with a slight up tone, I know it's not really a question, and this question that's not a question and the abrupt change in the direction of the conversation throw me. *Of course* I remember. Jacob stayed two extra days on his monthly trip to the East Coast—smack in the middle of a visit from his mother and Logan and Becca's regional soccer tournaments, which were being held hours apart. It was incredibly bad timing.

"Yes," I say, trying to not let the irritation from then enter now. "I remember."

"Right," he says. "So, I know I told you we went to a game and dinner, but there was more."

He looks down.

"We went out afterwards, it turned into a really long night, and somehow we ended up doing shots at this club on the West Side, at which point I was exceedingly drunk." He looks up to gauge my response. "I think the correct term would be wasted."

"*You* were *wasted,*" I say, "at a *club?*"

None of this is making sense. Jacob does not grimace or pound shots or go to clubs. He drinks fine wine at white-linen restaurants or a single craft beer after docking his sailboat.

"Yes," he says solemnly. "I was. I don't remember anything, really, after the shots. I must have blacked out or something, and as you can imagine, I certainly wasn't proud, so I put it out of my mind. But then, just now, I was talking with Ryan—that's who the call was from—and I mentioned how you've been worried maybe something's wrong, that you had these tests done . . ."

I stare at him, trying to process what he's saying, as the conversation veers further toward surreal. Questions spin along with his statements: Jacob blacked out? Why does he keep talking about the tests? And why is he talking to anyone, even Ryan, about such a personal thing?

What emerges from my lips with equal parts confusion and righteous anger is "Wait, what? You were talking to Ryan about—?" I look down. "Why? Why would you do that?"

"Why would I do that?" Jacob asks incredulously. "He's my best friend, Kate—no, he's *our* best friend—and I'm worried about you."

He does seem worried. Sympathy briefly flitters in; I would do the same thing if I were worried about him, and Ryan *is* our best friend—first his, then mine, then ours.

"So this *is* about me."

The grimace returns.

"There's no good way to tell you this." He presses his lips together and exhales audibly, shaking his head, like he can't believe he's got to say what he's about to say. "The club was a strip club, Kate. Apparently, the guys bought champagne for this private room and then, according to Ryan, they bought me a lap dance, for my birthday. And the woman, the stripper . . ." He pauses, repeats the exhaling head shake. "She gave me a, you know, a . . ." He glances down at his crotch and then back up at me.

No, I think, *no*. He swore he didn't need that from me, from anyone.

The bubble of fear inside changes shape and texture. Expanding. Creating pressure.

"I'm sorry, Kate," he says, reaching for me. But that can't be right; he can't be reaching for me, not as he tells me this.

I lean back, away, as I hear Jacob's voice go on, "I don't have any symptoms. But apparently that doesn't mean anything. She could have given me something, and I could have given it to you, unwittingly."

Comprehension is sudden. *How did I not see it?* This is about a sexually transmitted infection. After my last appointment, I told Jacob how the doctor had insisted on running a bunch of tests— standard procedure and all that—and how I'd objected, explaining it was impossible for me to have an STI. Now Jacob is telling me it was *not* impossible—that it is, rather, entirely possible that I could have a sexually transmitted infection. Contracted from a stripper. From a stripper's mouth. In a bar. From an act he does not remember. *This* is what is impossible. How can he not remember this?

The pressure builds inside and out. I can hear it, like a low buzz, the sound of a heavy freight train straining the tracks.

"Honey?" Jacob says, tentatively, breaking my stunned silence.

Questions fly, unprocessed, raw.

"Are you saying I have an STI? From a stripper? Is that what you're saying?"

Jacob, quiet, stands there with a pained expression on his face—like *he's* been wronged somehow—which angers me. My voice accelerates, crescendos.

"You've given me an STI from a stripper unwittingly? Is that what you said? *Unwittingly?*"

The train is thundering down, metal on metal, steel, smoke, and steam. The ground beneath me seems to move, triggering tremors from within. Darkness clouds the periphery of my vision. Jacob's face blurs.

"I didn't . . ." Jacob stops, starts again. "I don't remember any of it."

"How is that possible?" I ask, even louder. "How is it possible you don't remember a stripper giving you a—"

"Kate!" Jacob reaches for my arm. "Keep your voice down. The kids are right down the hall."

His tone is harsh, disapproving.

I jerk out of his grasp and step back. Although he's right, the suggestion that somehow, now, at this moment, *I'm* the one who is behaving badly only fuels the fire that has ignited inside my head, the cracking-open in my body.

"Are you saying I'm doing something wrong?" I say, seething but not yelling. "You've contracted an STI from a stripper, but *I'm* the one doing something wrong?"

The heat inside me swirls. I hear my mother, cursing at my father for wrongs done.

Don't, I think to myself. *Don't say it.*

I lower my voice to just above a whisper. "Fuck you, Jacob."

Jacob reels as if I have struck him. Foul language does not befit a Whittier. Swearing at your spouse is definitely off-limits. The Barton in me is rising, hot and dangerous.

I bring my hands to my chest as the room begins to spin.

"Kate, you need to breathe. You need to calm down and breathe."

Of course, he's right. Again. I need to breathe. Somehow, though, the fact that he's right about this makes me even angrier. I have a right to be upset, and he has no right to be right about anything.

"Seriously, Kate." Jacob stands in front of me with his hands palms up in supplication. A look of concern on his face. "Breathe."

So I do. I close my eyes, bow my head, and force myself to take a breath. But instead of growing calmer, in the darkness I see Jacob with his arms splayed across a black leather booth, the head of a dark-haired woman between his knees. Psychedelic blue and purple lights pulse across his face to bass-thumping music.

And then another image emerges from the depths, as if released by the train and the tremors, black and white and red, blurring with the first, a young girl with her hands held firm by others. Loud voices. Coarse laughter. Too many hands, everywhere.

I cannot stop it. I can never stop it.

Instant shame.

I breathe in through my nose, sparking an involuntary shudder. I blow out through pursed lips and bring my hands down, rigid and flexed, against my thighs.

"Bring it in, Kate," my therapist, Dr. Farber, has told me. "Focus on the here and now, and what you can control. Remove yourself from the situation if you can."

I try to focus on anything other than the images I've conjured and the rage now threatening to overtake me. I hear Jacob, mere feet away. I force myself to breathe—inhale, exhale. Another shudder. I move my arms and feel the hard, cold marble counter at the small of my back. I hear the tomato sauce and water bubbling on the stovetop. If I don't drain the pasta, it will be mushy, inedible. Jacob has ruined dinner.

Jacob has ruined everything.

Memories press against my will, but I need to stay here, in the present. Removing myself from the situation is not an option because I need to take care of my children. Logan and Becca need to eat so they can take their showers and go to bed. I cannot leave.

Jacob must remove himself. *He* has to leave. Now.

"Kate?"

I slowly lift my head and open my eyes to see Jacob's face, still concerned. *How often has he lied to me with that face on?* I think. *How often have I misread him?* What a fool I've been.

"You have to go," I say. "You have to leave. You can come back later, when the kids are in bed."

"Kate, please."

"Please?" I say, clenching my hands at my side. "I can't do this, Jacob—not like this. Not now. Please. Leave."

The colander is already in the sink. I placed it there a minute before Jacob derailed our lives with this, whatever this is. I reach into the drawer by the stove for the pair of yellow paisley oven mitts I spent twenty minutes choosing last Tuesday at Williams Sonoma— deliberating over yellow paisley, red paisley, blue stripe, Tuscan fruit print—when I thought oven mitts mattered.

"I'm not leaving," Jacob says. "I'll tell the kids it'll be a while till dinner. I want to explain what happened, so we can get through this and move on."

As I walk from stove to sink, the heavy, steaming pot in my hands, I see that he is now wearing his reasonable face, the one he uses when those around him—difficult clients, poorly informed partners, bickering children—are being unreasonable. His calculated effort to control the situation with a dispassionate demeanor has the reverse result: I feel accused, unfairly, and must stifle the suddenly conscious, entirely unacceptable Bartonesque desire to forcibly remove his composed expression. *Get through this? Move on?* Does he really believe that after a simple explanation, we'll sit down to dinner with our children as if nothing is wrong?

Overcooked pasta and still-boiling water pour into stainless steel, draining. Steam envelops me. It billows up, reflected in the window by the sink, the one that looks out over the pool. Just an hour ago, I was watching Becca and her best friend floating there, Becca's hand trailing in the water, creating gentle ripples.

I was chopping carrots.

"Hon?"

The pot is empty.

"I can't do this," I say. My voice is clipped, strained; not yelling is so much harder than yelling. "Please." I turn to face him, head-on. "Just go."

Before he can speak, I yell, loudly, "Becca! Logan! Dinner!"

Yelling feels good; a release valve opens, allowing me to breathe without feeling like a massive air balloon is residing in my lungs. I turn back to the sink. The window begins to clear. Drops of condensed steam fall, weeping across the surface of the glass—revealing my reflection and the familiar shadows of the backyard.

"Please, Jacob, before the kids come. You've got about two minutes. They usually come after the second call." Closed, the valve has begun to pressurize again. Turning only my head, I yell again. "Logan! Becca!" Release. My voice ricochets off the marble.

"Kate—"

"Now, Jacob." My throat constricts as I try to hold my shit together. I am shaking with effort. I pull the words out. "I mean it. Please go, just go."

We are both silent. I will not look at him. I stare out the window, watching a single, straggling drop of water trail down my face. I hear Jacob grab his keys and his wallet, slide his feet into the flip-flops he keeps in the hall by the garage, and open the door. There is a muffled *whoosh* as the door meets its frame in closing. Everything in this goddamn house is designed to shut softly—restrained, controlled.

I don't belong here. I never have.

TWO

"WHERE'S DADDY?"

Becca has been in the kitchen for fifteen seconds before she asks after Jacob. I am in the process of hurriedly removing the fourth table setting; I do not need a visual reminder of my absent husband. I cannot think about infections and strippers and betrayal—about the girl on her knees. Not now. I have decided to give Jacob what I call "the psychic silent treatment," a protective technique I've developed to block someone or the abuse they've inflicted. Though I have years of practice on others, with varying degrees of success, I haven't had to use it on my husband before, and I'm not sure I'll have the necessary willpower. It won't help that Becca and Logan expect him to be here.

"He had to go out, sweetie."

"But he said he'd read me the next chapter of *The Hobbit* tonight."

Normally, my daughter's petulance is endearing. We have countless photos of her with her lower lip stuck out, preternaturally blue eyes wide. She expects this expression to have a certain effect—an expectation that, I admit, we've reinforced consistently most of her life. Tonight, however, she will be disappointed.

"He must have forgotten. Sometimes Daddy gets caught up in his own life." I allow a small measure of bitterness and a generous portion of criticism into my voice. He let her down. He let us down.

He gets the blame. Then, remembering she's only eight and quick to register parental animosity, I self-edit. Warming my voice and expression, I say, "I can read it to you, if you want."

"With voices?"

"But of course," I say with an English accent and stiff smile.

On rare good days—bright, sunny, yellow days—my mother used to read aloud to me from our single book of classic Grimm's fairy tales using an elaborate library of voices for the characters. It is the only Barton family tradition I have embraced. Jacob has embraced it as well—his Gollum is magnificent, a blend of Scottish and Transylvanian accents. My specialties are the characters from the *Harry Potter* series, particularly Hermione, but I have a pretty good Gandalf, and my cuddles in the warm glow of her bedside lamp are just as good as her dad's.

"Yay!" Becca wraps herself around my waist from behind, the side of her face peeking out under my arm. "It's my favorite."

Becca's ebullience arises as quickly as her petulance. Despite appearances, her emotions are fairly balanced for a little girl; they do not run deep.

I know. I grew up with deep emotional imbalance. I live with the knowledge that my neurons might be fostering it, waiting for the catalytic spark. Life-altering events are never without risk: childbirth, moving, relationships changing. Jacob's confession. A sexually transmitted infection. Darkness descending. Struggling to breathe.

Stop, Kate, I tell myself. *Slow down. Stay here.*

"Did you see your brother, sweetie?" I ask, my voice tremulous. "I can't believe he couldn't hear me."

"I'll go get him," she says, skipping away.

"Thanks, Boo," I call after her, struck, as I often am, by my daughter's innocence and my fierce longing to preserve it. At her age, I was worrying about where on the color spectrum my mother would be on any given day: if she was feeling blue or violet, she might remain in bed, shades drawn; if she was feeling vibrant orange or blazing red, she might plan a backyard circus, frightening the neighborhood children with her frantic exuberance. Of course, there was the remote possibility, wonderfully tantalizing, that she might be yellow, and we would have a creative, love-infused day of joy and wonder. Although it wasn't intentional on her part, my mother gave me a glimpse of epic happiness every once in a while—just often enough to keep me hopeful. It's astounding how little it takes to keep a child believing and how messed up a little faith can make you.

Becca is back within three minutes.

"He was playing his game, and he was really mad I bothered him, but I told him it was pasta night, and that worked."

Although Logan looks like Jacob's mini-me—wavy chestnut hair, dark brown eyes, and classic English blue-blood features—he tends toward my side of the family when it comes to temperament.

Becca, on the other hand, is physically a Barton—honey-blond hair curling wildly about an open, expressive face—but with the personality I imagine Jacob might have had before his mother and her upper-crust expectations shaped him. Loving and beloved, Becca still believes the world is just as it seems and that life will be fair. I fear this perspective will all too soon be lost.

I spoon pasta into the bowls Jacob and I purchased two years ago in Italy while celebrating our fourteenth anniversary and remember how he chose the bright kaleidoscopic pattern in shades of cobalt blue, emerald green, and gold. How, while I wondered why we needed another set of dishes, he held up a plate across the showroom and said, "This is the one. Bold and beautiful."

Here and now, I feel the urge to throw each one of them against the marble backsplash and watch the red sauce and noodles splatter all over this perfect kitchen.

But I cannot.

I need to pretend everything is okay. That's the plan for tonight: Act like nothing is wrong. Block out Jacob. Do not fall apart. Do not let unloosed memories bring out the Barton. Do not channel my mother: yelling wild things, throwing plates, scaring my family shitless. Do not channel my father: drinking finger after finger of vodka, saying nothing, leaving without leaving.

No. I will place these bold, beautiful ceramic bowls of home-made food gently on the table. I will talk about school and soccer and having a barbecue this weekend. *Shit.* Scratch that last item—who knows what the situation will be this weekend.

"Where's Dad?" Logan asks as he shuffles into the kitchen, his scuffling, kick-the-heel gait just like his father's.

"He had to go out," Becca chimes in. "But Mom's going to read *The Hobbit*, if you want to listen."

"Why would I want to do that?" Logan scoffs, dismissively.

Going on twelve, Logan has adopted a preteen blend of mis-placed arrogance and bravado, a boy testing the waters of manhood without knowing the first thing about how to swim there. Normally, I find this endearing, like Becca's petulance. My firstborn, growing up. But tonight, I hear Jacob and his mother in Logan's scoffing dismissal.

The dishes. The scoffing. The shuffling. My psychic silent treat-ment is failing. Execution of the *Nothing Is Wrong, Block Jacob* plan is not going well.

"Logan, watch your tone," I say with a harsh tone of my own. "Your sister is trying to be nice." I gesture to the refrigerator with my head. "Get the water, please."

"Someone's in a bad mood," he mutters, though he does as he's asked.

I take a long intentional breath and say, "Perhaps we could *both* try to be more pleasant."

"I'm not being unpleasant," Logan responds evenly, pouring water into his glass.

And in an instant, I am transported back to my tiny childhood home with its paper-thin walls. I'm sitting at the mottled green Formica kitchen table my father bought at some garage sale, purchased because it was cheap and said to be indestructible, and being indestructible is critical in our house. My mother breaks things when she loses control, and she is on the verge of a blind rage. Aware we are all on eggshells, I try to disappear, but Daniel refuses to cow to her. "*I'm* not being unpleasant," he says, with an emphasis on the "I'm"—the most reproachful he can be of our mercurial mother. *Too much reproach.* Inside my head I'm begging him to *Shut up, Daniel, please shut up.* The air is sucked out of the room. I instinctively hunch my shoulders and hold my breath, shrinking my heart as far into my ribcage as I can. My mother flies into a fury, unencumbered by reason. "How dare you?" she yells. I look up and see the silent appeal in Daniel's eyes as the back of our mother's hand meets with the side of his head, right above his ear. I say nothing. Neither does our father.

Hurt people hurt people.

Daniel will learn to perfect this blow on me when she is gone.

"Mommy?"

Becca's voice brings me back to the present. She looks frightened. I turn to Logan. I cannot see his face, but he's stopped pouring water. He stands very still, his body stiff, defensive, which frightens me.

How must I appear to them?

I remind myself these molten memories are in my head.

I am here, now, with my children. The air is not thin.

I lift my hand from the polished mahogany table and rest it gently on Logan's shoulder. "Sorry, big guy."

I can see his inner deliberation. Should he shrug my hand off and hold on to his attitude or capitulate? Thankfully, he chooses capitulation.

Granting me a half smile, he says, "It's all right. It's not that I don't like it. I'm just not into the whole reading aloud thing anymore."

He rolls his eyes toward Becca. I recognize the gesture as an invitation to a detente of sorts, so I match his half smile with one of my own.

Nothing Is Wrong, Block Jacob is back on track.

Only a few hours until I can properly vent. I can make it.

Eating commences.

My children are enthusiastic about food—and dinnertime.

Dinnertime. When I first approached the idea of having children with Dr. Farber, I revealed my primary fear was that I had no idea what a normal family looked like. Countless therapeutic hours were spent in her hushed, dimly lit, slightly-too-warm office while we discussed how to establish healthy family rules and rituals: chores, reading on the couch, bedtime, and dinnertime—the last of which, according to Dr. Farber, was most important of all. Positive family dinners, she said, were linked to healthier, more connected children, less likely to do drugs or drink alcohol, more resilient in the face of life's problems, more likely to do well in school. As she went over the list of benefits, I remember thinking, *Just another reason I'm so fucked up.*

"Mommy, watch this!" Becca pulls a noodle in through pursed lips, leaving a small bit of it left at the end.

Logan laughs. "You didn't make it. Here, watch me again."

He demonstrates, inserting a noodle and inhaling it in one swoop. Then he looks at me and says, "Fish face."

I oblige—suck my cheeks in to create guppy lips, moving them apart and together, registering that this sort of behavior would have never been allowed at the table when I was growing up.

Until her own father's disastrous financial decisions led to an acrimonious divorce and subsequent fall from societal grace, my mother lived a life of privilege, and she resented losing it. Moreover, when she felt in control, she became intent on exerting it over us, as if this might keep chaos at bay. On those nights, dinner was executed according to her childhood remembrance of proper behavior: each bite to be chewed twenty-four times, to facilitate digestion; silverware to be placed neatly at prescribed angles on the plate; meaningful contributions to be made to conversation structured around the contents of the two newspapers delivered daily, the *San Francisco Chronicle* and *The New York Times*, the latter of which was always the final word.

Unless my mother disagreed, and then it wasn't.

If, on the other hand, Mom was in a mood, dinner could follow any number of scenarios: a feast of epic proportions with no identifiable menu plan, consisting of several meats, piles of vegetables, potatoes, and noodles; a slapdash, thrown-together meal of minimal nutritional value; bread and water, with a side of guilt; or, of course, no food at all.

Not surprisingly, considering Dr. Farber's emphasis, dinner was one of the first issues I tackled head-on. It didn't take much psychological layer-peeling to understand my mother's approach had been warped, and it was a relatively simple thing to put right with my own children—of all of the parenting tasks, cooking is by far the easiest to do by the book. I appreciate the predictability of recipes turning out the way they're supposed to, as long as you follow instructions.

And so, for our family, dinnertime is a comforting routine. We pass food around the table with basic polite behavior and have age-appropriate conversations about third-grade reading group and preparations for the sixth-grade science emporium, the latest game on the playground, and whether their soccer coaches are fair and good at their jobs.

Even tonight, struggling on my own, it is a relief for me to relax into the simple pleasure of listening to my children slurp long strands of spaghetti through pursed lips and laugh.

Nothing Is Wrong, Block Jacob has worked after all.

And then, right on the tails of that thought, comes another: *It won't last, this little piece of heaven.*

I should have known.

THREE

A DOUBLE BEEP TONE indicating an exterior door has opened lets me know Jacob has returned. I am curled behind Becca in her canopy bed, watching the curve of her back rise and fall. She is curled around our gray tabby cat, Ophelia.

I pull the sheet up over Becca's shoulder and maneuver off the mattress. She doesn't stir, but Ophelia rises, arches her back stiffly, and gives me a contemptuous look before leaping off the bed and padding out of the room.

Ophelia is a skittish creature. Jacob and I adopted her shortly after marrying. He'd begun traveling extensively and I was lonely, so he suggested a dog. Growing up, he'd always had Labradors and had a pedigreed puppy in mind. I insisted that we go to a shelter to rescue me a loyal companion, and once there I fell for an emaciated kitten that had been found in a trashcan full of rainwater—the only surviving member of her litter. The shelter had called her Ophelia. Although we found it a bit macabre, Jacob and I couldn't help but appreciate the literary reference, and the name stuck. With the exception of Becca, for whom she has a particular affinity, Ophelia bestows and receives affection on her own terms; her love is slow to develop and quick to be removed for even the slightest infraction.

I move over to dim the light on Becca's peace lamp with the

purple polka-dot shade, an item it took my daughter approximately five seconds to choose. Her room is a plethora of purple: walls, sheets, pillowcases, and lamps; shorts, dresses, tops, even shoes. It has always been her favorite color—"pup-ell," she called it when she was little.

One benefit of her obsession is the ease with which I can buy her things I know she will love. Another is that it has dulled the sensitivity I developed to the color as a child. Purple days were some of the worst: blue sadness with a tint of red rage, mixing to create the despair and hopelessness that ruled our lives when my mother slipped away.

Becca's purple is the color of lilacs and lavender—sweet, soft spring.

I pause, studying myself in the framed oval mirror on the wall over the dresser. The steam exposure earlier tonight wreaked havoc on my hair. Dark dirty-blond curls spin wildly, an outward manifestation of the pandemonium whirling inside my head. I pull my fingers through the curls, trying to exert some influence.

Stepping closer to the mirror, eyes blazing, I see a shadow in the hall. My hand pauses mid-pull. Irrational terror rises along with a memory. Daniel lurking outside my room. Voices. A fist to the door, popping the lock.

I am trapped.

I stop. Breathe. Tell myself quietly, "Be here, not there." Losing control is not an option. I gather my hair back into a ponytail, wrapping one of Becca's hairbands once, twice, three times—tight—around the curls, and stare again at my reflection, channeling the whirling thoughts, distilling them to *Love and trust can be dangerous. I'm not safe.*

Nonetheless, my heart tugs at the sound of Jacob's voice calling from the hallway, "Kate?" I can see his reflection in the mirror behind me as he peers into the room.

Taking a step inside, he gestures with his head toward Becca's sleeping form.

He wants to go to her.

Our faces are framed by photographs Becca has wedged between the mirror and the whitewashed wood: Becca kicking a goal as she falls to the ground; Becca, Logan, Jacob, and I on a snowy mountain-top, each lifting a ski perpendicular to the ground; Becca precariously balanced on a surfboard, Jacob standing behind her in a waist-high breaking wave; Jacob and I from the back, hand in hand at the edge of a trail. Becca took this last one with the purple Instax camera she got for a birthday, the kind with instant developing film. The image is crooked and too thick for the mirror frame; it is barely hanging on.

I'm reminded that the stable, happy family we've created is frag-ile after all. It could come apart at any time. It could be coming apart now. Because of a stripper. Because of Jacob.

As he takes another step, I turn abruptly and hold up my hand, shaking my head slowly.

I brush past him and walk down the hallway, contemplating which room to mar forever by the memory of what is about to tran-spire. Not much of a debate in the end—I enter Jacob's paneled office with the antique desk and plush, rich oriental carpet. It's his favorite room. *Go ahead*, I think. *Ruin this.*

I sense rather than hear Jacob following me. I flip the light on and see him in the window, his figure moving in the darkness of the hallway. As he closes the door behind him, squares of glare reveal one slight flaw in my room choice. The doors leading to the hall have beveled glass windows—no solid core soundproofing to protect my children's ears. I hesitate for a minute before realizing this may not be a flaw after all.

No yelling.

I slide into the corner of the couch across from the desk. Jacob stands awkwardly by the door. He looks to me, flicks his gaze toward his tall leather banker's desk chair, looks back to me. He takes two steps in my direction.

"Don't even think about it," I say.

"Kate, please. I'm sorry. You've got to know, I never intended for this to happen. I didn't mean to hurt you."

"Those are words, Jacob, just words. You're the one who's always telling the kids"—I imitate Jacob's contrived motivational speaker tone, the one he uses when schmoozing a client or imparting sage parental wisdom—"it's what you *do* that matters."

Jacob looks me right in the eye. "I know what I've told the kids. What I'm telling you is that this—this thing—it didn't matter. I barely remember any of it. If Ryan hadn't told me that it happened . . ."

His voice trails off.

I leave his hanging statement hanging there, watch him scrunch his mouth and face in what I interpret as a combination of injury and repentance.

"Barely remembering it doesn't change a thing. No one forced you. Drunk or not, you allowed a woman you didn't even know to do what I, what I . . ." The words catch. Like a hangnail, I press on; it hurts, and yet I can't help pushing on it. *The pain reminds you it's real, this life you're leading.* "I'm ready to hear exactly what Ryan told you about that night. All of it."

"All of it?"

"Yes. All of it. I think I deserve to know."

"All right," he says, drawing out the words. "But before I tell you what Ryan said, you've got to believe me—whatever happened, it meant nothing."

Jacob takes a step toward me, hands outstretched like he's holding or offering me an imaginary gift the size of a beach ball.

It meant nothing? Doesn't he see that makes it worse?

"Oh please, it didn't *happen* to you. You could have stopped it."

I think but don't say, *It's not like you were held in place. Or forced to your knees.* The image of the young girl struggling flashes again, black and white and red, at the edge of my consciousness. My body tenses. My gag reflex kicks in.

Block it. Block it.

Anger has the power to purge pain.

"For God's sake, Jacob, just spit it out."

As soon as the words leave my mouth, I recognize the irony of my word choice.

Jacob begins his story haltingly, his voice cracking after the first sentence. He called Ryan to check on the time of their doubles tennis match tomorrow, and Ryan, as usual, asked about me and the kids. Jacob told him the kids were great—terrific, actually—and that I was okay, though he was worried because I'd had some issues recently, so they were running tests to make sure it was nothing serious. How I was angry, railing at the medical establishment that mandates running tests for sexually transmitted infections on happily married women. Ryan was quiet, like maybe he was embarrassed, or this was too much information—but then he said, "You don't suppose it could have anything to do with what happened at your birthday party in the city, do you?" To which Jacob responded, "What do you mean? How could it have anything to do with that?" And Ryan said, "Hey, I get you don't want to talk about it, but you can get an STD from . . ."

Jacob pauses, looks at me intently. "Kate, are you breathing?"

I'm not. I'm not breathing. I'm doing my disappearing act, which by necessity involves holding one's breath.

I inhale and exhale.

"Go on."

Jacob sighs wearily. "So then, of course, I asked him what the hell he was talking about, and he said something like, 'You don't remember much from that night, do you?' and I reminded him I'd blacked out, which I thought he knew. I told him the last thing I recalled was the Patrón shots, thinking I should stop, go back to the hotel. That I'd had enough."

Jacob stops again. Looks at me. He wants me to acknowledge that he was trying to do the right thing, that if it weren't for peer pressure, he would have—that he is the good boy. Which is usually true. He is. My husband is even-keeled, responsible. He's the ballast in our relationship. That's one of the reasons I married him. Trusted him.

"Go on," I say.

"Then Ryan told me Alex and Christoph bought a magnum for one of those private rooms, and then, well, then they bought the lap dance."

I do not like Jacob's New York friends. Entitled society boys grown-up in name only. Christoph is an arrogant, womanizing cad—trust-fund enabled, better-looking than he deserves to be, and an unapologetic snob. And Alex is a lying son of a bitch. He cheated on his wife, Maria, my only good friend from our New York days. When Maria found out he was having an affair and, after some digging, realized it wasn't the first time, she was devastated—no, gutted. It took her weeks to get through a day without crying in her office or having to lock herself in the bathroom so their daughter, Maddie, wouldn't hear her falling apart.

"So Christoph and Alex paid for it," I say, my voice flat, matter-of-fact.

Jacob nods. "Ryan says he doesn't know how it went from there. He said the whole thing was getting out of control and he was uncomfortable, so he left and went to the bathroom or something. When he came back to the room, Alex and Christoph were gone and Ryan says he, well, saw the girl, you know . . ." Another goddamn pause. "And that's it. That's what he told me."

The image that's more of feeling returns: a dark-haired woman on her knees, my husband finally getting what he's been missing. Strobe lights flashing. Music thumping.

"Was it good?" I hear the words coming from my mouth, the trembling in my voice.

"God, Kate, it wasn't like that. Please, can't we stop this?"

"Stop this?" Hot, unbidden tears pool. "That's the problem, Jacob. I look at you and that's what fills my head. I don't want to see it or think about it—but I can't stop it."

My voice breaks. The tears fall.

"I can't stop it."

I close my eyes and put my hands over my ears to block out Jacob, and suddenly, without warning, I'm fifteen and back in the shower in our little house with the paper-thin walls. I'm there rinsing and rinsing my hair, trying to get the conditioner out. I'm in the shower—but I'm also watching myself in the shower. It's always the same. The girl in the shower closes her eyes. She hears the door open.

The plastic shower curtain sucks in toward her wet skin. "Daniel, Jesus, can't you wait?" She waits for her brother to respond, to peek around the shower curtain or pee or yell at her for taking so long. She prepares herself, covering her breasts with one arm, dropping her other arm so that her hand can cover the space between her legs. But it's not Daniel. It's Daniel's friend from college. She's only met him this morning. Adam, his name is Adam. He's taking his jeans and his underwear off and jerking the plastic curtain aside. The girl in the shower says, "What are you doing?" and then she screams when it becomes clear what he's doing and she screams and cries while he does it to her on the tile floor of the bathroom, her head wedged against the wall, looking up at the crooked toilet paper roll. The girl in the bathroom knows, and I know, that Daniel and her father are right outside, in the kitchen or the living room. They must hear her. They do nothing to stop the assault.

I don't do anything either. I never can.

I can never stop it. So it goes on—and on—and on. Jeans. Underwear. Trapped. Choking.

Memories burning through me. Pressure and heat building.

"Kate?" Jacob's voice calls to me. He is close by. I open my eyes to see him crouched in front of me. My head is bowed, lips pressed together; my shoulders are hunched, elbows tight against my ribs; my legs are locked, hands clenched at the top of my thighs. Every muscle in my body is tensed. Poised. Fight or flight.

"Don't touch me," I say in a menacingly soft voice. "Don't. Touch. Me."

I wonder if I will ever enjoy being touched by anyone again. I don't want to cry in front of him. And yet, and yet . . . sadness and rage wash over shame, salt in a wound.

Jacob's hands stop in midair. He sits back on his heels and then slowly stands upright.

"Please, babe. I know you're angry and have every right to be."

I'm not capable of saying anything. Fight or flight. My instinct hasn't decided which course to take.

"There's no excuse," he says. "But we can get over this."

This—this I can say something about. I rise from the couch, forcefully wiping my nose with the back of my wrist. "Get over it? This isn't an argument or a bad day, Jacob. It's a betrayal."

"A betrayal?"

How is there a question about this? His tone forces me to look directly at him. I must make him understand this.

"Yes, a betrayal. You cheated on me. With a stripper. In public. In front of your friends. I'll bet they remember it. I'll bet Alex and Christoph are thrilled you've finally sunk to their level."

He winces at the words *in public*.

"I'm not Alex. Or Christoph. I know what I did was wrong, but don't you think you might be overreacting? I didn't have an affair. It was just—"

Though he doesn't complete the phrase, I hear it, whispered in my ear, "Just a blow job." And the pressure cracks me wide open.

"Overreacting? Overreacting." My voice drips. "You let a stripper, a *stripper*, do what I, what . . . I . . ." I feel the heat again, boiling in my head. "And now you've given me a sexually transmitted infection—me, the wife you vowed to love and protect."

He shakes his head and I say, "Yes." My voice amplifies. "Yes, you did. So this . . ."

I cannot say the words.

"This *thing* that meant nothing, this thing you seem to think is inconsequential—well, it isn't. There are consequences, Jacob, consequences *I'm* going to have to live with, knowing the whole time you brought them into my life. You." My voice falters. "You."

I need to move. Flight. Get me out of here. I instinctively look at the door.

Run, Kate, run.

Jacob walks slowly toward me again, apologizing, and my instincts shift. It takes supreme control not to flail wildly at him. I hear him saying he'll do whatever it takes to regain my trust—give me space, make it up to me.

"I can't believe this is actually happening," he says. "This morning everything was good. Really good. Wasn't it?"

A clean memory of the morning flits across my consciousness. It *was* good. We had pancakes with the kids, with mini chocolate chips. We were talking about whether there would be good snow in Wyoming this year. Big Sky at Christmas. And now . . .

Silence fills the room. I stare without seeing at the gleaming wood-paneled wall across from me. Slowly, my eyes come into focus on a candid photograph of Jacob and me on the polished credenza behind his desk. Ryan took it. It's in a rough gray farmer's wood frame that doesn't quite work with the rest of the room's décor. Long curls blown back by the wind, I am looking right into the camera, smiling openly. Jacob is looking at me. We are joyful.

It was taken when I was nineteen, right after we met. Ryan had introduced us about a week earlier on an idyllic summer day. A cloudless, robin's egg–blue sky, glorious sunshine, a subtle breeze off the ocean, the smell of wet sand and seaweed. The kind of day that makes you believe forever could be real. Ryan was organizing a beach volleyball tournament. Jacob and I were a team. We came in third. Our first embrace was a victorious post-match, wrap-your-arms-around-me-and-hold-on one. Salt. Coppertone. Sweat. A kiss that took me aback. Then, I remember, Ryan came up and hugged us both.

I can taste my tears.

Jacob senses weakness. He reaches for me. I am within reach—until I step back, arms bent in a defensive posture, an instinctive move that has failed me so many times. Once again, hurt bumps up against rage. It was good. Now it isn't.

"What do you want, Kate?" Jacob asks. "What do you want me to do?"

I drop my arms to cross in front of my ribcage. Tight. I tell him the plan I began to develop while lying in Becca's bed, watching her and Ophelia sleeping. Well, the start of a plan. Hopefully enough of a plan to get me through this.

Enough to keep me from falling.

Separation. For a while, I don't know how long. Jacob will stay in the guest room in the guest wing. He will agree to never speak to or see Alex or Christoph ever again. We will go to see Dr. Farber—not some anonymous marriage counselor that will undoubtedly fall in love with my good-as-gold, handsome husband and view me as the unreasonable, overly sensitive wife.

Damaged goods, Daniel whispers. *Sloppy seconds.*

I tighten my arms again, holding myself together.

If I can get through this, not "over it" but through it—if I can look at my husband without seeing him splayed and lost to another woman's mouth under the blue and purple strobe lights, hearing the bass thumping, if I can heal this wound without reopening those that cannot be healed—then we will discuss the next steps.

Jacob will not fight me. If he tries, he will lose.

I may be broken, but I will never fall to my knees or go down for the count again.

I can't.

FOUR

I'M FLOATING ON A RAFT. Safe. Warm. Sunshine above, undulating water below. Without warning, the raft is overturned by force, spilling me into cold, churning waves. I come up sputtering, grabbing for something, someone, to hold on to. An undercurrent drags me down. I know he's there. I see his dark head under the water. I reach out and drift into consciousness, cocooned in a jumble of silky sheets and a down comforter. Safe and warm again, relieved, I hear Becca's and Jacob's muffled voices just outside the door before it opens a crack.

"Hold on, Becs—how 'bout we let Mom sleep a little longer," Jacob says. "She was up pretty late."

In the hazy shift from sleeping to awake, I think, *My husband is thoughtful.* Jacob must have heard me going into the kitchen to get a glass of water at 4:32 a.m. I roll over and stretch to look at the alarm clock on the opposite bedside table, placed there to stymie the compulsive time checking that accompanies my insomnia. My right arm and leg encounter Jacob's smooth, cool, un-slept-in side of the bed. Fully awake, it comes back to me: *Oh, shit, that's right—my husband's* not *so thoughtful.* There is a pile of superfluous decorative pillows he and the designer chose for the master bedroom stacked on the pillow where his head would normally lie. I rise up on my elbow to look over them at the clock.

7:14 a.m.

"But I need her to do my hair."

"I can brush it for you."

"No, we're doing a braid today, Daddy. A *braid*." Becca pronounces the word with reverence. "We've been practicing it and practicing it."

"Becca, listen, we don't have to leave for another half hour. How about you wait twenty minutes, and then Mom can do your braid."

I recoil back to my cocoon, performing my daily calculation of time slept versus time facing middle-of-the-night demons. Last night's were a new breed of malevolent creatures—conceived from the tumult of the evening, an ill-advised internet search on sexually transmitted infections, and unadulterated fear—that diabolically twisted my thoughts in the dark to dwell on loss and insecurity. Shame. Volatility. Lives spinning, upside down. Losing it all.

I am exhausted.

Assuming I fell asleep around five, I'm working on a little over two hours of sleep, and I can't afford to be fragile today. *Fuck me*, I think—and immediately realize that this response is not a good place to start my day. Time to get it under control.

Becca has not conceded defeat. "But I need her now."

"Becs," Jacob says. "Come on, honey—"

"It's all right, come on in, Boo," I call out, drowning out the rest of his response.

I sit up and throw the covers aside as my daughter bounds into the room, a flying lavender confection. She pounces onto the bed and wraps her arms around me, pushing me back onto my pillows. "Good morning, Mommy!"

I return her embrace, relishing the smell and weight of her. Jasmine and clementines. Daisy Dreamgirl is her latest body lotion fixation from Bath & Body Works. Her friend Haley gave out sample sizes in the ubiquitous, obligatory, over-the-top party favor bags at her birthday last month, and we had to "please go get more, Mommy" because of the packaging—purple with yellow daisies. We spent an hour there, browsing and spraying, before coming home happy and doused in sugar.

I fix my gaze on Jacob over the mass of unruly waves on my daughter's head. "Thanks. I've got it from here. You can go to work."

"I called and told them I won't be in this week."

"Daddy says he can pick me up from school and take me to soccer all week. Maybe even stay for practice and watch." Becca turns her face up to mine, her delight palpable. "So you can have more time to walk with Natalie and relax."

This pronouncement must have its source in Jacob. Hope springs eternal. As if picking the children up from school and taking them to practice so I can walk longer with a friend will address the root of our problem.

"We'll see, Boo. I've already made plans with Emily's mom for carpool."

Becca turns to look at Jacob as I'm speaking. He shrugs, as if to say, "I tried." I hear the pique in my voice, and my irritation amplifies. Rejecting his peace offering makes me look ungrateful and forces our daughter into taking sides. That was quick maneuvering.

Becca turns back to me, lower lip popped out, chin tilted down, big eyes—her classic, well-practiced, puppy-dog look.

I can nip this one in the bud.

I place one hand on each of her feather-soft cheeks, lean over, and kiss her nose, eliciting a giggle, as I knew I would. "No pouting. Lemme throw on some shorts, and then we'll do your hair. Go tell Logan we need to leave in fifteen minutes and meet me in your room, okay?"

Becca moves her hands to my face, mimicking the placement of my own. "K, k." Her return kiss is sloppier but sweeter.

Within a minute, Jacob is knocking on the closet-door frame as I'm changing. I yank a faded charity 5K T-shirt over my head as I push the door closed with my foot. "Don't," I snap through the door. "I'll talk to you in your office, later, after I take them to school."

"I can take them, Kate. I want to take them."

At the word *want*, the images from last night replay. Jacob's head tilted back over the edge of a booth. A woman's head between his legs. The pressure inside begins to build again.

"I don't need you to do that. I don't need you to stay home. I don't need you to pick them up and take them to practice. I don't need you." Harsh-toned words trip from my mouth—beyond pique, and louder than I would have liked since I've got to talk through the goddamn door.

This is why he needs to leave.

He's not angry. He's contrite and on his best behavior—taking time off, staying for soccer practice, which will please our children and their coaches. I am angry. I am not contrite, and I, for some odd reason that I've never been quite able to figure out, don't get any extra credit for staying for soccer practice. Classic. He looks good. I look bad. He is calm, and I am tempestuous.

Not this time.

Brushing past him as I leave the closet, I say quietly, "If you want to do something, get tested, so I know what I'm dealing with."

I don't give him time to respond; I immediately exit the room, calling out, "Logan, hey, buddy, did you grab your outline off the printer?" as I go.

Logan's room is next to ours. I can see him in front of his bathroom mirror, studying his hair from a "how will this look to others" angle. He sees me—behaves as though he hasn't. Pretends he wasn't preening.

"Yeah, I've got it. I'm not Becca. You don't have to remind me all the time." He scoops his bag from the floor by the strap and throws it effortlessly over his shoulder. "I've been ready for like thirty minutes. Can we go soon?"

"Give me three minutes to fix Becca's hair, and then we'll go."

"I wanted to be early, though. Can't Dad take me now?"

"No, Logan, he can't. That doesn't make sense—two cars leaving within five minutes to go to the same place. Besides, your father has other things he needs to do."

"But he said he was going to bring us."

"Well, he was wrong, and don't scowl at me. We'll be early enough. And since when do you want to be early, anyway?" I add, raising my eyebrows. Keeping it real. I don't want to appear too amenable, out of character. With change afoot, it's essential the kids know I can be counted on to remain the same.

It's essential for me to know I can remain the same.

———————

Twenty minutes later, we arrive in the school drop-off lane, technically not early but definitely not late. Becca's hair is in a tidy French braid. Logan jumps out of the car with a hasty, "Thanks, Mom. See ya," and makes a beeline for two friends who are standing near a cluster of girls in his grade.

That's what I thought.

Becca remains in her seat. "Can you please park and bring me in?"

She hasn't asked me this in a while. Per one of my parenting books, I've been trying to wean her off this practice—encourage independence and move her along on the developmental track. Today, however, I don't mind her neediness. A few more minutes of eight-year-old love and cheerfulness is a welcome distraction. It may also garner me a few additional parental points, and something tells me that as this whole sorry thing with Jacob unfolds, I may be glad to have some extras in the bank.

I watch a smile appear on Becca's face in the rearview mirror as I say, "That's an excellent idea."

Take that, Jacob, I think as I pull around the black Escalade in front of me, heading for a parking spot that has miraculously opened up.

My gloating is short-lived. As I throw the SUV into park with a flourish, my cell phone rings and "Incoming Call Dr. Brachmann" appears on my center console display.

The test results.

I turn the car's engine off and reach for my phone. Do I listen now or bring Becca in first? Obvious reasonable choice would be the latter. No question, really. Let it go to voicemail and call back.

Don't be a Barton—impulsive, irrational. The phone continues to ring . . .

Luckily, Becca makes the reasonable, Whittier decision for me. She is up, out of the car. The door closes behind her and I see her in the side mirror, awkwardly hoisting her backpack over her shoulders. Even though we bought the kid's size, it's still much too large for her frame. I turn off the engine and watch the purple-threaded RGW monogram settle across her narrow shoulder blades. Rebecca Grace Whittier. "Such a glorious name," my mother-in-law, Grace, purred when Jacob told her of our choice at a dignified Whittier Sunday brunch.

"She will undoubtedly be a glorious girl," Jacob responded, patting my swollen belly, a loving gesture Grace Rebecca Whittier obviously considered gauche.

"Jacob, please, some decorum."

Her words accompanied by a frown, a quick look around to see who might be watching. Jacob's hand lifting abruptly, as if he'd been stung.

Oh shit, I think as I open the driver's door. Any kind of separation will merely confirm what Grace has always suspected: that I am unworthy and incapable of being the right kind of wife. Despite my years of effortful good-wifedom, Jacob's mother has continued to make clear her doubts and reservations as to whether I will rise above my low social class and troubled childhood to meet the standards of her obviously superior son and his disciplined, storied family. Grace has made her concerns "quite clear, my dear," on many occasions.

And she won't be the only one to blame me.

I leave my cell phone sitting in the spare cup holder, malignantly beeping that a message has been stored, and shove the massive black door closed. I'm aiming for that satisfactory sound of metal slamming on metal. I must settle for a dignified "whumppf." I can hear my mother-in-law, still lurking. "Really, Kathryn." Haughty, proper, correct.

Her reversed namesake waits by the bumper of the car, hand outstretched.

Hold on, I tell myself. *Hold on while you can.*

FIVE

THE SCENT OF DAISY DREAMGIRL and sight of my cell phone greet me as I open the car door. Following Dr. Farber's advice, I try to focus for one minute on positive thoughts and emotions— shoring myself up. I sit and breathe slowly. Mandarin and jasmine, Johnson's baby shampoo and Crest toothpaste—how clean smells. The way my children's heads fit in the crook between my collarbone and my neck and the way their bodies melt into mine when they are tired—how love feels. How ordinary can be made extraordinary.

I open my eyes and glance down at my phone, the screen blank, black, silent.

Retrieving a message from your doctor's office confirming you have a sexually transmitted infection from your husband—how betrayal guts you.

I pick up the phone, scroll up.

Better to know.

I place my finger on the phone icon.

Treat it like a Band-Aid that must be ripped off.

I move my finger to voicemail, hover over Dr. Brachmann.

Get it over with.

Press 1 for reception, 2 for the nurse's line, 3 for test results.

A car door opens to my left. A petite, smooth-pony-tailed

blonde in color-coordinated yoga clothes opens the passenger door next to me. I recognize her instantly. Jessica Parker, committee chairwoman for fifth-grade cotillion. One of those things I'd never heard of until we moved here, cotillion is etiquette and dance classes for children, by invitation only. I laughed when Jacob told me he was hosting a pancake breakfast at school our first month in town—with Jessica Parker—because of cotillion. He'd heard she held the power over which children received the coveted vanilla envelopes containing the first invitation to social standing in this community. He was determined to win her over so Logan would receive one.

"Should I volunteer to verify parents' net worth before kids get a pancake?" I asked.

Jacob did not find this humorous. "These things are important, Kate. I know you don't see the point, but it's part of our kids belonging. We want Jess to like us."

I didn't see the point. I've since been enlightened. We live in a Southern California movie script, a world in which social climbing is as common as the bright bougainvillea lining the manicured lawns. In this world, I am a liability. I'm awkward, ill at ease; I dress the wrong way, don't know what to say on the sidelines during my children's soccer games. I was the only mom to show up in a swimsuit and shorts for the end-of-the-year pool party at Jess's house and proceed to finish off the last sips of a blue Gatorade. It was hot and, naively, I thought we'd all swim. The other moms wore designer sundresses or crisp white capri pants with cute tops. Drank chilled Chardonnay.

Thankfully Jess likes Jacob—a lot. Logan received the cotillion invite. And as his younger sister, Jacob informs me, Becca is a legacy, guaranteed a spot when her time comes.

My phone is repeating my options.

Jess is staring at me, staring at her. Her look says it all: Why is Jacob with me? I don't belong, never have, and probably never will.

And Jess is probably right, because I consider doing things like listening to a message about a stripper-contracted STI under her cool gaze while sitting in front of my children's school.

I cannot start the car fast enough. With quick mirror checks, I pull out into the semicircular drop-off, willing myself to go slowly in the school zone, heading away from home.

I listen as the recorded male voice, "Dave," instructs me on how to key in my code. I dig under the Visa card in my wallet for the slip of paper on which I've written our Dr. Brachmann codes, looking up at the road and down at my purse, all while driving 45 mph around a curving lane that winds around a horse farm. It takes multiple finger presses and deletions to get the code right—13440. I cross over a narrow two-lane bridge edging the fields that serve as a venue for large-scale soccer tournaments.

A young disembodied female voice greets me. "Hello, Mrs. Whittier, this is Donna, Dr. Brachmann's nurse practitioner? Can you please give me a call at your earliest convenience? Just ask reception to transfer you directly to my extension. Thanks. Have a good day."

They don't give negative results on the phone. Jacob's gut instinct was correct. I'm going to receive bad news.

I hit redial. Press 1. Ask for Donna. Give my name. Canned music plays. I drive on. The familiar bubble of anxiety fills my chest.

"Mrs. Whittier?"

"Yes?"

"Thanks so much for calling back. I wanted to go over your results. I was hoping you might be available to come in later today?"

"Can't we just do it now, on the phone?" I ask.

"Well," Donna says slowly, hedging, "Dr. Brachmann would prefer if you came in."

I take a breath, crowding the bubble. Try to squelch irritation. "Is something wrong?"

Donna sounds scripted. "We've found it is helpful to have these discussions in person—so we can address all of your concerns and questions."

I picture myself sitting across from Dr. Brachmann as he explains how I've contracted herpes or chlamydia from my husband. I try to see how this could be anything other than humiliating and awful.

"I'd prefer to know now." My voice is tight. "I don't really have time to come in."

So she tells me. All the tests came back negative, except one. There was a discordant result, she says: my Pap smear came back normal, but the HPV test was positive. She asks if I've ever tested positive for HPV in the past.

"HPV?" I ask.

Human papilloma virus, Donna begins explaining, the one they now vaccinate young people against. It's a common STI in adults that can, in some cases, lead to cervical cancer. She quickly adds that I shouldn't be alarmed; my test results show no cell abnormalities at this time, and the infection is likely to clear up on its own. She says many women my age have had it at some point.

"And now I have it," I interrupt. "I've never had it before, but I have it now. So I've gotten it recently?"

"Well, maybe, but it's also possible you've had it for a while. HPV often presents without symptoms, and since it's a virus, it can remain dormant for quite some time. It would be difficult to say when you contracted it." Perhaps remembering my indignation at the last appointment for even having to undergo these tests, she quickly adds, "It *could* have been recent, but you also may have had it for some time—months, even years."

I am quiet as she goes on—means of transmission, latency, stress-related flare-ups, chances of cervical cancer developing, follow-up testing in six months, and God only knows what else. A low, humming vibration starts inside my head, overriding her words.

My thoughts spin toward Jacob and his indiscretion, how his mistake has become mine.

"My husband . . ." I'm unsure of what to say next: *He caused it? He doesn't have any symptoms? He should be tested?*

"Discussing these matters with a partner can be difficult," Donna says. "If you'd like, I can send you a printable email that may help you explain how, given the nature of the virus, it's difficult to track when and where someone was exposed. Testing positive in a long-term relationship is not *necessarily* indicative of infidelity. Having said that, couples often share HPV. The thing is, unless your husband has symptoms, it will be impossible to know for certain that *he's* gotten it. There aren't any HPV tests for men."

Not necessarily indicative of infidelity rings in my ears, followed quickly by *impossible to know for certain that he's gotten it, with that slight emphasis on the "he."* It occurs to me that Donna may think I am the source. That I cheated on Jacob. I feel simultaneously violated and ashamed.

I hear a siren approaching, see an ambulance on the other side of the road, and realize I have continued to drive without any awareness of where I am or where I'm going. I've driven through traffic lights. Up and down a hillside. My hands are gripping the steering wheel, my knuckles white, my muscles taut, quivering. Negative energy sparks and travels across every nerve ending. I am literally going to explode. I'm in no condition to be driving.

All at once, it seems, there is silence. "Mrs. Whittier?"

Donna must have asked me a question, a question for which she expects an answer. I decide to go with "Can I call you back? I'm driving, and I should stop."

Stop. *Now.*

There is a parking lot ahead on the left. A Vons grocery store. A Starbucks. I pull in. Out of habit, I head for the Starbucks, but then I realize I cannot stop there. People hurrying in, hoping there's no line. People hurrying out, trademarked cups in hand, going about their un-ruined lives. And then I vaguely remember the back lot at the Vons.

Through a thin veil of tears, I find my way there and park near the street that runs behind it. The only other vehicle nearby is a dirty, dented pickup truck. A ladder sticks out over the bed, and a tattered strip of yellowed white fabric hangs from its end, a pitiful alert flag. The words "Wash Me" are written unevenly on the back gate.

I turn off the ignition. The purring of the engine ceases.

For a moment I listen to the ambient highway noise, staring at my left hand on the wheel and the two-carat alluvial fifteen-year anniversary gift sardonically sparkling on my ring finger. It takes a few painful twists and tugs to remove. One quick downward flick of my wrist to send it to the floor, where it wedges between the edge of the passenger door and the floor mat. I open my hands wide like starfish, breathing in. Grip the steering wheel tight, breathing out.

I unbuckle and lean onto the armrest, my forehead in my left hand. My knuckle is swollen. It hurts.

My chest moves in silent heaves. A volcano of emotions threatens: anger, shame, sorrow, defeat, and an overarching sense of futility. Trying hard has not worked. I have always been, and now always will be, damaged goods. The life I've tried to build can never be the same again.

How can I explain what this has done without revealing everything? What will happen if Jacob stays? Will I ever be able to look at him again in the same way? Have him touch me without . . .

But how can I survive it if he leaves? He is my constant. My balance. My chance at being something other than a thoroughly tragic, fucked-up Barton-mess of a person.

Another memory floats up. I am four or five, sitting cross-legged on the floor of my closet, knees hugged to my chest, listening to my mother rail against my father about the injustices rained upon her. I'm far too young to comprehend the Tolstoy-inspired vitriol spewing from her mouth, yet I know, my mother is mad. She screams her refrain, over and over: "I am ruined."

I bend. I bow. I tense up, elbows in against my ribcage, closed fists against my eyebrows. I begin to shake, and then I surrender to the pressurized forces I have struggled to contain for so long.

Once released, I am no longer in control. Waves. Torrents. I pound on the sturdy leather steering wheel until the bones in the palms of my hands ache.

I sob for the little girl at the kitchen table who tried so hard to disappear, only to find that she was the only one left. I weep for the girl in the shower who couldn't escape soon enough or hide well enough. And I cry for the woman who reluctantly believed she had found a safe place for her heart, only to have it run over by a freight train.

Trust built and destroyed. The inevitability of it all.

Coming apart.

Time passes. I'm spent. I hear my phone buzz, buzz, and buzz again. Jagged gulps settle to shudders. Sodden tissues litter the floor. The box is empty. I lift the hem of my brown T-shirt to wipe my face.

The pickup is moving. I watch the sad little flag at the end of the ladder wave limply as the wheels hit the first speed bump.

My cell phone buzzes again, a single pulse. Still sitting on the passenger seat, the screen briefly illuminates with a photograph of the ocean, taken along my favorite coastal trail. A breaking wave is obscured by "Home"—missed call, voicemail, and text: "Where are you?"

I cannot face Jacob. Not yet.

I pick up the phone, type in "HPV positive" in my browser, and a host of website options pop up. I flit from one to the next, changing search terms, querying diagnostic combinations, cancer rates, and latent periods. Charts. Frequently asked questions. Anecdotes from women facing similar news. Cheating spouses. Confrontations.

I do not feel better.

Run, that's what I should do.

I take an inventory. There's half of an energy bar folded in its foil packaging in the side pocket of my door, sticky and stale. There is a half case of water bottles in the SUV's cargo area, always at the ready for thirsty children. Spray sunscreen tucked into a mesh pocket. I'm wearing my shoes.

A decision quickly made: leave the iPhone behind. Jacob is home if the school needs a parent. I remove a credit card before placing my wallet and iPhone into the glove box. I don't need anything else.

Then I see a glint of light. I reach across the carpet in front of the passenger seat, retrieve my anniversary gift, and hold it between my fingertips. The irony of something so beautiful brought to light from spewing magma gives me pause.

The knuckle of the finger where this ring has lived for the last year is bruised, tender, so I slide it onto my right hand instead. I rub the sore knuckle before my fingers drift to linger over a small scar on my palm.

I reach up and flip down the visor, noticing the unnatural weight of the ring on the wrong hand as I do. Look at myself in the illuminated mirror—pale, blotchy, puffy.

God, I'm pitiful.

Run, Kate, run.

SIX

MY FACE IS DRY WITH a film of Coppertone residue, salt from tears and sweat, and dirt thrown up from the road. My sports bra remains wet under my T-shirt and my shorts are damp, clinging in all the wrong places. Hungry and slightly itchy, but relatively free of destructive energy, I arrive at the stone entrance of our community shortly before 11:30 a.m.

I manage a smile for George, my favorite guard, as the ornate iron gate swings open. George looks once, then twice, then three times. As I'm going through, he raises his hand as if to ask me a question, but there's a Tesla on my tail, so I use it as an excuse to wave and keep going. A friendly chat is not in the cards today. After losing my shit in the parking lot, ten miles of running, and turbo grocery shopping, I need a shower, some chocolate milk, and, as my mother-in-law would put it, a little piece of quiet.

I drive toward the house, trying to channel my thoughts.

The run served its purpose. I am not angry, ashamed, or afraid. I am resolute. Clarity came around mile eight, after I'd punished myself, pushing through a side cramp and my screaming left knee, rehashing past mistakes I've made in the trust/betrayal department. Someone once told me that when you're in pain, you focus on what hurts the worst. Maybe this is another reason I love to run—after a few miles, something physical is bound to hurt, and that pain brings relief from any emotional injury. Today, my pounding feet on the pavement were matched step for step with psychological pummeling, and although my thoughts initially banged against each other like bumper cars, order eventually began to emerge from the chaos.

Learn, Kate, learn.

Mile two—believing one day my mother would get better; waking each morning, looking through dusty blinds as light filled the sky, and thinking, *This will be the day.*

Mile three—hoping one day my father would put down the newspaper that blocked his sight and the booze that blurred it, that he'd notice me and keep me safe in my own house.

Mile four—moving in with my first boyfriend, a teaching assistant eight years my senior; letting myself be swept away by declarations of love, only to find him in our bed with another blonde, and then another.

Mile five—trusting the next boyfriend with too much of my past, only to have him throw it back in my face during every argument, convincing me that my brother's assessment of my value was all too accurate.

And miles six and seven—the litany of past wrongs, slights, and criticisms from Jacob, father of my children; warnings I did not heed that were not so inconsequential after all. Jacob, who put everything I've worked so hard to create at risk. Logan and Becca and my vow to give them stability and safety—because this is what is at stake.

At mile eight, as endorphins kicked in, I saw things clearly. If there is one thing I should know by now, it's that once someone has wounded you and gotten away with it, they will do it again. I must protect myself so I can protect Logan and Becca.

I spent the rest of the run—miles nine and ten—building my resolve. Conducting conversations and arguments in my head in which I sounded calm, logical, and justifiably righteous.

I am ready. Ready to face Jacob.

As I pull up to the house, I notice Ryan's Jeep and my friend

Natalie's van in the semicircular driveway, and then I see Jacob standing in the doorway, framed by the huge mahogany arch. Ryan stands behind him, his hand on Jacob's arm, restraining him. Natalie is in their shadow, in running shorts and a baseball cap.

She takes a few steps toward me, giving me the "oh, Kate" look she gives whenever I tell her something troubling, and I remember I was supposed to meet her this morning for a walk.

"Oh, shit," I whisper.

"Where have you been?" Jacob says, on me before I can even step away from the car, his arms around me before I can object.

It's an awkward embrace. I am stiff, unreceptive, my arms pinned to my sides. Before I can react, let alone respond, he backs away, keeping a grip on my shoulders.

"Why aren't you answering your phone?" he demands.

The surprise aspect of the greeting, combined with the frank concern on all their faces, catches me off guard. Why are they all here? Oh my God. *The kids.*

"The kids—" My breath catches. "Did something happen?"

"No, they're fine," both Jacob and Natalie respond instantly, simultaneously, before Jacob goes on alone, "They're fine, Kate. But how could you go off like that, without telling anyone?"

"I went for a run and left my phone in the car." I turn to Natalie. "I'm so sorry, Nat. I totally forgot about our walk."

"Jesus, Kate. You scared the shit out of me." Jacob's hand is on my arm. "I thought . . ." He swallows the next words.

"What?" I ask. "What did you—"

I stop short, taking in the expression on his face. He cannot be bringing this up, here, now, in front of Natalie and Ryan. But he is. My pulse quickens.

I grasp his wrist, pull his hand off, away. "I went for a run." My words are low, harsher than I meant for them to sound. I look behind him to Natalie and Ryan.

"Did you call them?" I ask Jacob, even lower.

"Yes, I did. I called Ryan and Natalie and the school and Dr.

Farber and the guard at the gate and anyone else that I could think of who might have seen you, that might know where you were."

My heart rate increases with every word. I can feel it pulsing in my chest.

"What? You called Dr. Farber? George? You called George? Jesus, Jacob. Why?"

"Why?" A pause, for effect. "Why?"

Because I am my mother's daughter.

"Do you want people to think I'm unstable?" I try to whisper. "That I need to be watched?"

The unspoken question hovers over us. *How desperate is she?* I am not even close. The post-run euphoria and clarity, however, have dissipated, and a familiar rush of negative emotions is sparking, pooling, spreading. *What did Jacob say to all these people?*

"No one thinks you're unstable," Natalie says in the kind of soothing voice I can't help thinking one would use to soothe an unstable person. She negotiates her way around Jacob to stand in front of me, her "oh, Kate" look still in place. "We were concerned, but only because we care about you, okay?"

When I don't answer, she repeats, "Okay?"

I nod, frozen in place. Another awkward embrace ensues. Over her shoulder I can see Jacob, still standing close enough to touch.

I feel trapped.

Natalie pulls back as Jacob says, "I didn't say anything to make people think less of you, Kate. All I did was ask if they'd seen you and if they saw you again, could they let me know and ask you to call home. I called Natalie to see if you were with her."

Natalie nods, one arm still around me.

Jacob goes on. "And I called Ryan to ask for advice. They both offered to come over. That's all. It's not some conspiracy to make you look bad."

He says all of this slowly, in an even tone, exercising control over his voice and emotions. I am wondering how *his* betrayal has so quickly turned into *me* doing something wrong. Again.

"Tell you what," he says, "let's both take a minute and calm down. Then we can go inside, off the street, and talk about this whole thing rationally. Okay?"

I say nothing. Words will go all wrong.

Natalie breaks contact, steps back, and looks over at Jacob, then up into my face from under the bill of her baseball cap. "I'm going to get going, let you guys talk, but I'll call you in a little bit." She looks over to Jacob, smiles tightly, then turns away.

I can feel him staring at me as I watch her walk to her car. I want to call her back. I want to scream, *He gave me an STI. He is not the good guy.* But I say nothing.

As she gets into her van, Ryan says, "I should get going too."

He pulls his keys from the pocket of his shorts.

Natalie's van door closes.

Talking things out with Jacob will not go well. I need a buffer.

"No," I say quickly to Ryan. "Wait. Don't go. Please."

My eyes meet his, lock on, begging him not to break the connection.

But he does. He gazes over at Jacob, posing a question without saying a word. This silent communication has been going on for two and a half decades, ever since Jacob and Ryan became roommates at their swanky East Coast prep school at age thirteen. They share an extensive vocabulary of gestures—eyebrow raises, squints, head tilts, grins, shrugs—used individually or in combination to convey a thought, a question, an inside joke. After years in their company, I have cracked the code; Ryan's asking, *What do you want me to do?*

Jacob answers him with a glance, then reaches a hand toward me. I instinctively shrug away.

"Come inside, Kate," he says gently. "I've got to go in. Call people. Let them know you're okay." He gives Ryan another glance. "I'll see you later, yeah?"

He's said his piece. Cool, deliberate, he turns to walk back into the house, leaving Ryan and me standing there on the driveway.

I bring my hands up to rub my face, longing to be back on the street, running. Self-abuse I can take. My hands smell like paper bag, dirt, and sweat. I remember the groceries and move toward the back of the SUV.

"Seriously, Katie Rose, are you okay?" Ryan asks.

Despite all the shit that is going down, I smile faintly at this nickname, bestowed upon me the very first day we met but rarely used since I had the kids.

Ryan and I were in an Econ 2 section together, Wednesdays at 1:00 p.m. There were only twelve of us, and during the first roll call, when the TA read out, "Kathryn Rose Barton," Ryan turned to grin at me. Green eyes tending toward hazel, a perpetual California surfer's tan, curly, light brown hair streaked with sun, and an irresistible smile. I couldn't help but respond in kind. After class he called out to me as I rushed out, "Katie Rose, hold up!"

Conversation led to coffee, which led to sitting together during the lecture and then to studying together in a library quiet room. He had a girlfriend, Sophia, a petite, raven-haired spitfire. Together they nursed me through two miserable breakups—listening, swearing, and sharing vodka, cranberry, and orange juice Sea Breezes on the balcony of their apartment.

It was Ryan and Sophia who introduced me to beach volleyball. Sophia taught me to dig. Ryan taught me to serve and kill.

The whole morning comes rushing back. Jacob in my closet, the conversation with Donna, the run, my resolve crumbling. I hear the concern in Ryan's voice, but I also remember that he was there in New York on that fateful night, and he didn't say anything. I shake my head and pop the back door. It swoops open, revealing several brown paper bags and a box of kitty litter.

"No," I say, "I'm not okay."

Ryan pockets his keys and walks around the SUV in my direction.

"Why didn't you tell me what happened in New York?" I ask. "I know he's your best friend, but really? How could you not tell me?"

Ryan reaches for my arms, turns me toward him. "Kate, I am

so, so sorry. Sorry that it happened. Sorry I couldn't stop it. Shit, I'm sorry I had anything to do with it."

Shrinking back, I reach up to remove his hands. "But you did. You were there, and you could have stopped it."

"It wasn't like that, Kate. The whole situation was out of control."

"You've got to be kidding. Not *one* of you was in control?"

"We'd all been drinking. You just don't know. You've never been in one of these places. It's dark and loud and people—well, I've seen guys totally change in front of my eyes. I didn't think there was anything I could say or do that would make a difference. I stepped out, which I know now, I shouldn't have done, but at the time . . ." Ryan looks down, his brow furrowed, his mouth a grim line. "Honestly, though, Kate, it wasn't my place to tell you."

His hands go back to my arms, his eyes rising to meet mine. "I know we've been friends forever, but he's your husband. That's a line I would not cross, even for you."

I drop my chin downward, staring at his Teva flip-flops, black with a blue wave pattern.

Ryan gently tilts my face upright.

"Having said that," he says, "it wasn't deliberate, not really. After that weekend, I had to go down to Brazil for a story, and I guess I assumed he told you and you forgave him, or he decided not to tell you. Either way, when I got back, it seemed everything was fine, and I figured it was between the two of you. The fact that what happened that night might have led to, well . . ." He wraps me in a hug. "I am so sorry, so, so sorry I didn't step in and stop Alex and Christoph, stop that girl. If I could go back and do it over . . . You have to believe me."

"Believe you? I can't believe any of it. I can't believe this is happening." I pull away, turn back to the groceries. I need to keep moving. "You know how he is." I gesture to the open door, where Jacob is not. "He's always reasonable, which makes me seem unhinged. I had myself together and was ready to talk, and now two minutes with him and . . . I don't know. It's all so complicated with the kids and—oh, shit." The paper straps break on the bag I've been lifting—maybe it's too heavy or I've yanked it too abruptly—and it tips over. I know *it's only a bag*, but I feel like crying, again.

"Do you want me to talk to him?" Ryan's shoulder bumps against mine as he helps me gather the contents that have spilled out: peanut butter, zucchini, a bag of baby carrots.

"God, no. Oh, I don't know. I don't want you stuck in the middle any more than you already are. I mean, what are you going to do if Jacob and I are . . ." The words "not together" stick in my throat.

"Don't worry about me. It's not like it's the first time I've had to deal with you two being on opposite sides of an argument, or a court."

"A court?" My heart jolts.

"Hey, no. No, no. Bad word choice. I meant a beach court, Kate—you know, opposite teams."

"Oh, right. I'm sorry."

"You're sorry? It's my bad. What I meant is I've had to negotiate a lot worse than this, and at least here we all have a firm foundation. Jacob's—well, you know, Jacob. And you, Kate?" He gives me a tight smile and wraps his arm around my shoulders. "You're an incredible woman. Smart. And stronger than you know."

"Strong?" I say as I stuff the baby carrots into another bag. "I'm not even sure how I'm going to get through this day. I feel like I'm losing it just being in the same room with him."

"Listen, I know it's hard, Kate, but you need to take your time figuring this out. It hasn't even been twenty-four hours."

The spilled ingredients become the focus of my ire. The peanut butter goes into a full bag, jammed on top of some grapes.

"Easy for you to say. I can't sit there at dinner acting like everything's fine. I'm not that good an actress." I pick up the raw chicken still sitting in the broken bag and try to force it into another, also full. "Last night was hard enough, and he wasn't even there."

"Hey, hey"—Ryan takes the chicken out of my hands and puts it down—"this bird is already dead." He grins with an eyebrow raised, and for a moment I feel a glimmer of hope. "Okay, let's take one thing at a time. How about I suggest Jacob hangs with me or stays in a hotel for a couple of days. Give you some space."

I lean against him, and he folds me into his chest, rests his chin on the top of my head. He smells fresh and clean, like eucalyptus, pine, and soap. I smell awful.

"God," I say, pushing back, "I'm sorry, I'm disgusting."

"I think I heard you say you went for a run, right?" he says with just the right touch of sarcasm. "Go, go—go take a shower." Exaggerated shooing motions accompany his words. "A long, hot one, preferably with soap."

He could patent his grin.

"Seriously, I've got this. I'll put these away, talk to Jacob, and then I'll go, so you guys can work it out. How does that sound?"

How can there still be tears?

SEVEN

I HAVE COLD FEET. Marble is not a warm, friendly flooring material; it's hard, unyielding, glass-breaking, and remarkably chilly. When we first looked at this house with the kids—showing them the pool, the yard with enough room for a sand volleyball court, and the home theater with the huge recliners, armed with cup holders (Logan's favorite feature)—they spent a good five minutes running down the halls yelling, "Hellooooo," marveling at the echoes. We've put oriental runners in the hall to cut down on the sound reverberation and the chill factor. Becca likes to leap from one to the next—thank God for nonslip rug liners. As I pad down the hall toward the kitchen, my bare feet go from hard marble to plush carpet to hard marble.

I stop when I hear Ryan's and Jacob's muted voices in the office. The door is closed but for a small gap.

"She's got a point there," Ryan is saying. "After all, if it weren't for them . . ."

"Yeah, I guess. I still can't get my head around why they bought the dance in the first place. They know I'd never go for that if I were in my right mind. And Jesus, they know Kate."

"Well, maybe it was because they do know Kate. She hasn't made any secret of how she feels about them, has she? And when she doesn't like somebody, she really doesn't like 'em."

I stiffen against the wall. *Is Ryan saying I brought this on myself?* Like the marble in this house, I can be hard, unyielding, glass-breaking, and remarkably chilly. There is a short pause in their conversation. I wonder if they've heard me.

"I don't know, though, it's probably more motivated by envy," Ryan continues. "You're the guy that has it all: high-paying job, cushy life, great kids, gorgeous wife. The green-eyed monster lurks within us all."

"You're not saying they did it on purpose?" Jacob, skeptical and—wait for it—"Nah, I don't believe that."

Denying the possibility. Of course.

"I know you don't like Alex and Christoph much either, but they're my friends, or at least they were."

"All I'm saying is it's not a big loss, as far as I can tell. Kate or them? It's an easy choice." Ryan's tone is soft, nonconfrontational. "How often do you see 'em anyway?"

"Christoph's out of the country most of the time, like you used to be. And Alex . . . not much since the divorce."

"Doesn't sound like much of a hardship to cut them out of your life."

A moment of silence. Maybe they're literally taking a moment of silence for this loss of Jacob's asshole friendships.

"And while I'm handing out advice," Ryan says, "you should give her some space, man. Just a couple of days. She's reeling, and it'd probably be good for both of you. Let things settle down."

Jacob doesn't answer right away. I can picture him, sitting behind his desk or standing by the window, looking out at the backyard, hands gently clasped behind his back, his face pensive as he formulates the proper response. I can see him with my eyes closed: level-headed, analytical, removing emotional volatility by will alone.

"I don't see how being apart helps us fix anything. How can we work through this if we're not together?"

"You're going to have plenty of time to talk this through," Ryan says. "You obviously know Kate better than I do, but it seems to me she needs some space to clear her head. She doesn't like being out of control, and this is spinning her around."

"So you think I should—what? Go away? Where? And what about the kids? I told them I was going to be around all week, take them to school and practice. It's not that easy to just go."

"I'm talking two or three days, dude. You take that kind of trip all the time. I'd offer to have you stay with me, but you've seen my place. I'm wishing I could kick *myself* out to have more room." Ryan began renting a stunning oceanfront condominium a few weeks ago. Stunning and tiny—a studio, really. A peripatetic journalist that specializes in outdoor stories, he's taking a year off, he says, to work on his first novel. "Why don't you go stay at that nice hotel in town for a few days? What's it called, 'The Inn'?"

"In this town? Staying at The Inn? All it takes is one spotting by the ladies who lunch or some book club or tennis team, and the rumor spreads like wildfire that Kate and I are separated."

I've heard enough. Jacob the Whittier, behaving as though what the neighbors think is the most significant consideration. I can feel the familiar creep of negative energy entering my lungs. I need fresh air, open sky.

I am better outside, always have been. Disappearing inside is much more difficult and less protective. As a young girl, hiding under the small back porch or along the side of the house, my back up against the siding, a book in my hands, I learned that getting out was the best escape. My mother encouraged absorbing literature, particularly the classics—Joyce, Hemingway, Faulkner—as an integral part of developing a rich inner life. No *Little House* or *Lemony Snickets* outside of school for me, however. According to my mother, once one could read by oneself, reading something worthy was the only option. Looking back at it now, with children of my own, I am stunned that I persevered through material so clearly over my head. But reading saved me. The need for escape is a powerful force. It's no wonder my brain operates the way it does, given that I cut my eyeteeth on *The Sound and The Fury*.

Tolerating spiders, the pervasive smell of decay, and concrete or dirt for a seat is a thing of the distant past. Here and now, orange trees, jasmine, and rose bushes surround the teak lounge chairs with fabric-covered cushions lined up along the edge of the pool. I lie down and watch the rafts Becca and her friend Selena were using yesterday drift and bump against each other.

The term "raft" doesn't do these things justice. They are Aqua Floats, made of leakproof nylon mesh filled with foam. When we ordered them from a catalog a couple of weeks ago to replace the inflatable ones from Target that hadn't lasted a month, the kids and their friends couldn't wait to test out the claim that they "are designed to keep their shape and last forever." Nearly every day for the last week, they've used the Aqua Floats as bumper boats, landing targets for jumping contests, and islands to be knocked off of by angry sharks. Yesterday afternoon's snack time may have been the first time the Aqua Floats were used for their intended purpose: floating.

Yesterday, before, seems so far away. I close my eyes, and a cloud of white light surrounds me, pulsing. Within a minute, the sun generates a hazy red pattern on the back of my eyelids. Birds call. Water falls from the hot tub into the pool. I think about Maria and her months of tears. I am less than twenty-four hours in. Palm branches rustle with the trace of a breeze that flutters over my skin. I hear and feel my phone vibrating in the back pocket of my jeans. And I haven't told Jacob about the test results.

Suddenly, there's a shadow hanging over me.

"Kate?" I squint up at Jacob. His face is dark against the bright sky. "I was talking to Ryan, and he seems to think it'd be good for you if we spent a couple of days apart. Is that right? Is that what you want?"

What *I* want? What I want is to go back—to yesterday, to before. Or is it? Would I want to go back, knowing that what I thought I had, I really didn't?

I sit up, nodding. He sits down, shaking his head.

"Okay," he says, resigned. "I called Dr. Brachmann's office. Made an appointment. They fit me in tomorrow."

My opening, I suppose. "There's no point."

"No, Kate, you were absolutely right. I need to get tested. I want to know. We need to know."

"We can't. That's the thing, we can't know." At these words, a wave of fatigue and defeat sweeps up and over me. We will never know. "There's no test for you. For men. For what I now have."

"What do you mean, what you now have? What do you have?" He stops short. "You talked to the doctor's office."

Where to begin. "This morning. That's why I went running. I needed time to—" I stop short too. "I have HPV, the virus that causes cervical cancer."

"Cervical cancer? You have—"

"No," I interrupt. "I don't have cancer. Not at this point. Just the virus."

Jacob leans forward, resting his elbows on his knees; his hand is over his mouth as if he can't bear to say the next words. "And I gave it to you."

The wave of fatigue and defeat crashes over what I remember from my conversation with Donna and what I found online—the statistics, confusing diagnostic combinations, symptoms and lack thereof, methods of transmission. I hear myself say what surfaces: "I haven't been with anyone else for sixteen years."

"God, Kate, I'm so sorry."

"Yeah, me too," I say, because I am. I am sorry for both of us. And I am so sorry for Logan and Becca. Our poor children are collateral damage, victims who haven't done anything wrong.

"What can I do?" Jacob asks.

"Nothing. There's nothing you can do. There's nothing anyone can do. Hopefully the infection will clear, but I'll never be rid of it. It may go dormant, but it'll never go away. They want me to come back in six months."

"Six months?"

"Yeah, so, until then." The wave washes over me again, over-whelming. Not just because of what I have but because of how I got it. The fucking strobe lights flash. The bass thumps. My chest begins to tighten.

We are both silent.

Jacob stands up, takes three paces, turns, and paces back. "What are you going to do?"

I'm not sure what he's asking. *Right now? Tonight? Tomorrow?*

"I don't know. Maybe rest for a little while—I didn't get much sleep last night, and the run . . . I guess I better call Dr. Farber. Let her know I'm okay, see if I can get an appointment."

"Do you want me to go with you?"

My chest retightens. I recall asking him yesterday to go with me to see my therapist. An awful idea. Clearly my decision-making is questionable. I don't trust myself to speak. Jacob is waiting, however, so I squint up at him and force out, "Not this first time back. I think it would be better if I went alone, okay?"

"Yeah, sure. Of course. Okay."

I take a long breath. The quiet between us allows the sound of water, birds, and breeze to return to awareness, along with the whir and hum of a propeller plane overhead. I can see it arcing over Jacob's backlit head. He looks up, following my gaze.

He breaks the silence.

"Do you want me to pick up the kids, take them to soccer?"

The sun is bright, and bringing my hand up to cover my eyes takes supreme effort. I am so tired. I must choose my battles.

"Becca's supposed to go with Emily's mom—it's her turn," I say. "But you can get Logan and take him to practice. I don't want to involve them in any of this, though. What will you tell him about why you're not coming home?"

This is all new territory. Jacob is a careful navigator. He gives the question consideration before replying, "I'll tell him I've got to go to a meeting first thing tomorrow so I'm heading out tonight. I go out of town often enough. That shouldn't raise any flags."

Jacob is probably referring to nautical flags, but it is the little white flag on the pickup that comes instantly to my mind. Surrender is appealing. There's a part of me that wants to give in, right now. A part of me that wants to say, *I still want to trust you. I long for yesterday.*

I am about to give voice to those very words when Jacob says, "This is crazy. I know you need some space, Kate, and I'll go, but we've got to fix this. It'd be crazy to let what happened ruin everything. Crazy. We can fix this."

And the memories come again—my brother's words, taunting, "You can't fix crazy." His palm on my forehead as I flail wildly, trying to defend myself. Helplessness mixes with fury, sweeping over the longing. *Crazy.* What power words hold. I shudder, and the hair on my arms rises like the hair on Ophelia's back when she feels threatened. I'm not sure what I'm more afraid of, the memories or the volatility of my emotions.

"Are you going to be okay?" Jacob asks.

I look away.

What if I'm not? And what if I can't fix this?

EIGHT

DR. FARBER'S OFFICE IS located in a building complex designed to resemble a Spanish mission, complete with an inner garden courtyard and fountain, arched windows with wrought iron details, and covered corridors with terracotta tiles. The massive wooden door on the outside does not quite match the more utilitarian ones off the corridors—plain dark wood with silver suite numbers. Dr. Farber is on the second floor in the back, which necessitates walking past five office suites once I've climbed the stairs. I've been making this walk for years, passing 201, 203, 205, 209, and 211. There is no 207 or 213—the latter, I'm guessing, because of superstition.

Many of the offices are occupied by mental health practitioners. In fact, this place is a discontented, depressed, or messed-up person's smorgasbord. With a few family lawyers thrown in for good measure, you could stay right in the building and exhaust your options for happiness—moving from therapist to marriage counselor to mediator to lawyer—simply by walking down the hall. Some of the names— Dr. Lawrence Keppler, PhD, in 205 and Marsha Presman, MSW, in 209—have been here as long as I have. Others have come and gone.

Depending on how deep in the shit I am, I sometimes think about what's going on behind these doors as I make my way to 215: how lives are being mended, relationships being analyzed and

healed—or quantified and torn asunder. Today I find myself thinking about how Jacob was a catalyst for my seeking out Dr. Farber the
first time, eighteen years ago. An intelligent, good-looking, nice guy
wanted to be with me, and it was inevitable I was going to fuck it up.

It was going well. We'd spent days and nights together, and then
a week, and then another. We fit like puzzle pieces. Jacob was serious
and a little shy. I was spontaneous and a little wild. He was a lifeguard
at the beach, watching out for others and saving lives. I was a waitress,
taking orders and serving fries.

That first summer, Jacob and I would sit for hours, reading, side
by side, in the apartment he shared with Ryan. We'd all grill burgers or
eat cheap pizza and drink beer and argue about the relative merits of
Rand, Faulkner, Rushdie, and Fitzgerald, the Beatles and the Stones,
whether Alanis Morissette had staying power. We were passionate,
impetuous, and self-important. We rewatched a video of Kiraly and
Steffies dominating Dodd and Whitmarsh in the Olympic beach volleyball finals and rushed down to the sand to play our own grudge
match, Jacob and me versus Ryan and Sophia. For the first time in
my life, I felt grounded and, paradoxically, like I was floating carefree.

It was going too well. So of course, I pulled out my habitual
relationship-killing maneuvers: flirting with other guys at parties,
drinking too much, giving Jacob the silent treatment when he didn't
deserve it—testing him, waiting for him to break. The end of the
summer meant his return to the University of Pennsylvania to finish
his senior year, and I was determined not to feel loss when he left.

Self-destruction preferable to abandonment or rejection.

But Jacob didn't give up. He was a lifeguard, after all. Undercut-
ting massive breaking waves and eluding riptides were second nature
to him. He dove right in, touched bottom.

"I don't know what you think you're doing or why you're doing
it, but it's not going to work," he said. Sincere, naïve, logical—classic
Jacob. "I know there's stuff that you haven't told me and you're scared
to trust me, but listen, Kate, I'm not going anywhere. I'll wait for you
to figure it out. I'll stay the course until you believe I won't hurt you."

I remember thinking, *Could he possibly be right? Can I find a way to work through enough of my bullshit to deserve being with a guy who says things like "stay the course"?*

Those were the words that led me to seek out a therapist for the first time. The university counseling center directed me to Dr. Susan Farber, and I made an appointment—to figure it out, to see if I could trust someone enough to let him love me. And now Jacob's words have brought me here again, to explain to Dr. Farber why she and Jacob were wrong—why trust and believing in others is just more bullshit.

The thing is, I know she'll try to convince me otherwise—and I'll want to believe her.

I still want to believe glimpses of epic happiness on the horizon can be real, that I can keep my demons at bay.

It's been a few months since I've been here, which isn't unusual. I'm a sporadic patient: in a crisis, my visits can be twice a week; when I'm feeling stable, it can be every couple of months. For several years, when our primary residence was in Brooklyn Heights, New York, I didn't see Dr. Farber at all.

Her office is always the same. Two black leather chairs for patients with a small table in between, holding a box of tissues. Dr. Farber's uncluttered desk facing the wall, her black leather portfolio centered perfectly upon the desk blotter, ready to be taken in hand and flipped open. What she writes on that pad, I will never know. I asked her once and she prevaricated. She doesn't write much, which is good, because it tends to make me uncomfortable. Whenever I say something and she makes a note, I think, *Well, that's obviously significant.* I wonder if she keeps a pad for each patient, stored in a file folder somewhere that she pulls out when they come in. Whether she reviews her notes for patients like me that come irregularly, so she can remember exactly what our issues are and where we are in dealing with them.

She has a pleasantly neutral expression down pat. Years of practice. I will say, "Hello, Dr. Farber," and she will say, "So, Kate." That's it, always, "So, Kate," followed by silence—which I fill.

Not today.

"Hello, Dr. Farber."

"Kate, how are you?"

Jacob's call to her yesterday morning has unsettled things. He has altered my safe place with its predictable patterns.

"Jacob called you," I begin, and then I realize that's not at all how I wanted to start. It's out there now, though, and I must complete the train of thought. "He had absolutely no right to call you, but he did it anyway. I guess that shouldn't surprise me, since he doesn't seem to care about what he has a right to do or whom he has a right to do it with."

I want to tell her what he's done, and yet I don't. I want her to ask me about it, so I can rationalize that the reveal is not of my choosing. Dr. Farber's eyes have opened a bit wider, creating an extra crease or two on her forehead, and a wild thought pops into my head: *I'm surprised she hasn't had Botox; it would help her maintain a neutral face so much easier.* Her hair is almost completely gray.

Dr. Farber waits for me to continue. I feel the story bubbling up—hot, roiling. *Ask me,* I think. *"What do you mean, Kate? What did he do?"*

But she doesn't. She just sits there, and I start to get angry with her too.

"And now everything's fucked up," I say. "I don't even know why I'm here, since you've been telling me for years it's okay to trust people, to be vulnerable and let your guard down, and that advice has gotten me right here, to this exact moment, sitting here telling you that my husband, the guy that was going to protect me and never betray me— well, he did. I knew it would happen, and it did. And now nothing can ever be the same, and it will happen again and again, each time worse than the last." I hear myself, on the edge. "It's all gone wrong, and I don't know what to do. I've got two kids to keep safe, kids that love their dad, and I don't want to hurt them, and I never, ever wanted them to be in a broken family like mine. I've worked so hard—so fucking hard—to do it right, and Jacob has ruined it, for nothing."

I gulp. Somewhere during the last minute, I started to cry.

"For something he claims he doesn't even remember. Something he says meant nothing to him, nothing. But it means everything to me, and now, now . . ."

Dr. Farber reaches across to the table for the box of tissues, hands it to me. I continue to talk as I put the box in my lap and pull two tissues out. I don't use them, just hold them, as the whole ugly story comes spilling out.

Tears spill with the words, and my nose starts to run. I tell her about Jacob's garbled confession while I was making dinner, the freight train, and the steam. I tell her about how this betrayal brought back memories about the rape in the bathroom.

I keep to myself, as I must, how I'm barely keeping the lid on Pandora's box of soul-scorching abuse I suffered for most of that year and the next.

Some things can never be revealed—to anyone.

I tell her about the flood of memories and the strobe lights and the flight/fight response that keeps repeating. I tell her about the STI, how Donna claimed it isn't a sign of infidelity, but I fail to see that it could be anything else.

I cannot wipe my face. I feel myself trembling as I think how Jacob called people yesterday when he didn't know where I was, what he assumed, and how frightened I am that his assessment of my fragile state could someday be accurate. I think about clinging to Becca's small hand.

I explain how I don't have a big army of people—only Natalie and my friend Maria in New York, maybe Ryan, but he's Jacob's friend too, and maybe Dr. Farber herself, if therapists can even be counted. Jacob has this huge contingent of people that love and support him: his god-awful mother, his two sisters who worship him and merely tolerate me, all his work people, and so many others who think he's the nicest guy, and will never, ever believe he's not. Ever. So they'll all think it's me. They'll think it's *all* me. And I knew this would happen.

As I say, "I knew this would happen," aloud, I am suddenly aware of how pitiful I must seem. My head tumbles forward into my hands as I rock down; my shoulders and ribs contract inward. The box of tissues falls to the ground at my feet. All the pain I thought I had washed out yesterday behind the Vons and this morning in the shower returns full force, gutting me.

"It's the story of my life. I'm a magnetic force for people's shit."

"You're dealing with a lot right now—so much pain," Dr. Farber finally says. She waits for this idea to settle in. "Do you want some water?"

Actually, I do. I do want some water. How did she know I wanted water?

"Yes," I say without looking up. "Yes, thank you."

I'm still crying and rocking. I hear her leave the room to go down the hall to the little kitchenette area, the soft sucking noise of the refrigerator door opening. I try to pull myself together, straightening my back, wiping my face ineffectually with the crumpled tissues I've been clenching in my hands before I remember the box on the floor. I realize Dr. Farber is taking her time, giving me time. I pull two clean tissues out, one for each hand, and press them to my eyes and cheeks, my nose, my chin.

I am upset but contained when Dr. Farber reenters the room, offering a bottle of cold water. I take a few sips.

"It sounds like you're thinking it was a mistake to trust Jacob. That it was inevitable that he would hurt you, and now he has."

"Not hurt me. I mean, of course I knew he would hurt me. We've talked about that often enough. I know"—I look to her for her trademark confirmatory nod—"that people are hurt by those who are supposed to love them all the time and that, mostly, it's not intentional. I get it. I'm not *good* at it, but I get it. Jacob and I are going to hurt each other. But this—this is different. I can't explain it, but it is. And it's so unfair. He's given me something that can't be treated and may never go away. But of course, *he* has no symptoms, and there's no test for men, so he doesn't have to go through the humiliation of facing doctors and nurses and knowing that they know."

"It's unfair, and you are hurt—deeply hurt."

I nod. I am deeply hurt.

"You said you found out about this the night before last?"

I nod again.

"It's very fresh, this new hurt, and it's bringing up old hurt," she says in her soothing tone.

I think about how I hit my shin on a cement bench at the kids' school a couple of weeks ago, and it felt like I had broken the bone. How the acute injury was so intense I couldn't walk. Now it's a receding bump and a purple bruise, warning me to be careful. I think longingly of how much easier it would be if injuries to our souls healed as quickly and with such a predictable pattern of recovery. Instant red to dark purple, lightening before shading green to yellow to healed. Instead, emotional wounds are just like silent viruses, lying hidden and dormant, waiting for a weak moment to burst open into red, gaping internal sores that no one can see.

Old hurt. Hurt people. Daniel. His anger mixing with testosterone and power—combustible. He calls out, "Kate, come on. You can't hide."

Laughter. He is not alone. There is no escape.

"Kate?" Not Daniel. Dr. Farber.

Block Daniel.

"A blow job." I spit out the vile words. "Of all things, in one of those private rooms, in front of people we know—in front of Ryan, in front of our oldest friend."

"I see." For the first time, Dr. Farber notes something on the pad. "That makes it worse for you, that other people witnessed it."

"Of course it does. I mean, it shows Jacob doesn't give a shit about me—on so many levels. How could he do that in front of Ryan? He's Logan's godfather. Like a brother to Jacob." Brothers. Watching. Darkness begins to descend, threatening the edges of my mind. I pull myself back. Block. Focus on Dr. Farber. "Ryan said he couldn't even watch. He said he was humiliated—for himself, for Jacob. He just left the private room until she came out."

Dr. Farber nods, her lips pressed tightly together. "So, you've talked to both Ryan and Jacob."

I nod. "I think Ryan apologized more, and it's not even on him. It was two of Jacob's other friends that set it up and paid for the whole thing. Jacob swears he doesn't remember it, that he blacked out, which makes no sense—he doesn't drink like that, ever. Maybe he just blocked it out. I don't know."

"Well, excessive drinking can cause blackouts, blocking entire events, even sexual encounters," Dr. Farber says. "Perhaps it was a surprise to Jacob as well, then, when Ryan told him what he had done." She says this as a statement, not a question. "Blocked memories are complicated. The fact that he doesn't remember it could make placing value on it more difficult, which is why he could be telling the truth when he says it meant nothing to him."

"Does that matter?" I am getting angry again with Dr. Farber. Maybe she's not on my side. And she is wrong; blocked memories are blocked for a reason.

"I'm simply trying to clarify the situation, Kate. I'm not making a judgment about the impact on you of his inability to remember the event or how he feels about it. What do you think? Do those things matter to you?"

Psychobabble on demand.

"Does it matter that he says it meant nothing? No. It doesn't. I've been in therapy long enough to know the subconscious is always working, lurking, influencing everything—everything—our thoughts and dreams, our actions. And I'll tell you what—I am working overtime to try to control my subconscious, to keep it under wraps. If Jacob couldn't do that, then subconsciously, deep down inside, he must have known he was betraying me. And if he has done it once, it will happen again."

"I don't know that the answers are that easy, Kate. Yes, some things indicate a pattern. Other times, people make mistakes. The behavior is unusual, an aberration. How do you see this?"

Dr. Farber looks over at the digital clock in clear view on the bookcase, under titles like *I Hate You, Don't Leave Me!* and

Schizoaffective Disorder Simplified and *The Oxford Handbook of Eating Disorders.*

Fucked-upedness of every stripe and color.

Four more minutes.

"How do you see it, Kate?" Dr. Farber brings me back.

"It makes me angry that he can't remember, and I can't *stop* remembering. He did something wrong, and *I'm* the one paying for it. I'm the one having tests. I'm back in therapy. I can't think straight when he's around, and I'm sad and defensive. And angry, so angry I think about doing crazy things that scare the shit out of me, like throwing plates and screaming at the top of my lungs—things that would definitely scare Logan and Becca. And the one thing I don't want is to scare my kids." I pause. Breathe. "You asked me what matters? They do. They're *all* that matters, and I'm afraid I can't be the kind of mother I need to be, that maybe I've been kidding myself and all these years of trying to be better have been for naught. Maybe I'll never be anything other than damaged goods."

Sloppy seconds.

I know as I say it that this sort of self-reflection at the very end of the session is common for me; knowing there's little time left, I finally lay out the real reason I'm here. Dr. Farber is used to it.

Two minutes and—go.

"Anger itself isn't bad, Kate. It's a normal human emotion. We've talked about this. It's about how we react to anger. This can be healthy, or it can be unhealthy—for the angry person and the people around them. Remember the strategies we've gone over: Breathe. Take your time, maybe even a time-out. Try to identify what you're feeling and why you feel it. Choose your words and behaviors, rather than letting them choose you." She holds my gaze. "And as for the fight or flight, it sounds like your response wasn't inappropriate. Fear serves an important purpose. It warns us that we're in a situation from which we may need to remove or save ourselves. Fight, flight, sometimes freeze— these are natural responses to perceived threats, whether physical or psychological. You've made more progress than you're giving yourself credit for. Just being aware, striving to protect yourself and your children, working at it—that's critically important."

I nod, though I'm not sure I believe her.

"We're all damaged, Kate. We can heal ourselves, but changing the patterns of our lives is incredibly difficult work." This last sentence is spoken with her conclusion tone of voice. She reaches down to the table next to her and pulls out her black leather planner. "Do you want to schedule an appointment for next week?"

"Do you have anything tomorrow or the next day?"

"I can see you Friday at eleven. Would that work?"

I nod. "Thank you."

I do not move. I need direction—a sense of control, even if it won't last.

As if she can read my mind, Dr. Farber stands and, with her hand on the door, says, "In the meantime, if you feel that asking Jacob to leave will make you feel safer emotionally, you have the right to ask for that. Take control, yes?"

"Yes," I reply.

But I don't.

NINE

I'VE AGREED TO LET Jacob come home tomorrow and stay for the weekend. Of course, as soon as I hang up the phone, I regret the decision. I seem incapable of holding on to an emotion. Perhaps that's why I said yes—with Jacob here, at least I may be able to settle on anger for a while.

Short term, I've got dough. Wednesday is homemade pizza day—from scratch. I mix. I knead. I wait for it to rise, anticipating the punch, punch, knit, and fold that precede the rolling. I think Dr. Farber would agree that this is a healthy mode of processing and expressing aggressive energy. When it comes to using my fists, dough will do. The first couple of blows take the air out. Punch, punch, fold, flip—repeat. It's a satisfactory sensory experience: warmth yielding under my hands; the smell of yeast, flour, and salt; the taste of the pepperoni slices I cannot resist popping in my mouth to go with my first glass of one of Jacob's expensive bottles of reserve Cabernet. *Reserved for what?* I thought as I pulled out the cork.

Habit kicks in. I separate the dough into two roughly equal balls and then separate each again. Logan likes pepperoni and sausage. Becca likes breakfast bacon. Neither of them wants anything resembling a vegetable on their pizza. I, in contrast, am partial to spinach and mushrooms. Jacob has dubbed his usual, which is piled with any and all toppings used by the rest of the family, along with whatever he can find in the refrigerator, the "Kitchen Sink Pizzette."

Tonight, however, the fourth pizza belongs to Ryan. He called and offered to come over tonight as I was heading out the door to pick up the kids from school. I'm looking forward to his company, since each night is more difficult in terms of executing *Nothing is Wrong, Block Jacob*.

I should know by now that absence can be more profound than presence.

For all the faults previously enumerated, marble is an excellent platform for rolling dough of all sorts: pizza, pie, cookie, biscuit, crois-sant (which is particularly tricky to handle). I cover the island with a dusting of flour and wipe down the four identical wooden rolling pins Jacob bought and personalized for our Christmas stockings the year before last.

"Finally, a practical use for the woodworking I learned from my grandfather," he said, brandishing a high-torque-power engraving tool he'd ordered online. Rolling pins, he said, were tricky to work with, given their cylindrical shape.

Surely it comes as no surprise that Jacob has a host of natural-ist-at-large skills: bird, plant, and berry identification; pitching a tent; starting a fire with flint. Added to his water lifesaving capabilities—how to identify, calm, and drag a drowning individual, how to clear water from someone's lungs and perform CPR—he's also a certified Wilderness First Responder. The man can identify the signs of a head or spine injury and splint a broken leg on a steep, icy ski slope. He's the perfect amalgamation of Smokey the Bear, a Canadian ski patroller, and a young *Baywatch*-era David Hasselhoff.

Blocking him is way more difficult than I ever imagined. I long for him, think about him being here, efficiently rolling out his dough without even watching, his eyes floating between me and the kids, taking us in, making sure we are all okay.

Shit.

I take two balls of dough and plunk them down, hard, onto the marble. Take the other two, plunk them down even harder.

Four workstations, four balls of dough, four rolling pins. I don't think Ryan will mind using Jacob's. It has a mountain on one end and cresting waves on the other. Logan's features detailed renditions of a surfboard and a game controller. Becca's displays a bunch of lilacs and a soccer ball. Mine, a pair of running shoes and a book.

"Eww—little fish?" I hear Becca exclaim in the hall. "You put little fish on your pizza? That's gross."

"Yep," Ryan says, "I don't know if your mom will have some, but anchovies are the best." He looks at me as he enters the kitchen, Becca on his back, her arms wrapped around his neck.

I've got to agree with Becca on this one. I hate anchovies. Hairy, salty little fish of dubious origin in a can. I scrunch my nose and shake my head. "No anchovies in this house."

Becca scrunches her nose back.

Oh, how I love her.

"Don't know what you're missing." Ryan tilts sideways and catches Becca with a slight wince as she slides off. "Shall I get my godson?"

"Please," I respond.

"Watch out, Uncle Ryan, he's gonna be mad at you if you stop his game."

"Not a chance. Be right back. Wait for us."

"Uncle Ryan says he and Daddy have been putting little fish on pizza since they were as old as Logan, and they ate it cold for breakfast. He says they would put it outside on the window when it was winter, and it would be like a refrigerator. Doesn't that sound double gross, Mom, cold pizza with fish for breakfast?"

Ryan is a storyteller. He loves to regale my children with his tales. He has his classics down pat: how when he and Jacob were thirteen, Ryan dreamed up an indoor slip-n-slide plan their second weekend at boarding school, and when the two of them flooded the third floor bathroom in their dormitory, Jacob's parents had to bribe the headmaster not to kick them out; how they won the lacrosse championship in overtime with Ryan scoring against three defenders with a brilliant around-the-back pass from Jacob on the assist; the time Ryan convinced Jacob to go for a late-afternoon sail in a sixteen-foot Hobie Cat and a sudden thunderstorm nearly took them to the bottom of the Atlantic, until Jacob's masterful piloting saved them. With every telling, the details of these stories grow more outlandish.

Over the years, Ryan has dropped in and out of Logan's and Becca's lives as he's gallivanted around the world—the Pied Piper, Peter Pan, and Indiana Jones all rolled into one. My children sit, rapt and wide-eyed, on the edge of their seats, waiting for the next twist, heroic feat, or astounding escape. Uncle Ryan fascinates them and then leaves them wanting more.

"Day-old cold fish pizza does sound double gross, Boo," I say.

Becca impishly bounces around the island, looking for her rolling pin, eyeing the round balls.

"Are they all equal, Mom? 'Cause I'm as hungry as Logan," she states, finding her spot, patting her dough.

"Did you wash your hands?" I ask.

"She better not have touched mine," Logan calls out as he enters the kitchen, glaring at his sister.

"Haven't seen *your* hands under running water," Ryan says, guiding him toward the sink, where I stand rinsing my own hands. "Let he who is without sin cast the first stone."

The running water washes over Ryan's admonishment, which is just as well: the kids would have absolutely no idea what he was talking about. Although Jacob and I were both raised Catholic, he hasn't gone to church in nearly five years, and as for me—well, let's just say a loving, protective God ceased to exist when I was fifteen. My brother belied his biblical namesake, becoming the lion, ensnaring me in a den from which I barely escaped. Standing here in my kitchen, watching my children's strong arms flex as they flatten their pizza dough into misshapen circles, I remind myself that I did escape. *Didn't I?* I pick up my rolling pin and trace my finger over the running shoes.

"You okay?" Ryan murmurs into my ear. I didn't even hear him approach. He rests his hand on the small of my back.

I nod, worried my voice will betray me.

"Let's make some pie," Ryan says, moving over to his station. He lifts his ball and begins to stretch it. "All right if I throw mine?" he asks.

Of course, the children follow suit. It's much harder than it looks. Logan has a pretty good toss. Becca gives in with a "Can you throw mine, Uncle Ryan?" As for me, I roll the dough out to about three-fourth the size I eventually want and attempt a few spins, only to have my fist go straight through it on the third toss. A hole that immediately stretches larger when I lay it down on the counter.

I groan and twist my mouth and face into an exaggerated grimace. The kids laugh. Ryan is undeterred.

"I can fix that," he says, moving around the island to my side. My pizza will have a thin spot, and the kids' resulting rounds are less round than usual, but I daresay we're having a better time than ever making our pies. Sauce is spread, cheese sprinkled, toppings placed and layered.

Dinner flies by. Ryan tells us all about his adventures in Tanzania, where he reported a story for *Outdoor* magazine about the porters that help tourists climb Kilimanjaro.

"We were in Barafu, on the sixth day of the climb. We didn't sleep that much in the first place 'cause we were in tents, the ground was hard like cement, there were animals howling and scuffling, and it was just hard to breathe. When our guides woke us in the middle of the night to make the final ascent, the sky was so dark and the stars were incredible—you could even see Venus, Jupiter, and Mars right above the horizon."

I love watching my children watch things that enchant them: movies, sunset at the beach, fireworks, and their Uncle Ryan. For me, their enthralled faces tend to be far more enthralling than whatever it is they are watching.

"It was cold, bitter cold, the kind that makes your lungs hurt and your fingers tingle. I had a headache and felt sick to my stomach—all of which are symptoms of a deadly illness that can strike mountain climbers. Do you guys know what AMS is?"

Both children shake their heads. Logan's mouth freezes midchew.

"It stands for acute mountain sickness. Acute means it comes up quickly, and it can be pretty bad. It happens because there's less oxygen in the air as you go higher, and dehydration makes it worse—which, since you play sports, you guys know means you have to drink lots of . . . ?"

"Water," Logan says confidently, his mouth still full.

"Water," Becca says half a second after her brother, sounding anxious.

"But dehydration by itself is pretty common, even down here at sea level," I add to the conversation. "And you are both really careful about drinking water."

Becca looks to me and then to Ryan. He nods.

"Absolutely, your mom is right. It's just when you're up high in the mountains, you have to be even more careful. The day before, they'd evacuated two people for AMS on gurneys. They had it bad, but I knew I'd be okay. I had to be okay to get to the top."

Ryan says this last sentence with gravity.

"How did you know you'd be okay?" Becca's face is etched with concern.

I raise my eyebrows at Ryan; time to make this less scary.

"Well, Becs, I've climbed lots of mountains. I knew the headaches and stomachaches and not being able to sleep are all pretty common when you get up that high." Ryan smiles encouragingly, his eyes crinkling. "The trail was empty, but you can't move as fast up there—each step is hard at some point—so I'm just putting one foot in front of another when, all of a sudden, a monkey came up behind me and passed me, running, with another monkey on his back. I could swear the hitchhiker monkey was grinning at me. He was eating this banana, the peels falling down over his hand."

"Monkeys climb mountains?" Becca asks, and I can tell Logan wants to ask too. He wants it to be true, but he's not sure this is believable, even for his Uncle Ryan.

"Absolutely, sure they do. Apparently, they *run* up mountains. There are monkeys all over the trail. Giraffes, leopards, wild dogs. It's crazy up there." Mingling fact with fiction makes for a great story. "Got to be vigilant, move slowly, don't startle them."

"See, that's why I want to be a writer, Mom," Logan says. "Uncle Ryan gets to do cool things. Way cooler than managing other people's money."

"Nah, you're wrong." Ryan shakes his head. "What your dad does is awesome. And if he had my job, you wouldn't get to see him much."

"Where are you going next?" Becca asks.

"Well, I was scheduled to go to New Zealand, where they filmed *The Hobbit*—which, I happen to know, is your favorite book."

Becca's mouth literally drops into an O, her eyes resembling an anime cartoon character. "You're going to Middle Earth?"

"I *was* going to Middle Earth, but now I'm going to stay here for a while."

"You're staying here?" She's over the moon, the stars, Jupiter, and Mars.

"Yep, I'm writing a book, and I'm staying right here until it's done. Didn't your mom and dad tell you guys?" Ryan shoots me a *Geez, Mom* look. "You two are part of the reason I'm staying put for a while. I want to watch you kick some butt on the soccer field and show me up out on the waves."

"But now," I interject, "I think Uncle Ryan wants to see you clean up these dishes."

Logan and Becca moan a bit as they comply with this one consistent chore that is asked of them—loading dishes. They even work together, sort of, until Logan becomes impatient with his sister for not moving fast enough.

"It must be nice having a sister to help you out," Ryan calls, watching the scene unfold. "I always wished I had a brother or a sister. . .

until I met your dad and then, boom, I had one, and an instant extra family."

What Ryan doesn't volunteer is that his parents died within eight months of each other, when he was fifteen. A scholarship student, Ryan was more or less adopted, unofficially, by the Whittiers. He spent every major holiday at either the Boston or Newport Beach estate and summered at the Whittier compound on Cape Cod until Jacob and I were married and we became his de facto family. Though, to be honest, we all still make the Whittier pilgrimage when Grace "calls us home."

I recall the first time I heard the word "summer" used as a verb. The April before his senior year, Ryan was explaining how his best friend/brother from another mother and he (and Sophia, by default) were going to be living together for the summer, and how I "would love the guy. He's literally practically perfect in every way." How, for Jacob, living in a rented house in Mission Beach represented "slumming as opposed to summering," but it was worth it to him to have a season of freedom before the real world and responsibility kicked in. Of course, Jacob would have responsibility all along—first as a lifeguard and then as the guy who decided to save me.

He saved me over and over. And now it's all gone wrong anyway.

I remember telling Dr. Farber years ago, before we moved to New York, after a particularly bad week with a baby, a toddler, and a husband that couldn't understand how postpartum mood swings scared the shit out of me, that for Jacob, life with me must seem a bit like being perpetually stuck in a riptide: every time you think you're about to make it safely to shore, you get swept back out, past the break. I recognize that it's been hard for him. I also recognize that if he knew the whole truth about me, he would have let the current take me out to sea a long time ago. What choice do I have now?

I won't find the answer to that question. The wound is too fresh, and I am too sleep-deprived. I look over at the kids and wish that Jacob were here, if only so he could help deal with making sure their homework is done and getting them into bed. Ophelia brushes against my leg, reminding me that I haven't cleaned her litter box yet. I am so tired.

"Mommy, we don't have to read *The Hobbit* tonight," Becca says, as if she can read my mind. "Daddy told me he's coming home tomorrow and he'll read two chapters. I told him he had to catch up first, and he said he already read *The Hobbit* when he was in school."

"You talked to your dad today?" I ask, though I shouldn't be surprised. Against my wishes, Jacob bought Becca her own cell phone last year, ostensibly so she could always reach us when at soccer or a friend's house.

"Yeah, he called me when I was in Ms. Bentley's car coming home from soccer. Uncle Ryan said he can stay and watch *The Voice* with us. Can we do that instead of reading?"

"You watch *The Voice*?" I ask Ryan.

Becca spins to witness his response, so he nods. "Absolutely, wouldn't miss it."

Becca scoops Ophelia into her arms and scampers down the hall to get her "'jamas" on for optimal viewing comfort.

As soon as she is out of earshot, Ryan confides, "I've never seen *The Voice*."

"You're awful," I kid, moving to the L-shaped couch in the family room, plush and wide as a bed. "Someday you're going to get caught. I may let you sink in front of Becca, ask you who's going to win."

"An idle threat, my dear, since I can easily find out." Ryan follows me, phone in hand, looking out from under a single raised eyebrow.

How does he do that?

"It's elementary, my dear," he adds with his classic Sherlock Holmesian English accent. "Just imagine, what if Watson and I had had the internet? Would have changed the whole dynamic."

And he's off. Ryan loves posing "what-ifs," as he calls them, for literary characters and real-life historical figures—things like "What if Ashley wasn't a gentleman and slept with Scarlett? What if Lincoln had listened to all of his advisers and decided not to go to the Ford Theater for the performance of *Our American Cousin* that fateful night in April 1865? What if the British Naval officer hadn't appeared on the beach to save Ralph from the other boys on the island in *Lord of the Flies*?" Fully developed, a what-if feels like an alternative universe, with Ryan pulling everyone in to play along.

Tonight, however, the game stops short. I give him a wan smile as I drop onto the couch and pull a throw pillow under my head. "What if I could go to sleep right here, right now?" I draw a fleece blanket up to my chin and close my eyes, sighing. "But I can't, and by the time the kids are in bed, I probably won't be able to. God, I wish I could pop some Ambien and be done with it."

"Kate?"

I open my eyes to see Ryan raising both eyebrows in a sharp, questioning arch.

"I mean one pill, Ryan. To sleep—which, by the way, I wouldn't do anyway, not when I'm the only adult in the house. That's a hard-and-fast rule: no sleeping pills when Jacob is gone. Though I could so use a good night's sleep."

"I can stay," Ryan says. He sits down next to me. "I could sleep here, on the couch." He moves his hand in a caress over the fabric. "It may be nicer than the bed in my rental." He gives me one of his classic grins. "Seriously, Kate—after *The Voice*, when the kids are in bed, go ahead and take your sleeping pill. I'll be your backup. No worries."

No worries, at least for eight hours. That's an offer I cannot refuse. *Sleep, Kate, sleep.*

TEN

JACOB HAS BEEN HOME for seven days. He sleeps in the guest room, making certain he rises early to remake the bed, including decorative pillow placement, so if one of the children happens to enter the room, they won't know anyone slept there. The emotional cover-up is more challenging. At my insistence, terms of endearment between us have ceased. Tension is building, filling the vacuum that sits where normal used to be. I run every day, miles and miles, in an effort to defuse volatile fears and feelings that ebb and flow with a rapidity that frightens me.

The kids provided a buffer over the weekend. Then came Monday, Tuesday, Wednesday. Despite my fervent requests that he return to work in the office, to give us both space, Jacob insists that spending time together is the only way to "fix" this. He makes lunch, waiting for me to come home from a walk with Natalie, a punishing run, or a sob session behind Vons. He clings and feigns, desperately holding on to his version of us. I, meanwhile, barricade, bury, and escape, fighting for my battle-scarred sense of self. Broken, weary, and plagued with doubt, yet unwilling to surrender, I notice every move, every mistake, Jacob makes.

I resort to Barton tactics: drinking more than I should, yelling, throwing things.

Today's battlefield is the aisle next to the second dishwasher on the back of the kitchen island. The casualty: a Churchill Blue Willow dish Jacob left out for our lunch, part of a set I received as a gift from Grace. Classic and elegant, in cobalt blue and creamy white. The catalyst: Jacob informs me he spoke to his mother and committed to Thanksgiving at her house back East, which he figured won't be a problem since "it's only the one issue; surely we'll have worked things out by then."

I feel his mother's judgment—instantaneous, indignant, and unforgiving.

"You told your mother we were coming without discussing it with me?"

"It's Thanksgiving, Kate," he says. "I mentioned it to Natalie, and she thought it was a great idea. She said doing things with family always helps her remember what's truly important."

"Natalie? When did you talk to Natalie?"

"She called a few days ago," he says, his voice matter-of-fact.

"Natalie called you?"

"Yes, Kate," Jacob says in the same "no big deal" tone. "She was worried, and honestly, it was good for both of us."

I imagine them talking about me, comparing notes, and I feel Natalie's judgment magnifying Grace's—wrapped in good intentions, yet no easier to bear.

Jacob goes on, "I appreciated hearing her perspective, and she was glad to hear my side of the story."

I am stunned.

"Your side of the story?" I repeat. "Wait, you told her what happened?"

Their imagined conversation takes a totally different turn in my head. No wonder Natalie's face has been permanently stuck in "oh, Kate" mode the last couple of days. How quiet she's been.

She's taken his side before she's even heard mine.

"You mean you hadn't told her?" Jacob is saying. "Honestly, I thought, for sure . . ." He shakes his head. "Come to think of it, she did seem surprised. She said something about trust issues—how hard it is for you, even with her. In fact, now that I reflect on it, she sounded hurt." His tone is of concern—for *her*, not me. "Maybe you should call her to explain."

"*I* should call *her* to *explain?*"

"It might help, Kate . . ."

Once again, I think, *Jacob does something, and the resulting consequences are my responsibility.*

"And she is one of your only friends," he finishes.

Though this last statement is true, it sounds like he's pointing out another failure on my part: my continued inability to make and hold on to friends. Heat rises within me, and this time fight wins out over flight. Before I know what I'm about to do, I pick up a plate and throw it in Jacob's general direction. The action is primeval—an expression of impotence and rage, not violence. Unconsciously aimed for the marble backsplash, the move is not designed to injure my husband. Not bodily, anyway.

And while his response, "This is not what Dr. Reynolds had in mind when he discussed appropriate expressions of anger," is not surprising, it does go to show how little he understands my current state of mind.

Jacob has no idea how satisfying the sound of china shattering upon impact with marble can be, nor does he have any appreciation for a physical manifestation of fragility that I can somehow control. Not to mention the added benefit of destroying something that represents Whittierness.

My response to his response is similarly unsurprising—his fuel to my fire. I pick up another plate, holding it in my right hand, eyes fixed on him. I cannot help but wonder, *Is this what he does to me or is this who I am?*

"This is crazy," Jacob says. "Kate, put the plate down." He holds his hands up, wrists tilted, palms facing me, as if he's calming a wild animal. "I know you're angry at me for telling my mother we'd come for Thanksgiving, for talking to Natalie. But surely you can see this is crazy. Please, can we just have a civilized conversation?"

Crazy. Civilized. With two words, he negates his attempt at empathic communication.

"Civilized? Like your parents were that first Thanksgiving?" I say, knowing where this will go, wishing I could stop it. "When your mother basically called me a bitch?"

I look down at the plate in my hand—feel Grace's disapproval emanating from it.

Jacob shakes his head slowly.

"Oh, right," I say, "strike that—it was a 'mangy mutt.'"

"She didn't call you that."

He's right, she didn't have to.

I was twenty. It was my first time visiting the Whittier compound "back East." I was struggling to be good enough, suppressing the Barton, trying hard to follow rules for proper behavior, hoping I would pass Grace's test of acceptability. Walking past the paneled library on the way back to my room after intentionally losing a card game to Jacob's little sister, I heard his father, James, arguing with Grace. She was, as she put it, "sharing her concerns" about my lack of breeding and pedigree, my questionable bloodlines. Those were the actual words she used—"questionable bloodlines and lack of pedigree," like I was some kind of dog. James told her she was being ridiculous, but that if she wanted to use that analogy, she might want to think about how purebreds eventually develop a host of problems like hip dysplasia and heart disease. He said, in a slightly ironic tone, that she might want to consider I could be a positive thing for their grandchildren.

I remember that, beyond being insulted, I was amazed that Jacob's parents were discussing our progeny when I wasn't sure Jacob and I would last another year, let alone have children. I looked down at my hands, saw them shaking from both anger and fear, and thought, *What if Grace is right?* And what would his parents think if they knew the truth about who I was? Hip dysplasia and heart disease would be a fucking picnic in comparison. I remember distinctly my first thought was *I can never tell Jacob the whole truth*, followed quickly by *Well, it can't get much worse than this, can it?* Then Grace said, "You're awfully quiet, Jacob," and I realized that he'd been there the whole time.

He didn't defend me. He didn't say a word.

"She didn't have to say the actual words, Jacob. The implication was clear enough. And as I recall, you didn't say anything, did you? If that's what civilized looks like, I'll pass."

"It was a long time ago, Kate." Jacob sighs. "I know you're angry and frustrated. For what it's worth, I'm frustrated too. I was hoping it would go more smoothly with Dr. Reynolds."

Jacob doesn't look frustrated. He looks completely unfazed.

I remain coiled, the creamy finish of the plate's lip between my fingertips. He doesn't realize how his behavior is affecting me—his composed demeanor, his careful words, like bellows. Mentioning Dr. Reynolds doesn't help either. Jacob found our new marital therapist after "making some discreet inquiries," and—surprise, surprise—I don't like him, and he loves Jacob.

What became patently obvious during our first joint therapy session was that if you chip away at Jacob, you get more Jacob. If you chip away at me, you find that underneath the careful construction of Kathryn Rose Barton Whittier is a whole lot of mess.

This would be bad enough except that I have been actively working, hard, on becoming and being a better version of myself for years. Literally, years. Struggling to bury painful memories and suppress paralyzing fears. Holding on. Grieving for the childhood I lost; piecing together the strands of what makes a happy family out of thin air, how-to books, and my therapist's advice; and trying to be the parent I never had. Convincing myself that love and trust have a place in my world and that I am worthy of receiving and giving them to others. Trust issues? Yes, I have trust issues. Serious trust issues.

This would take sessions and sessions to fully explain to the good Dr. Reynolds.

Jacob, in contrast, need only work on being Jacob. This took him a total of five minutes.

When Dr. Lawrence Reynolds, PhD, LMFT, asked my practically perfect in every way husband why he thought we were there in his office, Jacob answered, with a sincerity that simply couldn't be questioned, "I'm here because I want to work things out. I don't want one evening gone wrong to ruin our lives. Kate is angry, and I know she has a right to be, but I'm hoping she can find a way to let it go, so we can move forward as a family."

I imagined Dr. Reynolds's internal dialogue as I watched him watch Jacob, nodding in appreciative affirmation: "Such a good plan. Well done, Jacob. One, two sessions, tops, and we'll have this solved."

I don't trust Dr. Reynolds. He is in his thirties with a full head of hair, a beard, and a mustache—neatly trimmed, dark blond (why is he covering half of his face with hair?). At that first session, he was wearing a gray cardigan sweater over a button-down shirt and fleur-de-lis tie, pressed slate trousers, and black, lace-up wingtip shoes. No wedding ring. I found myself wondering, *How does he know anything about marriage, children, infidelity, abuse, a woman's point of view? How can he possibly understand instability stored in the very cells of my being, reawakened and careening about in ways I don't understand myself?*

"What about you, Kate?" Dr. Reynolds asked.

I distilled the sound and fury in my head. "Jacob is right. I am angry, and I am finding it difficult to let it go."

"Tell me more about that." Psychotherapy 101. Dr. Reynolds—Larry to his friends, I'm sure—and Jacob wore matching looks of sincere interest.

It didn't go well from there. According to Larry, it's all on me. I should try to be less accusatory, find ways to express my anger in a psychologically sound manner, focus on the positive, reflect on how forgiveness is an essential part of any healthy relationship. Somehow, *I* am to blame.

Back in the kitchen, Jacob hasn't moved. Nor have I.

He wants us to be happy together again, the way we were. But events change us. Sometimes forever.

Smooth, whole Blue Willow rests in my hand.

Sharp, broken shards of Blue Willow litter the floor.

"We should clean this up," Mr. Fix-it says, his face closed off. "Put the plate down, Kate."

I consider warning him, "Holding on to negative emotions in your leakproof soul can have consequences too." Instead, I place the dish on the counter and walk out of the room.

This cannot go on.

ELEVEN

THIS IS MY LIFE NOW, four weeks post-confession. Sunday, I wake to a whisper, Becca's face on the pillow next to mine. Monday through Wednesday, I wake to my iPhone alarm harp strumming and am reassured by the normalcy of school mornings, breakfasts to eat, backpacks and soccer gear to load in the car. On Thursday, Friday, and non-early-morning-soccer Saturdays, I awaken whenever I want, alone. I have claimed the center of the bed. With my spine on the firm island that runs down the middle, my outstretched arms and legs dip into the mattress depressions on either side—to the left is the slightly deeper one formed by Jacob's six-foot-two frame; to the right is my own.

Jacob takes the children home from soccer on Wednesday and returns them Saturday evening. He has rented a three-bedroom house, month-to-month, that can take him through the summer, if necessary. Becca informs me that "Daddy doesn't have a pool, but he says that hopefully we can all be together once spring comes anyway."

I will not rise to this bait. With a tight smile, I deflect, "Plus he's so close to the beach."

He is close to the beach. Three blocks. Logan reports you can see blue ocean from the second-story balcony off the bedroom, that he and his dad bought a telescope to watch the stars and check out the size of the breaking waves to assist in making early surfing decisions on Saturday mornings—surf or breakfast first. Riding bikes to get donuts or making Dad's famous omelets. It's an adventure with Dad.

We are courteous, Jacob and I, which is movement in a positive direction. We discuss logistics in polite tones: the soccer tournament snack schedule, Logan's birthday party planning (Jacob and Ryan are working on a go-kart racing outing), homework, orthodontia, sleepovers.

Larry, a.k.a. Dr. Reynolds, has suggested that, for the time being, we restrict our relationship conversations to the safe confines of his office, to prevent saying or doing things we might regret without a referee present. Given the charged atmosphere we have cultivated in his safe confines, I'm not surprised that Larry would be concerned. I have always wondered when I see people treat each other badly in public, *How awful must it be when they are alone?* So, while I do not like Larry, I think he may be right about this one thing. The forced compartmentalization of our marital issues to therapeutic zones has enabled me to behave in a manner that doesn't add credence to the idea that I might actually lose it.

Though I may lose it, still. There are days . . .

I miss the children when they're gone. The first afternoon they went to Jacob's instead of coming home, I found myself wandering around the house, going from room to room, the emptiness acute. I wasn't even aware I was calling out in grief until my cries echoed back to me. I want to say that it has gotten easier, and in some small ways, it has. But I miss my children so much it hurts. I miss the family we made. I miss Jacob. I do.

When the children were small and Jacob had to travel often for work, I used to say we had two lives, "Daddy-home" and "Daddy-away." As they got older, Logan and Becca knew which routines went with which lifestyle: Swimming at the beach followed by burgers on the barbecue was Daddy-home. Playing hooky from school on a lark and going to the zoo when we lived in New York or the Wild Animal Park here in California was Daddy-away. Lounging around eating donuts on a Saturday morning while watching cartoons so Mommy could sleep was Daddy-home. Breakfast for dinner was Daddy-away.

Now, Saturday evening through Wednesday afternoon is Daddy-away.

I don't know what they call it when they're at their dad's—maybe Mommy-away, though I'm not. Not really.

I'm home. They are away.

The transitions are always the hardest. I expect if it's hard for me, it must be even harder for them, but maybe it isn't. Then again, maybe it's scarring them for life.

I make plans to keep myself busy: walks with Natalie, laundry, grocery shopping, cleaning (I bought a steamer, which I find indescribably satisfying to use), going to see Dr. Farber (which is difficult but makes me feel better), going to see Dr. Reynolds (which is difficult and usually makes me feel worse), and hanging out with Ryan (which is easy and always makes me feel better).

I try to banish the memories and ignore the increasing frequency of nineteen-year-old-Daniel sightings. I try not to think about being alone in a big house with a maniacal older brother that may be trying to find me. I am grateful, in this one regard, for my neighborhood's gates and guards.

I even try to plan time for weeping—behind the Vons from 10:30 a.m. to 11:00 a.m. on weekdays when the children are home, and from 5:30 p.m. to 6:15 p.m. on days when they are away. Even though Jacob is gone and I could cry at home, I find it helpful to restrict my grief—or at least, to try.

Bedtime has been the toughest to conquer.

Early on, I would go into Logan's and Becca's rooms at night, where I would sit cross-legged on the floor, lie on one of their beds, or collapse onto one of Logan's blue denim beanbag chairs in front of the television he uses for video games. I'd sit or lie or collapse, remembering.

One night I pulled out some of their favorite books—*Dinosaur Fright*, *Paddington*, and *Guess How Much I Love You?*—and read them to myself slowly, trying to recall the smell and feel of their bodies. I allowed myself to dwell on their absence, yearning for Becca's pout or Logan's eye-roll, the arguing over homework, their bickering, and the inevitable "Mom, Logan's being mean" or "She's a pest; can you get her out of here?"

I imagined them curled up with their dad on a couch I've never seen in a room I've never seen, watching television or reading *The Hobbit*, an activity Jacob actually brought up with Dr. Reynolds. Jacob asked him if it was fair for me to restrict him from reading aloud to his children in the book of their choosing. His argument—"Isn't it better, with all this change afoot, to provide them with continuity whenever and wherever possible?"—garnered him yet more esteem in the good doctor's eyes. I could see it in Larry's earnest, beady eyes, all the more noticeable since the other half of his face is obscured by that beard.

I explained that the children associate certain activities with one or the other of us, and those should be sacrosanct. I wouldn't dream of trying to steal surfing or the donut shop. Why was it okay for Jacob to appropriate singing the lullaby I taught Logan and Becca or reading to them with voices?

Larry said, and I quote, "Healthy, comforting family activities, the things that make the children feel secure and grounded—these should not be restricted to one parent or another. If the children want their father to read to them, he should read to them. If they want you to take them surfing, you should be able to do that too."

Which would be all fine and good except that I am not a confident enough surfer to take my children out in the waves, and I would never take them out for donuts—which, I wanted to tell Dr. Reynolds, hardly qualifies as a "healthy family activity."

———

Last night, the end of the second week of our separation, I called Maria, my only true friend in New York. We met years ago in our neighborhood playground in Brooklyn Heights—on a Saturday, because Maria only came to the park on weekends. She looked as uncomfortable as I felt. We were like intruders at an exclusive club with opaque, unwritten rules of membership and behavior. It was remarkable how much a children's playground in an upscale New York City neighborhood reminded me of the Whittiers' country club.

I pointed out the similarity to Maria the second Saturday we met, telling her about the time I asked Jacob how one gained entry to their country club, and he replied, "There are only two types of new members here—the Bornwells and the Marriedwells." I explained to Maria that it had taken me a minute to understand these were not surnames and how it took a bit longer to comprehend that being a Marriedwell made the unfathomable rules even more critical to follow.

I wanted desperately to do it right—to be the right kind of wife and mother—and I needed Jacob to guide me. I told Maria about a time when our children were small, maybe five and two, and Jacob and I brought them to the country club swimming pool. We decided to take them to the snack bar for some French fries, and on the way past the clubhouse, we saw his mother, Grace, having lunch. I began to wave Becca's pudgy little hand with mine at her grandmother and encouraged Logan to wave too. Jacob scooped Logan up in his arms, literally pulled my hand with Becca's out of the air, and shushed me, adding under his breath that that sort of thing simply wasn't done. His mother was at a luncheon, he said, his voice low and serious, with the ladies that lunched. "Lunch" being a verb, like "summer."

Acknowledging wet children in bathing suits would be a great embarrassment.

I was shocked. Logan and Becca were little and adorable, and their grandmother, sitting less than fifteen feet away, would not—no, should not, could not—acknowledge them?

Maria got it, right away.

"That is seriously fucked up," she said.

It felt good to have confirmation of what I barely allowed myself to think—that maybe I wasn't the only one in my marriage with some messed-up issues.

In Maria, I found a kindred soul. We would sit on a bench away from the other mothers—discussing our children, to be sure, but also books and politics and her job. Maria worked full time, plus, in public relations. Brilliant, witty, and a tad cynical, she was, and is, a first-class spin doctor. Read one of her marketing brochures or press releases, and you are sold. Six years out of college, she started a firm with an associate—the Alex of New-York-stripper-club fame—who became her husband, and then her ex-husband.

"He'll regret the affairs someday, probably soon, much sooner than he realizes," she told me the day their nasty divorce became final. "They were all classic beauties. Did I tell you that? Two blond, blue-eyed skinny bitches and one brunette skinny bitch with, of all things, green eyes. That's the one I found out about first—of course. Letting me wax on about green-eyed monsters. It hurt, at first, since I know I'm not beautiful, or skinny."

"What?" I said. "That's not true, Maria. You're gorgeous."

"I'm not being self-deprecating or critical, Kate. Gorgeous? Come on. You—you're gorgeous. Me—I'm handsome, which is fine, truly fine by me. Handsome women grow old gracefully. Our strong lines and bold features become assets in the long run. The thing is, it shouldn't have surprised me that Alex isn't the sort to wait for the long run. I could kick myself for believing his promote. I'm in the fucking promotion business."

———

Last night, her voice far away, Maria told me she's into acceptance. That's how she opened the call.

"Kate, how the hell are you?" she said in her trademark husky voice.

"Okay," I said automatically. "How are you?"

"I'm into acceptance, sweetheart. Full-on embracing of acceptance. Letting shit go. I can thank yoga for that. It's my mantra, my intention, whatever you want to call it—radical acceptance of where I am, where Maddie is, the state of the world."

With a few well-placed uh-huhs, I got the whole picture. She's worked through all the stages of grieving: denial, anger, bargaining, depression, and acceptance. She read somewhere that not everyone goes through the steps in that order, the first one described by Kübler-Ross, but Maria did. And she's realized Alex was cheating for years, from the time their daughter was born.

"After Maddie," she said, "I just didn't have the energy for him. He's like a child, really—needy, insecure. You're so lucky with Jacob. He's an adult, an adult who cares about what people think of him, what society expects of him."

I hadn't told her about Jacob moving out. I'm going through the stages in a different order: I started with anger and have now moved into some kind of denial. At least when it comes to telling people about it. Meanwhile, Jacob, Mr. Appearance-Is-Everything, has surprised me. Though he hasn't told his mother, of course, he's discussed it with a few of his work colleagues, and Natalie, and, of course, Ryan, who was there, after all. As far as I know, he's abided by my wishes and hasn't spoken with Alex or Christoph. That Maria remained unaware confirmed this; Alex would be all over our separation, all "I told you Kate was a bitch and he'd leave her someday."

"Yes, well, I'll grant him that," I said, returning to the conversation. "Jacob does still seem to care what people think of him." I could hear how spiteful I sounded.

"Wait, you sound upset. What's going on?" Maria has skepticism as a natural undertone.

"It's nothing." I didn't even sound convincing to myself.

"Kate, come on. It's me. Spill."

"Jacob moved out a couple of weeks ago. He's got the kids for the next two nights."

"What? No shit," Maria said. "And here I am going on and on about myself. What happened? Are you okay?"

"It's not worth going into details. Let's just say . . . he betrayed my trust." That's how I should be explaining it to everyone. So succinct. Clean. Not ugly and complicated, as it really is.

"Betrayed your trust? What the hell. He cheated on you?"

"If there was anyone I'd tell, Maria, it'd be you. Something happened during one of his trips to New York. I'm just not ready to talk about it. Not yet."

"Are you sure?"

"Positive."

"Okay." She sighed. "It's your story. When you are ready, I'll be here to listen. Take it from me, though, Kate, don't hold on to it too long. Letting these things go is good for the soul. Meantime, anything I can do?"

"Yeah. Tell me how you get through the nights when Maddie is gone. Is it awful? Because this is awful. I can't seem to leave their rooms."

"Sweetheart, I wish I could feed you some line about how to view this as a good thing, you know—it's freeing, you'll have time to yourself, that sort of bullshit—but I wouldn't be fooling you, so I'm not going to lie. It pretty much sucks for a while. My advice, just be in it. Let yourself cry or get angry or whatever. Have a glass of wine or two—fuck it, three or four. Watch a sad movie. That always helped me. I would watch a real tearjerker, like *Out of Africa* or *Terms of Endearment*, and weep. Somehow it made me feel better to have an external reason to cry—you know, like I was kidding my subconscious into believing the tears were for Meryl Streep or Shirley MacLaine, not for myself."

"I think I have an old DVD of *Out of Africa*. Or maybe it's online?"

"Try to find it. It's the best, in my humble opinion. At the beginning, I would watch the whole thing. 'I had a farm in Africa'"—Maria slipped into a wicked impression of Meryl Streep's Danish accent—"'at the foot of the Ngong Hills.' But as time went on, I could fast-forward to one of the scenes that always brought on the tears—go straight there, cry, be done with it in ten minutes."

I told Maria about my Vons parking lot. She understood. We talked about her work and the kids. She shared a story about Maddie's latest swim meet and the swimsuit she absolutely had to have for her American Girl doll. We talked about how nice it would be to keep our daughters young and innocent for as long as we could, which led to waxing philosophical about the passage of time—how a toddler day could feel like a week, but it was all fleeting in retrospect. She reminded me of a quote: "The days are long, but the years are short." Then she told me about a book I absolutely must read and promised to email me a full list of the ones that helped her get through the first few months of her separation.

I hung up feeling marginally better. Then I found *Out of Africa* and let it work its charm.

Today is Friday. I woke at 11:42 a.m., went out to the driveway to collect *The New York Times*. Made a pot of coffee and toasted a bagel. Ordinary things. I ate breakfast by the pool, watching Ophelia prowl in the bushes, listening to the waterfall, the birds, and the sound of relative quiet. I read my way through the paper, finishing with an article about the mixed results of austerity economics in the European Union that ended on A12, corruption charges leveled against a big bank's CEO on B7, and a review of a new play starring a Hollywood actress who's trying to return to her roots on the stage on C4. I note these page numbers with thoughts of my mother and one of her favorite insults: "He doesn't read past page one."

Willful ignorance was an affront to my mother, as were laziness, impertinence, and moral laxity. Ironically, she was guilty of all of these herself: the first when it came to her children and their needs; the second whenever she was too blue to move; the third whenever she stated an opinion about another, lesser, human being; and the fourth, well, suffice to say mania doesn't necessarily jibe with taking the high moral road.

Yesterday, Dr. Farber and I spent a long time talking about the effects of affective disorders—how my mother was not able to control her moods, how she was as much a victim as we all were. For the first time, I told Dr. Farber about waking in the middle of the night to the sound of her playing the flute—Paganini, Debussy, and Prokofiev— the notes soaring in the dark. Or coming home from school to find her in the kitchen, music blaring, the smell of clove cigarettes in the air, her form bent over a table covered with sheet after sheet of yellow, college-ruled, lined paper, words spilling out faster than she could write them down. I knew my mother was a genius long before I knew how to describe her as such. I grew frightened of uncontained intellectual power, of its capacity to overwhelm and paralyze.

Family legacy.

As if on cue, I hear Natalie's voice calling from the kitchen— she's here to meet me for our daily walk. Lately, she and I have been talking a lot about family—the ties and expectations—in relation to her eldest son, Taylor. A senior in high school, Taylor's in the midst of the college application process. It's become an obsession for Natalie: the tests, essays, letters of recommendation, lists of awards. I am learning how much the process has changed since I applied, pinning all my hopes on one school, on getting away. Thankfully, Natalie's obsession has provided an ironclad distraction for our daily walks because I cannot discuss my life with her. She believes I am throwing happiness away, asking Jacob to move out because of—as she sees it—a foolish, drunken moment. I haven't told her about the HPV. I certainly can't explain the darkness this whole situation has brought to the surface or tell her anything about my past. A rift has begun to grow between us.

Today, as we pass manicured house after manicured house, Natalie tells me that she and her extended family are hoping Taylor will go to Amherst, a small liberal arts college in Massachusetts. The pressure is intense because he is a legacy. His father went to Amherst, and Natalie has told me that his essay, "Why Amherst?" was "beau- tiful, really," a tribute to the father he lost too soon.

About nine months ago, Natalie's husband, Michael, was involved in a freak auto accident. He was on a business trip in Germany, and the hired car in which he was traveling was hit from behind on the rain-soaked Autobahn between Hamburg and Bremen. The car spun and flipped twice. Michael died instantly.

It was truly awful—the phone calls, dealing with the consulate and the funeral home in Germany, details about embalming and shipping the body. Natalie and the boys were like a family of statues, their faces carved with grief, moving through the world in hazy shock. The unthinkable had happened: their husband and father left for the airport and never came home.

Compounding Natalie's sorrow was the fact that she and Michael had argued the morning of his trip about curfew enforcement for their middle son, Tanner, who at sixteen was pushing their buttons. Today, as she hugs me goodbye, she reminds me again how she hears her last words to Michael playing over and over, as if on a looped tape that will not stop, "You set me up, Michael—making rules that are too hard to enforce and leaving me to enforce them. Go, just go."

"Can you believe I said that?" she asks me. "Go, just go. That was the last thing I said. Not 'I love you,' not 'Have a good trip,' not 'I'll be waiting.'" She shakes her head. "'Go, just go.' Be careful, Kate. You don't know how much time you have, and no one ever told me to be careful about how I part with the people I love. That I should make sure my last words are loving."

Wanting to change the subject but also wanting to comfort her, I repeat words I've said a dozen times, fully aware I cannot convince her: "Most of us don't think about that, Nat. It could happen to anyone. Michael knew you loved him. He knew that above all else."

After she has gone home, I remember begging Jacob to "just go" the night of his confession. I try to think about my last words to my mother and draw a blank. Chances are it wasn't "I love you" or "I'll be waiting"—though I did, and I was. I was always waiting.

The truth is, however, none of us gets those moments back to do over.

What-ifs, if-onlys, and do-overs aren't real.

TWELVE

MONDAY. Eleven thirtyish. I am cleaning Ophelia's litter box when my cell phone rings. Distracted, I don't think before answering.

It's Daniel.

My father collapsed yesterday, presumably as he went out to get his Sunday paper. At some point—it's unclear how much time elapsed—a neighbor who didn't really know my dad called 911. The paramedics assessed his condition, performed defibrillation, and transported him to the nearest hospital. He is in a coma, minimal brain activity, on life support. The police were called in to talk to the neighbors in an effort to locate next of kin. One of them, an elderly schoolteacher three doors down, remembered Daniel, and the authorities managed to find him. A decision will need to be made as to what to do for our father—no one knows whether he had an advanced medical directive, what his wishes might have been in this regard.

This narrative is, of course, not what I hear from Daniel. His version is filled with Barton color, sarcasm, slurred words, and all the rest.

"Well, well, Mrs. Whittier, got some news for you. Dear old Dad keeled over, and some asshole took pity on him lying there sprawled out on the pavement with a goddamn *New York Times* in his hand and called 911. They used the paddles. Revived him. And the old fucker's still alive, but only barely. Thought you'd want to know since it looks like he won't be long for this world. The old bitch a couple doors down, Ms. Beckman, gave the cops my name, and fuck if they didn't track me down. Seems I'm in the system." He issues a brittle laugh.

Is this funny to him? I know from looking into his time at FCI Mendota that he's in the system for production and distribution of methamphetamine and heroin possession. Questions begin to swirl: *Where is he now? Why is this happening? What does he expect me to do?* Evoking decades of efforts to hide the entirety of my past from Jacob and clearly failed efforts to hide from Daniel, my thoughts spin wildly toward the familiar question: *How did he find me?* I'm not in the system.

Daniel's voice is in my ear, in my head.

"So some nurse calls me, and then I've got to talk to a doctor, some foreign guy, some Indian, says we'll need to make a decision about pulling the plug—the Indian guy wants to know whether Dad had ever 'made his wishes known,' and I'm like, seriously, I would have no fucking idea, and I'm guessing, since you bailed on him long before he kicked me out and haven't given a shit since, that you've got even less of a fucking idea than I do, but the Indian guy says he wants to talk to you, since we're both next of kin."

I would swear he is snarling and spitting as he speaks this one long run-on sentence—manic, or he's on something. I hold my phone away as if his words can reach out and touch me.

"Hey, little bitch, are you even listening? Aren't you going to fucking say something?"

"Little bitch" is just one of the many nicknames he has bestowed upon me: DG (for damaged goods), filthy whore, sloppy seconds. All I keep thinking as he goes on and on is *How, how did he get my cell number?*

"Fuck," he says under his breath. "I didn't need to call you. This is a courtesy I'm doing, and you aren't even going to answer me?"

A vise has tightened around my chest, making it difficult to breathe, to even contemplate breathing. Deep-rooted, primitive fear and disbelief flood my body. This cannot be happening.

"How did you get this number?" I choke out.

"Get this number? Jesus, you and your cell number–changing bullshit." He laughs.

Bile rises—bitter and burning.

"Some things never change; you still think you can fucking hide. I went to the public library, Googled you and Jacob, found his work number, and called his secretary, nice lady—wish I could say the same about you—yeah, nice, name was Shelly or Shelby or something like that. I told her I was your brother and I lost my phone and needed your cell. She was all, like"—Daniel puts on a fake high voice, imitating Shelby, the gravel in the back of his throat making the imitation appropriately surreal—"'Of course, I lost my cell phone last month and it was such a hassle to get all the numbers.'"

He's enjoying this.

"She couldn't wait to give me your number, your email, your goddamn mailing address."

I look around, half expecting to see him standing in my laundry room.

I must gasp or something. Instinct. He hears it. "What? Aren't you glad to hear from me? Your one and only loving brother?"

He laughs again, low, his voice cracked and raspy. I swear I can smell the smoke, feel his dank, sweaty breath on my neck. The thought of having to see my one and only brother, real and in the flesh, not some imagined nineteen-year-old version, is quite possibly the one and only thing I cannot handle.

I don't want to be involved in making any decisions about my father either, but—here's the kicker—I actually do know what my father would want. I know because he told me.

Daniel, however, does not know that I know.

I want out.

"Why are you calling? What do you want from me?" I instantly regret my word choice.

"Well, *that's* a loaded question, isn't it?"

Oh my God, no. *Hang up*, I tell myself. *Hang up*.

I move the phone down from my ear, look at the red circle. I can still hear Daniel.

"The old fuck is dying. That's why I called you."

I return the phone to my ear.

"It isn't really convenient for me to get to some hospital in San Jose to deal with this whole . . . situation. Don't see why it should all be on me, and I figured even you'd want to come pay your respects, say a proper goodbye."

"A 'proper goodbye'?" Words wrenched from a place I cannot name.

"Yeah, it'll be like old times: you and me hating each other, him silent like he's not even there. Only this time, when you wish we were dead, your wish will come true, at least for one of us." Another low, raspy noise, halfway between a cough and a laugh.

The END, I think, looking at the red circle on my phone. *I can do this. I can end this once and for all.*

"Where is he?"

———

I call Jacob. Tell him my brother, Daniel, called. My father is dying. I imagine Jacob's expression as he mentally searches for reference points from the heavily edited version of my life he's heard. I wonder if he has dreaded this day too, the day my lack of pedigree is exposed in all its ugliness.

"Your *brother* called you?" Incredulity is the order of the day. "Your dad is in a coma?"

"Yes. And yes," I say, harshly. "Daniel got my number, my cell number, from Shelby. I know you think she's the bee's knees, but you might want to tell her not to give out my cell number to anyone that calls claiming to be my brother. I wonder if she's done it before."

Anger is so much easier sometimes.

"He was your brother . . ."

Interesting choice of the verb "to be," I think. Was, not is.

Jacob changes course. "Yeah, of course, you're right. Shelby shouldn't give your number to anyone—but that's hardly the issue here, I mean." He pauses. I can hear him reconsidering and pivoting once again. His tone changes. "I understand what you're saying, and I'll talk to her, but Kate, isn't the real issue what you're going to do about your dad? I can go with you, or, well . . ."

This is the sort of situation in which I would normally look to Jacob to take over. He would tell me what to do, hold my hand, and help me do it. He'd dive in, bringing one of those red flotation devices, calling to me that everything will be okay; flip me onto my back; instruct me to stay calm and hold on; and then, with his arm around my chest, swim me to shore.

Now, although the surf is way over my head, I must keep Jacob away. Jacob cannot see where I came from. He cannot meet Daniel. He cannot know the truth about who I am, what I've done. The thought crosses my mind, for the first time, that he could use my past in a custody battle. Daniel's words ring in my ears. *Fuck.*

Fuck.

"Can you give me a minute?" I say before hitting the mute button and taking the first of several long, deep breaths, trying to drum up some Dr. Farber advice, any advice, that might help me. *Keep it vague*, I tell myself. *Stay calm. Choose your words.*

I un-mute.

"I haven't thought it all the way through, but I know what my father would want, and I'm thinking this is a chance for closure—you know, finality. Seeing this through to the end."

"I don't think you owe your father anything, babe, not from the little you've told me." *Just the tip of the iceberg.* "But if you think you can handle it, then I guess going up there makes sense."

I don't mind him calling me "babe" under the circumstances. It's oddly comforting. I am seriously messed up. I want Jacob and don't want him at the same time.

"Where is he—your dad, I mean?"

"He's at Good Samaritan in San Jose. That's where the ambulance took him. I called to make sure he was actually there, that Daniel was telling the truth. They transferred me to the nurse's

station on his floor, and he is there—on life support. I told them
I'd fly up."

"Do you want me to go with you?"

"No," I say, quickly. *Too quickly.* "No, thank you," I add. "I can
go alone."

"Are you sure you want to do that? What about Daniel?"

Shit, what does he mean? How do I answer?

"Won't he be involved in this decision?"

Oh. I sigh, hoping to release the tight feeling in my chest. It
doesn't work.

"As far as I know, he lives up there, but not near my dad. He
says it's not convenient to deal with any of this, and the nurse said he
hasn't shown up. But someone has to do it, and even if I don't want
to, I don't see that I have a choice. I know my father wouldn't want
this; I should go up, be there when he dies." Words spill, emotions
whirl. "The truth is, he was a shitty father, and if he had died without
my knowing, I probably would have felt bad but relieved, you know?
But now, knowing he's dying... I don't know. It's different somehow."

Then it occurs to me, there is a way to keep Jacob away from my
childhood home, my father, my brother—an honest reason for him
to stay away: Logan and Becca. I want to know that my children are
at home, safe, while I am away, unsafe.

"There is something you can do, though," I begin. "Could you
please take the kids tonight and stay with them here at the house
tomorrow after school while I'm gone? Selena's supposed to stay the
night tomorrow while her parents celebrate their anniversary, but if
you could pick them up tonight, I can leave early tomorrow, hopefully
go up and back in one day. Is that okay?"

"Sure, of course. But, Kate . . . I don't mean to say that you can't
handle this alone, but I'd feel more comfortable if you weren't—alone,
I mean. Are you sure I shouldn't come with you? I'd planned to work
a half day tomorrow anyway, for our date."

Our date.

I'd forgotten Larry prescribed a date for us and that Jacob and I had planned a walk on the beach while the kids were at school. "Oh, shit," I whisper to myself before saying, "I'm sorry about the date, Jacob, but at least the time off will make it easier to be there for the kids. I don't want the fact my father is dying to mess with their lives; you should be here, with them."

More quiet. "What about Natalie? Could she go with you?"

I consider this suggestion for less than a second. I don't think I could stand Natalie's heartfelt compassion—the product of a happy childhood, she simply cannot understand that not everyone loves their family. *And what if Daniel showed up—*

"No, not Natalie." I provide a sensible explanation, one to which Jacob cannot object. "It's too close to Michael's death to put her through that, and she's got the boys."

"Then what about Ryan? I'm sure he'd go with you."

Do I want someone with me? I allow myself to contemplate having Ryan there by my side. Do I want him to see all of this? All of me?

"Hey? You okay?"

Stop it, Kate. Stop it. Don't fall back.

"I suppose I could try calling him," I say—mostly to appease Jacob, but as the words come out, I realize that Ryan might actually understand.

Thankfully, the conversation turns to logistics. I need to stop feeling for a minute. I will fly up first thing in the morning. Southwest has flights all day. Jacob will take care of the children tonight at his place. They don't know their grandfather, so Jacob won't mention where I've gone. I can tell them when I come home if I ever tell them at all. Jacob will bring them here—home—tomorrow and explain to Selena's mom that I had a family emergency, but Selena can stay as planned.

I will call Ryan. See if he can go with me.

Go. Do what must be done. Come home.

My bookcase rivals Dr. Farber's. Sitting at my desk, preparing a list of things I need to consider for tomorrow, I look over to the packed shelves, wondering if Barnes & Noble has a book called *How to Deal with the Death of a Parent You Hate When Your Only Sibling Is a Drug-Addled, Alcoholic Sociopath.*

My eyes land upon a parenting book about raising resilient children. I remember one of the questions posed was why some children can overcome overwhelming—and often horrific—obstacles while others cannot. Why does one child persevere and grow stronger while another becomes a victim? The authors gave several fundamental guidelines, none of which I recall my own parents following—things like empathic listening, unconditional love, reframing negative messages. Although I wanted to follow them myself, reading this book was difficult, and I couldn't finish it. I recognized from the very first chapter that I am a mixed bag; the struggle not to be a victim of my particularly toxic nature/nurture combo continues to this day. The only quality of resilience I recall identifying with was the ability to focus my energy on the things I can control.

So, I make a list and cross things off. Call Ryan. Make flight reservations. Make car reservations. Track down information on end-of-life decisions. Call Natalie to cancel our walk and lunch for tomorrow. Lines through each one, except for Natalie, for which I indicate "left msg."

The second-to-last item on the list, "end-of-life decisions," evokes a stronger reaction than I thought it would. Bearing the responsibility for my father's death reminds me of feeling responsible for my mother's, which leads first to feelings of worthlessness and shame and then down the dark path to other sources of shame.

It is in this state of mind that I receive a return phone call from Natalie in response to my message. A call I do not handle well. Facing my own doubts about the tasks ahead, I find myself bristling from her first question.

"Do you think that's a good idea, going up there without Jacob?" she asks tentatively after I give her the condensed version of events. "I know how hard this sort of thing is. When Michael died, I remember thinking what I really wanted, more than anything, was for him to be there to help me. Such a strange thought, really, wishing for his strength to deal with his loss."

My rational self, which thinks, *Of course this is evoking memories of her own loss* and *Like her, I did think how nice it would be to have Jacob save me*, is overpowered in an instant by my irrational self: *Unlike her, with her perfect upbringing and perfect marriage, I am separated from my husband, who gave me an STD. I have a seriously dysfunctional family; I don't love my father and I'm not really anticipating sadness over his loss.*

What comes out of my mouth, in a tone more suitable for dismissing a minion than speaking with one of my only friends, is "This situation is nothing at all like yours. I'm not you, Natalie. I don't need Jacob, not like you needed Michael."

"I know that, Kate." I can hear the hurt in her voice. "I'm not trying to say . . ." She sighs, gives up without a fight. "Of course it's not, and you're not."

I look down at the second list I've started, things I cannot accomplish today but will have to be done. Will. Probate. Clean the house. Find a realtor.

I'm adding "Find a lawyer" when Natalie asks, "Will you have to stay up there to deal with his funeral?"

"Funeral?"

"Or maybe a memorial service? It's healthy to give people a place to grieve together—not only for you and your brother but also your dad's friends and other family. It's a lot, I remember, to deal with—writing an obituary, deciding whether to have a wake. If you want my help—"

"Natalie," I interrupt, "I appreciate your concern, but this isn't that type of situation. There won't be an obituary or a wake or any kind of service. As far as I know, no one will be grieving for my father."

And if my brother has to grieve, I don't intend to do it with him.

"Oh, I just thought . . ." Her voice cannot possibly get any smaller. "Oh."

I am wrong again. It can get smaller. I do not react well to this either.

"How about we talk when I get back because, despite not having an elaborate memorial to plan, I do have a lot to get done." Curt, mean, mercurial. I can hear it but cannot stop it.

Years of therapy and books and elaborate plastering work to create a Whittier facade, and still, at my core, I fear, I am a Barton.

Hanging up, I sigh. *Get it under control, Kate.*

I text a quick apology to Natalie: "So sorry—just not in a good place right now."

And then, with fingers flying over my keyboard—Googling, reading, scrolling, adding to my lists—I try to control what little I can.

THIRTEEN

RYAN IS NOT A FAN OF HOSPITALS.

"A few negative experiences," he says.

He offers to wait in the hallway outside my father's ICU room. The smell of antiseptic is strong. Dr. V. Bhatnagar methodically places his right hand under the hand sanitizer dispenser, his eyes on me as the clear liquid drops into his palm. He rubs his own hands together for a few seconds before reaching out for mine.

"I am so sorry, Mrs. Whittier." He has a beautiful voice. Melodic. "As you know, however, your father came into Emergency unconscious, following cardiac arrest that led to anoxic brain injury. You see, while his heart was stopped, his brain was deprived of oxygen, which resulted in irreversible damage. I spoke with your brother on the telephone about whether your father had a living will or other form of advanced directive. Your brother said he was not aware of any such document?"

This man is so polite. Daniel was probably a complete racist asshole on the phone. I shake my head. "I doubt my father had something like that."

"In that case, though this is difficult, Mrs. Whittier"—Dr. Bhatnagar is the picture of empathy, his tone gentle—"I have to ask you, as his daughter: what do you think your father would want us to do next?"

I look over at my father. Multiple tubes and lines connect to his body—an IV, a ventilator, a catheter. White walls, pale blue and white bed linens. My father is gray—gray hair, gray beard, gray skin. Bright green, purple, and red lines pulsate across the screens over his head on either side, a quick double beep every second or so, the sound of forced air keeping him alive. He is swollen, bruised, sagging. He would hate this.

"Perhaps he discussed his feelings about this with you at some point?"

I want to put poor, kind Dr. Bhatnagar out of his misery as much as I want to put myself and my father out of ours. "Yes, he did."

I fold my arms across my body and hold on. I recall holding myself in this way the day after my mother died. I hear my father's words echoing from the past: "When it's over, it's over. Stop crying. It's time to move on now. She's gone." He pats my back firmly. "She chose to do it her way. Guess she got that right. God knows, when it's my time, I just want to go."

His version of emotional support for an eleven-year-old girl.

"He told me once, 'When it's my time, I just want to go,'" I say. "He wouldn't want to be on life support. I am quite sure."

As far as I can tell, looking at my father, he's already gone, and as he himself would say, it's time to move on. Of this I am confident.

If Dr. Bhatnagar is alarmed at my seeming lack of sensitivity or grief, he doesn't let on. "If you are certain, then, I will have a nurse come in to explain the paperwork and how we'll proceed."

I want to tell him, "Please, simply get on with it; I don't need an explanation," but this seems inappropriate. Cold. Unfeeling.

Ryan follows the nurse in and wraps his arms around me, my own still crossed in self-defense.

I listen as more kindness and empathy are wasted on my behalf.

The nurse, Trina, first asks if we would like to speak to a member of the clergy—a priest or minister or rabbi? Are there any religious rites my father would want to be performed?

"No, thank you," I reply softly but firmly. "He was not a religious man."

Trina purses her lips and nods tersely. She goes over the papers on a clipboard, telling us how the monitor will be turned off first, no more beeping or colored lines. The curtain will be drawn for privacy. The lifesaving devices will be removed in stages, the ventilator being last. We will be left alone, if we wish, or a nurse or social worker can stay with us. Once the ventilator is removed, my father will likely pass within an hour. If we need a funeral home reference, they can provide one. They will come and retrieve his body, make the necessary arrangements.

"Thank you, a reference would be helpful," I say. "I'm not from here . . . anymore."

I forgot about dealing with his body. That's not on my list; *what else might be missing?*

"And I'd like to be alone," I add. I don't want to be judged for the manner in which I watch my father die. I glance over at Ryan. "Is that okay?"

"Are you sure?" he asks. "You don't have to be."

All this empathy is wearing on me. Though I cannot name or process what I am feeling, I do not love this old, gray man covered in tubes. I'm here for closure, a final goodbye.

My father does not last long. Far less dramatic than anticipated, more of an emptiness. In the end, I say nothing to him, but I'm thinking, *Go, just go.*

Now, there's only Daniel and me.

FOURTEEN

RYAN WILL WAIT OUTSIDE, AGAIN. His warm arms encircle me. He kisses my forehead. "Call out if you need me. I'm right here."

I nod. I don't want anyone to witness this part of my past.

"Just give me a few minutes," I say, my voice quivering. I think about the sanitizer dispenser at Good Samaritan. There isn't a container large enough to cover me for this.

The house is smaller than I remember. Uglier. Pre-fab, grimy beige siding; rusting drain pipes, some of which are barely hanging on; three concrete steps that lead to the faded black front door. No vegetation to speak of other than some scabby weeds where the small patch of lawn used to be. A chain-link fence has been installed since I lived here so long ago. The windows are noticeably dirty. Most of the screens are missing, and the ones remaining are ripped or warped, hanging in their tracks.

The inside is worse. The stench assails me—rotten, moldy, smoky, with a tinge of stale beer. Newspapers are piled chest high in the living room to the right of the door and all along the hallway leading to the kitchen in back, leaving barely enough room to pass. I see my father hasn't—hadn't—abandoned my mother's love of newspapers. The sofa sags in the one section cleared of debris, situated directly across from the television. It appears that any receptacle—beer can, paper cup, stained coffee mug—served as an ashtray. Empty bottles of vodka, a Russian-sounding brand I do not recognize with a red-and-white label, litter the floor along with black plastic compartmentalized plates crusted with the remainder of frozen meals and unopened envelopes with clear cellophane windows over my father's name, bills he clearly does not intend to pay—shit, *did* not intend to pay. I've got to get used to the past tense.

My parents' old bedroom is not much better. The whole room has been washed in gray and sepia tones—walls, sheets, carpeting, shades, and stacks upon stacks of newspapers. Atop the pile nearest the door is a paper from August 2006 featuring an article on bird flu strains found in wild swans. The next stack over is from June 2007, a story about an earthquake in Southern China. *Why did he keep these?* I can see the small writing desk by the only window on the far wall, its top covered with miscellaneous detritus. It is the only place I can think to look for a will or official documents pertaining to my father.

I try not to think about him or my mother as I shuffle sideways between the mattress and the wall of paper, endeavoring to touch neither. I have no choice but to touch the desk drawer knob. It is dry and cracked, yet strangely gummy at the same time.

The drawer is stuffed, difficult to open. Some old bills are rubber banded together at the top: PG&E, San Jose Water, Comcast. Underneath I see what appears to be a manila letter-size folder, so I lift the rubber-banded bundles and drop them on the bed. There are five or so file folders with no labels. A quick glance informs me that they hold what might be termed personal information about my parents: a copy of a 1040 and some attachments for my father from six years ago, perhaps the last year he filed; some ancient medical records; the title for the filthy Ford Focus parked in the driveway that may or may not run; some bank statements, again several years old. I grab the folders and shuffle back out, my eyes fluttering, wanting to close.

Muffled street sounds, water dripping. *A faucet?* Did my father leave water running when he went out for the paper? I was told the police came to secure the house. *Why didn't they turn off the water?* I take a few hesitant steps down the hallway toward the kitchen, the tiny bathroom, Daniel's old room, my bedroom. I wonder if my father's hoarding has filled these as well.

The kitchen is filthy beyond anything I could imagine—charcoal-tinged grime and rust-colored grease cover the stove and the Formica table. The microwave door is open, revealing food spatter that makes the inside appear mottled brown. The floor is sticky underfoot. I stand in the doorway, watching the drip in the sink.

I give myself instructions: *Do not touch anything. Get out.* I glance quickly at the closed doors lining the hall, imagining the bathroom tile, a moldy plastic shower curtain, and a corroded toilet paper dispenser, the piles of magazines, dirty clothes, and drug paraphernalia that defined Daniel's room.

As I return down the hall, a doorframe rattles, stopping me in my tracks, right next to my old bedroom door. *Daniel?* I stand still as a corpse, trying to quell the gagging sensation that threatens to overtake me as I confront the virulent combination of putrid air and memories.

Daniel is not here in the house.

Ryan is outside.

I am alone. *I should go. There is nothing here for me.*

My bedroom door is closed, the fake brass knob tacky as if a label has been removed, leaving glue behind. I try not to think of what substance has made it feel this way. I had forgotten how flimsy the door was, more like thick particleboard than wood. No effort required to open it, at least no physical effort.

I swing the door open, gasp, then hold my breath, feeling my whole body tense.

There are no newspapers or vodka bottles. The room is nearly exactly as I left it.

Why?

A thick film of dust covers everything—ashes to ashes, dust to dust.

Apropos.

I remember vividly thinking, as I closed the door the day I left, that a part of me died here in this room. Dr. Farber has informed me that trauma can freeze us in time, getting in the way of emotional and psychological growth. She would find this room fascinating: a physical manifestation of the theory.

My father and brother freezing me here.

A worn, pale-blue chenille bedspread covers the single mattress. A darker blue pillow, about eight inches square, lies diagonally against the headboard. This dark blue pillow and the black-and-white picture of the Eiffel Tower hanging over the desk were my pathetic attempts at decorating. Oh, how I dreamed about going to Paris, going anywhere, away from here. I begged my father for the desk from IKEA, some assembly required, for my birthday. I knew my only hope was to do well in school and get the hell out of Dodge.

This room was both sanctuary and the place where Daniel could find me. The sorry lock on the door, a push-button in the middle easily dislodged by one hit of the side of his closed fist to a spot three inches to the right of the knob—a thud that cracked the framed mirror hanging on the back a bit more each time. No point in calling for help; Daniel figured out how to shut me up. This is what facing your demons must feel like—body blows to the mind, spinning me this way and that. Fragments of memories like small chunks of colored glass that don't quite form a complete mosaic. I can't breathe. I'm dizzy, disoriented.

I'm dying little by little, but I'm not dead yet. I scream, "NO!" Eyes closed, I reach my hand out blindly—connect with the sharpened pencils on my desk. I grasp one and jab toward the person on top of me, hoping the pointed end is facing the right direction. He yelps.

"Kate? You all right in there?" Ryan is at the front door.

Answer him, I tell myself, *or he'll come in and see this.*

"Don't come in. Please." My throat hurts. "Don't come in. I'm fine. I'll be right out."

The top of the desk is empty, save for a single pencil lying behind and partway under a cheap digital alarm clock I bought at the drugstore when I was ten so I wouldn't be late for school. This clock displays 9:19 a.m. It is not the correct time, but, remarkably, it's plugged in, still working. There's power in the house. Dad paid the electric.

The closet door is ajar, beckoning me. As I reach for the knob, I recall how I used to hide in this tiny space, sitting on the floor, my arms wrapped around my knees, trying to be as small as possible. The futility of it all is obvious to me now.

Two cheap dresses hang on wire hangers in the back. A short polyester one with three-quarter sleeves, black with white trim, the uniform from the diner where I worked part time, still bearing the name tag "Kate." The other is longer, in red satin, torn at one shoulder—the prom dress I saved tips to buy and wore once. I hated both and left them behind, along with the memories they held. And here they have stayed, entombed in this closet, this house.

But on the floor under the dresses there is a box I have never seen before. A plain, dust-covered cardboard box with a cover. "For Kathryn" is written on top in thick black marker in my mother's unmistakable handwriting.

This is not mine. My father must have put it here after I left. I can picture him, his figure bent, gut hanging over the edge of his faded blue uniform pants.

I should not have come.

Yet here I am, looking for closure and finding something crying to be opened. I place the manila folders on the ground and kneel down. My hands hover over the box. *Pandora's box.* I shudder as my fingers touch the lid.

Inside, I find yellow lined pads to the brim, a proliferation of my mother's handwriting. On top, a plain white envelope bearing a single word in what must be my father's handwriting: "Kathryn." Shaky script—old age or alcohol. The envelope isn't sealed.

A two-page document, handwritten. At the top of page one: "Last Will and Testement." *If you spell it wrong, is it still valid?* It will take time to decipher his handwriting, small and uneven, like chicken scratch. I will read this later.

Then I see the letter underneath, on the top page of the top note-book, that begins, *Dearest Kathryn. I don't know exactly when you will read this. I've asked your father to wait to give it to you when you are older, mature, at least eighteen, although you have always been an old soul, you probably could be reading it now.*

Dizziness, lack of adequate oxygen, and shock come together to form an inner tornado, whirling upward.

I try to slam the box closed, but the cardboard lid catches, bends inward.

My cell phone rings.

I lean on the crooked box top and rise awkwardly to my feet, pull the phone out of my pocket. It is a number I do not recognize. The hospital? The funeral home?

"So, you did it." Low, raspy, like sandpaper on raw skin. "You actu-ally killed the old man. Bit of a surprise. I call, planning on heading over to see him, and the nurse tells me he's passed away but not to worry, his daughter was with him." His harsh laugh, a sound I can never forget. "Got to hand it to you, little bitch, didn't think you had it in you."

Get out, Kate. Get out now.

Flight.

"You there?"

Hang up. What does he mean—am I there, am I here? Is he here?

"Guess I'll need to come and find you."

"No." A reflexive response, harsh. *Kate, shut up.* Fight kicks in. "No, don't. Don't come here."

I sound so much stronger than I feel. My hand is damp with sweat on the phone. My heart is racing.

"Wait, you're in the house?"

Fuck.

I hang up, cutting him off. Too late.

I spin around. A buzz of fear and fury fills my head, blocking out all sound. I bend to pick up the box with its crushed lid and, rising, see black and white and red, and then . . .

Nothing.

FIFTEEN

THE DOOR SLAMS SHUT behind me. Terrified, the hair along my temples and skin wet with cold sweat, I slip and then fall down the cement stairs, clutching the moldy-smelling cardboard box, thinking, *This is where my father fell, where his soul left his body, if he had one to lose.*

I scramble up. Try to regain some sense of balance and order. Based on the look on Ryan's face—his eyes are bright with alarm, greener than I've ever seen them—I must be a sight.

"Are you hurt?" He moves toward me hesitantly, as if he's torn between scooping me up and running for it. "What happened in there?"

That is a loaded question. Too much. Impossible to explain. I don't trust myself to speak. I hope he can see that what I need is to get in the rental car and get away from here.

"Kate!"—his voice filled with urgency—"Kate, you're bleeding."

I look down but cannot see over the box. I didn't feel it at first; however, now that he has mentioned it, the backside of my right calf is burning.

"It's nothing."

The car is my goal.

Get in. Get away. Go. Just go. I pin my hopes on Ryan receiving my psychic communiqué, understanding my overriding need for self-preservation and the fragility of my grip on it. He must, because he changes course away from me, in the direction of the driver's side of the car, matching his pace to mine. I throw open the rear passenger door and drop the box on the floor. As I sit down in the front next to Ryan, I can feel the box like a lead weight behind me.

"Here." He hands me a few rough brown Starbucks napkins from our airport-to-hospital drive this morning. Starts the car. "You sure you're okay?"

I debate answering, then choose silence—looking out the window to avoid his gaze. He won't believe me if I say yes, and he'll worry more if I say no. I'm trembling, forcing down nausea; I'm clearly incapable of doing anything remotely useful to stop the bleeding from my leg.

"Should we stop at a drug store? Get something for that?"

"No, it's only a scrape."

It isn't—it's a gash. I fold two napkins to fashion a compress, which I push firmly against the wound. I barely feel it—too many open wounds are taking precedence over this one. I can hear it now: "Try to process what you are feeling: identify it, name it, address it." Fucking Dr. Farber. This is impossible. Giving up and giving in, I look out the window, here but not here, until the acute adrenaline-rush curtain lifts. We're passing a parking lot, rows divided by trees and bits of grass, about to get on 87 North.

My phone rings. I take one look at the incoming number—it is my father's, the number of my childhood—and drop it on the floor. My hand is blotchy red with blood that seeped through the napkins. In my peripheral vision, I see Ryan glance over.

The ringing begins again. I leave the phone where it lies.

"Do you want me to get that for you?"

"No." I do sound like a little bitch. *Jesus, Kate*, I tell myself. *Stop that.* "No, no thank you. I think it's my brother."

"Your brother?"

"My brother. Daniel." Merely saying his name causes the adrenaline to course through my body again. Heart racing. Sweat forming. Skin instantly clammy. "I have nothing to say to him."

Cut to my manicured street—a drive, a flight, and a drive away. I have little to no recollection of the journey.

What a difference a day makes.

Dearest Kathryn.

Four hundred–odd miles separate me from my father's body, lying in a box awaiting the furnace, and my brother, lying in wait at our childhood home. Less than four feet separate me from the box in the backseat of Ryan's Jeep, wrapped in the Southwest Airlines tape that kept it closed in flight, my mother's words and my father's will, waiting to be revealed. Forty yards separate me from my children, probably lying on a couch or a beanbag, waiting for me.

Silently, we pull up the circular drive. Before I can open the door, Ryan is up, out, and opening it for me, offering his hand. Just as quickly, I am wrapped in his arms. He kisses the top of my head, murmurs, "You're so brave."

I lean into him, my arms around his waist, feeling his strength and the solace he offers. I am not brave. I am numb. "I don't know how to thank you for being there."

I realize that he has seen more of my past than Jacob has. *What must he think of me now?*

I pull back slightly, tip my head; my forehead brushes the soft whiskers on the underside of his chin. Outdoor lights in the shape of rustic lanterns shed a glow over the entryway, but Ryan's face is shadowed. I cannot read his expression. I turn and rest my cheek on the curve of his shoulder.

"I'd do anything for you, Kate."

The haze parts briefly. *He would,* I think. *He would do anything for me.* As I would do anything for my kids, for Logan and Becca.

I am still.

"Mommy! Mommy's home." We break apart and turn in tandem as Becca runs toward us. "And Uncle Ryan's here, Dad," she calls over her shoulder as she launches herself into me, curls her body into mine.

I stumble slightly. Wince. I smooth the top of her head with my hand. Her damp curls are silky with the familiar smell of jasmine and clementines. My Daisy Dreamgirl.

"Mommy, I got two goals today at the scrimmage, and one of them Coach Riley said was indefensible. *Indefensible.* And the spelling test for tomorrow got canceled because Ms. Garrett said we're all doing so well that she's giving us a break. Selena's here, but she got tired. She goes to bed way earlier than me, so Daddy got her settled and said I could wait for you, but I'm kind of tired too, so I'm glad you're home now."

Becca winds down like a toy running out of batteries, everything slowing until she simply stops. Sleep will be right around the corner.

Jacob and Ryan clasp hands, and their bodies close in a half hug.

"Thanks, man," Jacob says quietly.

Ryan pulls away first. I can barely hear his response. "Tough day. She's got to be beat. She fell and cut her leg somehow. I bought some bandaging, but the wound should probably be cleaned." His voice lowers even further. "Oh, and her brother's calling her."

Over Becca's head, I watch Ryan retrieve the box from the backseat. My defense system goes on high alert. I don't want Jacob to question me about Daniel or the box. I don't want anyone to see what's inside. *Please don't give it to Jacob.*

"I'll bring this in and put it in your closet, Kate." Ryan heard me. He holds the box with the lid facing his chest, bottom out, so the black words are hidden from view.

"I can get it for her." Jacob's arms are outstretched.

Don't ask. Not in front of Becca.

He does. "Is this stuff from your dad?"

"Nah, dude, I've got this." Ryan's eyes rest on mine, confirming the connection. He deflects attention from the box to the children. "You guys go on in, get this pipsqueak in bed. Tear Logan from his Xbox."

Then he gives Jacob another use for his open arms.

"Looks like she could use a ride from her dad." He gestures with his head toward Becca's sleepy form, resting against me.

The warmth of her body is whisked away. I am lost, bereft. Our little parade makes its way across the stone walkway, Jacob draped with Becca, Ryan with the box, me limping behind.

SIXTEEN

SUDDEN AWARENESS ON a curving trail. Sand underfoot, the sun hot on the top of my head. I am running—parched, dripping. My lower right leg and hip throb.

Panic goes off like a bomb.

How did I get here? Where are the kids?

There is music playing, Michael Bublé pleading with someone to let him go home. I have my phone.

I reach behind my back and pat the zipper pocket. I have my keys. Where did I park?

Call the school, I tell myself. *Try not to sound terrified. Breathe. Do not say, "This is Kate Whittier. I've lost my mind and wanted to check if my children are there at school."*

The phone is ringing on the other end. The perky receptionist, what's her name? What's her name? Sharon? Yes, Sharon, answers.

Breathe.

"Sharon, hi, this is Kate Whittier. I was out of town yesterday, and my children were with their dad"—this is true if today is the day after yesterday, if yesterday was the day my father died—"and I just wanted to make sure they made it to school on time and everything's okay."

Oh my God, what if I brought Becca in?

"I didn't receive their names as being absent, Mrs. Whittier, so I'm guessing they're here. Do you want me to call their classrooms to check if they're okay?"

"No, no." *They're at school, breathe.* "That's fine. Thank you. Thank you, Sharon."

"No problem, happy to help. Have a good day."

I take a few more steps along the trail. There is another call I need to make. I look at my phone. It is Wednesday, 11:30 a.m.

Today is Wednesday. My father died yesterday.

I remember leaving the hospital with Ryan.

I remember Becca's smell, her wet curls.

Then, now.

What is happening to me?

Am I losing my mind?

"Hello, you've reached Dr. Susan Farber. If this is an emergency, please hang up and call 911"—*Is this an emergency? I have little to no recollection of the last twenty-four hours*—"I will return your call as soon as possible. Thank you."

I leave a message. I walk on. The trail takes a sharp right at a cluster of scrub oak. My car—solid, imposing—is a welcome sight.

———

Breakfast dishes in the sink, Ophelia's litter box cleaned—I clearly went through the motions of an ordinary day.

My laptop is open on the island. There is an email from Natalie, responding to one I sent her this morning. *I sent an email?*

"Kate, I am so sorry for your loss. I do understand you need space right now, but please don't push me away. Call me whenever you're ready to talk."

What did I write to her? I open my outgoing email: "Natalie, I need space. I cannot handle calls or texts. Kate."

Why did I write this? Did something happen with Natalie?

———

Dr. Farber returns my call. I begin to shake but do not cry.

"I think I've had some sort of psychotic break," I say.

"Are you thinking about hurting yourself?" she asks.

"No, I'm just scared. I don't know what's going on."

"Where are you now, Kate?"

"I'm in my house. I was on a run when I just kind of . . . woke up. Like, I was there suddenly, and I had no idea how I got there."

"Are you alone?" She sounds worried. "Where are your children?"

"Yes, I'm alone. They're at school."

"Do you know what day it is?"

"Wednesday. It's Wednesday, just after twelve, right?"

"Yes, that's right. I can clear time and see you at two, but I want you to call someone, your husband or a friend, someone that can come stay with you, maybe bring you to the appointment. Can you do that?"

I tell her yes, ticking off the possibilities in my head.

Jacob? *No.*

Natalie? *I guess no, though I don't know why.*

Ryan.

In my bathroom, I kick off my running shoes and see an awkward, thick, haphazardly applied bandage over the back of my right calf. Hence the throbbing.

I remove the bandage. There is a large scrape and gash on my leg. A scab has begun to form over the edges, but a section is still open. *Why did I go running?*

Steam covers the glass shower door. The stingingly hot water feels good. I watch the skin on my chest and stomach flush red. A thin stream of watered-down blood runs down the drain from my leg. There is a bruise on my hip and another one on my arm. I do not know how they got there.

I find gauze under my bathroom sink, some pale-blue Johnson & Johnson antiseptic cleanser I used to use on the kids' scrapes. Part of my boo-boo basket, pulled out for all minor injuries, the sight of which was often enough to quell their tears. "Blink, blink, blow. Blink, blink, blow," I used to say, doing it along with them, blinking and blowing cool air through pursed lips on their injury, distracting them. Now, I am distracted beyond effectiveness. The bandage will not stay on.

How did I hurt myself?

————

My bed is meticulously made except for two missing velvet throw pillows. The housekeeper, Ana, doesn't come on Wednesdays. I must have woken early enough to make it myself.

I walk into the closet and discover the two missing pillows before me on the floor, along with a lightweight down comforter that I keep stored with the summer linens in a zippered plastic drycleaner bag on a top shelf, now made into a makeshift sleeping bag.

I slept here, not in the bed. I didn't make the bed. Ana made it yesterday.

The indoor campground is not as alarming as the pile of canary-yellow lined notebooks bearing my mother's handwriting. An open cardboard box, with more yellow inside, is wedged against the hamper. My clothes from yesterday are not in the hamper. I see them stuffed into the small garbage pail in the corner, a dark splotch visible on the blouse, another one, barely visible, on the pants leg—stains I do not wish to acknowledge or wonder about. I remember putting the clothes on, just not taking them off. A pair of short gray capris, a gray blouse. *What do you wear to face your past and kill your father?*

The lid of the cardboard box lies a couple of feet away. Strips of Southwest Airlines tape crisscross the surface. A few letters show in the gaps: "For Ka."

A partial memory flashes, my cell phone rings. I'm in my old room, and it looks exactly as I left it. *How is that possible?* It must be a faulty brain circuit, some sort of errant flashback.

I can acknowledge this, and yet my heart races. Sweat forms instantly between my breasts and at my temples.

"Katie? Are you all right in there?" Familiar words in a familiar voice, bringing me out of the closet.

I am frozen. Images flash and vanish—newspapers piled high, empty bottles, a chain-link fence, a navy-blue pillow placed at a jaunty angle, two dresses on wire hangers. Smells hover—rusting iron, beer, rancid grease. My hands feel sticky. I randomly think, *Out damned spot*. My phone rings.

Ryan finds me there, clinging to my towel as if it can save my life.

"Hey, hey." His voice is tender, as if he fears startling me. "Hey, it's okay."

He doesn't say anything about the fact that I'm standing naked but for a towel in the middle of my closet, surrounded by linens and notepads, visibly shaking. I can feel it, the shaking. Tremors initiated deep within. His hands are warm, his breath soft on my face. I am covered with softness. My robe is suddenly around my shoulders.

"Let's put your hand through here. Can you do that for me?" he asks.

I watch him from above, and yet I feel his touch as he coaxes me into my robe and then turns me toward the bedroom, away from the camp.

"Jacob told me you were really, really angry. You broke some wine-glasses and demanded that he leave. He said he didn't want to go, but you insisted, so he finally did. He called the kids this morning, though, and they said everything was okay. You don't remember any of that?"

I am sitting on the edge of my bed, bewildered, my left leg folded in toward me, my right leg dangling, re-bandaged. Ryan is sitting next to me, his body the mirror image of mine, our knees touching. He holds my right hand in both of his.

I shake my head. I don't remember any of it. Wineglasses? *We were drinking wine?*

Ryan and I are working backwards. I don't remember getting the children ready for school. I don't remember waking up. I don't remember reading or sleeping in the closet.

"Okay, what do you remember from yesterday?"

Tears form in my eyes. I'm disappointing Ryan. He helped me yesterday, and I don't remember.

"Hey, sweetie, it's okay, relax. We're going to figure this out, and you're going to be okay."

Am I?

"I remember the hospital, leaving the hospital after my father"—I hesitate—"after he died. The nurse gave me his things, and you and I talked about calling the funeral home to make arrangements. There were questions about my father, things I didn't know, like his social security number." I can hear my own voice, desperate-sounding, looking for reassurance.

"Yes, that's right. We left the hospital and then"—he studies my face—"do you remember anything after that? Before running today?"

I stare at the sand-colored carpet and remember the sandy trail. I close my eyes, trying to picture myself leaving the hospital. Ryan's arm is around my shoulder, we are walking across the parking lot. A siren blares and falls silent. He's checked the flights back. Do I want to stop to get something to eat? I'm not hungry, but I am terribly thirsty.

"We stopped on the way to the airport."

"Yes, we did." I'm confused. He's so serious.

Denny's—*we went to Denny's.*

"We went to a Denny's. You ordered me pancakes and bacon, told me it was comfort food and I should eat it." I glance over at Ryan's face for confirmation. Maple syrup. Ryan had a burger.

"And then?"

I look past him, away, to the bathroom and closet. I want to know. I want to give him the right answers. I think about those fleeting images. *Could they have been real?* Where did the box come from?

"The box."

"Yes?" Ryan's eyebrows rise; his hands stop rubbing mine. *Please don't stop.*

He thinks I know something about the box. He wants me to, but I don't.

"Where did it come from?"

Wrong thing to say. His face clouds over, closes off. It is my mother's writing. We must have gotten it from the house. There's no other explanation. "We went to the house, didn't we?"

Ryan's nod is barely perceptible. "Yes. We went to the house. We discussed it first, whether it was a good idea or not, but you said it would be helpful to know if he had a will or any other records you might need. You said that maybe if you could see it and put it all behind you, you'd have closure, once and for all. I wasn't sure, but, well . . ."

My heart pounds. I choke out, "And Daniel was there?"

"Your brother? No, no, we didn't see him. He didn't show up at the hospital, and you said he wasn't at the house. The door was locked when you got there, and you said it locked on its own when we left. You had the box when you came out, and you were bleeding. You wanted to get out of there. You whispered, 'Just go, just go' while we were driving and then again on the plane, like a mantra."

I must look quizzical, because he says, "You probably don't remember that, though—which is okay. It's okay that you don't remember it, Katie. It must be some kind of psychological protective mechanism, keeping you from overloading, you know?"

Protective mechanism. Ryan shifts his position and moves my leg so that he can sit next to me—one arm around my shoulder, the other holding my hand.

"And I came home and fought with Jacob."

Ryan nods, slow, steady. "He said you were angry because he had some wine with Natalie."

I remember this now. I saw the bottle and asked Jacob who had been there, and he was evasive, like he was hiding something. He didn't admit it was Natalie until I pressed him. Natalie and Jacob together, drinking wine, while I was losing my mind. My husband and one of my only friends. Natalie stole my date with Jacob. Not that I—

"Hey, hey." Ryan turns my face toward his own.

I still have Ryan.

"Let's get you dressed and get out of here, huh? Get some fresh air and go to your doctor's appointment."

And Dr. Farber. I still have Dr. Farber.

SEVENTEEN

RYAN TAKES ME TO Dr. Farber's office and waits, again, for me. When I tell her that he was with me yesterday, during the time I don't remember, Dr. Farber asks me if it's okay if she speaks with him for a minute or two. I say yes, and she leaves me alone in the room.

I don't want to think about yesterday, about forgetting, about death, about my father, my brother, the possibility of losing my mind, my children, everything. I go over to the bookcase—open above, closed cabinets below, where I imagine she keeps her patient files. I scan the titles on the shelves, wanting to focus on something other than myself. The word "disorder" appears multiple times. An interesting word choice that could mean an illness or lack of order or messiness—or an illness characterized by a messy lack of order. It must be exhausting, dealing with people like me all day long. We come here, all of us, looking for order, for answers that elude us. I think of that old saying about crazy people not playing with a full deck. It's unfair, really. We're expected to use our disorderly brains to fix our disorderly brains—to successfully play the game of life without having all of the cards. And, here's the rub, we're bound to lose—you'll even lose at Solitaire if you don't have a full deck.

My attempt at profundity is interrupted, thankfully, before I get sucked into the riptide. Dr. Farber reports that Ryan gave her an idea of what transpired yesterday and says she'll try to talk me through it, as appropriate. She asks me a few questions about my physical health: Did I take any new medications in the last couple of days? Am I anxious or confused about basic things—who I am, where I am, that sort of thing? She recommends a visit to my family physician or a psychiatrist to confirm the etiology, tells me she's mentioned this to Ryan as well. I focus on the word "etiology." I've always liked it—a fancy word for the cause of disease.

"We'll talk today for a little while," Dr. Farber says. "And then I'd like to go over a few concrete strategies that may help you. How does that sound?" Her normally even, measured tone is tending toward overly sensitive. Like she's talking to a crazy person, someone with a serious disorder with complicated etiology.

"Will it happen again? Is that why I need coping strategies?"

"It's hard to say, Kate. Have you had memory loss like this before?"

"Like this? No, not like this."

"Not like this."

"Well, no, I mean, I've forgotten bits of time before—like arriving somewhere without remembering the drive, or drifting away from a conversation and someone asks a question and I don't know what they're talking about. You know, flashbacks that don't make sense—things like that. My problem is usually that I can't forget, not that I can't remember."

Dr. Farber is writing on her pad.

"My mother left me a box—my father had a will," I say reflexively.

Her notepads. She is sitting at the kitchen table, canary yellow against the green Formica, swirling curlicues of white clove smoke in the air above her like airplane writing that doesn't say anything meaningful. I wonder if my mother's writing has any meaning. *Canary yellow—canary in a coal mine, warning.* I try to recall it. Apparently, I read some of it last night. Her image blends into me on the floor of the closet, wrapped in my summer-weight comforter, flipping the pages up and over, page after page. But the closet is wrong; it's tiny, like the one in my old bedroom. Dresses on rusty wire hangers, black and white and red. My cell phone is ringing.

My cell phone. I was there, that's why I am seeing, smelling, and feeling these things.

I was there.

Dr. Farber is waiting. *Did she ask me a question?*

"Like that," I tell her.

"Like that?"

"I don't know what you just said. I was having some kind of memory, a flashback, of my mother. She left me this box in the house. I was in the house yesterday, Ryan says. These images keep coming in and out—my cell is ringing, but I'm in my old room, in the closet."

"These images, they're of the house where you grew up?" I notice that she doesn't ask about what was in the box.

"Well, yes, and no, not really images. I mean, I can see them, but it's more than that." I can smell the papers and the stale smoke, feel the cloying air, the tacky knob. "It's like I'm actually there, with the smells and the noises—everything."

If I try hard to focus on right here, right now, maybe I can stop them. I stare at Dr. Farber, take in her black boots (suede with fringe), a long black-and-brown-patterned dress, the smell of lavender and—*what is that*—vanilla, her gray hair in a braid that disappears down her back.

Gray, disappearing. *My father.*

"Ryan probably told you, I watched my father die yesterday."

Dr. Farber's nod is almost imperceptible. She does not say, "I'm sorry for your loss," thank God. No, she doesn't say anything.

"His heart stopped sometime on Monday. The police tracked my brother down, and he found me." With blunt, declarative sentences, I tell Dr. Farber about the call, the decision, the plan, the execution, and then the disappearing of the rest. It doesn't take long.

She is impassive, but writing more than she normally does. Taking it down. It obviously took *me* down.

"Your brother didn't come to the hospital," Dr. Farber says, her voice neutral, her features unchanged.

I find it ironic somehow that with all I just offered up, this is what she chooses to comment upon. *Daniel.* Perhaps in most healthy families, children that could be there for the end of their parent's life would want to be. I don't suppose this a good time to mention that I wasn't sure *I* wanted to be there. That I wasn't sad or reflective or contemplative—nothing positive. I just wanted him to die.

Go, just go.

Dr. Farber is waiting.

Ah yes, *Daniel.* I try to parrot her tone and expression.

"No, Daniel didn't come to the hospital. He was not there." Ryan says he wasn't at the hospital. But I talked to him, didn't I? My cell phone ringing, *it was him.* He was—

"We haven't talked that much about your brother."

No, we haven't, I think, and I prefer to keep it that way. There is nothing good to say about my brother. *Nothing.* Grace's voice floats up, giving advice to her grandchildren: "If you can't say something nice, don't say anything at all."

Best, then, not to say anything at all.

Should I tell her that? That I have nothing to say, don't want to talk about Daniel? Or will that merely put undue importance on him, increase the morbid curiosity factor? More fucking absence meaning more than presence. Will she write that down?

Block Daniel is failing. *Daniel. There.* Me hiding in the closet. A rattling doorframe. *Again.*

Fear.

Freeze. Fight. Flight.

I watch Dr. Farber watching me.

Dissociative amnesia related to post-traumatic stress. That is what she is calling what happened to me. It's a new one. *First HPV, now this.* I'll have to Google it when I get home. Should I go home? Stay with Ryan? It's Wednesday. The kids will go to Jacob. Good thing. *I need to get my shit together.* I look back at the bookcase, searching the titles and the subtitles for my new diagnosis. These books are tricky that way, with subtitles. The title will be something like *Get Me*

Out of Here or *Night Falls Fast* or, my personal favorite, *ElectroBoy*, giving you no idea what the book is really about. It's the subtitles in fonts a fraction of the title size that will reveal the truth: *My Recovery from Borderline Personality Disorder* or *Understanding Suicide* (as if that's possible) or *A Memoir of Mania*. To me this is symbolic of the disorders themselves: like unfair business contracts, you don't really know what you're dealing with until you read the fine print. Except narcissism. Those titles are quite upfront. Guess that makes sense, though—after all, it's all about them.

"Kate?"

Oh shit, that was a major digression. Dial it back, Kate.

What did she ask me? *Oh, yes, Daniel.*

"I'd rather not discuss him. Can we talk about something else?"

Dr. Farber makes a note. I imagine it says something like "Does not want to talk about her brother. Never does. Something there."

Oh yes, there is.

"Of course, we can talk about something else. How are your kids?"

"They're at school. It's Jacob's day to get them, and they'll stay with him until Saturday, which is good. It will give me time to . . . do you think it's okay for me to have my kids?"

My kids.

"Can your husband keep them longer?"

"I can ask him. Or if they come home, maybe I could ask Ryan to stay with us."

Dr. Farber nods.

"It would be good to set that up." She looks down at her pad. "Do you mind if I ask you a few more questions about yesterday?"

"I don't know how much I'll be able to tell you." I laugh uneasily. *That's the point, Kate: find out what you know, what you don't—try to get at what's being blocked.*

"You said earlier you watched your father die."

Here we go. How did I feel about that or tell me more about that—but no, Dr. Farber is better than that, better than Larry. Silence is her tool of choice: drop a statement and then just wait until the emptiness in the room makes me uncomfortable enough to say something.

"He was already gone, really, I think, when I got there. That's why they call it life support, right? Without it, he wasn't alive."

The story of my father's life would be titled: *There But Not There: How Alcoholism and Neglect Lead to Abandonment.*

"So, when they turned it all off, he faded away." My voice fades. *Go, just go.*

I'm not being completely honest. There was a moment when he seemed to struggle for breath. I remember thinking, *Yeah, how does that feel?* The thought made me feel a wave of guilt, followed by a bigger wave of resentment, followed by an even bigger wave of hostility—if he'd been a better father, protected me just a little, cared just a little, hell, even noticed me, I would have protected him and cared back. I am capable of those things: I protect and care for Logan and Becca. I would die for them. *I would kill for them.*

I decide to share only part of this, couched in acceptable psychobabble. "I suppose I had mixed emotions about it. A little guilt, resentment, even some anger, if that makes sense."

"Guilt, resentment, and anger are common when someone dies."

This goes on for a while. Dr. Farber asks questions. I think, digress, couch. I realize that I am protecting myself from *her*, which I often do—choosing what to disclose, what to keep hidden. This suddenly strikes me as unhealthy, given that this room and Dr. Farber are supposed to be safe. A safe place for me to let it all go. Even here, I can't do it.

So, with two minutes left, I tell her that.

"Dr. Farber, I'm not being honest with you. It's like I'm afraid to talk about yesterday, afraid to be judged or analyzed, afraid of what it all means."

And . . . go.

She simply nods. As if she already knew. She looks at the digital clock. "You may not ever have another episode like this one, Kate. You may, though, so let's go over a couple of the coping strategies I mentioned earlier."

She closes the black leather portfolio and places it on her lap, leaving the other shit there, hanging, but, to her credit, she's not judging or analyzing, at least not openly.

"Some of them I think you are doing naturally, which is great. Avoiding being alone, reaching out to others that have shared the experience, like Ryan. Hugging those you love, which you've told me you do often with your children. Crying to let things out. Hard exercise." She smiles faintly. "Which I know from your running, you do very well. You might consider hot baths or meditation, watching a funny movie—laughing truly is excellent medicine. What do you think?"

I do not know what I think—my thoughts race about, spinning out of control—but what I say is "That all sounds doable."

I am giving her a picture of myself that is far more secure than I feel.

"We will take all the time you need to work through this. I can make space for you more often, if you'd like." As she reaches for the black leather planner on her desk, the caftan-style sleeve of her dress falls open, revealing her arm—age spots, jiggly triceps. I realize, as if for the first time, that she is probably the age my mother would have been had she chosen to live. I search quickly for the pertinent Freudian concept . . .

Transference. Dr. Farber as maternal, accepting, constant, with firm boundaries. *Another fucked-up relationship.*

Yet I find myself saying, "For the first few days, yes, that would be good, to know I have a safe place to come."

"Good, let's say Friday at twelve ten?" She's giving me her lunch hour. She told me once, years ago, that she saves that time slot in case a client is in crisis. This is confirmation; I am in crisis. She stands up, hand on the door.

"Friday, two days from now, twelve ten," I say. "I'll be here."

If I don't lose my mind again.

"Please make sure you see your doctor."

Shit, I must have said that last thought out loud.

"Ryan will help you with that. You seem to be stabilizing, Kate, but if you feel, at any time, that you aren't—that you may be losing your place in time and space—call 911."

Losing your place in time and space. Poetry.

"Try not to be alone."

Try not to be alone, I echo silently as I follow Dr. Farber's back and her gray braid to the waiting area.

Ryan rises to his feet, drops an *Entertainment Weekly* on the glass coffee table. "Thank you, Dr. Farber," he says to her.

I realize that in all the years I've been coming here, she's never met Jacob. She wouldn't be able to pick him out of a lineup. With a single, subtle drop of her head and a restrained, tight-lipped smile, she acknowledges Ryan's words.

He holds out his hand. "You okay?" Quiet, tender.

Dr. Farber turns to go. Pass-off complete. Patient in good hands.

Ryan pulls me into his body; his arm settles securely around my shoulders. "Let's get out of here. Take a walk on the beach, and then I was thinking maybe we could go by the kids' soccer practices. I'm no doctor, but seeing them, being able to see they're okay—it might ground you."

I am not alone.

EIGHTEEN

THE WEATHER HAS TURNED. The marine layer rolled in while I was in talking with Dr. Farber—fog closing in while I was trying to clear the fog.

I smile to myself.

"I knew this would make you feel better," Ryan says.

He's right. The ocean comforts me; it always has. Its vagaries resonate. The power of a ten-foot wave that can rag-doll the most experienced swimmer contrasting with the gentle lapping at my toes of that same wave after it has spent itself. The impenetrability of a riptide that won't allow me to reach shore contrasting with the soft undulation of a swell lifting me as I float out past the break on a calm day. Constancy coupled with variability—always here, always changing. And then there's the mystery of what lies below—what I can see on a clear day and what lies in deep sea trenches, where crushing pressure and darkness demand adaptations.

Transparent and revealing, murky and opaque. Supportive buoyancy. Merciless pounding. Stimulating and soothing. Ebb and flow.

Today, the ocean is not calm. A brisk offshore northwesterly wind creates white caps: six- to eight-foot plunging waves run parallel to the shore, unrideable, turbulent, dangerous. There are no surfers bobbing on boards. A symphony of sounds—the hissing of the wind,

149

the calling of the gulls, and the steady, uninterrupted spilling of waves over it all, water on water, fluid velocity, crests collapsing.

Ryan and I walk slowly, side by side. The Pacific cools the moisture in the air; it is invigorating, but I am not dressed appropriately. Neither of us is. When Ryan puts his arm around me, pulling me in close, I welcome the warmth. A few minutes in, with the wind pushing us along, he says, "I called Jacob while you were in with your doctor."

Crash. My mood curls and drops in a regrettably predictable fashion. I stop sharply, tugging his shoulder back.

"What?!"

He slows but does not stop, scoops me back into his embrace. "Hey, it's okay, I didn't tell him everything that's going on. That's for you to do when you're ready. I just said you're dealing with a lot. Mentioned he might need to keep the kids a little longer. Asked about their soccer practices and told him we might come by."

Ryan stops then, spinning me toward him. "Kate, I'm on your side."

My hair whips into my face, into his. Reaching both hands up, he gathers the swirling curls loosely behind my head in a makeshift ponytail. His eyes, a kaleidoscope of green and brown and gold, and his mouth—lips slightly apart—are just inches away. I feel my breath quicken in a way I haven't felt in such a long, long time. Not in panic or anger, but in bracing exhilaration.

Time stops. I want him to—

"I'm on your side," he repeats, his voice a whisper, a caress.

I cannot breathe.

A gull screeches.

Ryan sighs heavily and releases the ponytail, his hands dropping to his sides. He steps back, looks deliberately at his watch.

"We should go. You're cold, and Becca's practice has started."

He doesn't want me. Not like that. Who would?

I hear Daniel's voice: "Filthy whore, no one's going to want you now."

I will never be rid of him.

NINETEEN

AN AWKWARD SILENCE fills Ryan's Jeep. He rolls down his window, and as if the discomfort is welling in the air itself, a rhythmic thumping noise replaces the silence.

"Can you open your window just a crack?" he asks.

I comply, wordlessly, feeling responsible for the unease and the unpleasant pulsing. The noise stops.

"Thanks."

"Why does that work, opening another window?" I wonder aloud.

Ryan smiles.

"I actually know the answer to that," he says. "I researched it once for a piece I was writing for *Outside*. I was in this convoy of vehicles, and the driver insisted on having his window open, claimed it kept him alert. Would have been fine except the conditions were ridiculously bad—dry and windy; unpaved roads, littered with pot-holes. Open windows resulted in dust everywhere—your hair, your eyes, your mouth." He wipes his mouth as if the memory is creating dust. "Closed windows meant cloying heat and shared air, but we actually preferred that to the dust. Anyway, none of us wanted to open another window, but eventually that thumping noise drove us nuts, so we had to."

I am grateful to Ryan for filling the silence. I try to focus on what he is saying, thinking perhaps this is a question Logan will throw at me someday, and when he does, I'll be able to impress him—something that is harder to do now than when he was little, when he accepted my loosely fact-based answers to questions like "Why does pumping a swing work?" or "Why is the sky blue?"

Ryan goes on. "My editor at the time loved having scientific shit woven into stories, gear-head stuff most of the time. So I looked up the open-window thumping phenomenon, and here it is—well, what I remember. When you open a window, vortices of air are created—you know, like oscillations—and when they hit the trailing side of the window frame, another, second wave is created. Part of that second wave is projected forward, triggering another vortex at the open window. Still with me?"

His eyes dart over for my nod.

"That vortex feedback interacts with the resonant frequency of the air in the car, which is relatively fixed, and that creates the unpleasant pulsing noise. When you open another window, you change the resonant frequency, and the vortices' feedback is broken. Hence"—he flourishes a hand in the air—"the noise ceases."

"I don't think I'll remember any of that," I confide. "But I may pull some of it out of thin air to impress Logan someday."

"I only remember because I wrote about it and had to answer questions from my editor, Harvey. What a name. Fit him though. Anyway, if you can't remember the whole explanation, here's an interesting factoid you can sock away: the police and the military have experimented with low-frequency acoustic oscillations for crowd control. The noise is so uncomfortable, people will move to get away from it."

Moving away from uncomfortable things.

I am reminded of my behavior on the beach and Ryan's deliberate step backwards.

The traffic light ahead is turning yellow. Ryan guns the engine into the intersection, abruptly downshifts as he spins the steering wheel to the right. Propelled by momentum, my body veers left, toward his. I glance down at his tanned arms and hands, imagine him touching me, scooping my hair up. Despite my embarrassment and shame, I cannot quell the return of pooling desire. I look up to find his eyes on my face. *Is there a question there, in his eyes?*

But he takes the next right turn slowly. Deliberately. We pull into the parking lot next to the athletic fields, and he exits the car without a word.

Get yourself together, Kate.

———————

Inland, the sky is blue. In less than a ten-minute ride, we have entered the 72 and sunny microclimate.

Becca's team is practicing along the fence near the back of the closest field. I see her immediately and am relieved when my rush of feelings for her takes precedence. Ryan and I walk over, stop well back from the sideline, and watch for a few minutes as the girls run a practice drill, coordinating passes among four players as they progress down the field. The coach calls out encouragement: "Hustle, Selena! Keep moving, girls, keep moving! Eye on the ball, Becca!"

When they get to one end of the field, they begin again, going in the opposite direction, methodically changing their group and order across the width of the field without additional direction. Disciplined. That's why they win.

I am not a good soccer player. I'm good as a standing target. The irony of this is not lost on me. According to Logan, I don't even have a proper instep kick since I don't bring the upper part of my leg back at the hip, with my lower leg bent, before driving both forward with an efficient coordinated effort.

"No power, Mom, if you don't use your whole leg," he told me last week.

Apparently, I also don't place my non-kicking foot correctly. It's much more complicated than it looks.

Isn't everything?

I wanted to explain to Logan that I didn't play any organized sports when I was young, certainly no school or club sports that would have required parental support: driving to tryouts, providing snacks, paying dues, showing up on time. Logan, however, has reached the age when every story about my childhood, or Jacob's, for that matter, is met with rolling eyes and the exaggerated, "I know, and you had to walk to school in the snow four miles, uphill each way," a phrase provided to him by none other than the man standing next to me.

Ryan and Jacob both played nearly every sport as kids, organized and otherwise. Prep schools are good for that. Football, hockey, basketball, baseball, tennis, golf, swimming, lacrosse, soccer, even broomball (whatever that is). Add in cycling, surfing, and beach volleyball, picked up during their college years, and there aren't many sports they don't have firsthand experience with, at least on a basic level. Giving credence to the phrase that life is not exactly a fair playing field for the poor or the disadvantaged.

The girls are taking a water break. I see Becca approach Coach Riley, gesturing toward me. He nods, pats her on the back. My little sprite darts down the sideline, gripping her bottle of water, arms pumping. She reaches Ryan first and leaps into his open arms. He spins her halfway round and sets her back on the ground. And now she is mine. Her arms strong around my waist.

"Are you feeling better?" Blue eyes open wide under her brow—knitted, worried.

She knew something was wrong this morning. *What did I say? What did I do?* I long to make it right.

"I'm fine, baby. Uncle Ryan and I just wanted to see you practice a little bit. Your team looks good, and you're working so hard," I say in my best *nothing is wrong* voice, despite the catch in my throat. "So proud of you, Boo."

I hold her, hugging tight per doctor's orders, my left hand around her, my right cradling the back of her head, the ponytail holder centered in my palm as I gaze upon her face. A thin sheen of sweat, beading at her hairline, dampens tendrils that have escaped the elastic band. She smiles. It works. We are both reassured.

"Are you staying and bringing me home? 'Cause Dad said he was coming to get me."

Before I can answer, Ryan interjects, "No, Becs, your dad's still coming. We're just here to watch for a while."

She looks to me for confirmation, pulling back slightly. "K, but I'll see you on Saturday, right, Mom? At the game? We're playing this traveling team called the Hornets. Coach Riley says we all have to play our best 'cause they're, like, super good, and we need lots of fans to cheer for us, so you should come too, Uncle Ryan."

Ryan's smile tugs at my heart. "I'll be here, Boo. Now get back over there before Coach Riley yells at your mom and me."

She grips me hard, quick. "I'll call you on my cell phone tomorrow, Mommy, and the next day too. To say hi, okay?"

"Okay, Boo." Tears form. "I love you," I say into the top of her head, closing my eyes, bottling it.

Visiting Logan's practice is another story.

As we pull into the dirt parking lot next to the middle school field, I notice Jacob's pearl-gray BMW sedan parked along the wooden fence.

Ryan sees it too. "Hey, no worries. He knows we're coming by. Let's keep the focus on Logan, okay?"

There is no reproach in his words, but my own thoughts are a different matter. I shouldn't need someone to remind me of this: maternal self-focus isn't healthy for children.

Ryan hops onto the top rail of the fence and pats the space next to him. "Best seat in the house."

I climb up and we sit in companionable silence. I look for Jacob along the sideline. Not surprisingly, he is friendly with both of our children's coaches. He doesn't appear to be here, however, which is strange. I turn and look back at the car in the lot: his plates, his car. I consider saying something to Ryan, but right then he puts one finger on my cheek, turning my head back toward the field.

"Logan," he says softly.

Logan's team is scrimmaging with another team. I recognize Natalie's son—Trent, her youngest—in the goal. The dynamic is completely different here than at Becca's practice. More bravado, testosterone pulsing in the air, energy oscillating and reverberating. Good thing they are playing out in the open, so some of it can escape. I watch my son, no longer a little boy, his limbs long and lean, athleticism mixed with the grace and confidence of youth. He runs down the field, receives a pass with the inside of his foot, dribbles, and then, bending his right leg at the hip and knee, brings the upper leg forward as he forcefully accelerates his lower leg, executing a seemingly effortless, powerful instep kick.

"That's the way," Ryan calls out.

The sound of a car approaching, crunching gravel behind me, proves to be too great a temptation. Curiosity kills the cat. I see Natalie's van, Jacob in the passenger seat. Natalie and Jacob together again. I tense and slip forward. Gripping the wood with both hands, I am suddenly aware of the rough texture under my palms and the back of my thighs. Ryan reaches over, touches my left knee—to steady, calm, or restrain me?

In a flash, I am in the kitchen, flooded with light. Cool night air blows through an open window. Still in the clothes I have worn all day—in the hospital, at the house, on the trip there and back. I can feel the layer of grime on my cheeks, the back of my neck. I notice an open wine bottle on the counter, two used glasses. Barely perceptible lipstick prints on the edge of one, prints that do not belong to me.

I don't wear lipstick, unless I'm at a wedding or one of Jacob's benefits.

My husband drank wine with someone, here in my house, while I was gone.

A question, an answer, an argument.

The offensive wineglass precariously balanced in my palm.

"Who were you having drinks with, Jacob? Natalie? You were having drinks with my best friend while I was gone?"

And then, ah, the feigned innocence, topped with pity. Poor, irrational Kate.

"Babe, please don't do that. We weren't having drinks." Jacob's reasonable face returns. "Listen, she was feeling bad, this thing with your dad brought back memories for her, and for me, about losing people. Her grief is still fresh, Kate. You may not see it all the time, but she's mourning Michael every day."

What? Now Jacob is an expert on Natalie's emotional well-being? I don't see her grief? I was with her through all of it, doing my best. I'm not a good friend and somehow he is? *He's* there for her?

She's taken his side through this whole thing. She hasn't called or texted me—but she's been in my house, in my kitchen, drinking with Jacob.

And here—and now—she is with Jacob. Again.

A small voice that sounds remarkably similar to Jacob's whispers in my head, *"You are being irrational."*

I am up, off the fence.

Fight or flight.

A cheer goes up from the boys on the field.

I hear Coach Lowry: "That-a-boy, Caleb! Nice assist, Logan!"

I hear Dr. Farber in my head: *"What are you feeling? Why are you feeling it?"*

Betrayal. Anger. And now I've missed Logan's moment. *Fucking Natalie, fucking Jacob.*

Natalie waves as they approach, white Starbucks cups in hand. *First wine, now coffee.*

Jacob's attention is on the field as he calls out, "Go Logan," prompting a proprietary smile from her.

"Hey, guys, just in time," Ryan says.

What is wrong with everybody? *This is not acceptable.*

My veins are filled with ice and yet heat rises in my chest, my neck, my face. Red hot. The chaos in my head surges, overpowering sense and sensibility. Everything slows to a crawl and time is suspended, eerily soundless, as if we've all been pulled into a vacuumed vortex spinning the wrong way. I look back and forth between Jacob and Natalie and Ryan and the field, where even the boys seem to be moving in slow motion.

"So, this is how it is?" I hear myself say. I feel my shoulders hunch, my hands form loose fists, my arms come up, crossing in an X at my forearms so that my right hand lies directly over my heart.

"Kate?" Natalie's "oh, Kate" face is back, her arm is moving toward me—but its progress is halted by Jacob's hand.

"I got this," he says. "Can you two give us a minute?"

Ryan is off the fence now, behind me. I sense him rather than see him. Jacob reaches for me. A glance passes between them, over me, through me.

"No, dude, I think it's better if . . ." Ryan's hand is there, grasping mine, breaking the X.

Jacob falters. Pity and practiced compassion turn to confusion and frustration. His orderly world, his disorderly wife.

"Trust me on this," Ryan says, pulling me gently away.

It doesn't occur to me until we are back in the Jeep and I can breathe again that I didn't get to hug Logan.

On the heels of that thought comes another: *Will I remember this tomorrow?*

TWENTY

JACOB IS WORRIED about my mother's notebooks. I heard Ryan talking to him about them Wednesday night. To read them or not to read them, that is the question. Maybe Dr. Farber should read them first, Jacob told Ryan—make sure that there isn't something there, something that could trigger another episode. That's what Ryan is calling my dissociative amnesia with Jacob, "an episode" in which "Kate blocked out some of the shit that was going down."

On the way home from the debacle at Logan's soccer practice— after I calmed down enough to speak rationally—I mentioned Dr. Farber's coping strategies. Ryan, ever supportive, suggested that I develop a plan built around those strategies for the next couple of days. Take control. I thought back to the night Jacob revealed his betrayal with the stripper—lying in Becca's bed, conceiving a plan, determined not to fall.

Ryan is right. I'm having some serious control issues. The notebooks are part of that. After all, they are for me. *For Kathryn*, my mother's letter said, not *For Kathryn's psychologist to screen and filter.*

"You know," Ryan said as we pulled up to the garage door, "anyone would have felt overwhelmed by yesterday: losing your dad; going back to your old house; dealing with your brother; and finding your mom's stuff, which I'm guessing may be pretty intense, from what

I've heard about your mom. Reading all that will be good eventually, but right now, maybe not so much."

He tempered this message with a classic Ryan grin, head tilted forward so he could raise his eyebrows over the top of his Ray-Bans, à la *Risky Business*. *Risky business indeed.*

"As for tonight, I'm thinking maybe some take-out sushi, a few Asahis, and a couple half hours of mindless comedic television. What say you?"

"Sounds very coping-like."

"Yes, methinks it will be, fine lady. Your Dr. Farber mentioned you shouldn't be alone just yet. I'll stay so we can all rest easy, yeah?"

So that is how I got through the evening: lying on the couch, drinking beer, trying not to acknowledge the undercurrents swirling like those damn open-window oscillations, creating a thumping noise in my chest I worried Ryan would hear. Three Asahis and an Ambien later I collapsed into bed, shrouded in a pre-sleep cloud of whispery half thoughts, impossible to corral. *Is something going on between Jacob and Natalie? Can I resolve things with Jacob? Do I want to resolve things? How could I not want to? My poor children. Can I protect them from Daniel? From myself? What happened in that house? What more might I lose?*

Am I on the edge of falling?

If I fall, where will I land?

Jacob, Natalie, Daniel, Becca, Logan, Ryan.

Jacob. Ryan. Logan. Becca. Logan. Becca. Loganbecca.

I drifted away.

Today, Thursday, is going by in a bit of a blur. Ryan stayed with me at the house last night, borrowing an old T-shirt and a pair of shorts from a bag of things Jacob left behind that I intended to give to Goodwill. I slept in late. Ryan made me breakfast to eat out by the pool, and then he sat with me while I read my father's will. It wasn't professionally written and clearly not lawyered, though my father must have watched a television movie that had a will in it, because some of the language is not his:

"I, Nicolas Xavier Barton, being of sound mind and body, do hereby leave everything I own including the house located on Locust Street in San Jose, CA, all of its contents and the Ford Focus parked there, to my daughter, Kathryn Barton Whitter." (Again, spelled wrong, *shit*.) "She has my permission to do with this property as she sees fit. I hereby disinherit my son, Daniel Xavier Barton. If Kathryn sells the house, all of the money is to go to her and none to him (Daniel). Kathryn will also be the person responsible for figuring out what will be done with my things and with me."

The document is signed at the top of the second page over a line. Under the line he has printed his name, NICOLAS XAVIER BARTON. The date reads May 26, 2010.

It's been in here for over eight years.

"What will be done with my things and with me," he wrote.

"I need to make some calls," I say aloud.

First on the list, the funeral director. I apologize for the delay in contacting him. Ryan walks away to grant me privacy when I lower my voice to provide instructions for the cremation—no funeral, memorial, or obituary. I provide my credit card information from memory.

Now I can hear Ryan inside, cleaning up the kitchen. Images of my father's kitchen surface, along with the realization I have to make arrangements to de-hoard the house. Within moments, I find a San Jose realtor online who specializes in my father's neighborhood.

Lindy Wortham's webpage photo is daunting. Big blond hair, nipped and tucked to the point of pinched, she looks like the sort of person that won't take any shit from anyone. I dial her number.

———

Forty minutes later, Ryan gives me his rapt attention as I describe the equal parts illuminating and frustrating conversation I had with Lindy about the necessary steps to prepare my father's house for sale. He commiserates with me on how futile it seems to spend any time at all on a place I'd prefer to see razed to the ground—a likely fate, given it is the lone holdout in a sea of gentrified homes.

"Did you call the doctor?" Ryan asks me.

I hadn't. So I do.

Dr. Brachmann's scheduler squeezes me in with Donna, the nurse practitioner.

Donna conducts a basic physical examination and takes some blood— for what, I'm not sure; she admits there isn't really a laboratory test for dissociative amnesia. The words "no laboratory test available" reminds me of the inability to test Jacob for HPV, which isn't helpful.

She tells me the only injury that can be seen—the cut on my leg—will heal on its own.

Late in the afternoon, Ryan and I go for a slow, easy run together, each listening to our own playlist.

Afterward, showered and clean, we grocery shop, steering clear of Vons.

Back at the house, we make an early dinner, assiduously avoiding discussing anything of consequence.

"How about a walk?" Ryan asks me as the sky darkens. "As my mother would have called it, a little evening constitutional."

I put on a sweatshirt while he rummages in the Goodwill bag for something warmer. Side by side, we walk slowly down the driveway.

Before we reach the street, Ryan says, "What you did on Tuesday for your father, being there despite your feelings, was a decent thing to do—the right thing. I know someday you'll be glad you were there."

He sounds so sincere I don't have the heart to tell him that I definitely wasn't being decent; pushing your father out of this world into whatever comes next with a "go, just go" does not qualify as decent or kind or anything of the sort.

"I wasn't there, you know, when my parents died." Ryan hasn't talked to me about his parents' deaths in any detail before. I know that his father died of pancreatic cancer and his mother from an accident several months later. He tells me now that when his father was diagnosed, he wanted to leave boarding school and head home, but his parents, eternal optimists, were convinced that his dad would beat the odds and convinced him to stay. At first, it seemed they were right. Then, quite unexpectedly, the cancer bloomed. His father went from lecturing in front of two hundred students to feeling unwell and a bit shaky to comatose in a hospital bed in less than two weeks. Eight months later, his mother, an avid walker, was hit by a drunk driver at six thirty in the morning as she rounded a corner in their neighborhood. No sidewalks, an early-morning fog, and his mother's dark gray sweats were all considered contributing factors, but the bottom line was that an overly stressed lawyer going through a nasty divorce with a blood alcohol level of .15 had left an all-night restaurant with three cups of joe and a Denver omelet in his system as an antidote for hours of whiskey neat.

"Not that it would have changed the outcome, but it might have given them some peace, knowing I was there. Or maybe it would have given *me* some peace, I don't know. At least for my mom, anyway—my dad had my mom there. My mom was alone."

We have that in common, I think but do not say. *My mother was alone.*

"I've read about it, that moment when someone dies, how profound it can be." Ryan slows his pace to a crawl.

"Profound" is not the word I would have chosen, yet I suppose there is something to be said for witnessing that moment: it is both simple and inscrutable—the cessation of living as we know it, passing from this world into the unknown.

For Ryan, it would have been profound and meaningful. He is a good and decent son.

As a daughter, I am clearly lacking.

I am clearly lacking in many ways.

"I'm sure it can be profound," I say. "For most people, it probably is. For me, though, it was simply putting finality on something that had already happened. My father wasn't just gone before I arrived, he'd been gone a long, long time—he abandoned me years ago. The thing is, Ryan, you miss your parents. As painful as it must have been to lose them, to be alone, at least you had them. I can't imagine what that feels like. I know how much Jacob misses his dad, and I've always envied him that, in a strange way." I realize as I verbalize these unedited thoughts that I trust Ryan, perhaps more than anyone. "I don't miss my parents, not really. Not the way you or Jacob do. It's like, how can you miss something you didn't really have?"

He doesn't answer. He is quiet for a minute. "I do miss my parents," he finally says. "I don't think about them every day, but there are times when I wish I could call them, just to hear their voices, like Becca does with you. You know, they weren't much older than I am now when they died. I was still a kid. I don't know what they would think about most of the adult things in my life. They never had the chance to know who I've become."

"They would have been proud of you, Ryan."

He shakes his head.

I reach for his hand. It is warm and dry.

Walking along in the dark, looking in on homes warmed by golden light, hearing only the scratchings and buzzings of the night, I feel an emptiness that is freeing. Like there is a vacuum sucking the truth out of me.

"Sometimes when I was reading stories to Logan and Becca at bedtime, with their bodies curled into me, smelling all clean and innocent, and I heard myself say the words on the page about mother bears or bunnies or birds, I would feel this ache, this longing for something I never had," I say slowly. "I guess in a way, my mom dying meant the death of some wild hope—of a mom that would actually be there for me, you know, someone that would take care of me, listen to my stories, and hug me good night. I do miss that. I miss that wild hope."

Ryan squeezes my hand, stops, and turns. His face is shadowed.
"I understand. I'm so sorry, Katie Rose."

My heart stops.

"We should head back, make sure you get a good night's sleep."
He begins walking in the opposite direction, toward the house.

I certainly know how to push people away.

TWENTY-ONE

IT'S FRIDAY, I think when I awaken.

I confirm this on my cell phone and am insanely grateful to be fully aware of my surroundings, of "my place in time and space." I roll over, delighting in the firmness of the mattress under my back, the coolness of the sheets on my toes, the sound of pool water trickling down the waterfall entering through an open window, the school photos of Becca and Logan in silver frames on the dresser—Becca in a purple dress the shade of frozen blackberries, her hair sunlit, with a smile that speaks volumes about her open view of the world; Logan in his favorite electric-blue Hurley T-shirt, wearing a smile that's more of a concession than an expression of happiness.

I miss them. I miss getting them ready every morning. I miss Logan's grouchiness and Becca's hair, miss watching them at the counter spooning breakfast cereal into their mouths: Cheerios, plain, no sugar for Becca, Honey Nut Crunch for Logan.

Tomorrow is Saturday. They will be here tomorrow night. I should ask Ryan to stay, as a precaution. In case of another "episode."

I hear myself sigh; the noise is amplified by the stillness in the house. Before I see the note on the bedside table, I know I am alone.

Written on the back of one of Jacob's monogrammed notepads, clean white with a nautical-blue stripe under his name, Jacob William

Whittier: *KR. Hope you slept well—early am surf report epic! Meet you after dr. appt at my place. Dinner on me.* Signed with a huge, sloppy X and a trailing R. I imagine him going into Jacob's office where the notepads reside, pulling one off, flipping it over and jotting these words, coming in and watching me sleep for a second before dropping the note here beside me.

I close my eyes. Feel the back of his fingertips gently tracing my jawline.

Did that happen, or am I only wishing it had?

Jacob calls me on the way to my appointment with Dr. Farber. He wants to discuss the timing of the kids' games tomorrow. Becca's game will still be underway when Logan needs to be delivered to his field for pregame warm-up. If I can't be there, Natalie has offered to fetch him on her way.

I bristle at the mention of her name. "I will be there. You won't need Natalie."

"Kate, listen, this thing you've got toward her doesn't make any sense. She's one of your best friends."

"Really?" I can hear how nasty I sound. "One of my best friends would hang out with my husband, drinking wine, while I'm away? One of my best friends would choose not to call me during one of the most troubling times of my life, after I was there every minute after her husband died?"

"Kate, Natalie told me you asked her not to contact you. You can't have it both ways." His reasonable voice has a hint of frustration. "And the wine thing? You're making something out of nothing. Nothing happened."

He and Natalie must be talking often.

"I think we ought to follow Larry's directions," I say aloud, silently thanking our marital therapist, who was wearing a truly hideous maroon-and-tan argyle sweater at our last appointment. "We're not supposed to discuss issues like this on our own, only with him, in his office."

"Dr. Reynolds? You want to wait and talk about this with Dr. Reynolds? You're not listening, Kate. What I'm telling you is there isn't anything to discuss. Natalie came over on Tuesday because she wanted to know how you were."

"And she couldn't simply call and ask? And you had to open some wine while you talked about me? That's what you're saying?"

"Jesus. How do you do that—make an entirely innocent event sound immoral? Your friend comes over to our house on the day your father dies to ask me how you are doing—something that, honestly, no, she doesn't feel comfortable doing over the phone, because she remembers how hard it was to accept sympathy over the telephone when her husband died. Which, you'll recall, was only a short time ago. You were there, as you've pointed out. She stays to talk because it makes her sad, and you behave as though she's done something malicious. And on top of that you're mad at her for not contacting you these last two days when you specifically asked her not to?"

He doesn't know how Natalie questions me, makes me feel unworthy. I am getting angry, and I don't want to be angry. I hear myself becoming an ugly person. I don't have time to process this.

"I told you, I don't think we should discuss this because, as always, you're making me sound awful. I'm not going to do this, Jacob. I'm on my way to see Dr. Farber, and I want to be in a good place when I get there, so, please, can we not do this?"

"Dr. Farber," he says, with a tinge of huffiness that reminds me of his mother. "Kate, do me a favor. Ryan told me the box you brought back was filled with things your mother left for you—things she wrote, he said. I'm not sure it's a great idea for you to be reading that kind of thing right now. I mean, it's been a rough couple of days. I was thinking maybe you could bring the box to Dr. Farber and she could look through it, kind of make sure it's not going to"—a pregnant pause—"you know, put you in a bad place." He says these last few words uneasily, as if aware the words themselves might put me in a bad place.

Which they do.

"You think I can't handle reading my mother's writing?" I hear myself say and instantly regret.

I don't like myself. Don't want to talk to him anymore.

"It's not that. It's—"

"Jacob," I interject, my voice softer. "Let's not do this, okay? Let's talk on Monday, at Dr. Reynolds's office. I'll see you tomorrow at Becca's game, all right?"

"Yeah, okay." There is a quick pause, and then he says, very gently, "Kate?"

Oh my, I think. His voice can still break my heart. "Yeah?"

"I'm really sorry about your father. I'm sorry I wasn't there for you. I should have gone. I should have been there."

I realize as he says these words that had this happened a year ago, it would have all gone very differently. *What-if.* Maybe he would have been there. Maybe I could have told him the truth. I am sad, suddenly, and then I realize something else: I am changing.

———

I mean to start with this. "I am changing" is how I intend to start the session with Dr. Farber. But I don't.

What comes out of my mouth is "The coping strategies actually worked."

They did. I feel stronger, grounded.

"On Wednesday, I hugged, laughed a little, had a few beers, and slept through the night." I keep a running tally on my left fingers with my right, clicking off each assigned task, finishing with a flourish, both hands open like a magician—*ta-da*.

"I did have to take an Ambien to achieve the last one." I move my pointer finger to my chin and roll my eyes up in affected contemplation before I return my gaze to her. "Still counts though, right? Saw the doctor—nothing physically wrong with me, other than the cut on my leg, which is healing nicely. Oh, and I ran the last two days. A reasonable amount at a non-punitive pace. I even thought about trying the meditation thing this morning when I woke up, but honestly, I'm not sure that will work for me. Focused quiet is not my strong suit."

Dr. Farber does not appear impressed with my litany of successful coping. "You seem rather energized."

Definitely not impressed, almost sounds concerned.

"Well, yes, I am energized. You make that sound like a bad thing. Is being energized a bad thing?"

Is energized a euphemism for manic?

"No," she says, with a little shake of her head, "simply an observation."

"Thank God." I mean to sound relieved, but it comes across as a tad too enthusiastic. "You had me worried for a second."

"Other than energized, how are you feeling today?"

"Good." I am, I'm feeling good. I've dealt with Jacob. Daniel hasn't called again. I'm actually looking forward to the rest of my day: talking to Boo after school, walking on the beach, dinner with Ryan. "I'm feeling remarkably good, which, now that I think about it, is probably some kind of reaction, isn't it? Some kind of boomerang or whiplash after the last few days."

Dr. Farber engages in the silent treatment. That was fast. *I must be on to something.*

"That's what you think, isn't it? I'm reacting. No, actually, I've decided to put it out of my mind for a while. I even thought about turning off my phone or leaving it behind—you know, to avoid having to deal with any of the shit."

"The shit," she repeats.

"Yes. The shit: Jacob, Natalie, my dad's ashes, the house, my mother's 'gift'"—that last word punctuated with air quotes—"which, by the way, Jacob doesn't think I can handle reading. Did I tell you about the gift?"

Years of therapy and I am still taken aback at how often, when basically left to my own devices, I surreptitiously identify my own issues, the things I should discuss, if I let myself go there. Today, energized, I'm going there.

"No, you didn't."

"Well, apparently, my mother left me a box of her writing, with a note."

As I speak these words, I am there—the smell of rust and rot, the cloying polyester fabric of the red dress brushing against my face as I crouch over the box, reading the top page: *Dearest Kathryn* . . .

"'Dearest Kathryn,' that's how she started it. It's pages and pages..." My voice trails off as I try to re-root myself in the present, studying the neutral beige wall behind Dr. Farber's head, the sepia picture of a covered bridge that hangs there. I've never really noticed it before.

Dr. Farber waits.

I shake my head. "She must have left it for me, with my dad or hidden somewhere. I guess he found it after I left and put it there, in the closet, along with this handwritten guilt-ridden will. Strange, though, that he would care about some box of her shit when it was obvious he didn't care about anything else. Did I tell you he'd become a hoarder? There were newspapers, bottles, trash—everywhere."

No, not everywhere. Not in my room. It was pristine. Exactly as I left it. No clutter. I stop talking, struck by the clarity of this image: my bed, desk, lone poster, pencil, alarm clock.

Not much ever, no more now.

I sigh, audible recognition that I have left my good mood behind. Such a tenuous grip on everything: my mind, my mood, my emotions. I want to remember but don't want to remember. I want to read what my mother left for me but am petrified about what I will find. I want my father's house sold but don't want to talk to the realtor or the waste removal company she recommended. I want Daniel out of my life but wonder if I will ever truly be rid of him, whether I can ever move past what he represents.

I trip onward.

"Apparently, there are companies that deal with hoarders. Who'd have known? The same companies that take care of crime scenes or hazardous waste or when someone dies alone in a house, and there are regulations for how it all has to be cleaned up. Turns out, if my dad had died inside the house, I would have had to disclose that to a future buyer. Not sure if there's a statute of limitations on that or whether I have to tell them about my mom." My throat tightens. "The things you learn."

So true; I'm learning things I never really wanted to know.

"Anyway, this company, Aftermath—which, well I don't know what to say about that name—they come in, check for biohazards, clear the shit out, clean and sanitize everything according to these regulations, and then? Then they actually give you a certificate that says it's safe and habitable." As if that house was ever safe and habitable. "They are going to my father's house tomorrow to assess and set a schedule. The irony is, it'll probably be ripped down before anyone lives in it again, so it's all a huge waste of time. Too bad they can't just bulldoze the whole thing, newspapers, bottles, trash, and all."

Including Daniel, lying in a drug-induced stupor—that would be the best.

"Is your brother involved in this at all—in these decisions about the house?"

Did I say his name? I definitely did not. Why does she want to talk about him so badly?

"Daniel, no, he isn't involved. Thank God. I don't want to talk to him any more than I want to talk about him. He hasn't called again since Tuesday. Hopefully, he never will. Though I'm learning, slowly, that you can't hide, can you?"

Hiding from Daniel. Hiding and being found. *Fuck.*

"I've decided to hire an attorney," I say, "to deal with the sale of the house. Maybe I'll just give Daniel all of the proceeds. Get him out of my life for good." *Make it possible for him to buy a shitload of heroin and blow his brains out.*

"Do you think that would work?"

"I don't know, but it's certainly worth a try. I don't want him anywhere near me, or my children. I don't need any money from my father. I went up there for closure and now . . ." I stop; how did we get here from "the coping strategies worked"?

"But then you found the notebooks and the will."

"Yes, then I found the notebooks and the will."

"And a letter from your mother." A statement, not a question, again. Do I remember the letter? That's what she should have asked. Do I?

"Mm-hmm." Maybe I should give her the silent treatment. Make her uncomfortable enough to tell me what she's thinking. I sit, hands folded, ankles crossed, waiting. It strikes me that this is how I sat, waiting, the day my mother died. I feel the vise tightening around my chest.

She was lying on her back, the bed made beneath her, the coverlet pulled tight. That's where I found her. Her body pale white—all color in her finally drained away.

Memories of that day are murky and, at the same time, crystal clear. Walking into the silent house after school, uncharacteristically neat as a pin—the kitchen counter and table cleared and wiped down, the newspaper folded, the smell of lemon and pine overwhelming, as if the whole house had been doused in industrial-strength cleaner. All of the bedroom doors were closed. I don't remember if I called out for her; that part is gone. Perhaps I knew she wouldn't answer. Perhaps I knew she was there but not there. Shaken and forsaken, I distinctly remember thinking that my mother—still, quiet, her face smooth— looked peaceful. Even then, as a young girl, I knew that contentment, peace, and grace had eluded her while she was alive.

I didn't cry, not at first. I went into the kitchen to wait for some- one to come. I didn't think to call anyone. Who would care? Daniel stayed out as much as he could by then, avoiding my mother and her increasing rage toward him, coming home only when it was dark, like a rat. So it was my father who found me there in the kitchen. I can see myself, sitting at the Formica table, back straight, ankles crossed, hands folded in my lap, staring out the window for hours as the light and color drained from the sky.

I am crying now. Sitting here, in Dr. Farber's office, in my black leather chair. And I don't want to be crying over my mother. What did I tell Ryan? I don't miss her. I really don't.

I remain in my perfectly poised position, but my hands are clenched, my ankles pinned together. I stare at the bridge over Dr. Farber's head. I'm holding on for dear life.

"What's going on, Kate? Can you tell me?" Dr. Farber places her notebook and pen on the desk beside her and leans forward.

I can't, not really. I don't know what to say. Now that my mother is back in my head, I want to get inside of hers. I want to know what she wrote. She left me behind without a hope or a prayer of surviving in a house that was never safe or habitable. I want to understand why she left me there—how she could do it. Because I never could. I couldn't leave Becca and Logan. I miss them as it is, every night they are gone. I miss their touch. And I realize that despite all the pain and loss associated with her memory, despite all her imperfections, I still long for my mother. The wild hope. If this is as close as I can get to feeling a mother's touch, I want to read her notebooks.

Dr. Farber's face is open, caring, which only makes me feel emptier. I am bereft.

Words slip out: "She didn't love me enough to stay. I wasn't worth staying for."

A soft exhale. "Kate, your mother suffered from a mental illness. The feelings you are having are completely understandable—that somehow if you had done something differently or been different, your mother wouldn't have taken her own life, but you need to know that isn't the case."

She waits. Gives me time to say something.

I don't.

She continues, "Those with bipolar disorder are more likely than nearly any other population to die by suicide. Their family members are not the reason for it, nor can they prevent it." Her voice slows, quiets with compassion. "You got the worst of it—losing your mother, feeling abandoned by your father, feeling unsafe, and, I get the sense . . ." She pauses. When she continues, I can hear a tremor. "I get the sense there's more, things that you are keeping deep inside that you feel you cannot share, even now. But you're a survivor, Kate."

Strength returns to her voice. "Not only have you survived, you have done so much work to consider all of these things, to shore yourself up, to create a healthy environment for your children, and to be a good mother."

To consider all of these things. To be a good mother. Am I? Am I a good mother? What if I snap and plunge? What if that has already happened? What then?

"What you decide to do with your mother's pages, that is up to you—not Jacob, not me. If you want to read them, just remember they are words on a page. They will only have as much power as you allow them to have. Having said that, place yourself in a safe situation when you read them. And if they trouble you, stop. Put them away. We can talk about them here, if you want to do that."

"Do you think it's a good idea, to read them?" I am afraid to ask, afraid not to.

Dr. Farber looks down for a moment. "I don't know what they contain, so it's difficult to say. I don't know if they will answer the questions you have or give you the understanding you seek. I do worry that you will be disappointed or that it may muddle things further, but then again, you won't know if you don't read them."

Muddle. An excellent word. The truth is, I'm already muddled. More than muddled—that's the problem.

In the end, we don't discuss how "I'm changing," despite my original intentions. We do talk about why my father left my room untouched, why he left me his will. "Perhaps he was waiting for me to come back," I speculate, which makes me feel sad about my father for the first time. We glance over my anger at Natalie and Jacob, why I have such rigid loyalty issues, which makes me feel uncertain.

Although she probes delicately again about Daniel, twice, we do not discuss my brother.

I do not tell her about actually being *in* my room, exactly as it was back then—the bed, the desk, the pencil and clock, the broken mirror, the dresses in the closet. Hearing his voice. I do not tell her that I remember some of it now. I do not tell her that I think I know what triggered my dissociation. I do not tell her that I can see myself there, then, dying a little each time they came for me.

How that was the worst.

I don't tell her about the last time and the vow I made that day. I do not tell her about Daniel contacting me in the past or that seeing him, whether in the flesh or as a paranoid ideation, is frightening on a visceral level.

The last two minutes, we sit in silence as the volume of what I must not reveal swells and rises to the surface, looking for a weak spot to break through.

TWENTY-TWO

A FIERCELY COMPETITIVE pickup game of volleyball at Moonlight Beach proves to be excellent therapy recovery. Ryan has been playing regularly and knows a few guys that are willing to show up on a random Friday afternoon. I haven't played in a while, yet by the end of the first game, Ryan and I have found a rhythm that works.

The insides of my forearms are almost instantly sore, and I dread which muscles will be barking at me tomorrow. We lose badly, but somehow it doesn't matter—there is no agony in this particular defeat. Whether from the exercise-released endorphins, the thrill of a few perfectly executed points, the fresh and slightly salty air, the sand under my feet, or the celebratory ass slaps and sweaty embraces, I feel vibrantly alive.

In accordance with the agreement we forged Wednesday night before I went off to my Ambien/Asahi-induced sleep, Ryan brought my mother's box back to his condo for safekeeping. What to do about them comes up as we drive back.

"Kate, there's probably as many ways to look at those notebooks as there are people giving you advice about how to look at 'em; we're all just bringing our backstory to it. Jacob, he's afraid they'll be destabilizing. Come on, we both know the guy. In his worldview, notebooks from long-dead relatives are like a beehive—best not disturbed. There may be honey in there, but fear of getting stung keeps you from getting at it."

Ryan effortlessly parallel parks his Jeep in a tight spot, the loaded words delivered as he spins the wheel, glancing over his shoulder.

He turns his head back, settles his gaze on me. "As for the good Dr. Farber, it wouldn't take a genius to figure she probably thinks you'll gain insight into your mom. All those pages and pages when she was manic, and if maybe she wrote some of it when she was in a dark place, that's pretty fascinating shit for a psychologist. And, well, let's be honest, it might"—he gestures with fingers and palms to his own chest—"help her"—then opens his palms to me—"help you."

His intonation is a spot-on imitation of one of our collective favorite movie scenes of all time. In *Jerry McGuire*, Jerry, played by Tom Cruise, says "help me, help you," repeatedly, with dramatic flair, until his client, played brilliantly by Cuba Gooding, mocks him before saying, "You're hanging on by a very thin thread, and I dig that about you." Jacob, Ryan, and I have been known to use both of these phrases to defuse many a desperate situation.

Tilting his head, he opens his car door. "Shall we?"

I climb out. Before shutting the door, over the top of the car, I ask, "And you—what do you think?"

"Darlin', to be sure, I'm coming at it from a different place—a complicated one." He walks to his front door, pauses as he unlocks it. Sighs. "Full disclosure"—he glances over at me—"I'm a little envious."

"Envious?"

"After you," he says, gesturing toward the steps leading up to his unit.

He says nothing more until we are both inside the living space. Then his eyes drop, and he says, quietly, "Like I told you yesterday, I never really got to know my parents as people. If I had the chance now to know what they thought and felt, I'd, well . . ." He turns to me, his green eyes shining. "I'd view it as a gift."

I reach for him. He reaches for me. Our hands meet in the middle.

He soldiers on. "Having said all that, I'm not naïve. I get that this could bring up all sorts of stuff. Some of it you may not want to deal with, but then again, some of it—well, some of it could be amazing." He gives me a rueful smile. "The way I see it, though, your past, your parents, that house—they are all a part of you. But, Kate, this is important"—he grips my hands tight, as if to emphasize the point—"they don't define you. It may be a trite phrase, but it is for sure true when it comes to you: the whole is so much greater than the sum of its parts."

This is what unconditional love must feel like.

I want to dive in.

He drops my hands, heads into the kitchen area. As he talks, he snags a Brita pitcher from the refrigerator and fills two tall plastic glasses with water. "As for whether you're ready to read them, I disagree with Jacob and Dr. Farber. I think being able to take a good hard look at where you came from, facing your past the way you have—going back to San Jose, being there for your dad, even bringing the box back here—those are all signs of strength."

He hands me a glass, takes a long pull from his own.

"You're fiercely strong, Kate. Fiercely strong and capable of handling the notebooks. On your own, if you want, or with me by your side. I mean, not looking over your shoulder"—he lifts his head and lengthens his neck, as if he's lurking over me—"just here." He points to the couch behind me. "Or over there." He points to a modern leather-and-chrome slingback chair in the corner. "Or we could take 'em outside on the porch with an ocean breeze there to keep the air clear and waves to wash the shit away. You can read, and I can write."

This sounds perfect, actually.

So, with the sun warm on my face and a background mix of symphony and surf, I read—sitting cross-legged, my knees sticking out under the arms of the wooden deck chair, the box by my feet, a yellow pad on the low table in front of me. Ryan sits across from me, gold-touched hair flopping over his forehead, tipping the edge of his sunglasses, his laptop open, keys clicking. It's both surreal and so real.

The letter.

To start, the letter.

———

Dearest Kathryn.

I don't know exactly when you will read this. I've asked your father to wait to give it to you when you are older, mature, at least eighteen, though you have always been an old soul, you probably could be reading it now. You are my muse, darling girl, a little version of me that hasn't been tainted by the world and the madness. So as I write for you, I write for me. I wish I were stronger, that I could contain the shifting, draining sand as it spills out time and sucks me under. Today is an in-between day, on my way from one place to another. I don't know how long I will be here, transitioning. I just need long enough.

Words often fail me, being able to explain what I'm feeling, seeing, hearing, believing. How difficult it is sometimes simply to breathe. How brushing my teeth can seem an insurmountable task. And then I wake up one day and there is light coming through the shades and I want to open them, to see the sky. For a short while, the world is sane again. I listen to the birds and cars and my children's voices without being overwhelmed by a cacophony of chirps, roars, whines, and cries; flavor returns to food and hunger can be satisfied without invoking shame and guilt; I cherish the delicacy of your touch when you tentatively return my embrace; and colors appear with hues and tints that don't throb and pulse.

Often, I hear you and Daniel discussing my moods as colors in the rainbow, as if they fall somewhere distinct along a predictable spectrum. If only that were so or, since it is not so, if only I could describe it for you, do it justice—you see, it's not that clean or simple. And yet, and yet, I feel compelled to try. If I were going to use a color analogy, this one comes closer.

Do you remember the time we went to that arts fair in Carmel? You called it a golden day. You begged me for this wooden kaleidoscope, decorated in tiny stone mosaic. You chose it so carefully. All the way home, you held it, spinning it, watching the patterns emerge, each turn a new design. You pronounced it magical and insisted I look inside. Held to the sunlight streaming through the window, the images were bright, jewel tones of royal blue, purple, rose pink, gilt gold, and emerald green. When you tilted it toward the floor, the colors darkened, dimming with lack of reflected light. That's what I feel like sometimes, the inside of a kaleidoscope that I do not control. Tumbling colors, ever-changing, bright one moment, tilted down out of the light another, arbitrary patterns that appear symmetrical because of reflections that bump up against one another.

But that isn't quite right either. Perhaps if every sensation were included—smell, taste, touch, all represented in the flowing bits of colored glass—then maybe it would begin to convey what it's like.

You came to me in my room one sluggish, muddy, gray morning, holding shards of mirror, broken pieces of glass, and splintered wood. The kaleidoscope broken, smashed thoroughly by Daniel. Your hand was bleeding. I tried to push aside the funereal drape that threatened to cover everything. I tried to care. You needed me to scoop you up in my arms, to comfort you—but I was comfortless.

There are days when my emotions, my thoughts, even my actions, are like those broken shards: ragged, dangerous, capable of cutting deep. I know that I have hurt you. And Daniel. That I will scar you both in ways I cannot fathom.

On days like today, when the window opens, I look into your clear blue eyes, lit from within, and I want to burrow inside your skull where the light originates, to inoculate your brain against the madness that has engulfed mine. I want to take you away from here, away from me, but if I bring you, there I'll be. One day, though, you will be far, far from here. Perhaps you will read this letter and know that despite it all, I loved you. I'm just not strong enough.

I will fail you. I know I will. That knowledge has become the worst part of these precious, precarious days in between.

I'm not sure when I start to cry. Silent, slow tears, not dramatic heaving. I look down at my left hand to the tiny crescent-shaped mark near the base of my palm, under my lifeline. I remember picking up the pieces, making a small mound of them to show my mother. I knew the toy was irreparable, yet back then I still hoped my mother could fix things.

The letter ends there, "*in between.*" The rest of this notepad seems to be blank. I wonder when she wrote this, how old I was, whether it was closer to the golden day of the kaleidoscope, when I was about eight, just a little older than Becca, or the end of her life, three years later, when I was just about Logan's age. I wipe my face with the edge of my sweatshirt sleeve, reach for the next notepad in the box, and read on.

Poetry, prose, random scribbling, all of it infused with my mother's unique perspective—a perspective I now recognize as part byproduct of her bipolar disorder. Dazzling descriptions of dappled light on leaves, crystals of salt on a hard twisted pretzel, the crisp flesh and tart sweetness of a green apple, inner dialogues that alternatingly confuse or catch at my heart, musings on hope and despair, promises and lies, death, existentialism, and the illusory nature of pure joy.

She is a wonderful, lyrical writer—at times.

What price genius? Or is it simply insanity—a rich inner life run amok?

Jacob and Dr. Farber need not have worried. I do not even pretend to understand much of what I read. This does not cause alarm or spark disappointment; rather, I am relieved. Intensely relieved. Were I to relate to it all, feel at one with my mother—that would confirm one of my worst fears.

I place the yellow pads back in the box and sit quietly. My thoughts still, distill, to two questions: *I may not be my mother yet, but is this where I am headed? How much of my mother is inside of me?*

I shiver and pull down the sleeves of my shirt over my wrists, shoulders hunching forward against the chill in the air. The sun drifts low in the sky, deeper blue and inky violet painted with wisps and puffs of pink and gold.

A glass of wine appears before me, held in Ryan's outstretched hand. "I thought you might be ready for this."

He is right. I am. Holding the glass by the bowl, I raise it up to the light and swirl, watch it spin crimson and garnet in my palm.

Ryan reaches for my empty left hand and pulls me over to the porch railing, overlooking the sand.

"It came highly recommended. Dominus. I read a review before opening it to breathe. It's supposed to be . . ." He turns on his haughty country club lady voice—a bit like Grace's, but with a horrific French accent—"Refined, with ripe black raspberries and rich fruit." He grins. "But I liked this part the best," he says, back to his own voice. "They said the finish is like a crescendo in a Beethoven symphony—long, elegant, and inspirational, leaving you wanting more."

His eyes glow.

"Nice, huh?" He lifts his glass in a toast. "Perfect for tonight."

Long, elegant, and inspirational—leaving you wanting more.

TWENTY-THREE

IT IS, AND I DO.

Dominus, living up to its review.

A sliver of moon and a panoply of stars hang high in the vast sky over the ocean. Candlelight glows over the table creating an island in the darkness, a cocoon of light. The low murmur of the coastal train and its echoing horn; country roads that curve off and away; a bouquet of homegrown roses; the mellow and sensuous tones of cello or oboe. To this list of things that fill me with longing, I can add the flickering of candlelight on the face of my oldest friend.

Yearning pulses through me—the power and possibility of desire.

As if he knows I need a mental break, Ryan talks about nothing weighty: the sunset, the water temperature, and a triathlon he's thinking about racing in early May. Packing as much as he can into each day, he says. He admits that while I was reading, he mostly checked out event websites and read blogs and reviews on a new bike he's had his eye on.

"If anything," he says, "I've become an expert procrastinator the last few weeks."

"How is your book coming along?" I ask.

He grimaces.

"Sorry, sore subject?"

"Turns out the deadlines I've always cursed are good for something. With time at my disposal, I'm wallowing in protracted writer's block." He admits he hasn't written a page worth reading in days. "I suppose I'm literally running from the problem. Or, should I say, cycling and surfing from the problem."

He explains how he has tried every cure for writer's block he can think of: rereading novels that top various "best of" lists to acknowledge, again, the talent of writers he admires; studying passages in which an author creates a mood or a vision with what seems like an effortless command of words; torturing himself with comparisons in which he will always come up short (Rand, Joyce, Tolstoy, Steinbeck, Dickens); or listening to Rachmaninoff or the Rolling Stones, exceedingly loud, to drown out the critic in his head as he writes freehand on legal pads.

"My mother always wrote to classical music," I pronounce. "Always."

Ryan gives me a quizzical look. "I don't know why, but I'm surprised to hear you talk about your mom writing. I guess I thought the existence of this stuff was swathed in secrecy."

I instinctively hesitate; *how much do I want to share?* Other than in therapists' offices, I have always conscientiously avoided discussing my mother, my childhood, the whole nature/nurture mix. But with Ryan, at this precise moment, it feels different somehow. I think about how I wouldn't have my mother's box at all if it weren't for him taking me back home.

"My mother . . ." I stop. Start again. "She wasn't like other mothers—baking cookies, meeting you after school, asking about your day. She didn't really do anything the way ordinary people do things."

I picture her with instant clarity: the front of her dress white with flour, tendrils of strawberry-blond hair curled around her face, moist from exertion and the heat in the kitchen. Every surface in the small space covered with mixing bowls, cookie trays, and bread pans.

"When she baked, it was as if there were display racks to fill and customers lined up to buy. When she read to me, it was as if a theater company had taken up residence in her body. And when she wrote"—I am transported back and my voice slows—"it was as if the words were erupting from her brain or her soul, I don't know which— maybe both. Pages and pages on those yellow legal pads. Music so loud I don't know how she could think. Smoke so thick I don't know how she could breathe." I shake my head, trying to clear my thoughts, still unsure whether my mother's essence has the power to invade, take over. "And then it would all come crashing down and she'd sleep for days and days."

"The stuff she wrote, in the box," Ryan says. "What's it like?"

"Oh." I look down at my nearly empty plate, trying to compose a description that takes in the depth and texture—and failing. "It's hard to say, really. She wrote about broken promises."

Talk about irony.

"And despair." I dig a little deeper. "Desolation, the divine, long- ing for more. You know, light stuff," I say, mocking my own seriousness.

"It's okay, Kate. I really want to know."

I reflect back on a few lines I read and reread this afternoon, trying to capture my mother.

"She wrote this poem about flowers blooming unseen, their scent lost to the wind. I won't do it justice." I am using my mother's words. "But it was something like 'delight dimmed by neglect.' No— hold on."

I dart inside to search for the right notepad. I find it two note- pads down in the stack. The poem is on the top page, a first draft or only draft, with no lines drawn through or words crossed out, nothing discarded.

I step back through the French doors and squint at the words in the candlelight. "'Delight dimmed by neglect, petals soft and willing, for none, for naught, for night will come, descending dark . . .' I sup- pose she meant to say something about unrequited love or innocence and beauty betrayed."

I feel the familiar prick of tears, my new status quo.

"I don't know, though, maybe it's about her depression." I hold the pad to my chest. Shrug. "And that's something I can make sense of."

Ryan waits, silent and still, struggling to conceal his curiosity with compassion.

"I didn't get through much of it." I turn away, lean inside the open door to drop the pad back on top of the others. "But it looks like there might be a short story, or maybe the first couple of chapters of a novel, but most of it is like a journal—not a 'today I went shopping and bought ten pairs of dressy shoes I couldn't afford' type of thing, more like philosophical musings or recordings of some dialogue in her head that's either dazzling or . . ." I shrug again. "Quite honestly, a lot of it, well, it's just gibberish."

When I return to the table, I find I can't look at Ryan. I look to the left of him, into the darkened window that reflects back my own blurred image—his profile, the candlelight, the table.

I confess to him, to myself, though I'm not sure why, "It feels like I'm trying to touch her somehow, the wild hope thing. But to be honest, it's a mixed bag: I'm not sure if she was brilliant or insane. Earlier, when I was trying to decipher it and some of it made sense, even a little, I wondered if it's a gift, as you suggested, or a curse."

Ryan reaches for my hand, his voice reassuring. "I think it sounds fascinating. She must have been fascinating."

He has no idea.

"I kind of wish I'd known her," he says.

I look away. "I wish I had too," I say, wistful, my voice barely above a whisper, not to be heard.

Enough of that. I begin stacking the plates and serving dishes to clear it all away.

"Would you be willing to let me read some of it?" Ryan asks tentatively.

"Oh, I don't know. I mean, most of it is raw, unedited, often incomprehensible—Faulkneresque." I stand and balance the dishes on my wrists and arms with the expertise of long-ago waitressing days.

Ryan watches me intently as he rises to his feet and moves around the table, blowing out the candles, gathering the empty glasses and bottle. "Well, it might help if you could talk about it with someone. And God knows I could use some brilliant Faulkneresque inspiration."

The kitchen counter, like everything else in this unit, is tiny. I stop, unsure of where to put it all. Ryan is there behind me. He brushes past me, his chest against my back, his hands resting briefly on my hips as he squeezes by, and I nearly drop everything.

Next to me, he lifts the top plate, turns on the tap, then reaches for another.

"You know, when you talked about your mom and the music and the legal pads," he confides, "my first thought was *a kindred spirit.*"

I must look startled, because he holds up a hand. "But I get it if you don't want to share it. Seriously, it's yours and yours alone."

I open the dishwasher. Ryan hands me the rinsed plates one at a time, and I busy myself with loading dishes. *Kindred spirit?* He has no idea what he is suggesting. Nevertheless, on some level, I want him to understand her—maybe that would help him understand me. I have never felt this way with Jacob. I have always been so busy protecting us from my past, as if avoiding it denied it its power. Though there was certainly some truth to that, with all the junk we've had to sweep under them, we've never been able to have rugs that lie smooth on the floor. Maybe sharing it, revealing it, would be better. Sweep it out and vacuum it away. I know it will never truly be gone, but less dust and dirt I might be able to take.

Everything is loaded.

I close the door, straighten up, and Ryan is there.

"Kate, I'm sorry, I shouldn't have asked." He brushes his fingers lightly along my jawline, *like this morning,* and turns my face toward his as if to bring me back from wherever my thoughts have taken me. "Enough intensity for one week, huh?"

My breath stops for an instant. "No, you're right. It would help. I want you to read it. I do."

It takes real willpower to move away from his side. My mother's letter is a few notebooks down on the pile. I retrieve it and the one with the poem I'd left on top.

"You may as well start where I did." I present them to Ryan.

He holds the notepads in both hands. "Now?"

"Yes, but I don't want to watch you reading them. I'll just sit here obsessing, *Which part is he reading? What is he thinking?* Maybe I'll go take a shower, if that's okay?"

"Sure, yeah, of course. Come on." He places the notebooks on the side table by the sleek armchair.

———————

A hot shower helps clear my head. With the slate-gray and sea-foam-green tile, tiers of small brown bottles of body wash, shampoo, and conditioner, and three varieties of loofah, I feel like I'm in a spa, not a bachelor's condominium. It is obvious Ryan leaves no bath product behind when he travels.

The lather smells of him. I look at the label: eucalyptus, sage, and mint.

Yes, that's it. That's Ryan.

Perhaps a cold shower would have been more appropriate after all.

I step out to find a stack of clean towels, two small brown bottles of body lotion, a fluffy white bathrobe emblazoned with *Spa, The Peninsula*, a snifter of brandy, and a simple message on a yellow sticky note: "Thank you for trusting me."

Dried, lotioned, robed, and fortified by a strong pull of liquid courage, I clear the steam from the window and confront my reflection. My eyes are bright (*lit from within*, my mother wrote) and my skin is tingling—whether from the heat, the eucalyptus and mint, the alcohol, or the knowledge that Ryan is waiting for me in the next room, I don't know. As I stare, the steam returns, fogging over my image. I rub my head with a towel, brush my fingers through my hair, retrieve the snifter, and pad out to the living room.

Ryan is stretched out long, his feet up, intent on my mother's words, his hand poised, ready to flip to the next page.

Some mood lightening is in order.

"The Peninsula, huh?" I move to the far corner of the couch, curling my left leg under my body, keeping the right one open to the air. The last bandage fell off in the water. I'd looked in the cabinet under the sink for another, but all I found was an open zippered travel bag of what must have been old prescription medications tucked behind a veritable trove of the little brown bottles of hair products, body wash, and lotion. I had to smile. Doubtless, there is a story behind how he has obtained so much eucalyptus, sage, and mint.

Ryan looks up, his face slowly transitioning from pensive concern to boyish charm.

"I know what you're thinking, but no, I didn't steal it," he says when I raise my eyebrow, giving him my best attempt at looking askance.

"One of my last pieces was for a men's magazine on the best spa treatments for guys—you know, best facial, manly mani-pedi, sports massages—and somehow"—he grins—"the Peninsula made the list."

"And the treasure under the sink?"

"Under the sink?" he says, looking briefly alarmed.

"All of the body wash and lotion?"

"Oh, that." He shakes his head. "I'm hoping it lasts a while, 'cause I haven't been able to find that exact blend anywhere else."

"How, exactly, did you get so much of it?"

"Ah, well, that was not as difficult as you may think. It just so happens the hotel staff at that particular establishment found me a likeable fellow. I may have smooth-talked the ladies in the hall a bit; every time I saw one of them, I would explain that, in all the world, I had never found anything like their luxury cosmetics. I thought I was dividing and conquering, getting them each to give me a little extra, but these women were way ahead of me; the last day I was there, they left me this huge stash in my room. Not a word, and, when I tried to thank them, they were like, 'What are you talking about?' Loved them."

Ryan always has a story. Always.

"And the robe?"

"Bought it."

My eyes widen in surprise.

"Right? You're thinking that I finagled it out of the spa staff, aren't you? But no, simply out-and-out purchased it. I didn't actually have to pay for it myself, though, 'cause it was a write-off for the story. Is it not the most comfortable robe you've ever worn?"

"It is." It is, though I have to admit, when he looks at me this way, I'm thinking about why he left it in there for me. I imagine him naked under this same robe.

I've left too much silence in the air, and now the lighthearted mood is lost. He looks back down to the yellow notepad in his lap, lifts it, and places it gently, reverently, on the ground next to his chair. As he effortlessly rises to his feet, thoughtfulness returns.

"Kate, that letter from your mom. Wow. No wonder it made you cry." He sits next to me on the couch. Lifts my hand. Studies it. "I saw you rubbing your palm."

He follows suit, resting his fingertips over mine, his thumb making small circles over the crescent. "Is this scar from the broken kaleidoscope?"

I try to pull my hand back, nodding stiffly. He does not let go, continues to rub the scar, easing the pressure until it's a caress. I'm not sure what he's aiming for, but the feeling goes from comforting to erotic in less than five seconds.

I am finding it harder and harder to breathe.

Without dropping my hand, Ryan leans forward, bringing his mouth within an inch of my neck, directly below where his fingers marked a trail before my shower. He breathes in, "Holy fuck, it smells even better on you."

I sigh and my eyes drift closed as my head tips away. Anticipation is heady. I wait, and then his hand slides around my waist, easing me closer, lifting me, as his lips make contact with my skin, soft as a whisper.

"Kate." His voice is low, broken. "I . . ."

I open my eyes and look into his, green and gold and brown. My fingers curl into his hair as his mouth covers mine. This first kiss rages with tenderness, as if we are both trying to contain something. I can feel the controlled power in his hands as he moves them down over my back in a gentle caress. When they stop, just below my waist, he bends toward me and pulls me into his arms.

I have never been kissed so softly before, and it is disarming. Tantalizingly sweet. Slowly, so slowly, the kiss deepens until I feel I may never be able to breathe again. Desire pools where anger and fear customarily reside. I am aching inside, longing for his touch.

I shudder involuntarily and Ryan backs away, his face clouded with passion and uncertainty.

"Katie Rose," he murmurs, "tell me this is okay."

I don't trust myself to speak. I don't know what to say or how to say it. *I want you. I need to feel you everywhere. I'm sorry.* Actions will have to speak for words. Holding his gaze, I reach down and loosen the belt on the robe. He blows out his breath as if he's been holding it a long time. I lean back before he can touch me and tug on the hem of his shirt.

"I need to feel you," I manage to say.

He removes his sweatshirt and T-shirt with two quick yanks over his head before his mouth finds mine again, this time with an intensity that obliterates all rational thought. He encourages the robe farther open, and I can feel his chest against my breasts. Warmth envelops me, radiating inwards, alight.

His lips and tongue explore my mouth. My hands roam over his strong back and shoulders. He pulls away from me slightly, dislodges my hands from his shoulders, and drops them to my sides. He gazes at me. "God, you are so beautiful."

Almost tentatively, he strokes his fingertips down my sides, then up across my belly to my breasts. Over and over, a delicate symphony of touch. He finally lingers there, caressing my nipples with the pads of his thumbs in the same small circles he used on the scar.

Exquisite. Erotic. Overwhelming.

I feel as though I am spinning, falling. Out of control. Then I remember.

"Wait, I need to tell you. After New York, I found out—"

"I know," Ryan says. He lifts me and slides me onto my back. Resting on his elbow, he stares into my eyes. "I need you to know, Kate, I will always love you," he whispers, "all of you."

Before I can respond, he captures my mouth again in a tender, deep kiss while he traces a new pattern down my side with the fingers of his free hand, slowing over the spot above my hipbone before arcing across and down to the sensitive skin on the inside of my thigh. He bends his head to kiss a path down my neck, along my collarbone, as his hands continue to move, setting me on fire.

I surrender, moaning, pressing myself upward into him—his hands, his mouth, his chest. I grab his hips and pull him down. My legs, my eyes, and my heart open. I breathe in salt and sweat and the smell of grill smoke. Sensations dip and soar.

I want his touch everywhere. I want all of him too.

I am undone.

TWENTY-FOUR

WE'VE MOVED TO THE BED—naked, limbs intertwined. A wall sconce in the hallway near the bathroom sheds barely enough light to allow me to make out Ryan's features, the outline of his leg resting over mine under the sheet. Sated, safe, I slowly tilt my body away to turn on my side, my back nestled into the curve of his body. I wrap his arms around me and close my eyes to sleep.

"I've wanted to do that for a very long time," he murmurs into the back of my neck.

I startle, ever so slightly. "You have?" How long is a very long time? "Since when?"

"Oh, I don't know. Suffice it to say a long, long time."

I roll over onto my back, pulling the sheet tight to my chest, my arms over the edge. Suddenly I am not so very tired.

"A long, long time?" Jacob and I have only been separated for a couple of months.

Ryan props himself up on his side. He rubs the thigh closest to him.

"Don't look so alarmed. Just because I've wanted to doesn't mean I intended to or thought I'd be able to. Believe me, I completely, totally understand the difference between wanting something and realistically expecting to have it. I mean, it's kind of like wanting to have millions of dollars: you know you probably won't ever have it, but that doesn't stop you from wanting it."

Having millions of dollars doesn't make people happy. Jacob and I have more money than we need, and look at us. Shit, I am a mess. I am lying naked with my husband's best friend. *What am I doing?*

"Hey, where'd you go?" Ryan lifts his hand from under the sheet and strokes my cheek with a tenderness that makes me want to weep. That's the word, *tender*. This whole experience has been tender. No one has ever made me feel so precious.

"What are we doing, Ryan?" I say despite wanting this feeling to stay, wanting to keep reality at bay.

"It's okay, Kate. We're okay. Don't overthink it. Let's enjoy this moment, right now, and let tomorrow's worries come tomorrow. For me, this has been the most incredible night of my life, and I want to stay present—here, now—loving you. Having you in my arms."

"Loving me," I repeat, muddled, like Dr. Farber warned me about. *Oh God, what will she have to say about this?* Self-doubt blossoms. Tears form.

"Hey—hey," Ryan whispers. "Yes, loving you." He moves closer to me, runs the back of his fingers gently down the side of my neck, lightly swirling in the hollow above my collarbone. "I love the curve of your neck."

He pulls the sheet away, continuing the trail down between my breasts, up and over each one in turn, before placing his palm flat over my heart. "Your heart."

I feel myself moving.

"Please," I say, even as my body molds into his. He silences me with a petal-soft kiss before he continues his lazy tour of my body.

His hand nearly floats as it drops down over my breasts to my belly.

"I love this curve," my hip, "and this one," my thigh, over my knee, down to my ankle, and then back, "and this one and this one and this one."

A long, flowing caress that takes my breath away. "And you have the most amazing legs I've ever seen." He lifts my right leg and, with two fingertips, traces the contours of the gash on my calf.

"I love your courage"—he looks up—"and your ferocity."

He places my foot flat on the bed, leaving my knee bent. He reaches for my left hand, returns to the small crescent scar.

"I love the little girl that's still inside you and that young woman I met in Econ 2. Most of all, I love who you are now. So yes, Kate. Loving you—all of you."

The tears pool, threaten to spill. I reach with my free hand to press down on my cheeks as if I can stop them, knowing I cannot. So muddled. I struggle to understand when our relationship shifted in his mind, in my own. I want him. How long have I wanted him? How long has he wanted me?

As if he has read my mind, he goes on, "I've probably always loved you, though I didn't know it right away."

"Always?" I've been with Jacob for nineteen years.

Ryan's expression is so open and vulnerable, I am overwhelmed. I look up, away, to the juncture of the wall with the ceiling. I am reminded of some advice Dr. Farber gave me: "Conversations that are difficult face-to-face are often easier if your visual focus is elsewhere." This topic, with Ryan, may be easier with visual disengagement.

He must agree, because he turns to lie flat on his back. But he keeps hold of my hand, lays it over his own heart before saying, "Yeah, pretty sad, huh? I mean, I didn't realize how I truly felt until you'd been with Jacob for about a year."

A year?

"I was with Sophia then, and we fit, you know?"

I hope this is rhetorical, because I am holding my breath and unable to answer.

Ryan's voice slows, as if he is traveling backwards through time. "But then that second summer, we were all at the Cape for like a week— you, me, Jacob, the whole Whittier clan. There was this gorgeous day. Not a cloud in the sky. Hot, with a light easterly wind. Ideal for sailing."

I can feel his heartbeat, his chest rising and falling.

"Jacob was at the helm on an epic broad reach, so the boat was nice and balanced. You were heading up to lie on the deck, and as you passed Jacob, he pulled you in to kiss you. One hand on the wheel and the other wrapped around your waist. I can see you now, wearing this nautical-blue-striped bikini with your hair all loose and blowing in the wind. Do you remember it?"

"Mm-hmm," I murmur, thinking back to that summer, recalling the mood of those days as opposed to the specific one Ryan is mentioning. One of the only places I truly felt free at the Whittier Cape Cod compound was on that boat, far away from Grace's discerning and all-too-often critical eye. I do remember the swimsuit. I spent hours shopping for a modest bikini, trying to find the right balance between exposed skin, minimal tan lines, and Whittier societal expectations. In the end, I gave up and settled on one that was at least the right color combination.

"Well, that moment will be imprinted on my heart and mind forever. God knows it wasn't the first time or the last that I was envious of Jacob, but that was the first time I truly wished I could be him, you know?" He rolls onto his side to look at me. "I wanted to be me—being him—having you, if that makes any sense at all."

He hovers over me, propped on his elbows. He tangles his hands in my hair, his eyes locked on mine. Complete and total engagement. "I wanted to feel your skin, warm under mine. I wanted to run my fingers through that hair and down your back. I wanted to feel the curves of your body and your legs wrapped around me."

He does, and I do.

"And, man oh man"—he smiles—"I wanted to kiss you. I've wanted to kiss you all these years."

As his lips touch mine, I am reminded of his words earlier this evening: *long, elegant, and inspirational, leaving me wanting more.*

Afterward, as Ryan sleeps, memories keep me awake. Ryan standing next to Jacob at the altar, both of them resplendent in tuxedos. Me walking down the aisle, clutching my all-white bouquet of gardenias, garden roses, and lilies of the valley (chosen by Grace after she put the kibosh on my yellow daisy idea, as well as pretty much every other idea I had, as far too common and pedestrian), wilting under the gaze of dozens of Whittier family members, friends, acquaintances, and business colleagues. I was sure many of them wondered, as Grace did, *Who is this girl, really, and why is Jacob marrying her?* A reasonable query, given that there was no "bride's side" at our wedding. I had no guests—family or friends—in attendance, other than Ryan and Sophia, who, along with Jacob's two sisters, served as a bridesmaid.

"Focus on Jacob," Dr. Farber told me. "You are marrying him, not his family or the upper-crust society they inhabit."

On that score, she has been proven wrong.

But I did focus on Jacob. Jacob standing there, waiting for me. Ryan, best friend and best man, next to him. I recall observing that, though they were not blood-related and didn't resemble each other physically, they looked more alike than ever that day. Now, reflecting back, it was the look on their faces (well, that and the matching black tuxedos) that made it seem so. A look of love and devotion. Why didn't I notice it then: as I approached and Jacob reached out for my hand, Ryan's expression darkened before he looked down, away.

And later, the overly emotional, topsy-turvy toast that we all attributed to a few too many glasses of vintage champagne and Martha's Vineyard Cabernet '78. Jacob's father, James, had been reserving cases and cases since the year of Jacob's birth for this specific occasion. The expansive and expensive wine cellar in the basement has a special section for these particular cases of wine and champagne— labeled for graduations, weddings, grandchildren's births. Not only for Jacob but also for his two sisters, Jennifer (1975) and Corinne (1983).

All eyes were on Ryan as he held a flute of Dom '78 aloft and regaled us with a tale about the day he met Jacob, how Jacob and his family welcomed him, made him one of their own—an honor, privilege, and gift—and how, though he could never repay Jacob, introducing him to me was as close as he could ever get. That he hoped we would go on to create an amazing family of our own, one in which he would be lucky, again, to have a role. Laughter and tears all around, but now I can see Ryan—so clearly, as if I am watching a video—and the pain is there, just under the surface.

Memory after memory. I'm curled up next to Jacob, whose arm is draped over me, at a post-volleyball-tournament beach bonfire, and Ryan disappears for a long walk, saying the smoke and flames are making his eyes water. Ryan is visiting us in the hospital the day of Logan's birth, and he tears up while holding him for the first time. When Jacob asks if he will be Logan's godfather, Ryan bows his head over the bundle in his arms for at least a full two minutes before finally looking into my face with that same combination of love and pain. Why did I not see it?

Ryan and I have lunch before he has to leave for another end-of-the-world assignment in Patagonia, and he tells me that traveling helps him survive the loneliness that defines him—that a job that requires him to remain unattached allows him to convince himself it's by choice. When I ask him why he hasn't married one of the many gorgeous girlfriends he's had through the years, he laughingly takes my hand and replies, "The only girl I'd have ever married is already taken."

And then, last year, Ryan flies in from Costa Rica and Jacob can't pick him up at the airport as previously arranged, so I'm the one who pulls into the passenger arrival zone and steps out of the SUV, calling his name. He turns, and the expression on his face silences me. At the time I labeled it as surprise, but now I can see him standing there—duffel at his feet, worn backpack slung over a shoulder—and he looks as though he's just won the lottery. Lifting me off the ground, breathing in as though he hasn't had adequate oxygen in hours, he says, "So this is what it feels like."

The past collides with the present as Ryan awakens and rolls over. "Hey," he murmurs, pulling me into him, "can't sleep?"

"Just thinking." *And remembering.*

"About?"

"You. Me. This." I should be happy. I want to be, but sadness, crushing sadness, overtakes me. He loves the person he thinks I am. He doesn't know how fucked up the real me is. Maybe I'm not safe from the abyss. "I'm not the person you think I am."

"Hey, hey." His voice sounds like love. "What is it? Really, come on. I've told you my deepest, darkest secret; whatever you're thinking, I can deal with it."

"You don't know what you're saying, Ryan. Honestly, you don't."

He puts a finger to my lips. "Let me stop you right there, Katie Rose. I may not know everything about you yet, but there is nothing you could say to stop my loving you."

I shake my head slowly, eyes closing over brimming tears, my lips pressed together as tight as I can make them, holding in words. *Don't tell him, Kate. Don't.*

Ryan watches me intently.

"Okay, give me a second," he says. He gets up, picks up his boxers, pulls them on, and throws me his T-shirt, saying, "For you."

As I pull it on over my head, he says, "Okay, here's what we're going to do." He leans against the wall and, spreading his legs into a V with his knees bent, he pats the space he's created between them. "You sit here—facing that-a-way so you can talk into the open, let it all go—and I'm going to be here, right behind you, holding you. And I'm not going to let you go."

I settle into the spot he's designated, and he wraps his arms around me.

I've never talked about this with anyone, not even Jacob. The closest I ever got was when I alluded to it once, and Jacob said, "Put it behind you, Kate. No point in reexamining pain, is there? The past is the past."

Except when it won't stop impinging on the present.

Here goes nothing. How do I tell Ryan? He has no idea.

"After my mother died," I begin, "our family fell apart. Not like we'd ever really been together. My mom was—well, you read the letter. She mostly took out her anger on my father. She'd berate him and scream how she wished she'd never met him. I don't remember him ever defending himself. He'd just sit there and drink. Even when she'd start in on Daniel. And Daniel challenged her, almost as if he wanted her to get mad at him, like any attention was better than nothing. I think he hated me already then, because I didn't stand with him against her. Anyway, after she died, the rest of us well and truly fell apart. My father behaved as though he'd forgotten Daniel and I existed. He went to work. He drank. That was it. At first, I waited for him to shake out of it—thinking, you know, that as soon as he finished feeling sorry for himself, he'd wake up one morning and remember, oh yeah, I've got these kids. But that never happened." I swallow. "Some things I'd been doing even before my mom died—like laundry and figuring out what to eat. I learned to buy a lot of soup when I could get my dad to take me to the store; it's got a long shelf life. Daniel spent most of his time out; he only came home to sleep. Sometimes, on the weekends, he might sit with my father to watch sports on TV. I don't know what he ate or where. He was mostly on his own."

Ryan is still, his arms steady around me, his chest moving in and out with mine.

"For as long as I can remember, though, Daniel hated me. When we were young, it was little things: he'd pinch me or tear pages out of a book I was reading. Maybe it was because my mom was so mean to him, I don't know. Once she was gone, he started hitting me. His favorite thing was this quick blow with the heel of his hand, right above my ear. It would come out of nowhere. I never knew what might set him off, so I tried to just stay out of his way. I'd hide if he was in a rage."

I feel Ryan tense and think to myself, *This isn't the bad part.*

"The thing was, at the beginning, Daniel was smart. He did well in school, got into college, left home when I was fourteen. He joined this fraternity and started drinking and smoking. We hardly saw him, but he came home once in a while. Then, one visit home, he brought along one of his fraternity brothers. He and my dad sat watching sports on TV while he raped me in the bathroom."

Ryan's arms stiffen. He recovers, turning it into a tighter embrace. "Your brother?"

"No, no. The fraternity brother. Daniel and my dad knew, though, because I was screaming—but they didn't do anything. They just sat there, watching TV."

Ryan begins to rock me, imperceptibly. He doesn't say anything.

"I don't know why I was surprised by that, but I was. Daniel must have decided that since I didn't fight back or call the police or say anything, it must have been okay with me, so the next time he came home . . ." I can't go on.

Ryan waits.

I recover enough to say, "The next time he brought this other guy. 'Another brother,' he said. I was so naïve. I didn't think anything like that first time could ever happen again, but in the middle of the night, the guy came into my room." My voice doesn't sound like it belongs to me. "I had . . ."

A voice inside me screams, *"Stop. Stop now."* I force myself to ignore it.

"I had my period," I whisper, embarrassed and ashamed. "And I told him, when he was on top of me, holding my hands over my head, that I was bleeding. At first, he didn't understand or something, so I repeated it, and he got this look on his face. He rolled off of me and walked out. I was shaking, but I bolted out of bed and locked the door. I could hear him yelling at Daniel, saying, 'You owe me, man.' And then, a minute later, there was pounding on my door.

"There was this spot on the door that, if you hit it just right, the lock would pop open. So they both came in and Daniel said, 'Get up.' I tried to fight but Daniel slapped me, hard. I was stunned. He pushed me down onto my knees with the other guy watching, and then he went around behind me and whispered in my ear, 'It's just a blow job.' And then he pulled my hair back, and the other guy—"

I'm not crying, but my body starts to shake as if racked by sobs. My voice sounds broken. "I could hear Daniel behind me the whole time. Laughing when I choked."

Ryan tenses. I hear him whisper, "Jesus Christ."

"Afterwards, Daniel called me sloppy seconds. Told me that no one would ever, ever love me."

"That sonofabitch."

"I believed him. I mean, he was right. Who would want me?" The pain comes roaring back. "I tried to think, who could I go to? Who would believe me? And I realized I didn't have anyone. I didn't really have friends; I never wanted anyone to know what went on in our house. The only person who seemed to know I existed was the librarian at the high school. I used to go there, to the library, to do my homework, and after I was done, I'd wander through the stacks, pulling books out randomly, sitting on the floor to read them. She noticed, Ms. Brawly. B. Brawley. I asked her once what the B stood for and she said, 'Beatrix, as in Beatrix Potter, the author of the children's books.' I told her I'd never read them, and she gave me a copy of the first one, *The Tale of Peter Rabbit*. Beatrix Brawley. She was this lovely older woman."

I wait for a question or some kind of interruption from Ryan. Hoping that I can get off topic and abandon this confession. But he is still—still and constant, holding me.

"There was no way I could tell her what was happening. No way. But then Daniel came home late one night. He brought these two other guys, and they were high on something; they were loud and wild, like animals. They held me down, and afterwards, one of them told Daniel I was the best payment he'd ever had."

I squeeze my eyes shut. "The next few minutes, I've tried harder to forget than anything else. The guy said, 'But you probably already know that.' And Daniel said, 'She's my sister.' And the other guy was like, 'Yeah, right, so what, you can't do your sister?' Maybe he needed to prove something, I don't know, but they actually had this conversation while they were standing right above me in my room, this surreal conversation about how it wasn't incest if it was a blow job because a blow job wasn't sex. So the two guys got me on my knees, like the other time, and one of them held me, and the other one pushed Daniel in front of me. He unzipped his pants." The words stick in my throat. "I was crying, begging him, 'Please, no, no.' I said it over and over, and finally Daniel just hit me over the ear. Really hard. I saw stars. And then he said, I remember this, 'She's not worth it.' And they left me there on the floor."

"Sick bastards," Ryan says under his breath.

I rush on, "So I went to the librarian. I didn't tell her what happened. I couldn't. She was just this nice old lady. All I said was I needed to get out of my house. She didn't ask me a bunch of questions. She helped me figure out the UCs and decided I should apply to UCSD. She called Admissions, made sure that I took the tests, read my essays. She threw me a lifeline. And I started to envision escaping. I didn't know if or when Daniel would be back, but I started to feel like I could change things, so when this trumpet player in the jazz band asked me to go to prom, I told myself I should go. Of course, it was awful. When the guy came to pick me up, my dad was falling-down drunk. Slurring his words. I was sure the guy wished he hadn't asked me, I was wishing I'd said no, and we ended up barely speaking. I told him I wasn't feeling well and asked him to take me home early, which turned out to be an even worse decision than going in the first place. Daniel was there with another brother, a guy I'd never seen before. I managed to get to my room, but it was like they were lying in wait. The other guy was on me so fast. He ripped my dress and pushed me against the wall and then to the ground, but something rose up inside me. I grabbed for one of the pencils on my desk and stabbed him with it, and then I bit him, and he was furious. He told Daniel he'd make him pay for it. Daniel came into my room."

I reach up to cover my cheeks. Ryan's embrace tightens around me.

"For the first time, he hit me with his fist closed, again and again, until I fell down. All I could do was curl up on the ground and pray I'd survive. Finally, he kicked me, really hard, and then again, even harder, and then he left me on the floor. I stayed there in my room until I heard him leave the next day."

Telling the story, I remember the flood of emotions—rage, humiliation, resignation, fear, and the tiniest bit of something I didn't identify until much later, when I'd been gone for months: hope.

"I left a few days later, my face still bruised. My father gave me all the money in his wallet, but he didn't say a word about what had happened. I never went back—well, until Tuesday—and I've never told anyone the whole story. Not Jacob, not even Dr. Farber."

Now Ryan knows. Now he'll wish he never told me he loved me.

Ryan scoots forward off the wall and turns me sideways in his arms.

"I'm so sorry. If I had known," he whispers into my neck, his voice thick. "Your brother was wrong about no one wanting you or loving you." He holds my face in his hands. "Look at me, Kate. I love you." He kisses my forehead. "You didn't do anything wrong. You were just a girl. Those men were animals. And your brother? Jesus." He tucks my head into his chest. "What they did defines them, but it doesn't define you. You are beautiful and smart and brave and strong. You make me see the world in a different way."

He doesn't say anything about putting it behind me.

He doesn't tell me that I need to be fixed.

I am suddenly very, very tired. The days that have come before catch up with me. I cannot keep my eyes open.

Ryan lays me down to sleep on my side. He lies alongside my body, leg to leg, hip to hip, chest to my back. He strokes my hair.

"Try to sleep, Kate. I am not going anywhere. I'll be right here. When I was little and I couldn't sleep, my mom used to rub my back like this." It feels like a figure eight—looping, repetitive, soothing. "She called it an infinity back rub, to remind me she would love me for all time. She called it McCann magic. It always worked."

McCann magic.

As I drift off, I swear I hear him whisper, "He'll never hurt you again."

TWENTY-FIVE

McCANN MAGIC CANNOT dim the harsh light of day, which floods in through the bare French doors. Nor can it calm the agitation I feel when I awaken next to Ryan's still-sleeping form. I slide to the edge of the bed and ease my body off the mattress.

I am tempted to grab my clothes from yesterday and head home, alone, putting off the "what does this all mean" conversation.

Leave him before he can leave me.

Tempted until I look at Ryan's face. Calm and unlined in slumber, he looks like a younger version of himself, and I think about the years that have passed since we first met. Unbidden, my mother's poem comes to mind—the one that might, or might not, have been written about unrequited love—and I reconsider my plan.

Ryan deserves better.

Then again, he deserves better than me. Everyone does.

The coastline is shrouded in a thick, pale gray marine layer. I grab the Peninsula robe, step out on the porch into the bracing, moist, chilly air, and silently close the door behind me. Wrapped in the robe, I face the ocean, hoping its meditative magic is stronger than the McCann version. It isn't.

What am I doing? What are *we* doing? How can I face Ryan now that he knows the truth? How will I be able to face Jacob? Will he know simply by looking at me, at Ryan? What have I done? *What have I done?*

My poor children.

I feel uneasy standing still at the porch railing and debate whether I can walk down onto the beach in a robe with only a T-shirt underneath. *Probably not the best idea*, so I ever-so-carefully and slowly reopen the French door and tiptoe over to the bathroom. My wrinkled shorts and T-shirt are lying on the floor in the corner. I put on the shorts, consciously avoiding looking into the mirror.

I pick up the sticky note Ryan left for me last night, flip it over, and jot a hasty message: *brb—walking on the beach*. I drop it on the table next to Ryan's bed, then retrieve my phone and grab his sweatshirt off the floor, just in case.

The sand near the staircase is damp and heavy underfoot, straining leg muscles already sore from yesterday's volleyball matches. I head to the firm, packed area of beach along the water and walk south, hoping to stay in sight of Ryan's porch.

A stiff breeze blows my hair behind me. I recall Ryan's revelatory moment on the sailboat, so many years ago, and my thoughts begin to swirl, buffeted by an internal wind whose direction is hard to gauge. Gale-force gusts of memory, a course dictated by my past, and an iffy forecast do not bode well for smooth sailing. I consider the ramifications of my actions and words last night, the inevitable tumult that will affect us all.

After several minutes of brisk walking, I turn around and look back at Ryan's porch to check for any movement. In this direction, the wind whips my hair into my face. I will have a tangled mess to deal with when I reunite with a brush.

A tangled mess indeed.

I continue on.

"Kate!" Ryan's voice over the sound of wind and surf.

I turn. He waves. He's wearing the robe.

Longing returns full force.

I don't want to walk away. If he still wants me.

Two newspapers—the *San Diego Union Tribune* and, all too familiar, *The New York Times*. A mug of steaming hot coffee with milk, oatmeal with agave syrup and fresh blueberries, a glass of water with lemon.

"Hydration, antioxidants, fiber, carbs, and a caffeine boost—this," Ryan says, waving his hand across the counter, "is the true breakfast of champions."

I can only manage a weak smile in response.

He pulls me into his arms. "Are you okay?"

"I don't know," I say into his chest.

He tilts my head up. "I love you, Kate. Nothing will ever change that," he says, firmly. "I wish I could stay here with you in this room the whole day."

I pull back. "I can't—"

"I know," he says, smiling. "We can't stay in this bubble forever."

The trouble is, a part of me wants to do just that. Stay here in this room. Escape. Be loved, this way.

But I can't. We can't.

"Hey, hey, there you go again, disappearing on me. Don't." He releases me, pulls out a stool. "Come sit down. Eat. Read the paper. Try to relax. Give yourself a few minutes."

I manage a few bites of oatmeal—it's delicious—and a sip of coffee, which is joltingly strong. I watch Ryan. He follows his own directions. He eats. He reads the paper. He looks relaxed. I try to do the same—but unfortunately as soon as I am left to my own thoughts my appetite wanes, the printed words of the *Times* become incomprehensible, and the myriad questions tumbling through my brain give me a noticeable case of the jitters.

"Okay," he says, looking at me. "Okay, darlin'. Let's do this."

He puts the newspaper and his empty oatmeal bowl aside. He takes my hands and, resting his thumbs in my palms, begins to make the same figure-eight shape on my palm that he made on my back last night.

"You're worried about how this is going to go, so let's talk about it. First things first, another confession." His tone and expression are serious, but there is gentleness in his eyes, bright green and shining. "I wouldn't have believed that it was possible to love another human being more than I loved you yesterday, until last night."

I look down at the breakfast remnants, the newspapers.

"Don't let this calm, steady demeanor fool you," he says. "I'm trying to contain myself, because what I really want is you—*all* of you, body and soul."

At this, I look up.

"I want to wrap you in this bubble and keep you safe. I want to take away anything that hurts you. I don't want to share you." He gives me a rueful smile. "But I know that's completely unrealistic. We have to live our lives in this world, and you have other people to love, people who love you back. People who need you. So right now, you're going to go home and get changed for the kids' soccer games. Then we'll meet there and behave the way we have for more than twenty years."

I shake my head, ever so slightly, and he nods in response.

"Yes. You're going to go home after their games, and for the next few days, nothing'll be different. Be with Logan and Becca—take them to school, help 'em with their homework, referee their arguments, and try to keep Logan from playing too many video games." He makes it sound so easy. "Talk to Dr. Farber, run, go to the grocery store, read more of your mom's stuff. Inspire me."

Dr. Farber. Do I tell her about last night? About Daniel? About my mother? And Dr. Reynolds. Shit, Jacob and I have an appointment with Larry on Monday, and we were supposed to have gone on a date. *Jacob. Oh my God, how am I going to do this?*

My chest tightens. "And Jacob?"

"Yeah, that's going to be tough—for both of us."

I don't know what to say. I'm a bundle of contradictions. I dread facing my husband. Will he sense that I am different somehow? Haven't I betrayed him worse than he betrayed me? Yes, I have. And yet I love how my hands feel in Ryan's. I love looking at him over a breakfast table and imagining the feel of his lips, the slightly rough texture of his unshaven face, his hands holding my hips.

As if on cue, he rises to his feet and makes my imaginings reality. His mouth tastes like blueberries and lemon.

Hands still on my hips, he pulls back to look at me. His eyes are more hazel than green. *Perhaps he's as muddled as I am.* "Listen, I'm not trying to pretend that last night didn't happen or that it didn't change things." His voice is restrained, without a hint of the typical Ryan playfulness. "I only love you more. As much as I don't want you out of my sight, if it's too much to handle combining this"—with one hand, he gestures back and forth between us—"with the kids and Jacob and dealing with everything that's going on and you need some time today to be by yourself, then we'll wait to see each other until it's Jacob's turn to be with them."

There it is: he's finding a way out. Daniel's specter looms.

I drop the top of my forehead to rest on his chest. "If that's what you want."

"That is absolutely not what I want. I told you, what I want is to protect you, to keep you with me twenty-four seven . . . but that's not realistic. So I'm asking you what you can handle."

"I don't know. I want to see you . . ."

His hands move to the small of my back, instantly evoking a host of riotous yearnings. Holy shit. I reach around for his wrists, grasp them firmly, and pull them away.

"But you cannot touch me around other people. You have to promise not to touch me."

"Not even an arm around your shoulder?" He moves as if to do just that, and I skirt away.

"I'm serious, Ryan; unless you want me to melt in front of everyone, no touching." I hold my arms out, wrists flexed, hands up.

"Okay, okay. I'll go take a cold shower. And you're going to go change and meet me at Becca's game, right?"

I nod.

"Excellent. Now, can I have a kiss before you go?"

Jesus, what he can do with a smile.

"A chaste one. Can you do chaste?"

"I can do 'em all, darlin'."

He can. Tender, lips barely touching, once, twice, three times. Even chaste is electrifying.

"Now," he says, backing away, leaving me standing there with my eyes closed, "you better go before I come out or this cold shower will be for naught."

TWENTY-SIX

WITH FOUR MINUTES LEFT in the second half, the score of Becca's game is 2-3; the dreaded traveling-team opponents, the Hornets, are winning. Becca is in the attacking midfielder position, and she is exhausted. Last weekend, Logan spent a solid hour explaining all the positions to me—an effort to "bring me up to speed," he said. I was grateful to have his attention for more than a few minutes, so I expressed an unrivaled level of interest.

"It's pretty cool Becca's coach put her there, Mom, 'cause an attacking midfielder is a critical position. Becca has to play both defense and attack, so she's got to be super fit and see the whole field. The nickname for her position is the 'playmaker' or the 'armador'—that's Spanish."

Becca as the playmaker may be one of the first times Logan has a reason to be proud of his little sister. I am proud of him for working on his Spanish. When I tell him this, he gives me a sheepish grin. "Mom, I learned that from playing FIFA '18, not in Spanish class."

Of course he did.

My playmaker is not giving in to fatigue or frustration. She is one determined little girl. An errant kick from a Hornet, and she is on it—legs pumping, body angled as she turns to intercept the ball, looking left, right, center, to identify a teammate to target with a pass.

Jacob and Ryan are standing next to each other on the sidelines, Logan in between them—all three are yelling encouragement.

My cell rings. I look down and see a vaguely familiar number. The waste removal company, Aftermath, is scheduled to be at my father's house, and Lindy has promised to call with an update, so I answer it.

"You think you can sell the house out from under me?"

My heart stops. I realize I'd hoped against all reason that I might never hear from Daniel again.

"This isn't a good time for this conversation." I turn from the field, take a few steps away, covering my other ear with my hand.

"Go, Becca!" Jacob's voice booms.

"Too fucking bad. You think I'm concerned about what's convenient for you? You don't seem particularly concerned about what's convenient for me, messing with my house."

"Your house? You haven't lived there in years."

"Yeah, Becca, great pass." Ryan's voice this time.

A roar erupts behind me. I spin to watch Becca and two of her teammates in a jumping group hug in front of the goal.

"Go, Becca," Logan yells, repeating his dad's cheer.

"Becca's your daughter, isn't she?" The raspy voice grates on every nerve. "Sounds like you're at some kind of game. I forgot she's old enough to play competitive sports. What, nine, ten?"

As if there is any way I would tell him a single, solitary thing about my children.

"What do you want?"

Hearing my tone of voice, Jacob and Ryan both turn toward me. Jacob looks alarmed. Ryan looks pissed. He takes a step in my direction. I hold up my hand, shake my head.

"What do I want? I want you to call off the fucking cleaning crew. The guy in the navy-blue uniform with his gloves and questions, I want him off the property."

I briefly, ever-so-briefly, consider mentioning that it's not his house, that in fact our father specifically stated in his will that he did not want anything to go to Daniel. Perhaps that is the real reason for my father's will—not so much to give things to me as some sort of guilt-assuaging gesture but to keep them from his son. I decide it is better not to add fuel to this confrontation. Just stick to the inarguables.

I walk away from the field, putting distance between my family and my brother. Jacob puts his arm around Logan's shoulder, turns to watch the game. Ryan watches me.

"The house needs to be cleaned. It's filthy. The hoarding shit has to go—the newspapers, the bottles. I would have thought you'd be glad to be rid of it."

"I'd be glad to be rid of your interference in my life."

He wants to be rid of me? Is he fucking kidding?

"You think I want to be involved?" I say. It feels like grit is lining my mouth. "I'm only doing this because I have to."

"You don't have to do anything. I didn't ask for your fucking help."

Shit. He's not going to like this.

"Unfortunately, you're wrong. I do have to deal with it because our father left a will, leaving the house to me. Not to you. Which means—"

"What the fuck are you talking about—he left the house to you? That doesn't make any fucking sense. I stayed with that asshole for years—fucking years—and this is how he repays me? And now you think you can take what's mine? You don't even need it, you fucking bitch."

I move farther away from the sideline. The sound of my brother's voice in my ear seems to create a force field that traps me outside of my surroundings. The girls on the field, my daughter running, the cheers and conversations of the onlookers, the smell of freshly mown grass and wet dirt, even the warmth in the air—all have been removed from me, like in one of those scenes from a sci-fi movie when a vibrating barrier separates a character from the world.

I watch Ryan say something to Jacob, who then begins to walk in my direction. I wave him off, but he continues to advance across the grass. I wonder if he will be able to penetrate the barrier. I lift my hand in the universally understood stop gesture the same moment Logan calls to him, "Dad, come on, we've got to go. I can't be late." Jacob looks at his watch. I nod and shoo him.

Daniel is still talking. "You've got more than you need. And mark my words, if you take what's mine, you can bet I'll come and take what's yours. Do you hear me? I will come there, and I will take what is yours—you better watch that little girl carefully, because I will always find you. At any moment, you can turn around, and I'll be there. For all you know, I could be there right now. Turn around, go ahead—"

My hand goes to my throat as I gasp and spin around, wildly looking for him, even though I know on some level it is just a threat. I hear Daniel laughing. I hold the phone away, press the red circle, and instinctively drop it on the grass.

Jacob and Logan are walking toward the parking lot. Jacob looks over his shoulder, sees me spinning, dropping the phone. He hesitates, touches Logan's shoulder, says something I cannot hear.

Logan's voice is louder. "I can't be late." His body language is clear: he is angry.

Nevertheless, Jacob is turning back toward me when Ryan calls to him, "It's okay. Go ahead with Logan, I got this."

The cell phone rings, vibrating like a snake in the grass. I stare at it, thinking, *Stop ringing. Stop ringing.*

A bee buzzes by my ear. Ryan approaches. I see Jacob and Logan getting in Jacob's car. Hear the doors slam. See Becca running.

"Hey, you okay?" Ryan bends to pick up the phone. "Who's calling you? Is it your brother?" He turns the face of the phone so I can see the incoming number. It's not the vaguely familiar number. It's my father's number. The phone number from my childhood. He's switched phones for reasons I cannot begin to fathom, but it couldn't be clearer; he isn't here. Of course he isn't. He's there, at the house.

I nod. Exhale a shaky breath.

Ryan's finger hovers over the screen. "How 'bout I tell him to fuck off?"

"No, no. Don't."

The ringing stops. Another cheer rises from the fans on our side of the field. Another group hug in front of the goal. I look for Becca and she is there, in the middle of it. *I will come there and take what is yours.* Pulling away from her teammates, she glances to the sideline. Her head turns, looking for me. I want to be over there, cheering, not over here, staring at my phone in Ryan's hand. I want to wrap my daughter in my arms and keep her safe. I hate my brother.

"He won't care what you say." I hold my hand out for the phone, palm up, fingers vibrating as if the force field hasn't been broken.

Instead of giving me the phone, Ryan takes my hand. "Okay, that's not the way this is going to go. You're shaking. What did that piece of shit say to you?"

I do not know how to play this. Should I tell Ryan? He knows about Daniel now. Should I explain about Daniel's threats? Acknowledge the unacknowledged, Dr. Farber would say—reveal it and rob it of its power.

"He said he'll come and take what is mine," I say in a very soft voice.

"Take what is yours?"

"Becca. He said, 'You better watch that little girl carefully.'"

"What? He's threatening you? Threatening Becca?"

"He sounds crazy, or maybe he's on something, I don't know. I told him about the will, which was stupid, but he's in the house, and that Aftermath company is there to do an assessment, and the realtor told me that I'm responsible for the house, and the insurance, and anything that happens there, and I don't have the insurance policy updated or paid, so if he does something or—"

"Hey, slow down. One thing at a time, please. What insurance are you talking about?"

Becca turns to look for me again. I don't want to do this—*fucking Daniel.*

"The homeowner's insurance. She told me that when someone dies, the policy ends, and as the responsible party, I have to extend it in my name, but I don't want to be responsible for him, and apparently he thinks he's going to live there." The game is nearly over. "I want to watch my daughter play soccer."

Though I know Daniel is far away, I want to be near her.

"Yeah, of course you do. Come on." He pulls my hand gently and puts my cell phone in the pocket of his shorts. "Let's go watch the game."

If Becca is tired, the adrenaline of winning must be pulsing strong. She is a dynamo. Determination shines on her face; there's a sense of purpose in her every movement. I try to focus on her. I try to still the swirling thoughts and emotions. I try to silence Daniel's voice reverberating, *I'll come and take what's yours.*

———————

The girls are stoked. Listening to Coach Riley's postgame wrap-up, they are the picture of barely contained perpetual motion: slurping on orange wedges and popsicles brought by Emily's mom, fidgeting on the grass, lithe limbs stretching and twisting, on their knees and then sitting cross-legged and then lying down. I stand a few feet from the cluster of other parents, watching their easy manner with each other. Ryan left only a few minutes ago to head to Logan's game, and I am not adept at blending myself into an existing social circle.

"Can the team come back to our house to swim?" Becca pleads, puppy-dog eyes primed.

"I'd love it, Becs, but we've got to go straight to Logan's game."

"The girls can come over to our house," Emily's mom, Patrice, says with pitch-perfect tone and timing. She is daunting—immaculate, flat-ironed blond mane, Hermes sunglasses, fitted white jeans, and a pale pink T-shirt with strategic shirring to maximize her curves. I don't want to like her but cannot find a valid reason not to.

"We decided to start heating the pool again since the solar is simply not enough with these shorter days," she says. "The water is the perfect temperature."

Of course it is.

"Can we, Mom? Is that okay?" I hear other girls clamoring for approval, can see and hear said approval being granted by the other parents. I don't want Becca out of my sight, but that would be selfish. Daniel is far away, hours away, in San Jose. Becca wants to go to Emily's.

"I wish I could say yes, sweetie, but I promised Logan I'd be at his game too, and I don't know how I can bring you home and then to Emily's and make it back in time to see Logan."

Patrice is coordinating with the other parents—timing for drop-offs, pickups. Turning in my direction, she smiles with her super-straight, gorgeous white teeth, an expression that doesn't quite make it to her eyes.

"I can bring Becca with me, so you can go on to Logan's game. Emily's got extra suits."

There is no reproach in her words or her demeanor, yet I feel instant guilt. It's a kind offer, though, and Becca is already with the other girls, smack in the middle, excitedly talking about I don't know what.

"Thanks. That would be great. I'll come by on my way home from the game to get her."

"Take your time, really. Emily loves having her friends over"— she lowers her voice a notch—"and Becca is her favorite."

"That's very sweet of you to say," I hear myself sounding so fake, so patently obvious, but Patrice just keeps smiling. "I'll have my phone, so . . ."

I realize as the words leave my mouth that I don't have my phone. Ryan has it in his pocket.

Becca darts over for a hug.

"Thanks for letting me go," she says into my chest. I hold her tight. As she pulls away, she adds, "I'll be waiting for you at Emily's."

Waiting for me. I know she'll be so busy that I won't cross her mind, yet it's lovely, the idea of someone waiting, for you. And then I hear Daniel's voice and realize that the same thing can be horrifying, depending on who's waiting.

But then I also realize that I know where he is now. I can serve him with a restraining order.

I can choose not to freeze or flee. I can fight back.

It's time to stop running and hiding.

TWENTY-SEVEN

NOT HAVING MY CELL PHONE feels like I'm missing a limb. I have become accustomed to having it at all times, checking it more often than I need to, relying on it to feel connected. It's odd, really, since I have always considered myself a loner, more likely to feel irritated than reassured by the constant presence of others.

It dawns on me, not that it should be a huge insight, that this new desire for connection stems from the kids—and Ryan.

Over the course of our marriage, Jacob has never been a big "touching base" sort of guy. He might call once during the day, if ever, to check on the kids or to inform me he must stay late at the office. Even when traveling for business, he could go two or three days without calling. When life is predictable, going according to plan, extraneous calls are just that. Extraneous.

As of late, though, now that they aren't always with me, Logan, Becca, and I have taken to texting and calling each other—particularly Becca, who likes to hear my voice nearly as much as I like to hear hers.

And Ryan, I have learned in the last few weeks, is big into touching base.

I like this, but I am also aware that this means he is likely to answer my phone if it rings in his pocket. If Daniel calls again.

I need to get my phone back.

When I arrive at the game, Logan's team is blowing away the competition, and Ryan and Jacob aren't even actively watching; rather, they are sitting, side by side, in two of our folding chairs from REI, chatting about something on Jacob's iPad. I see Natalie with her eldest son, Taylor, several chairs downfield. She gives me an expectant look, her brows knitted together—her "oh, Kate" face again. I definitely do not have the energy to deal with her or her judgment.

I debate which side to put my chair on and then opt to go with Ryan since, prior to last night, that's what I would have done.

As I pull the frame out of the carry bag, Ryan hops up. "Let me help you with that."

His fingertips graze mine and I'm shocked, literally—little electric charges fire from fingertip to groin. I feel faint.

How can such a simple touch mean something today that it wouldn't have meant last Saturday? His face, his lips are merely a foot away. Behaving as if nothing has changed may well be impossible.

At least for me. Ryan doesn't look fazed.

He covers for me—unnecessarily, since Jacob is still looking at his iPad—by saying, "Whoa, I don't think you ate enough for breakfast. You look like you're going to pass out."

Jacob glances at me, begins to rise from his chair. "Are you okay? Here, sit down." He points to the chair Ryan was in.

"I'm fine," I say, shaking my head lightly.

Ryan raises his eyebrows at me. "Jacob's right, Kate. Sit, sit. I'll take this one."

He is nearly done opening my chair.

Sitting in between them is not appealing. Making a scene is even less so. I sit down.

"What was that call from your brother about?" Jacob asks, in a hushed voice.

I sigh. "Oh, he's angry—really angry—about my arranging to have the house cleaned. Claims it's his and I'm interfering in his life.

As if I would want to do that. I want him out of my life, forever."

Jacob quickly looks left, right. Frowns. "Maybe we shouldn't talk about that here, huh?"

Ryan stops his chair assembly to stare at me, trying to read me.

It's not that I want to discuss Daniel's veiled threat with Jacob. He has a way of processing this sort of situation with a practicality that lacks empathy. I can hear him in my head, explaining in an entirely reasonable way that Daniel, as a mentally-ill drug addict who can't even function well enough to keep a roof over his head, couldn't act in a concerted manner on any threat he might make. And even though this assessment might be correct—even though, in all fairness, it's what I have told myself over and over—I wonder if Jacob could ever understand the psychological threat my brother presents.

Ryan, on the other hand, is a wild card. Given the emotionally charged air between us, I think it's best not to agitate or even ask for my phone.

"Agreed," I say simply. "After all, he's far away, in San Jose. What's the score?"

Behave normally. Breathe, Kate. Watch the game. You can explain it later, or handle it yourself.

Ryan gives me a penetrating, quizzical look, which I try to ignore. Jacob sits back down, glancing over at the other side of the field.

"It was four to zero a few minutes ago. The coach took Logan out after his third score." Jacob lowers his voice. "Moved Randolph in as striker since he doesn't get to play there much."

Still staring at me, Ryan nonetheless matches Jacob's decibel level and tone of voice, though it comes off as somewhat ironic: "To be honest, we stopped watching a bit ago, started working out some issues for Logan's party next weekend."

"Let's switch places, then, so you can keep going." I am acutely uncomfortable sitting in between them.

"Are you sure?" Ryan says.

But I am already up and moving away from the chair, putting

distance between us so as to avoid direct contact. We drop into the exchanged seats, and Jacob leans over to show Ryan some video of the go-karts the kids will be driving. I watch the game halfheartedly, wishing I had been here to see Logan score or at least play.

I realize that a few months ago this would have seemed like the most normal thing in the world to me: sitting here like this, the three of us together. To an outsider watching us, it still looks that way. Yet now every interaction is marred by confrontation or crisis or undercurrents, without the benefit of posted signs like those at the beach—red flags for dangerous conditions, yellow for fair, checkered or green for safe zone.

I should come with beach flags.

Even better, I should come with sailing flags, which are more descriptive by far. I can't recall the colors or shapes of most of them, aside from the two Jacob insisted we all learn before our first family sailing trip last year: "man overboard"—a red triangle stacked on top of a yellow one, and "diver down"—blue and white with an edge that looks like a capital K.

I do, however, remember my introduction to the whole set of colorful, graphic flags, so long ago.

As an engagement gift, Jacob's father purchased sailing lessons for me with a private instructor, Gus, a cantankerous old white-haired friend of his. Gus had tan, leathery skin and wrinkles around his eyes that bore witness to endless summers without sunscreen or a hat. I learned how to turn a rope into a line (by putting it on a boat), how to tie basic knots and cleat off, how to tack and jibe, all onboard a fifteen-foot sailboat—or, as Gus described it, "a JY 15 centerboard dinghy." He told me time and again, "Katie, you must always know the vessel you're sailing and how to steer her, the direction of the wind, and the forecast where you're headed."

My final test had been to sail him out for lunch at a neighboring yacht club, where, as we sat on the dock eating lobster rolls, he quizzed me on the flags. I can clearly picture Gus, chuckling as he told me he often wished his wife carried one, warning him of her state of mind—some of the lesser-known flags with messages like "keep clear," "stop instantly," "desire to communicate," or, his personal favorite, "standing into danger." I told Jacob about it that night. He smiled faintly and told me that we didn't need flags since we could talk. Now, as I sit here between him and Ryan, I recall that even then I thought the one flag Jacob should pull out more often was "desire to communicate."

As for me, I should be displaying "standing into danger."

———

Final score 5-1. Postgame, Logan seems to be happy with the result, sheepishly acknowledging his coach's high praise and high-fiving his teammates. As soon as we get into the car, however, it's a different story. He's angry.

"Six minutes. I sat out for six minutes, and then he puts me in at center back when they've got, like, no chance of scoring. I'm the best attack player on the team, and he takes me out of position for practically the whole second half. It's bullshit."

"Logan!" I'm sure it's not the first time my son has used profanity. It is, however, the first time he's used it freely in front of me. "Please don't swear."

"Why not? You do."

"I'm an adult. You're not." It's a bullshit excuse, and yet it's the only thing that pops into my head. "Besides, it's not bullshit for your coach to pull you or move you when the team is up by such a large margin. It shows good sportsmanship."

"Sportsmanship? I thought this was competitive soccer. I thought we were supposed to be competitive."

"You are, Logan. Your team is very competitive. You played really well."

"You weren't even there when I was playing well, so how would you know?"

This conversation is not going in a positive direction. I haven't seen or talked to Logan since Tuesday night, and I don't remember what transpired that night. It's time to dial it back.

"You're right. I wasn't. I came as soon as I could after Becca's game, and I was disappointed—really disappointed—that I missed your goals. Dad and Uncle Ryan told me that the second one was, how did they put it . . . 'really sweet.'" I glance over at him with a smile and am relieved to see his face clear. "Can you tell me about it?"

"Yeah, it was pretty sweet, Mom. So we had just scored a couple of minutes before—not me, I didn't score, but I had the assist. Blane intercepted a long pass at midfield and dribbled it, like, maybe ten feet or so before he passed it to Jeremy. Jeremy had a guy on him, probably their only decent player, and he was, like, all up in Jeremy's face. He was this obnoxious kid—did you see him? He had reddish hair, and you could tell he thought he was the shit."

I give Logan a sideways glance.

He smiles. "He did, Mom—he definitely thought he was."

I try to focus on Logan's sweet goal story. My thoughts wander, though—from how much I love hearing his voice and his enthusiasm to the fact that he's a gifted storyteller, like his godfather, to last night, to Daniel's call this morning, to my phone. I reach for my phone in my waistband. It is not there.

"Are you even listening?" Logan is justifiably pissed off.

"I'm sorry, I got a little distracted, honey. I heard the whole thing."

"Yeah? Did you hear what I asked you, then?"

"No. Just the last bit, I got distracted. I'm sorry, Logan. It's been a long week for me. What did you ask me?"

"Where are we going? This isn't the way home."

"We have to go get Becca at her friend Emily's. It's not out of the way, not really."

"Is she going to be ready to go or will we have to wait for, like, ever for her to get out of the house? Can you call and tell her to be ready?"

"I don't have my phone, but you can call her."

"Where's your phone? You had it at Becca's game. I saw you talking to somebody."

"I dropped it, and Uncle Ryan grabbed it for me. I forgot to ask him for it at your game, so I'll have to get it later."

"Dad said that he and Uncle Ryan are going by the go-kart place this afternoon to check it out for next week. Maybe you could bring me over there and get your phone?"

"We'll see, Logan."

"We'll see, Logan," he mimics me, doing a rather good job of it. "Why do you always say that? Why can't you decide now and tell me? If you're not going to take me, just say so."

He's mad again.

"You seem really angry." Dr. Farber tells me it's important to let my children express their anger—even Barton-style, inappropriate-scale-to-the-event anger—so I can help them learn how to vent it in a healthy, responsible manner.

"Yeah, maybe I am. Mostly I just don't get you. You're acting really weird lately, and you're making Dad feel bad."

"Did he tell you he was feeling badly?"

"Not like you'd say it, but the other night he told Becca and me we can talk about stuff with him—anything—that he's trying to get better at listening and whatever we feel is okay. I can just tell that he feels bad. He doesn't really like living in that house. Why can't he move back home? What'd hc do, anyway?"

I should have known this question would come. It's surprising, really, that he didn't ask it sooner.

"Dad told me not to ask you. He said it's between you and him and has nothing to do with us, me and Becca."

We're pulling up to Emily's house along a cypress-lined driveway. A palatial Tuscan masterpiece with an enormous dark wood gate, stucco walls with stacked stone accents. There is a keypad encased in a separate pillar. I pause before pressing the call button.

"He's right. It is between your dad and me; it has nothing to do with you and Becca." I lean out the door, intending to press the button.

"Yeah, well, it may not be about us, but we're the ones that have to go back and forth. And she's not happy either. She cries all the time at Dad's. Just so you know. Not to be mean, but I hope you're happy, 'cause nobody else is."

Guilt washes over me like a sudden downpour, drenching. I look over at my son. For an instant, he reveals his sadness. Then he turns to the window, and when he turns back, he's wearing a mask, Whittier-like, as if he's shaken an Etch-a-Sketch and blanked his emotions.

"Logan . . ." I try to think of the right thing to say.

"Whatever. It's not like I thought you'd tell me what I wanted to hear."

"What would that be?"

"It doesn't matter." He's closed off completely now, staring out the window as if his favorite 3D movie is playing on the other side and he can't take his eyes off it.

I press the call button. "I'm sorry."

It's true. I am. For so many things.

I think about my mother's letter: *I will fail you. I know I will.*

I see Becca come running out the front door in a swimsuit I don't recognize, curls flying. I look over at my son, trying not to be hurt.

My mother was not able to do the right thing for her children. *But I can.*

TWENTY-EIGHT

BECCA SERVES AS Ryan's welcoming committee late Saturday afternoon, running to the front door when she hears the double beep.

"What's that?" she asks when he steps inside.

"This?"

I listen from the kitchen, gripping the countertop, grounding myself to combat the odd wooziness I now feel hearing his voice.

"Some stuff of your mom's, Becs, and her phone," he answers. "Here, pipsqueak, how about you go give this to her and tell her I'm putting the box in her closet?"

Becca doesn't leave his side. "Are you staying for dinner?" I swear I can hear her skipping in her voice.

"I wish I could, but something's come up." I swear I can hear his smile in his. "I've got to meet somebody for dinner."

"What somebody?"

"A work somebody."

Their voices fade as they make their way toward my room at the end of the hall.

Ryan cannot be here, I realize with sudden surety. He cannot stay here, with me, with my children.

Not tonight. Not ever.

I need to text Jacob, ask him if he can come get the kids after dinner, keep them until Monday. Until I know I am stable, or at least until after my appointment with Dr. Farber.

———

With the help of a large swallow of yet another bottle of reserve Cabernet, some strong psychic silent treatment voodoo, and, believe it or not, Lamaze breathing, I try to present some semblance of normal Mommy/normal Katie Rose.

Inside, I am reeling.

Becca comes around the island to hand me my phone and then wanders off to the family room to go back to the multiplication game she was playing on my laptop before Ryan arrived. I look down at the phone and press the screen. It remains black.

Ryan stands in the doorway.

"It's out of power, and I'm an Android guy. You got a few calls before it went dark," he says. "One from that company that's cleaning your dad's house and one from Maria. Oh, and a text message from Natalie. I know things are rough with her right now, so I didn't answer the text. I did take the calls, though. Hope you don't mind. I realized I haven't talked to Maria in years."

As I plug the charger cord into the phone, Ryan moves closer to the island. "In fact, I forgot you were such good friends. I told her I picked up your phone at the game and hadn't had a chance to return it. She said it's probably just as well since she's in the middle of some huge project and was using you as a procrastination technique."

He looks nervous; maybe he's reeling too.

"The call was a tad awkward." He actually looks very nervous. "But she sounded good."

"Yeah, she's okay, I think. I talked to her yesterday morning, told her about my father."

I take another sip of wine, recalling the conversation with Maria.

"You've really gotten hammered, haven't you, sweetie?" she said. "Give yourself time and permission to feel whatever you're feeling. It's all valid, and don't let anyone tell you it's not."

I glance at Ryan. "She offered to come out here, have Maddie stay with Alex—said it would be good for her too. So like her to not mention anything about a big project. Anyway, I told her how great you've been, how you went with me to San Jose, and, well, everything."

"She and Alex are getting along, then?"

"Yeah, they're better. They talk now."

Ryan looks away. I don't tell him how, when I mentioned Ryan's increased involvement in our lives, Maria said, "I see," and then, "Be careful, Kate," which somehow ruined the mood of the call.

"And the call from Aftermath?" I ask.

"Yeah, right, the guy said they weren't able to get into the house to assess the situation. But they did have some suggestions. They could hire a security guard or have someone from the public health department go with them. The guy said even loose cannons usually respect someone in a uniform with a badge. He also said that sometimes the police have to be involved. He wants you to call him on Monday, said you have his number."

"Did anyone else call?" I ask in a low voice.

Ryan moves closer to me and says with quiet intensity, "Kate, I don't think you should take his calls anymore. I talked to him. You should block any number he calls from. You know how to do that, right?"

"You talked to him?" I mean to whisper. It comes out like a hiss.

"Yes, he's a real prince, your brother. Don't worry," he says before I can interrupt, "I didn't say anything to rile him up. Quite the opposite. Tried to calm him down. Told him you just wanted out of the whole situation. That you were only trying to clear the house of your dad's shit, which seemed to work. He said all he wants is to move on with his life."

"That might have been enough once," I say. "But not anymore. Although he hasn't followed through on threats before, this is—"

"Before? Wait, he's threatened you before? Does Jacob know?" Ryan grips my forearms, his volume rising.

I pull away. "We shouldn't talk about this here. I don't want the kids to hear us." Beckoning to him, I leave the kitchen and walk down the hall toward the guest wing.

Ryan falls into step with me. "Kate," he says, his voice imbued with urgency—or is it anger? "How long has this been going on?"

"I don't know exactly. Years, but—"

"Years?" He stops abruptly, reaches for my arm.

Instinctively, I pull away. We aren't far enough away from Becca yet. I put my finger up to my lips. Four long steps later, I say quietly, "It was different. Not like this. It was like a game for him, scaring the shit out of me. He called, left messages, just to let me know he could always find me. Once, a long time ago, when we were still in New York, he sent a threatening letter from prison."

As I say this, I hear how bad it sounds.

"Prison? Jesus, what was he in for?"

"Possession with intent to distribute." I recall researching this, heart in my throat. "Meth, heroin. He was an addict himself. Maybe he still is, I don't know."

"Jesus, Kate. That's serious shit. I know. I lived on the street in Nevada a couple of years ago for a story. Meth and heroin addicts don't follow rules. They flirt with death like it isn't real. Did you tell Jacob?"

"Tell Jacob?" I am shocked he would ask this. "How could I tell Jacob anything without telling him everything? You know him. Can you imagine if he knew the truth? Don't you see? That's the power Daniel holds: he could ruin my life in one conversation with Jacob." I stop and look down at the marble. "All I could think to do was stay away from him, from there."

Ryan places his hands on my shoulders, bringing me closer, forcing me to look at him. "And you are. You are away from there, from him and what he did. You aren't like him, Kate. And he's not going to hurt you or your kids, not on my watch."

I shake my head, pull away. "I don't want you involved. I don't want anyone involved with my brother. What I'm saying is it's time for me to stop hiding. It doesn't work. I'm going to hire a lawyer, get a restraining order. Or, I don't know, something else." I think about

Daniel threatening Becca and the extreme solutions that have flitted along the dark periphery of my consciousness. "I'm done running. It's time to fight back."

"Kate, what are you talking about? Now, more than ever, you have to stay away from him. Promise me—for right now, you won't do anything."

"Mommy," I hear Becca calling. "Mo-o-om, come see this."

I exhale forcefully, try to smile. "I've got to go see."

"Yeah, I know. But first, promise me. And then block your dad's number and any of the ones Daniel has used."

"I will, tonight, after Jacob gets them."

"Mommy," Becca calls again. It sounds like she's in the kitchen now, not the family room. "Your phone is ringing."

We both turn and start toward the sound of her voice.

"Don't answer that, Becs," Ryan calls loudly before lowering his voice to add, "Now, Kate. You've got to block them now."

Becca is standing next to the island, the open laptop before her. My phone is sitting on the counter, no longer ringing. My heart is in my throat.

"I didn't answer," Becca says. "I almost did. It was Aunt Maria. Look, Mom, look how good I did on this game!"

I resist the urge to sweep her into my arms, not wanting to alarm her. "How *well* you did, honey," I say, striving to sound as normal as possible. I can see from the screen that she has a new low score. "You do a good job, you did well." I rub her back. "And look at that—you did, you did so well."

"See, Uncle Ryan?" She points to the screen. "I got a new best low score, which is good." She looks to me for confirmation; I nod with a forced smile. "'Cause you want to go as fast as you can. It's bingo. Want to try, Uncle Ryan? My mom is good—she does well—but my dad is even better."

"I'm not a math man like your dad, Becs, but for you"—he looks up at me—"I'd do anything."

Ryan is not a math guy, not at all, and I know he's just pretending to care, but he puts on a game face and plays along. A few rounds of multiplication and division, five minutes, and four Becca laughing-fits later, he closes the laptop cover in exaggerated exasperation and shoos her off to her room to "give us a minute or two to do something boring, okay?"

"I could stay, though, and wait for you to finish," she says.

"You could," Ryan says, "but we'll finish faster if you go read a book or something. If you're here, we'll just be distracted by how cute you are, and it will take way longer."

She looks at me, and I nod. "It's okay, sweetie. I'll come get you as soon as we're done."

We stand at the island, a Becca-size space empty between us. I pick up my phone and, with a few clicks, block my father's number. I pull up recent calls, find the two I think Daniel has used, and block those too. I see that Maria left a voicemail, so I quickly read the transcription.

"She's hunkering down tomorrow to finish her project while Alex has Maddie. Says she'll call tomorrow night or Monday," I tell Ryan.

Ryan half nods, then drops his face into his hands and rubs his temples with his fingertips, hard. When he lifts his head, his complexion looks blotchy beneath his tan, and his face bears the look I have seen for years without recognizing it—a mixture of love and pain.

"Are you okay?" I ask.

Ryan gives another half nod.

A surprisingly uncomfortable silence settles between us until a muffled, deep-bass boom comes from the direction of the kids' bedrooms.

"Logan," I say. "He has some friends over. They're playing a new game. I figure I'll let them play until Jacob comes to get them."

At the mention of Jacob's name, I feel my chest constricting. The uncomfortable silence expands.

Ryan steps closer, eliminating the empty space between us. His fingers brush the back of my hand.

I move away.

"Kate," he says, his voice nearly a whisper.

Holy shit. I turn and gesture for him to follow me.

Down the hallway—marble, carpet, marble—to the guest room. I stand by the door until Ryan follows me inside. The door closes with the house's trademark hush.

I shake my head. "We can't—"

His mouth crushes mine. He entwines his hands in my hair as his body presses mine against the door. *Why does something so wrong feel this right?* I ask myself before the ability to think is momentarily obliterated. But then, as quickly as it began, the kiss is over, ending with the same raging tenderness that characterized the first one.

Ryan steps back, breathing hard.

I want him. Cannot have him. Logan and Becca are down the hall. This is Jacob's house. Our family house. Even if Jacob no longer wants me, I cannot have Ryan, not ever. Everyone is unhappy.

This—this is crazy. I feel tears forming.

"We can't do this, Ryan. We can't. I can't do this."

We both look straight into each other's eyes, and then, as if burned by my tears, he looks away.

"No, you're right. I know, but I don't want you to be alone, not with . . ."

He folds me back into his arms, rests his chin on top of my head.

"I'll be fine," I say. "I'll be here, behind the gates and the locked doors, and Becca and Logan will be with Jacob." I begin to pull away from his embrace. "I can't do this, though. We can't be alone together." I try to convey strength and confidence, but my voice catches.

"I've got you," he says, holding on. Then, silently, he slides his left hand down from my waist, rests it on my hip, while with the fingers of his right hand he traces the curve of my cheek and outlines the shape of my lips, as if he's memorizing them for later. "You're right. I'm sorry. It's all going to be okay. Lemme say bye to the kids, and then I'll get out of here."

Ten minutes later, he's gone.

TWENTY-NINE

I AM PAST THE BREAK, floating on a lime-green Aqua Float—sunshine above, softly undulating water below. Without warning, the raft is overturned by force, and I am spilled into deep ocean. I come up sputtering, grabbing for something to hold on to, but the raft is out of sight—and he is there. I see the top of his dark blond head and lean limbs under the water. Reaching up from the depths, his fingers, like talons, close around my ankle. He turns and swims straight down, his grasp tightening. I try to swim upward, my arms and free leg arcing through the water with inefficient desperation. Pressure builds inside my head and lungs. I look to the surface; the light is fading. Dark spots appear and camera bulbs flash.

Drowning, I will not be saved.

I awaken on Monday bleary, disoriented, my upper arms and thighs sore, as if I've been up all night deadlifting or actually fighting someone far stronger than me. I long to see Becca's sweet face, half obscured by her favorite stuffed animal—a large, floppy-eared gray elephant with a purple sweater that she uses as a combination pillow and security blanket. But the kids are still with Jacob.

Yesterday, Sunday, went by in a bit of a blur. I recall going for a run, gardening, steaming—trying, and failing, to come up with a reasonable yet ironclad way to rid myself of the reality and specter of my brother. I look over and see a pile of dark clothing on the floor; I do not recall taking it off or leaving it there. I must have been exhausted when I came to bed. I am exhausted still.

The dream lingers. I lie quietly, waiting for thoughts of underwater demons to dissipate.

As a child, Logan suffered from night terrors. He would awaken in the wee hours, screaming and panic-stricken. His eyes were wide open, yet he remained trapped inside the dream. Inconsolable, he would thrash about as if he did not recognize me or Jacob, as though we were the source of his fear. The next day, he often only vaguely remembered the incidents and could not name or describe the horror into which sleep had delivered him. I could remember, however, and his terror was frightening to behold. I worried my son was doomed to suffer from the insomnia and nightmares that have plagued me throughout my life—or worse.

Dr. Farber reassured me that night terrors are not directly linked to other mental disorders and most children outgrow them. And, indeed, Logan did. Of course, this led to an extensive discussion with Dr. Farber about my dreams, dreams in general, and the predominant analytic theories related thereto. So, while I will never be an expert, I know a thing or two about Jung's view on the collective unconscious. And Freud? Well, shit, dear old Sigmund would have a field day with me.

Having said all that, my latest recurring dream doesn't require paid analysis. I've got this one covered. Which is a good thing, given that I have more than enough to fill hours with Dr. Farber and I'm limited to fifty minutes per session.

I stare at the ceiling, considering the wisdom of composing a list to bring with me to my appointment this morning, an attempt to perform triage on my increasingly complicated set of issues. The idea is appealing, on a couple of levels. It would eliminate the often seemingly chance nature of what my subconscious chooses to bring to the fore, and it might compel me to discuss things I'd otherwise avoid. Moreover, I will have a written record afterward in case my memory goes wonky.

Competing for the top, should I decide to try this approach: Item one—my deranged brother: what he did, what he represents, what I need to do to prevent him from hurting me or, worse, my children. Item two—despite a seemingly valid premise, my self-preservation efforts have turned into cowardice and selfishness, ruining my marriage and my children's chance for a happy childhood. And item three—my deep-seated longing for unconditional love coming to fruition with Ryan could destroy not only my husband's longest-standing friendship but also the whole fabric of our lives.

This has got to stop. *Enough, Kate, enough.*

Time to get up. Eat breakfast. Feed Ophelia. My cell phone buzzes a reminder to call Aftermath. As I search for the number in recent history, I see the activity from Saturday, the calls and text messages I received while Ryan had my phone. He spent four minutes talking to Maria, nearly seven talking to Daniel. *What did they talk about?*

Entering my closet, I touch the screen over Aftermath, put the phone to my ear, and trip over my mother's box. I don't remember leaving it where it now sits.

"Fuck," I say, breaking my fall on the shelf over the hamper, just as the phone is answered, "Aftermath, this is Rick."

Shit, I think, rubbing my hand on my thigh to mitigate the sting. *Not a great start to this conversation.*

"Hello? This is Rick Engle?"

"Yes, hi, this is Kathryn Whittier. I'm so sorry about that, I just tripped over a box. So sorry."

"No worries, Mrs. Whittier. I've tripped over a few boxes myself. Comes with the territory in my line of work."

Rick Engle is a nice guy. Thank God.

I push the box up against the wall as Rick talks. It's an illuminating conversation. They will work with me to figure out a way to get back into the house. Daniel isn't the first difficult client they've had to handle. Mr. Engle explains that hoarders often resist the removal of the dangerous, often toxic, detritus of their lives. They cling to it as if it gives them meaning and structure, and they panic when Aftermath sweeps in. Hoarders do not believe what they are told—that ridding themselves of unhealthy junk is freeing, that they will have space to move and breathe, that they will rediscover and appreciate valuable belongings long hidden underneath.

As I listen to him, I realize his words could easily apply to me. Time to get rid of that which is dangerous and toxic. Make room. Save that which is valuable.

As soon as we hang up, I compose my triage list.

THIRTY

I DON'T EVEN WAIT for Dr. Farber's "So, Kate" cue.

List in hand.

It's time.

"I want to talk about Daniel."

The spillway opens. Dr. Farber has either perfected neutrality of expression or she is truly unsurprised by the torrent of words from my mouth. I talk, without stopping, for several minutes. I start with the first time Daniel forced me to perform oral sex and move on from there—the threat of incest, psychological and physical abuse, living in shame and dread. My brother damaging me and then blaming me for being damaged. My mother, and then my father, abandoning me again and again, leaving me alone in the house—that unsafe, uninhabitable house—and then my father, dear old dad, leaving me the house itself, forcing me to deal with Daniel again now.

I tell her about my vow the day I left home to never fall on my knees again. How I've failed in so many ways.

As my voice trails off, I notice that Dr. Farber's stoic face is showing some cracks. There is softness in her eyes, a slight tightening in her mouth—compassion, and maybe a little stifled anger?

"Kate, you are not responsible for the actions of your brother or his friends, or your parents. None of these things are your fault. You were sexually abused and raped. You didn't do anything wrong. Do you understand what I am saying?"

I want to believe this, but shame washes over me nonetheless, settling like floodwater. I am up to my neck in it.

"Kate, do you understand what I'm saying?"

I nod. Rationally, I do. Emotionally, I am not there. I don't know if I ever will be there. I wonder if anyone ever gets there.

"I have never done it willingly—oral sex. I can't. I tried a couple of times with Jacob." I wince, remembering. "The first time was awful. I thought maybe with time, it might get better, but it didn't. The second time was horrific, really. I couldn't touch him for days, didn't want him to touch me. There are a lot of times, actually, when I don't want him to touch me."

I almost feel guilty, telling her about Daniel after all of these years in this safe room, as if I've committed a lie of omission. The trouble with being in therapy as long as I have is that you start to believe you deserve some sort of honorary degree in psychology. As Maria might put it, "you believe your own promote." Or you believe in your own diagnosis and treatment regimen, as the case may be.

"And then, when Jacob, well . . ." More shame rising, cutting off my words.

"Does he know what you've just told me?"

"Some of it."

"Some of it," Dr. Farber repeats—not a question, exactly, but I answer.

"He knows I was raped that time in the bathroom. I think he assumes I was forced to give the guy, well, you know, which isn't entirely wrong since that happened too, later. The next time. I haven't told him any of that. I'm not sure how he would react—after all these years. In fact, it could be worse, since so much time has passed. If there is one thing I'm sure of, whoring for your brother isn't fixable, and I can't imagine he would love me if he knew. I am definitely not worthy of the Whittier name."

Dr. Farber leans forward. She speaks slowly, calmly. "You were raped, Kate. Though I don't know your husband, from what you have told me, he's a good and decent man. You may find that talking about this here, with me, gives you the strength and comfort to talk about it with him. Whether you ultimately stay together or not, he is the father of your children and will be a part of your life. Consider giving him the chance to be a part of your healing. I'm not suggesting you rush into it. Just consider it."

"Part of my healing."

"He's been with you for a long time. I would venture that he subconsciously comprehends you've been hurt and are protecting yourself against it. Knowing the source, acknowledging it to him, with him, will give you a chance to see how he truly feels. His true feelings—not the ones you imagine he will have—these are the ones you can address openly. Tilting at windmills is rarely productive, and although dealing with the truth is hard, it can be freeing."

Tilting at windmills.

"Jacob doesn't like messy, broken things. He likes order and decency."

"But, Kate, you've told me he loves you—and your truth is part of you."

I am messy and broken.

"Maybe. Maybe he doesn't love me anymore."

Dr. Farber does not respond.

"Then again," I think out loud, "maybe he'll be glad to hear my disinterest in sex really is, as he has said a couple of times, a 'PTSD' thing."

Dr. Farber's face is drawn like a bow. "It isn't uncommon for rape and incest victims to suffer from post-traumatic stress. And you, like many survivors of rape and incest, have closed off parts of yourself to others—it's self-protective, and completely understandable."

I know this on some level. I've known it for a long time. I simply don't like to dwell there.

"Then a trigger—like Jacob's behavior or going back to your childhood home, hearing your brother's voice—brings it back, and your coping mechanisms are overwhelmed."

"And I fall apart."

"With trauma like this, triggers can set off memories or flash-backs and nightmares that are vivid and real. You experience it all again—as if it is happening here, now."

I nod. I do feel I'm experiencing it all again.

"It's like I can't breathe and a freight train is headed right for me," I say. "I want to disappear."

Escape. Swim to the surface. Face the reality of lost time.

"Sometimes, I can even forget where I am."

"Well"—Dr. Farber seems to be choosing her words carefully—"your body and your mind react to protect you. Reactions you are familiar with: anger, fight and flight, dissociating yourself from the situation, and even, ultimately, the amnesia, where you literally shut it down."

Sitting here, listening to her, I remember being inside the tiny bedroom closet in my father's house: seeing the torn red dress, hearing my phone ring, hearing Daniel's voice, the instant panic setting in, feeling like I was going to choke. And then I remember the rage I felt, still feel, toward Jacob whenever I think about him getting "just a blow job" from a stripper in public, in front of his friends. How the vision of him unloosed a memory for me: being watched by my brother as his fraternity brothers violated me.

My heart beats madly. There is a wounded part of me that wants to cry and scream and hurt someone all at the same time. Another part of me feels like an observer, watching that wounded version of me, trying to keep myself in control. Maybe this is what crazy feels like? Slipping into the abyss. I focus on the picture of the bridge over Dr. Farber's head, trying to remember her strategies to ground myself back here, in her office, in this leather chair, safe.

"What he did . . ." I think I'm about to say something about Daniel. Mid-sentence, I realize I'm also talking about Jacob. "I can't forget. Ever."

"No." A shake of her head, a gentle tone. "You probably won't forget. But revealing it begins to address the power of the memory.

While closing off parts of the self is protective, it can be helpful to open them up—to face them, even when it is painful. Sometimes, Kate, we hold on to our hurt and shame and anger because we believe they are our very foundation, that if we let them go we won't know how to be. What I hope you find, however, is that while these experiences may remain a part of you, they don't need to define you."

She sounds like Ryan and Mr. Engle, or they sound like her. I think about the house, Aftermath, my mother's box. My mother.

"Except opening up and facing the truth scares the shit out of me." I hear my voice quivering. "Being overwhelmed, it's, well, it's..." *Overwhelming.* "When my mind goes wild, my thoughts dart all over the place, and I can't control my emotions." I stare again at the bridge over Dr. Farber's head. "I wonder if maybe I'm just finally falling into the abyss."

Silence for a moment, and then: "The abyss."

Tears form. The bridge blurs. "Like my mother. I've been reading it—the letter, some poems and journals—and the whole time I was petrified, petrified that I would see myself in her."

"Do you?"

I blink slowly. The bridge remains blurred.

"Only a little. I understand some of it. The rich inner life, the volatility—I have those too."

Dr. Farber leans forward. "Kate, you are not your mother. But you are her daughter. That relationship, well, you can't undo it. Acknowledging things you share with your mother, maybe some of them even good things, doesn't mean you are destined to become her."

I continue to stare, waiting for the bridge to clear.

"Throughout the years we've been talking together, the things you have described to me—the feelings you have, the worries and fears—have rarely been unusual for the circumstances. Strong, serious, conflicting emotions are part of being human. Being aware, expressing them instead of holding them in, naming them, putting them in perspective—these are signs of a healthy psyche. You are aware. You are expressing them. You are exerting control. Your mother could not do this."

"I will fail you." My voice is so small.

"What do you mean?" Dr. Farber asks quietly. When I don't answer, she asks again, "What do you mean by that, Kate?"

"My mother wrote that in her letter—'I will fail you'—and I know now, that's my biggest fear, that I will fail my children. For a while now, it's seemed like I can't avoid it—like I have to choose between a broken family or a broken me. The separation, the not-knowing, I know it's not healthy. It's not good for them. And I've done something else, something that could hurt them." I look down at my list, crumpled, dotted with wet spots. "I brought a list."

I hold it up, as if for her approval.

"Yes." Dr. Farber smiles. "I noticed that." She puts down her pen. She nods at the piece of paper I am stretching tight between my hands, as if I want to rip it apart.

"I slept with Ryan on Friday," I read, not daring to look at her. "I shared everything with him, even the stuff about Daniel."

I realize as I say these words that they cannot convey what I mean. I shared *everything*: my body, my heart, my mother's writing, my past, my pain.

"He told me afterward that he's been in love with me for a long time, years, since before I married Jacob. He's carried it around all this time."

I summon the courage to look at her.

"I betrayed my husband, even worse than he betrayed me. I know you probably think it was a horrible idea getting involved with him, with Ryan, and I'm an awful person. And you'd be right. I know that. But I also know I've never felt"—my voice cracks—"so loved . . . for exactly who I am, not someone that needs to be fixed. Just me, broken. All of me."

"I don't think you're an awful person, Kate." Her face is back to neutral.

Another moment of silence, of feeling all the loss.

"As for feeling loved for exactly who you are," she says softly, "that kind of love is extraordinary—and empowering."

Extraordinary and empowering.

"Yes, it is. I've felt it before, you know, on the giving end—for my kids, for Logan and Becca. Receiving it, though, from him, from Ryan—it was different, another kind of extraordinary." I remember Ryan's eyes as he told me I made him see the world in a different way. I reflect on what he meant, on how my children do the same thing for me. "Love like that, it changes everything, doesn't it?"

Dr. Farber's face opens, revealing a softness I rarely see. "Yes, it does."

I inhale deeply, allow my eyes to close. I hold my breath at the top, recalling the feel of Ryan's fingers tracing over the curves of my body, my jawline, my lips. I exhale with a sigh and open my eyes.

Facing the truth sucks.

"The thing is, I can't be with Ryan. I know that. I can't have his love, not without hurting all of the people I love. Not without destroying my family."

I am grateful for Dr. Farber's silence. I welcome it. Don't feel a rush to fill it. I am sad, but I don't cry.

This is my life.

"I know you've told me this so many times. It's not that I haven't been listening. I guess I've been so trapped by my own shit that I haven't been able to understand what you meant: we're all broken—me, Ryan, Jacob—aren't we."

It's not a question. It's a statement of fact.

"I've always known that I am, because, you know, my damage is easy to see. And Ryan, he's got this loneliness he wraps around himself. But Jacob is broken too—he's so worried about how things appear, he cuts out whole parts of living. You know, when Ryan told me about him the first time, he called Jacob 'practically perfect in every way,' and I remember thinking, *Like Mary Poppins.* Back then, I thought practically perfect was an amazing thing."

I shake my head at my ignorance and romance novel naiveté.

"I wondered why someone like him would ever want to be with someone like me. But now—now I feel sort of sorry for him. I mean, it's not like I've got it figured out, and I dwell too much on anger and sadness and fucking despair, but at least I'm embracing all of it."

I look Dr. Farber in the eye. *Here's what I've learned.*

"I think that's why he loves living here and I hate it sometimes, with the perpetual sunshine and all the perfectly manicured everything. It seems to me that rainy days make me appreciate sunny ones. And unhappiness, well, it highlights being happy. Cynicism from people like Maria reminds me to marvel at the delight Becca has in simple things like her favorite ice cream—or a new purple anything. With Jacob, I don't know, he avoids anything more negative than mild disappointment. Do you know, I've only seen him cry once? Once. When Logan was born. He didn't even cry when his father died—and he *loved* his dad. I honestly have no idea how he feels about any of this marital stuff other than that he wants to fix it, to fix me. To make the situation go away and go back to the way things were before. And I'm not sure I can do that."

I blow out a breath. "Logan told me on Saturday that everyone is unhappy—him, Becca, Jacob. Do you know what he said?"

Dr. Farber shakes her head. Of course she doesn't know; she wasn't there.

"He said, 'I hope you're happy, because no one else is.'"

I realize I am running up against the fifty-minute mark. Any second now, she will stop me with the glance at the clock, pick up her appointment scheduler.

Two-minute warning. Unlike in football, there is no automatic time-out when two minutes remain. Other than the ones I used to impose on Logan and Becca—time-outs during which everyone retreats to their corner and I can figure out what to do next—these are rare in real life.

Rare time-outs, no do-overs, no what-ifs, and no if-onlys.

"I can't stop thinking about that, because even if I were happy, I'm making the people I love unhappy. In the end, how could I be happy if that's the price? How do you know when to do what's right for you and when to buck up and do what's right for others, even if it's not right for you?"

"If I had the answer to that, Kate, I'd write a book and retire from practice on the proceeds. That would be a book nearly everyone could use."

I glance at her bookcase and smile. "Well, between us, we probably have every psychological self-help book in existence—and I can tell you, it hasn't yet been written."

Dr. Farber smiles in return—a real smile that spreads across her face, reaching her eyes. "Truth is, what you asked is such a difficult question to answer. Balancing one's own happiness with the happiness of others, balancing independence and a strong sense of self with togetherness and belonging, examining the past enough to find understanding and compassion without letting what you find dictate the present and the future, embracing each moment and accepting it for what it is—these are things each of us has to figure out for ourselves."

God, she's good.

Time is up.

"We've covered a lot today, Kate," Dr. Farber says in her closing-things-down voice.

I don't want to see her reach for her appointment book. Proactively, I stand. "Yes, we have." The crumpled list is still in my hand. "And yet there's still such a long way to go, isn't there?" I try to smile. "At least I'm sure about one thing: I want my children to be safe and know they are loved. I want them to have what I didn't."

"I know," I add when she opens her mouth to speak. "See you on Thursday."

THIRTY-ONE

"HOW WAS YOUR DATE?"

I never thought it would happen. I actually feel sorry for Dr. Reynolds. I must be channeling a new level of empathy, one of those traits of resilience. A week ago, I would have simply been irritated by his lack of intuitive power and sensitivity—and his shades-of-gray-patterned sweater vest. Though he couldn't possibly have known, I would have expected him to divine that my father died last week. That I'd had an episode of dissociative amnesia, slept with my husband's best friend, inherited a house I don't want, and discovered a link to my mother's inner thoughts. I would have expected him to intuit that going out on a date with my estranged husband was not high on my list of priorities.

Sitting here now on his intentionally nondescript, neutral beige couch, however, I recognize that he has no idea how absurd his question is; he cannot divine anything about the past week, and *it's not his fault*. Even the most perceptive, experienced therapist wouldn't be able to discern all that, and Dr. Lawrence Reynolds is far from a perceptive, experienced therapist. I *have* changed. Pity replaces anger. He's a young, unmarried marital therapist who is in way over his head and relying on textbook strategies like husband/wife dating.

I have to tell him what happened. I open my mouth to do so, just not in time.

"Kate had a tough week, Dr. Reynolds." Jacob sits in his corner of the couch, but he reaches out his right hand and touches the back of mine. He is dressed immaculately in a pale blue pressed shirt, shimmery silver tie, and black slacks. His voice is measured, calm.

"Her father died this past Tuesday. She's had to deal with her brother, who is not well—mentally. The date, well . . ."

"Oh." Dr. Reynolds's brow furrows. "I see. I'm so sorry. So sorry for your loss, Kate. Are you . . . how are you doing?"

Okay, I'm not a saint. Larry Reynolds, PhD, still makes me feel like snapping. I don't, though. What I do is look down at Jacob's hand over mine.

"I wasn't particularly close to my father, Dr. Reynolds, but it was . . ." I sigh. "It was a difficult week."

"Yes, I see." A pregnant pause. "Would you like to talk about your week—your father or your brother? It was your brother, right?"

In this moment, it hits me.

Yes. I want to talk about my week. My brother. Acknowledge it all. Here and now. Give Jacob a chance to be part of my healing, as it were.

Or not.

Jacob and Larry both look at me expectantly, wearing matching masks of neutral concern. Here goes nothing—giving the phrase "nothing is wrong" new meaning. In this case, nothing is indeed very wrong.

I take a deep breath and begin: "I know we haven't really talked about my family. It's complicated. I am, well, I was estranged from my father and my brother. His name is Daniel, my brother. My father, he was an alcoholic, and he checked out after my mother committed suicide when I was eleven. She—my mother, that is—took an overdose of pills one day when I was at school."

I stare past Dr. Reynolds. My voice is flat, monotone.

"I found her. Things got worse after she died, although to be honest, my childhood was chaotic when she was alive. My mother was erratic, to say the least."

My words slow.

"Demanding, angry, depressed, wild sometimes. Probably bipolar, though not diagnosed as far as I know."

The two men remain silent.

"Anyway, after she died, my father, who wasn't a good parent before, well, he didn't try very hard. He went to work. He drank. He didn't seem to care about me, and he definitely didn't care *for* me."

I stop to take another deep breath. Here we go.

"I see," Dr. Reynolds says grimly.

"No, I don't think you do; you see, I'm not quite finished." I am polite. I am a model of decorum: ankles crossed tightly, hands gripped in a fold on my lap with Jacob's hand resting on top. "One of Daniel's college fraternity brothers raped me when I was fifteen."

Again, I hear my own voice—calm, dispassionate, as if I am telling someone else's story. But this is my story. This is my life.

"My father and Daniel did nothing to stop it, even though they were in the next room and heard me screaming."

Jacob moves his hand away from mine. He stares at me. I think I know this face, the "maybe we shouldn't talk about that here" message unspoken, yet loud as a bullhorn.

Where else would be an appropriate place?

I am making him uncomfortable, which is unfortunate.

After all, this is who I am.

"Jacob knows this much. There is more, though, things I haven't talked about with him or well, anyone, even my therapist, until this morning—I told her this morning." *And Ryan.* But I can't say that here.

Jacob glances at me, surprised and clearly not happy with me, with this state of affairs.

I understand. This does not fit his worldview.

Poor Jacob.

"After that first rape, Daniel must have told his fraternity brothers they could have me as payment—for drugs, I think, but it could have been other things too. The second time I had my period, so

Daniel held my hands while one of his fraternity brothers forced me to give him, well, as Daniel put it, 'just a blow job.'" I hear his voice. I pause, breathe, open my hands, and press my palms down on my thighs. "I was sixteen."

Jacob folds his arms across his chest. He is no longer looking at me. Rather, he is staring at Dr. Reynolds—or maybe he's staring at the black-and-white picture of a tree over Dr. Reynolds's head, right next to his framed diplomas.

Jacob refuses to look at me. His lips are pursed together tightly. His face is a death mask.

I look at Dr. Reynolds's beard, the point under his chin, then down at the ground between us.

"I lived in fear for almost a year, dreading when my brother would come home with a friend, or friends. I tried to think of someone I could ask for help." I sigh audibly. "But I came up empty. My father never tried to stop them—not once—even though I'm certain he knew what they were doing."

I leave that statement hanging for a moment.

"When I finally fought back, Daniel punched me and kicked me. He told me no one would ever love me, that I wasn't even worthy of his abuse. He said *I* was crazy. I left home a few days later and didn't ever go back. Until this past week. It was, as Jacob said, a tough week for me."

Jacob, the prince of understatement—though this time unintentionally.

Silence fills the room like a cloud of volcanic ash—making it difficult to inhale, numbing us all, freezing us in place.

I look to Dr. Reynolds. It may have been only a few seconds or several minutes since I spoke. I could not say for sure. He opens his mouth and then immediately closes it again.

Emotions return, raw honesty pulling them forward. I feel tears forming as I go on, my voice getting quieter and quieter.

"Despite years away, I suppose I still believe my brother was right. That I am damaged goods. Sloppy seconds. Crazy."

Hearing my brother's names for me come out of my mouth, I repeat in my head, *This does not define me, this does not define me*— a new mantra. I wonder whether my husband can see it that way.

Dr. Farber's advice resounds: *Tilting at windmills is rarely productive.* If I want to know, I will have to ask him. I turn to look at him.

"Jacob, you must be thinking something, feeling something, right now," I say. "Please tell me."

Dr. Reynolds sits back.

Jacob bows his head, looks at his hands. He says nothing. He doesn't know how to feel this. When he took those marriage vows— for better and for worse—he had no idea. This is beyond worse.

"Jacob," I practically whisper. "Whatever it is, I just want to know so I can . . ."

So I can what? I don't know. Dr. Farber and I didn't cover this. So I can defend myself? So I can understand you? So I know whether you can love me?

"I, I . . ." He finally looks at me.

I have often wondered in the past what it would be like to see Jacob feel a negative emotion deeper than mild disappointment or frustration. *Here it is—and it is devastating.*

"I don't understand. Why have you never told me this before?"

His eyes cloud over. He leans forward, covers his face with his hands, rubbing his temples, up into his hairline, as if to erase his thoughts.

"If I had known . . ." He shakes his head.

I want him to finish. If he had known, what? He wouldn't have married me? He wouldn't have had children with me? He would have run for the hills?

I cannot see his face, and I want to. I want to see if there is a battle of emotions playing out there. Not because I want him to feel horror or pain or disgust or anger, but rather because I want to know that he can. Then it hits me like a lightning bolt, though it's so obvious: I sought him out for his lack of emotional swings. I envied his ability to live in the yellow and green zone and never venture into red, blue, or purple. The product of a volatile nature/nurture environment, I needed his stability and then blamed him for the very thing that drew me to him.

And he undoubtedly did the same. I gave him the full rainbow: the good, the glorious, the bad, the ugly.

"Jacob, I didn't keep it from you to hurt you. I didn't tell you because I was ashamed, and I didn't think you'd be able to love me if you knew." Suddenly, quite desperately, I want him to love me. I want to be that girl in the nautical-blue-and-white bikini on a sailboat with his arm around me.

Before I can explain any further, he looks at me as if I am a stranger. Then he turns his face toward Dr. Reynolds—to acknowledge him, or perhaps to avoid my gaze—his hands clenching and unclenching.

"Excuse me." He stands abruptly, walks briskly to the door.

Before either Dr. Reynolds or I can say a word, the door is closing behind him.

The ash hasn't cleared. I briefly consider whether Dr. Reynolds's stillness is an indication of advanced therapeutic technique that is quite out of character or if it is borne of inexperience and ineptitude. I decide to go with the former and wait for him to provide analysis or advice or, fuck, anything at all.

After a moment, it becomes clear it was the latter.

He opens his mouth, closes it, opens it again, like a bearded guppy, before finally saying, "Well, I would have encouraged Jacob to stay, but now that we are here, just the two of us, maybe we can work through some of what's happening with you now—or, if you prefer, we could discuss what you've just shared."

No thank you, I think but do not say. How do I get out of here?

My cell phone vibrates—once, twice. A phone call. I reach for it in the side pocket of my purse. It's Maria.

Following Jacob's lead, I stand abruptly. "Excuse me."

Walking out is much easier than I would have imagined.

THIRTY-TWO

BEFORE I GET OUT the main office door, I have return-dialed Maria's number. There is a reception area near the entrance in a small internal space designed to look like a courtyard, with fake palm trees in pots. I sit down, relieved to be out of Dr. Reynolds's office, relieved to be done with therapy for the day.

Enough is enough.

Though I hope it isn't anything serious, I realize I'm looking forward to hearing about someone else's problems. Connection through shared pain.

"Kate, thank God. Are you okay? Where are you?"

"I'm sitting outside our marital therapist's office, having been abandoned by Jacob—though I can't really blame him. He was blindsided."

"Blindsided?"

"It's a long story."

"So you're alone then?"

"Yes. Why? What's going on? Are you okay?"

"Me? I'm fine." She doesn't sound fine. "We're all fine here."

"You don't sound fine."

Silence.

"Maria? Can you hear me?"

I look down at the phone and see time continuing to tick along. I haven't dropped the call.

I am getting tired of all these awkward silences.

"Yes, yes. I can hear you. Listen, Kate, can I ask you a personal question?"

"Have you ever not been able to?"

"Right, yeah. I'm sorry." This is a very strange call. Maria doesn't apologize for anything. "Okay. Here goes. Is something going on between you and Ryan?"

Oh. That's right. They spoke on the phone. For four minutes. And he seemed uncomfortable telling me about it, I remember that now.

I frame, quickly reframe, an answer. "He has been helping me get through the last couple of months, particularly last week. We've gotten closer. Why?"

"It's been a long time since I talked to him, but he sounded— well, he sounded odd on Saturday."

"Odd?"

"Odd—uncomfortable. Super protective, almost proprietary."

"Proprietary?"

"No, that's the wrong word. But sort of like you're more . . . more than just a friend. Even a best friend."

"What are you trying to say, Maria?"

"I'm sorry, Kate. I am probably not handling this the right way. I've been thinking about something, something I think you need to know, but I'm just not sure how to tell you."

In an instant, I am back in my *Architectural Digest* kitchen the night of Jacob's confession: *I don't know how to tell you.*

"Whatever it is, just tell me. Nothing can be worse than what I'm dealing with already."

"I know, that's the thing—you've got enough on your plate and, I don't know, I could be way off base about this, but if I'm not, it could make you very, very angry."

"Angry? With who? With you?" I'm so confused.

"Maybe. Oh, shit, there's no easy way, so I'll try to do this long story short. After I talked to Ryan on Saturday, I thought he sounded overprotective, like I said—maybe, I don't know, overinvolved. Cagey. I know it's not my place, but I was worried about you, so I mentioned something to Alex last night when he dropped Maddie off."

"Alex?"

"I know you don't trust him, Kate. I get that. It has gotten much better lately, though. I suppose because we've both accepted how this is going to be, we're actually talking about things again. Anyway, that's off topic, and I need to just get this out. I told him about my phone call with Ryan, and he made a comment like 'Well, it didn't take long for him to capitalize on Jacob moving out, did it?' So I asked him how he knew about Jacob moving out, and he said he called him a while ago—about something else, not personal at all, about a potential client—and Jacob was brusque with him, told him he couldn't speak to him or Christoph, that he'd promised you he wouldn't after the birthday thing in New York last spring. So Alex asked, 'Why—what happened to upset Kate?'"

I am speechless. *What happened to upset Kate?* He helped it happen.

"Jacob repeated that he couldn't really talk, that he had promised you. Then he said something Alex didn't get at the time, but it's what got me thinking. Jacob told him he didn't remember it, made some cryptic comment about having Ryan to thank for the details, and said you had asked him to leave because of the lap dance that went too far. Then, apparently, he hung up, and since then he hasn't answered any more of Alex's calls or texts."

At least Jacob is abiding by my wishes to disassociate himself from Alex.

"Alex told me he thought it was unfair you would kick Jacob out over a failed ten-second lap dance, but that he never did understand women. I told him your separation must have been for something else—that you wouldn't ask Jacob to move out over a failed lap dance."

The words that come out of my mouth are uncensored: "A *failed lap dance* is not what happened. The stripper your ex-husband bought for my husband"—I grip the phone—"she gave him a"—no matter what, I will always hate this phrase—"she gave him a *blow job*, right there in front of all of them, during which he acquired an STI that he then shared with me."

A pause. "Jacob told you he got a blow job from a stripper?"

Déjà vu, again.

"Yes, he did. Well, no. Jacob says he blacked out and doesn't remember it. Ryan told him." My voice slows. "Ryan told him, and he told me."

There is a long pause. I am about to ask if she's there again when I hear her voice.

"Oh, Kate."

God, she sounds like Natalie. *Fuck "Oh, Kate."*

"Oh, sweetie, I don't think that can be right. Alex admitted that he and Christoph bought champagne and paid for a dance—believe me, I gave him some shit about that—but not surprising to me, he says Jacob got really uncomfortable and practically shoved the stripper off his lap. He said it effectively put an end to the evening. Jacob was furious, said he was leaving, and told them to get out, which they did. Then just a couple of minutes later, they saw the stripper in the main bar, and Alex went over to apologize to her for how Jacob had behaved. He said she was like, 'It's not the first time a guy didn't want me, but tell your friend I tried and I'm not giving the money back.' Alex said he and Christoph didn't expect her to give the lap-dance money back, and she said, 'No, but the other guy, Brian? He paid for more.'"

Though my mind begins to race, I try to follow what Maria is saying.

"Then Christoph got a cab, and Alex was flagging one down for himself when he saw Ryan and Jacob on the opposite side of the street, getting into a cab heading the other way. He said he tried to wave, but neither of them saw him. So—"

"What are you trying to say, Maria?" I break in.

She pauses, moderates her voice, as if that will help defuse the message as she says, "I'm saying that Ryan may have paid for more, but it didn't happen. There wasn't time. Alex saw the girl leave the room right after he did, and if something else had happened . . . well, Alex has no reason not to tell me. He was really clear about how furious Jacob was—he said he'd never forget it 'cause, even drunk, Jacob doesn't do angry. He's Mr. Calm, Cool, and Collected."

The silence is on my end this time. *What?* is all I can think. *What?*

"Kate? Are you there?"

I try to come up with a response. Breathe. "Yeah, I'm here. I don't understand. This doesn't make any sense."

Ryan paid for more, but there was no more? *How did I get the HPV, then?* My thoughts race back to the first call from Donna at Dr. Brachmann's office, her emphasis that HPV can go undetected for years, and that testing positive while in a long-term relationship doesn't necessarily indicate infidelity. I remember the FAQs and message boards I found online about how a diagnosis raises doubts and accusations. Confrontations.

"I'm sorry, sweetie. I just wanted to make sure you had all the information. I think Alex is telling the truth. For what it's worth, he told me Jacob was really, really drunk—he used this vulgar phrase, something called 'whiskey dick,' which he said means a guy's so drunk he can't get it up, regardless of the temptation."

My thoughts veer from Donna to whiskey dick. *Alex* would *know about something like that.*

When I don't say anything, after a moment, Maria goes on. "The thing is, Kate, Alex has no reason not to tell me the truth. He knows you don't like him. As long as you're around, he can't see Jacob, and he adores Jacob—so from his perspective, if you were out of the picture, things would actually be better."

"So what Alex is saying is that *Ryan* paid the stripper for . . . more . . . but Jacob didn't want it?" I ask. My brain has started to work again, but I still don't understand. Ryan said Jacob was a willing recipient. That he saw it. Why would Ryan say that if it wasn't true? "Are you saying Ryan is lying? That doesn't make sense. Jacob is his best friend. Ryan wouldn't do anything to hurt him—they're like brothers."

A wave of guilt and shame crashes over me as I say these words, followed quickly by another wave of confusion.

I can hear the hesitation in Maria's voice when she answers, "I don't know, Kate. This may sound crazy"—shit, that word again—"but is it possible that maybe Ryan set up this whole thing on purpose? To break you guys up?"

No. That couldn't be. Disbelief hits, threatening to suck me out past the break to deep water.

"At the beginning, when I told him about how Ryan was behaving, Alex said he's always suspected Ryan loved you—not like a friend, like a wanting-you kind of thing. I just thought he was envious of what you and Jacob have and that was why he acted the way he did sometimes, but . . . Did you ever see that? I mean, could Alex be right?"

Do I tell her? Do I admit to what Ryan said last Friday, what we did, how I trusted him?

"This doesn't make sense," I repeat. *Does it?*

Ryan lying on purpose goes against everything I've always thought of him. Then again, I obviously don't know him as well as I thought—he admitted to harboring these intense feelings for me, for such a long time, and until a few days ago I had no clue. *Could he do that to Jacob—oh, God, could he?*

"Jacob has always been there for him, his whole family has. They took him in, and he's Logan's godfather, and . . ."

And . . .

"Listen, we don't know what happened for sure. You should just ask Ryan. Call him. Ask him. Tell him what Alex said—that there wasn't time, and how the stripper said a guy named Brian paid for more, but Jacob wasn't interested in any of it. Ask him why he told Jacob something different. You need to clear it up, get the story out there."

At the word "story," my stomach drops from my throat, into which it has been steadily climbing over the last few minutes. Ryan and his stories, his "what-ifs." What if this was one of Ryan's what-ifs, brought to life? *What if Jacob got a blow job from a stripper, and Kate found out about it? What if I was there to pick up the pieces?*

The what-ifs multiply.

What if I was wrong about the identity of the man in my dreams pulling me under?

What if the safe, warm, floating sensation symbolizes my life with Jacob, the family we created?

What if it is Ryan who toppled me off and is pulling me under?

"I have to go, Maria," I manage. "Listen, please don't say anything to Alex, to anyone, until I can talk to Ryan. And Jacob."

Oh my God.

"Yeah, of course, it's not mine to tell. Listen, sweetie, please call me later, let me know you're okay. Whatever this is, whatever happens, I'm here. You're not alone."

———

I call Ryan. He doesn't answer.

In fact, my call goes straight to voicemail.

"Your call has been forwarded to an automated message system." *Where is he?* "At the tone, please record your message. When you have finished recording, you may hang up or press one for more options. To leave a callback number, press five."

What happened to "Hey, it's Ryan. Leave me a message, and I'll call you back. Have an awesome day"?

I debate about what to say for a few seconds and end up with "Call me. I need to talk to you."

I send a text saying the same thing. His last message, sent last night, is stacked above mine: "so sorry – don't forget – laoy."

Last night, it took me a second to figure out the acronym—"love all of you." Now I focus on the "so sorry" part.

I sit—silent, numb, unsure of what to do. I don't know what to think. What to feel. I wait for anger, despair, or sadness to boil up to the surface. For some reason, I see Jacob's face from just a few minutes ago—was that just a few minutes ago?—and I am filled with empathy. What if we've both been blindsided?

I get up. It's the only thing I can do.

Maria's right, though. I'm not alone.

The tinted glass door sucks inward as I open it to leave the building. The sunshine is so bright it hurts my eyes. I fumble for my sunglasses, squinting. And then there he is, leaning up against the side of my car. I can see the top of his head, dark hair glinting with reflected light, his eyes on the phone in his right hand.

My heart rate increases with each step. If Maria is right, what have I done?

———————

"Jacob?"

My husband looks up, drops his phone in the pocket of his black slacks, and pushes away from the SUV. Without a word, he opens his arms.

Without a word, without thinking, I walk into them.

THIRTY-THREE

MY CHEEK RESTING on his shoulder, I close my eyes and breathe in Davidoff Cool Water. It's as familiar to me as the sound of his voice or the feel of his hands holding me close. He's been wearing the same scent since I met him. I used to buy him a new cologne every Christmas for his stocking. He would thank Santa and dutifully try them, and yet he always returned to the Cool Water. A few years ago, I quit the new cologne campaign and learned to appreciate that wearing this was so Jacob. Calm. Cool. Collected.

His embrace is warm.

Where do we go from here? What am I going to do?

"I'm sorry," he murmurs into my hair. "I shouldn't have run out of there."

Run out? I had assumed he was angry or disgusted. The idea of Jacob running away is shocking to me. Jacob, the lifeguard and first responder, running away from a crisis?

"I couldn't stand being in there with that guy hearing our lives bare and open like that. It's not that I . . ." I feel him sigh. "I'm not good at this, Kate. All I knew was I needed space. I wanted to scoop you up and run with you. I would have, if I'd thought you'd let me."

Jacob releases his hold, tilts my face up toward his. His eyes are damp.

"What happened to you, what your brother did, and his friends…"

I watch him trying to contain himself and failing. Seeing him in pain is painful; I don't want to see it, and I suddenly realize how awful it must have been for him all these years, watching me fall apart.

"You have nothing to be ashamed about. What they did to you was criminal, unforgiveable." His face contorts into an unrecognizable mask. "I want to kill the sonofabitch."

Jacob enraged is frightening; I believe he could do it.

The last few days, I've believed I could do it too.

With some effort, he begins to reassemble his features into the Jacob I know.

"And when I . . . well, it all makes sense to me now, why what I did . . ." He pauses. "I'm so not good at this. What I'm trying to say is that I can't comprehend the shit you've had to overcome. And all these years. That you didn't think you could tell me? That you were keeping this all inside? It makes me feel this—I don't know how to explain—this hole in my chest, like I've failed you in some incredibly big way. But the idea that what your brother did could make me love you less? That's simply wrong." His voice breaks as he goes on, "I know I've told you before, and I'll keep telling you—I love you, Kate. These last couple months, even though we've been fighting, my world just seems flat without you."

A car pulls into the parking space next to mine, reminding me where I am. Where we are. I have grown accustomed to crying in public, but the idea Jacob would do so adds to the surreal nature of this day.

"All I want," he says, his voice unsteady, "*all* I want is for us to be together again. To be a family. You, Logan, Becca—you are what matters to me, nothing else."

Nothing else matters. Oh, how I hope this is true. But how much can he take? My fucked-up past, potential betrayal by his best friend, definitive betrayal by his wife with said best friend?

When I don't say anything, he looks out over my shoulder, back at the building. With the back of his hand, he wipes along his cheekbone.

"Look, like I said, this introspection thing is hard for me, but"—
he drops his gaze back to me—"I have learned a couple of things these
last few weeks. When I said I want to be there for you and the kids . . ."

He tilts his head downward, pulls his lips into a taut line: his disappointed face. "I don't want my family to feel like they can't tell me
things that matter. It's not only you and what you said in there. I heard
Becca crying the other night. When I went in to talk to her, I could
tell she was forcing herself to stop. She told me nothing was wrong."

Wait, I think, *he's disappointed with himself?*

"I want to be better, and if you give me the chance, I promise I
won't hurt you ever again the way I did."

But what if he didn't hurt me that way at all?

I have to tell him about Maria's call, about what I've done. Just
not here, not in the parking lot.

I need to do this right—no blindsiding, no rogue waves.

"Can we get in the car?" I ask, opening the locks with a press of
the button on my key. "I need to talk to you."

——————

Jacob hasn't talked to Ryan since Saturday afternoon. They parted ways at
the indoor go-kart track after taking a few practice spins. "He said he was
heading over to the house to return your phone. Did he not show up?"

"No—I mean, yes, he showed up." He showed up, helped me
block Daniel, kissed me, and left. "I tried to call him just a bit ago and
it went straight to voicemail, a new voicemail."

"Do you need him for something? Can I help you with it?"

My phone buzzes, vibrating. I look down, see *Rick Engle.*

Aftermath.

Daniel.

Not now. I press decline.

Oh, how I would like to have a book on how to handle this
situation. I am ill equipped. Should I talk to Jacob about my call with
Maria and Alex's account of that fateful evening? Should I talk to
Ryan first and get the story from him? And what about the rest?

"Kate?"

"Jacob, there's something I need to tell you."

As these words leave my mouth, I remember Jacob saying these same words to me in the kitchen when he told me about the stripper. I remember the confusion and rush of emotions. I remember how I wished I'd never known. I want to spare him this. *Is not telling protecting him or deceiving him?*

Jacob's expression is not from his normal set, though I think I recognize it—it's openness.

"Okay," he says softly. "It's okay."

I am about to hurt this man in ways he does not deserve.

"It's complicated. I'm not sure how to even start."

Jacob's eyes and mouth scrunch slightly, like he's trying not to say something, before he restores, with some effort, the open look, with a hint of an encouraging smile.

"Just start and you'll find your way."

My phone vibrates again. Rick Engle again.

Why?

Daniel.

I pick up the phone. "I'm so sorry. I need to take this. It's the company that's cleaning my father's house."

"The what?" Jacob asks.

"I'm so sorry," I repeat before answering, "Hello?"

"Mrs. Whittier? Rick Engle here. I'm afraid—well, ma'am, I'm afraid I'm calling with some very unfortunate news."

"Unfortunate news?"

Jacob is not yet as numb as I am. His expression changes from open to concerned. I feel nothing. Well, that's not entirely true. I actually feel a bit relieved, since for this one moment I can stop thinking about Ryan. The irony that anything to do with Daniel could be a relief does not escape me.

"Yes, ma'am. I'm actually not sure about the protocol in a situation of this nature. Perhaps I should have waited to speak with the police."

"The police? What did my brother do? Did he threaten someone?" Jacob cocks his head. His body has stiffened.

"No, ma'am. Our crew showed up a bit ago at the property with a private security guard, as we discussed, and, well, they just called me. Apparently, there was no answer, so they used the key to enter the premises and found your brother unresponsive in one of the bedrooms. They called 911, and, uh, they're waiting there for the police and the paramedics."

"Unresponsive?"

"Yes, ma'am. No longer alive. Dead, ma'am. Your brother is dead."

"My father had a heart attack on the front porch." I don't know why I say this. My mind has begun to review the litany of deaths that have occurred there. My mother, my father, my brother, pieces of me throughout.

I stare straight ahead, through the windshield. A bright scarlet hedge of flowers blurs out of focus to a red haze as I process his words.

"This does not appear to have been a heart attack, ma'am. More likely drug-related. Security officer said something seemed off though. The room was oddly clean. Nearly empty, he said. Other than, well, you know, spoon, needle, they found a pencil, some used duct tape. Guy said it looked like maybe the deceased had been stabbed with the pencil—maybe stabbed himself—which also doesn't make a lot of sense. But you know, with users . . . guess what I'm saying is, probably an overdose, though with the circumstances, could have been something else. Either way, I thought you ought to know. It seemed wrong to me you wouldn't know what was happening."

That I wouldn't know what was happening. *Do I know what's happening?* Does anything in my life make sense? Something else, he said. An overdose or something else. The pencil. The pile of dark clothing on the floor. A box in the wrong place. Associations and disassociations. Did I do something to Daniel? No, I couldn't have. There wasn't time. Wasn't time. It would have been impossible for me to fly to San Jose, devise a plan to play a role in my brother overdosing, somehow execute that plan, and return home in time to sleep in my own bed.

The sound of Mr. Engle clearing his throat brings me back. I need to say something.

"Oh, yes, well." Do I thank him? I guess that would be appropriate. "Thank you for calling. I know this goes beyond your job." *Think, Kate, think.* "Maybe . . . could you ask someone to give my number to the police?"

"Of course, ma'am. I am sorry, Mrs. Whittier, truly sorry, to be the bearer of such bad news."

"Thank you," I say. Then I look down at my phone and think, *End this.*

THIRTY-FOUR

MY BROTHER IS DEAD. Of an overdose. Or something else. He died in a super clean bedroom, which must have been mine because every room in the house except my bedroom was filled with shit. I think about the pencil and the frozen alarm clock, lost time and how I wanted him to die, the dark solutions that have been floating in the periphery of my mind. How I prayed Daniel would never talk to Jacob. And though now he never will, it does not matter; I spilled the story to Jacob on Dr. Reynolds's couch—a totally unnecessary preemptive disclosure that cannot be taken back.

Things can never go back to the way they were before.

And it occurs to me everything would have gone so differently if Jacob had not preemptively disclosed his transgression that wasn't actually a transgression before I got the results from Dr. Brachmann's office that fit Ryan's story.

Disclosure. Disassociation. Deceit.

My mind spins to all the things I have yet to tell my husband.

We are sitting in my car, Jacob and I, still in the parking lot. After I finish relaying the conversation with Rick Engle, I notice the radio is on softly in the background. It's tuned to NPR; *The World* is on. I listen to this program on my way to school when I pick up the kids. It registers that Jacob or I need to go get them soon.

"We need to pick up the kids," I manage.

"Let's go together," Jacob says. His voice is gentle. "I'm going to stay with you. I think that's best, for you and the kids."

I nod. Dr. Farber is right—my husband is a good and decent man. How am I going to tell him what Ryan and I have done?

"I'm sorry," I start to say, "about the other things I need to tell you—"

"That can wait, I think," Jacob says, "maybe till we get home? You're right, we need to get the kids, yeah?"

I reach to turn the key in the ignition, my fingers trembling.

Jacob reaches for my hand. "How about I drive?"

I get out of the car, walk around the back. As I pass him, Jacob stops me. "We're going to get through this, Kate. We are."

He is wrong. *I'm going to lose him.* I'm going to lose him, but he deserves the truth.

———

Becca can't stop smiling when she sees we are both in the car to pick her up. Logan tries to behave as though he doesn't even notice, even shushes her when she says, "This is the best day ever."

I'm going to lose this too.

———

Before we get home, the police call. Jacob pulls over and I get out of the car, standing by the side of the curving road that leads to our community entrance. I ask him to take the kids home; I'll walk the rest of the way.

As I listen to the detective assigned to the case talk, my thoughts drift to the times I imagined Daniel following me on this road, and so many others, and it hits me: *Daniel is dead. Gone.* He will never hurt me again. He will never harm my children. He cannot take what is mine.

My phone buzzes as the detective hangs up. A pulse of anticipation darts through me as I glance down at the screen, hoping it is Ryan.

It isn't. It is our wireless carrier with an automated message. I stop walking at the elaborate stone entry façade. Phone Ryan. Standing in front of the iron pedestrian entrance, I punch in the code on the keypad and listen for the click of the unlocking gate. Jarring bell tones fill my ear, followed by a computerized woman's voice—"We're sorry, you've reached a number that has been disconnected or is no longer in service . . ."

And I realize immediately that Maria and Alex's theory is correct. And then another realization hits, equally life-altering: *If I do not tell Jacob the truth about Ryan, I will simply be running and hiding from a new set of dark secrets.*

———

Dr. Farber's tips and techniques for handling stress and her advice regarding tilting at windmills resound in my brain, competing with the swirling emotions that feel like those damn oscillating vibrations Ryan explained to me in the Jeep. It is a wonder that no one else can hear it. I have decided to wait until the children are in bed but now appreciate how difficult it would have been for Jacob to stifle his confession while I was making dinner so long ago. Once you decide to come clean, it is hard to resist the urge to do it straightaway.

———

Jacob and I share the nighttime rituals, alternating rooms. Jacob starts with Becca, reading to her before I tuck her in. Logan no longer wants to be read to or tucked in. Tonight, though, when I am standing in his doorway wishing him a good night's sleep, he leans on his elbow and asks me to come talk to him. I sit down on the edge of his bed.

"Is Dad staying?" His voice is hushed, hopeful.

"I don't know yet. He might stay tonight." I don't want to sugarcoat the situation or make promises I can't keep. I am fully aware that Jacob is not likely to want to stay after I tell him about Ryan. "But you'll see him tomorrow either way."

Logan lies back on his pillow. "I hope he stays."

I hold back tears watching him trying to emulate his father's equanimity before he turns on his side, toward the window.

"Good night, Mom."

I don't trust myself to speak. Silently, I lean over and kiss his temple.

———

Becca's eyes are drifting closed when I enter her room, her hand resting on a sleeping Ophelia. Jacob's voice trails off when he sees me.

"Keep going, Daddy," Becca says through a yawn. "I'm not tired, really."

Jacob closes the book, places it on the night table.

"Mom's here to tuck you in, sweet pea. It's late." He gives her a hug. "We'll read more tomorrow."

Our paths cross. Shoulders touch.

"I'll just go say good night to him," he says. "You okay?"

I nod, turn to Becca. I recall Dr. Farber's advice about shoring up, so when Becca's arms reach out, I hold her close. Ophelia doesn't move.

———

Jacob is in the kitchen, looking out the window, reflected light bright around his darkened figure. I remember the night of his confession—the overcooked pasta, the steam billowing, the condensed water tearing on that very window. I remember the devastation and know that whatever happens, after this night, we'll be forever changed, again.

"There are some things I need to tell you," I begin. "I was going to tell you in the car, before the call about Daniel."

I talk fast, not wanting to lose my resolve.

"I spoke to Maria. She called right after you left Dr. Reynolds's office, before I came out to the parking lot. She called about, well, that night in New York."

"That night?" Jacob's face blanks for a moment, and then he gives me a quizzical look, his eyes narrowed. "Kate, please, with everything else that has happened, can't we—"

"This is different." There isn't a good way to do this. "After my brother called on Saturday, Ryan had my phone. Maria called, and he answered. She thought he was acting—well, 'cagey,' she said, so she talked to Alex about it, and they think—Maria and Alex, that is—they think Ryan lied to you about what happened that night in New York."

The quizzical look is frozen on Jacob's face. "What are you talking about?"

"With the stripper, the . . ." It still hurts to say it, so I don't. "Alex told Maria you weren't interested, that you pushed the girl away and were furious with him and Christoph. He said you'd had so much to drink that you couldn't—well, that maybe that was why you pushed the girl off. Maybe you were embarrassed, or . . ."

Quizzical has dissolved into thinly veiled anger—an expression I don't need help identifying.

"I'm just trying to explain what Maria told me." The irony of the turnaround of this story and the storytelling does not escape me. I trip on, wanting him to know everything she said. "There was no blow job, Jacob. You made it clear you weren't interested, and Alex talked to her after they left the room. She left too, right after they did. Alex apologized to her for you pushing her."

"What?"

"And then she told him Ryan had paid for it—she thought his name was Brian—and she wouldn't give the money back, even though it didn't happen. Alex said only a couple of minutes later he was waiting for a cab on the other side of the street, and you and Ryan came out to flag a cab . . ." My voice slows. "There was no time. It didn't happen. Ryan lied to you."

Jacob's hands go up, fingers spread, in a defensive position. He gives his head a shake, as if to dislodge his thoughts. "That doesn't make any sense, Kate. What about the infection?"

"I don't know for sure, but it's possible I've had it for a long time—since before us—and it just showed up now, maybe because I was stressed. The nurse told me sometimes that happens; it doesn't need to mean someone cheated. She told me when she called with the results. I just couldn't believe it because, well, with what was happening, it made more sense that—"

"So," Jacob says, shaking his head again, slowly, "you're saying Ryan paid for something he knew could ruin our marriage, lied to me about what happened, and let us both believe I gave you an STI? That's not possible. Ryan wouldn't do that—not to me. Hell, not to you either."

"I know it's hard to believe—it's hard for me to believe—but there's no reason for Alex not to tell us the truth, Jacob. No reason at all."

"And there's a reason for *Ryan* to not tell the truth? That makes even less sense. Think, Kate," Jacob says, his tone blunt, forceful. "What you're saying is our best friend tried to make this happen, lied to us both, and watched our marriage—no, our family, *his* family—fall apart." He's indignant. "There's no way he'd do that. No way."

As he speaks, I feel my shoulders rising up, folding in as if to protect my heart. I force myself to exhale.

"I mean, it makes no sense," Jacob goes on. "What possible reason would Ryan have to do that to me? To us?"

What he is saying is a logical argument but an odd one. Jacob would rather believe he did something he didn't do than believe Ryan knowingly did something to hurt him. My husband is beyond a good and decent man. He is a better person than I will ever be. I don't deserve him. This is a truth no one will ever doubt.

"Alex and Maria are wrong, Kate. Ryan would never do that." His hands drop. His expression hardens. His eyes narrow again. "They're wrong."

"I don't think they're wrong, Jacob." It's time. "There is a reason." I can feel my insides splintering. "A reason for Ryan to want our marriage to fall apart."

Jacob stares at me.

"He told me he's in love with me, that he's been in love with me for years." My chest is crushed between an internal balloon and an external brick. I take a shallow breath, hoping it will lessen the pressure. It doesn't. It is a familiar yet odd feeling—because while I am accustomed to the pain, this time it is not just for myself; it is for Jacob. The thought crosses my mind—*Have I made a huge mistake telling him this? Would it have been better to lie?*—followed almost instantaneously by *You owe him the truth.* And then I am overcome with empathy—not only for what is happening here and now but for what he went through the night of the overcooked pasta, when he confessed to me. I want his pain to stop. And I cannot stop it.

"What?" Jacob breaks his silence. "He loves you? You mean—"

"Yes, that's what I mean."

We both fall silent. He looks down. So do I.

Jacob breaks the silence again. "When did he tell you this. When did he tell you he loved you?"

I knew my confession would lead to this, yet I am crushed. *Get it out, Kate, get it out in the open.*

"He told me after . . . after we . . ."

Jacob gives me a "Don't go there" look, and I stop. I think again about that night, the night when I began to fall apart, and how our roles have now reversed. How I am destroying my husband.

"Do you love him?" he asks.

"I thought I did . . . that night. It was just one night. I know," I say quickly as Jacob opens his mouth to speak, stopping him, "I know that doesn't matter. Please try to understand, I thought we might not figure things out, you and me, and I was so lost, and he was there through that whole thing with my father and the house and . . . and he was so . . ."

It comes back to me, the longing, now like a punch in my gut.

"Do you love him, Kate?" Jacob repeats.

Honesty sucks.

"I did," I choke out. I look at my husband, recognize my own anguish in his face, almost unbearable. "Right then, I did."

He is moving before I understand what is happening. Toward the door.

"Where are you going?"

"Are you kidding? I'm going to find him."

"He won't be there," I say, with conviction. Somehow I know—he won't. "He disconnected his phone. He's gone, Jacob."

I reach for Jacob's arm. He jerks it up and away. I follow him to the door leading to the garage. He slams his hand against the square gray panel, and the door behind my SUV swings up. I reach again for his arm. "Please don't go. Please. He's not there."

"You don't know that." He turns, gives me a withering look. I drop my hand. "Go back inside, Kate. Give me *something* here. Go back inside."

Seconds turn to minutes. Minutes to an hour. I pace for some time—marble, carpet, marble—thinking how it has all gone so wrong. Wondering how anything can ever be right again. Finally, I sit on the floor in the front hallway, leaning against the cold marble wall. Waiting. Waiting. Trying not to think about deceit and death and disassociation.

When he returns, I don't need the house's double beep alert. I've been watching for the lights of the SUV.

"Go to bed, Kate," he says when he sees me. He's solemn; his eyes are dark. "I've got nothing to say."

"Was he there?"

"No, he wasn't." He turns his back to me and moves toward the guest room.

"I need to explain," I implore. "Please, can we talk about this?"

"I can't do this right now." He continues to walk away. "You need to give me some time."

I stand there, in the middle of a carpet runner, and watch him enter the guest room and close the door behind him. Firmly but quietly.

THIRTY-FIVE

THE CLOCK READS 6:04 A.M. when I hear the double beep.

I make the marble, carpet, marble walk down the hallway. The guest room is empty. There is no trace of Jacob having slept there. His car is still parked at Dr. Reynolds's office. He must have called a car service to come get him.

At seven fifteen, he sends me a text message: "I think it would be best for the children to stay with me tonight. I will pick them up from school. I will let you know when I am ready to talk."

He does not answer his phone. I try his office. Shelby tells me he called to say he wouldn't be coming in, that he was working from home. "Isn't he there, Mrs. Whittier?"

He is not. And there is no sign of him at his rented house. I drive by twice before parking, ringing the bell, knocking, calling out to him.

I go through the motions of living. Trying not to feel. Hoping I stay here. Now.

Waiting. For what, exactly, I don't know.

———

Aftermath takes care of drug-related death cleanups as well. Mr. Engle calls to tell me they can incorporate the second job into the first without any additional costs. *Two for one*, I think, though Mr. Engle wouldn't

281

use such a tacky phrase. I think he feels sorry for me. Two sudden deaths in the same family within the same week in the same house.

———————

On Wednesday afternoon, Jacob sends me another text, asking if I can pick up the kids from school. He will fetch them from our house at five thirty when he gets done with a meeting he cannot cancel.

Running doesn't help. Steaming doesn't help. I can't read the newspaper without my hands starting to shake. I find myself longing for an episode of dissociation.

The pickup line is long. When I pull into the curved driveway at the school, there are only twenty or so children left, standing in small clusters. Logan is with Becca, his hand protectively resting on her shoulder. The moment he gets in the car, he tells me he received an email from Uncle Ryan saying he's nailed a huge, undercover, "can't pass it up" assignment, that he's terribly sorry he won't be able to make it to his go-kart party. He sent something.

"Can we go check the mail?" Logan asks.

So we do. The box is full: catalogs, grocery circulars, a few bills, and two packages from Amazon—a small white box bearing Logan's name and a small brown cardboard box addressed to me, which Becca begs me to open right away. Inside is an amethyst-colored kaleidoscope with a swirling curlicue design, made of some kind of heavy plastic or Plexiglas—unbreakable outside, broken bits inside.

Logan is distracted, reading the cover of the game box he received.

Becca asks me how the kaleidoscope works, so I show her, and she sits spellbound, holding it up to the light as we drive away from the post office.

"It's beautiful, Mommy. And it's purple. Is it for me?"

"It is, Becca," I decide without hesitation. "It's for you."

My eyes fill with tears as I glance back at her in the rearview mirror, remembering myself at her age, fascinated by the shifting shapes and colors, amazed that I could create such beauty.

At home, I sort through the mail and find a plain white envelope stuck between two bills and the Costco magazine. Addressed to me: Katie Rose Whittier. Block letters, no return address, postmarked San Jose. At first I think it is from Daniel, one last posthumous Barton family gift. Then, rereading the name, "Katie Rose," I rip it open.

Folded inside is a single sheet of paper. Ryan's unmistakable handwriting.

At the top, centered: "What If." Under that, "Burn After Reading."

KR—

Last year, I was following some climbers for a story on El Capitan, and one night, as I watched a star fall in the dark expanse over the valley, revelation struck—I was about to outlive my parents' lifespan, but only just, because I, too, was running out of time. I lay there, recalling an interview with a woman who'd lost her husband on Everest. She told me she knew, from the start, that loving him was risky and conflicted. That he would never stop climbing, never stop taking chances. But she loved him enough to lose him to the only thing he loved as much as he loved her. She said having him for a short time was worth all the pain. I lay there, thinking of you.

Of you, and Jacob.

And I knew right then that if I died without loving you, I would not have lived. I had nothing—and everything—to lose.

I have hurt the two people I love most. I will carry this with me until the day I die.

But when that day comes, I will know, now, that I have lived.

And you are safe. You and Becca and Logan are safe.

Remember this, Kathryn Rose Barton Whittier . . . you are beautiful and eminently loveable. All of you.

Forgive me. Love him fully. He's the better man.

Signed with a huge, sloppy X and a trailing R.

THIRTY-SIX

AT 5:30 P.M., the doorbell rings.

It is Jacob, which shouldn't surprise me, because he makes it a rule to be prompt. I wonder, though, why he rang the bell.

"Are the kids ready?" He stands outside the doorway, his expression inscrutable. I yearn for the old, open-book Jacob.

I nod. "I think so."

He turns, takes a step back toward his car. "Can you tell them I'm here?"

"Do you want to come in?"

He continues to walk away.

"Jacob, please," I plead. "There's something I need to show you, a letter from Ryan."

He stops, still facing away. "Jesus, Kate."

"It's postmarked from San Jose." I wait for a response that doesn't come. "About hurting us both, about why he did it, about his parents dying and keeping me and the kids safe. It's cryptic, but I think he may have done something to Daniel."

I do not say that until I received Ryan's letter, I'd continued to wonder if it might have been me that had done something to Daniel. I do not mention the dark clothing I don't recall wearing or my mother's

285

box being moved without a memory of moving it or imagining Daniel blowing his brains out on heroin. What I say is "I may not deserve the chance to ask you for anything, but I want you to understand what happened—at least I want to try to explain it."

He turns. His face is hard, stoicism personified. With four strides, he is past me. "I'll be in my office."

I follow him in, watch his straight back as he makes his way down the hall. I walk past his office and into my bedroom and then into the closet, where I open the top drawer with the hidden jewelry compartment where I stashed Ryan's letter.

And then I go to find Jacob. He is sitting behind the desk in his office, reading glasses on. I hand him the envelope.

"I'll be outside," I say, gesturing with my head to the lounges by the pool.

I sit there, upright, at the edge of a lounge chair, listening to the waterfall, feeling the sun on my face. It is there that Jacob finds me, a piece of paper in one hand, a black gas lighter in the other. He hands me the letter, then reaches for my free hand.

"Shall we?" he asks, looking over at the fire pit we rarely use.

Together, we watch Ryan's letter burn. My eyes smart. I tell myself it's because of the smoke.

"I'm . . . I'm so sorry," I say, softly, as the flames flicker out.

"I talked to Alex and Christoph," Jacob says. "And Maria. He betrayed us both, Kate. He betrayed us all." He picks up the lighter from the edge of the pit. "I've been doing a lot of thinking the last couple of days, well, the last couple of months, but this last bit was . . ." He sighs. "It wasn't easy. It's going to take time, and I don't know, I can't promise anything—but we've got to start somewhere. Maybe tomorrow morning we can try to talk—here, or maybe take a walk on the beach?"

Sadness washes over me as I look at him, trying to keep his face a mask and failing.

"A walk on the beach," I repeat.

He nods, just barely.

Tears prick. I nod back, just barely.

"Tomorrow morning, then, eight thirty, by the stairs where we used to meet when I was a guard," he says.

I nod again, daring to hope, wondering, *Can we possibly fix this?*

THIRTY-SEVEN

THE SMELL OF ROASTING TURKEY, melted butter, and sage lingers in the kitchen after I close the oven door and check the time. One hour in and it's starting to turn light brown inside the huge plastic oven bag Maria suggested using, claiming, "It seriously could not be any easier." My only experience, admittedly limited, is with the traditional basting method—the one to which Jacob is accustomed, the one he's seen Grace's cook, Ellie, use year after year. I so wanted Jacob and the kids to feel they hadn't given up the tastes of a Whittier Thanksgiving that I actually called her— Ellie, that is, not Grace— and asked for advice.

"Use the bag," Ellie whispered before giving me the recipe for the stuffing. "Trust me, it's what's inside that matters to your husband."

This morning, Jacob watched me for a minute before he offered to finish cutting the apples and walnuts, murmuring, "Ellie's stuffing."

All four of us are fully engaged. Starting with our "super big brunch," so labeled by Logan, the kitchen has been bustling all day. Logan is on the sweet potato and carrot puree. The carrots are sautéing in a pan of water and butter and the sweet potatoes are in the bottom oven. Becca has the mashed potatoes. The potatoes are peeled and in the pot of water, waiting to be turned on when her phone alarm alerts her. Jacob has pulled a bottle of cellared vintage reserve wine from our wedding-year stash intended for anniversaries, saying "it seems appropriate somehow to celebrate we're here together—trying—don't you think?"

The table is set with Whittier china, glistening antique crystal and silver, though the placement of each plate, glass, and fork is far from Grace-approved alignment since the kids were in charge. The flowers, selected from our garden and arranged by Becca in a purple plastic container that used to hold straws, are splendidly colorful and haphazard—a little bit of Barton.

———

We aren't all better yet, Jacob and I. We're taking it slow, learning new ways to fit together again, and we have a long way to go—but we're moving in the right direction. Literally, moving. This Thanksgiving weekend will be our last in the big house. The truck is coming next Friday to relocate the essentials to a rental the kids and I found in an eclectic neighborhood near the beach, not far from Jacob's.

"A fresh start," Jacob calls it.

He and I are looking into joining a coed beach volleyball group, as a team. Logan is thrilled we'll be biking distance from the donut shop. Becca worried about changing schools next year until Jacob explained she'll make friends in the new neighborhood, adding, "Change can be good."

I tend to believe he means it. I have heard the conversations he's been having with his mother. Not overheard—no need to lurk outside his office after he scoots off to "take the call somewhere quiet," as he used to—no, this past week Jacob has called Grace or taken her calls within my earshot intentionally. Until yesterday, I'm pretty sure Grace thought the whole Thanksgiving-on-our-own thing was a cruel hoax or ploy and Jacob would call her from the airport announcing we had landed and were on our way to the compound. Until yesterday, I admit, I was worried he might cave—even after I bought the turkey and all of the fixings. He hasn't, though. In fact, if anything, he actually seems to be enjoying this new approach to his mother.

"Mother, please, you're obviously not listening to me."

Head shaking.

"No, you're not."

Pause.

"Okay, well then you're not hearing what I'm saying. We're not coming. We're going to give thanks for being here, at home, with the kids."

Another head shake.

"Yes, just the four of us. No, not Ryan, he's away."

A glance my way.

"Because this is home, Mother, this is our home. My home is with Kate and the kids."

A bittersweet, tight-lipped smile in my direction.

"I'm sorry that you aren't happy about this."

Loopy hand gesture, indicating she's going on and on.

"Yes, I understand this isn't how it's always been done, but change can be good."

And with that, his features shift, and I recognize a look from the unspoken vocabulary he always shared with Ryan—the "we're in this together" glance.

We are, I hope.

Jacob has also expressed an interest in reading some of my mother's writing. Last night he asked if maybe I could find a piece or two that would help shed light on who she was. So, after checking on the turkey's progress, I pull a few of the notebooks out of the box and head outside. I find it's still easier to read them outdoors. Besides, it's a gorgeous day—bright, sunny yellow, with a Crayola sky-blue sky. The scent of freshly mown grass mingles with rosemary bushes blooming near the pool.

I lie on the pale-green Aqua Float, listening to Logan, Becca, and Jacob playing a game of sorts in the sand nearby as I flip page over page of lined paper, dry and crinkly on the edges from years lying in that mildewy cardboard box. I've begun debating what to do with most of it after I've read it once over.

Some of it is worth keeping—fascinating, illuminating, bright, broken, and beautiful. Some of it is viscerally frightening—at times, it seems, my mother's mental illness negatively refracted her thoughts like some sort of fun-house mirror, twisting her internal reflections. While I'm not afraid, per se, to keep the entire box, I also don't want to become a hoarder, holding on to things solely because they exist. On the flip side, if I throw pages away, I wonder if my vivid imagination will take me along with them from trash bin to truck to landfill, decaying slowly. I consider Dr. Farber's suggestion about burning them and throwing the ashes in the ocean—how it might be therapeutic, liberating.

The jury is out as to whether that particular technique worked with the last written gift I received.

I still think about Ryan. I wonder where he is and whether we will ever see him again. What he did and what he might have done. Why. I think about whether there were clues I didn't see or want to see. I think about the box of prescription pills I found under his sink and the sorrowful tinge of his skin the last time I saw him and the words "only just" in his letter. I found myself weeping in the Vons parking lot a few days ago, questioning what was real and what was just a story, thinking about the tension on that fine line between love and hate.

He wrote to Jacob and each of the kids, postcards sent from faraway lands, no return address expected. Promised to write again. Though it's our first Thanksgiving without him, Logan and Becca have bought the undercover trip story Ryan has provided. To them, he will remain Peter Pan and Indiana Jones rolled into one.

Jacob and I have begun to discuss Ryan's Pied-Piper characteristics—his willingness to lead people to destruction. What it all means. Where we would be without his what-ifs.

Back to the task at hand.

Though I find poetry exposition daunting, I figure that at least my mother's poems are brief and a few of them have lines that rhyme. Also, I recall from my one miserable foray into poetry in high school that there can be myriad interpretations. We can't really get it wrong; who is to say how the words speak to each of us?

Today I've chosen something from the notepad on which her letter to me was written—well toward the back, in blue ink, the only other composition on the pad. Not a single word scratched over, but it appears to be another first draft, this one titled "Life: Repeat as Necessary."

broken
a promise made
shifting shapes
lights fade
teasing, pleasing, fighting, appeasing
remembrances of things that were
and then,
were not
blurred fates
inextricably bound
I am lost.
I am found.

I repeat it several times, falling into its rhythm.

I paddle to the edge of the pool, drop the notebooks on the stone edge, and push off into the center of the water. Floating, I close my eyes, watch the pattern of light change on the back of my eyelids.

The poem echoes in my head until my children's voices break the reverie.

"Cowabunga!" Logan shouts, and I hear a series of three splashes in quick succession. Waves rock the raft. I hold on, watching their bodies, like seals, spinning under the water until the two smaller shapes arc toward me, one on each side. Becca and Logan's slick, wet heads emerge.

"Come and swim with us, Mom," Becca says.

"Marco Polo, I'm it," Logan calls. He dips under the water, his hands up, fingers counting down from ten to one.

I let go. Slide off into the water. My tiptoes reach the bottom as Logan pops up again. "Marco."

Jacob is underwater on the other side of the pool. I can feel something moving below the water's surface on my left—Becca.

I haven't moved fast enough. "Polo" is barely out of my mouth before Logan's hand reaches out to touch my side.

I am found.

His eyes open. "Mom, you didn't even try."

"Maybe she wanted you to find her," Becca says, hiding behind me.

The words of my mother's poem swirl in my head—the cyclical nature and challenge of life. Shifting shapes, promises, memories we allow and those we block, things that are real and those imagined, how intertwined we all remain—Jacob, Ryan, Natalie, Maria, me—how broken, and yet . . .

As the kids swim away, Jacob comes up for air. "You're it?"

I nod and watch my children for a second before closing my eyes. I hear a soft splash as Jacob dives underwater. And then, with my feet firmly on the bottom of the pool, I begin counting backwards from ten, feeling the current of my family all around me.

EPILOGUE

MY FATHER'S HOUSE has been declared safe and habitable, and it will be torn down as soon as probate clears. I've already contracted with a demolition company. They'll pull the permits, raze it with a hydraulic excavator, and remove the debris "down to the dirt."

When I was getting an estimate from my new contractor, Wendell ("Call me Dell") Brandt, he asked if there was anything inside the home we wanted to keep or donate.

"Any family heirlooms, antiques, or picture albums that might be tucked away on a closet shelf?"

"If there is one thing I know for certain, Dell, it's that there's nothing in that house I ever want to see again. Maybe you could send me a photo of the empty lot when you're done."

"I get it, Ms. Whittier. And you ain't the first. I always say not everyone can be the Waltons. I did notice a bit of wild grass and clover in the back—maybe we should leave those, eh?"

Dell has a folksy way about him. I'll probably never meet him in person, but I can imagine how he appears—salt-and-pepper hair, solid build, face and hands that bear witness to hard work outdoors. Straightforward. No bullshit. And he did get it—not everyone can be the Waltons.

It will be a while before I get the photograph of the lot, down to the dirt, with some wild grass and clover.

I can wait.

RESOURCES

Mental health resources

- NAMI (National Alliance on Mental Illness) https://nami.org

- NIMH (National Institute of Mental Health) https://www.nimh.nih.gov/

- DBSA (Depression and Bipolar Support Alliance https://www.dbsalliance.org/

If you or anyone you know has suffered from abuse, you/they are not alone. Listed below are **a few of the resources available.**

National Sexual Assault Hotline – 1-800-656-HOPE (4673) is a partnership between RAINN and more than 1,000 local sexual assault service providers. RAINN also operates the DoD Safe Help-line for the Department of Defense. They have programs to prevent sexual violence, help survivors, and ensure that perpetrators are brought to justice.

RAINN (Rape, Abuse & Incest National Network)
https://www.rainn.org/after-sexual-assault

The National Sexual Violence Resource Center (NSVRC)
is a nonprofit organization that provides information and
tools to prevent and respond to sexual violence.
https://www.nsvrc.org/find-help

More resources for survivors:

https://www.nsvrc.org/sites/default/files/2014-09/nsvrc_
publications_resource-list_online-resources-for-survivors.pdf

A Guide for Friends and Family of Sexual Violence Survivors:

https://www.pcar.org/sites/default/files/resource-pdfs/friends_
and_family_guide_final.pdf

ACKNOWLEDGMENTS

OVER THE LAST several years, this novel has been in and out of the proverbial drawer, and there were times I doubted it would ever be read by anyone outside my circle of fellow writers, friends, and family. I owe so much to the people who believed in me and encouraged me to put it out into the world. If I have missed someone in compiling this list, please know that if you were there for me at any point, I am grateful.

Thank you—

To the Feisty Writers for their strength, empathy, and wisdom, many of whom beta read this novel at some stage in its life cycle: Donna Brown Agins, Elizabeth Eshoo, Tanya Jarvis, Kimberly Joy, Jen Laffler, KM McNeel, Andrea Moser, Phyllis Olins, Tania Pryputniewicz, Nicola Ranson, Lindsey Salatka, Gina Simmons Schneider, Suzanne Spector, Barbara Thompson, and Nancy Villalobos.

To Marni Freedman, fearless Feisty leader, San Diego Writers Festival co-founder, brilliant writing coach, and dear friend, for her courage to dream big, her energy and enthusiasm, and her unflagging support.

To the writers, coaches, and audiences of So Say We All's VAMP, who gave me the space to tell my stories and tell them better. I never imagined myself repeatedly spilling my guts to a bar full of strangers, but this has turned out to be one of the best things I've ever done—illuminating, healing, and just plain fun.

To those who provided invaluable feedback as beta readers, including my sister Amy Zadeik Anderson, Elizabeth Appelquist, Anisha Bhatikar, Laurie Champion, Noel Dwyer, Michelle Furtado, Tracy J. Jones, Cassandra Morgan, Shiloh Rasmussen, and Janey Williams.

To Kathryne Squilla, Janice Tan, and Krissa Lagos, for their keen editing eyes.

To Jeniffer Thompson, co-founder of the San Diego Writers Festival, host of *The Premise* podcast, and my final beta reader, for her friendship and assurance the novel was ready to go.

To my publishing team at She Writes Press, including Brooke Warner and Samantha Strom, and to my publicist, Caitlin Hamilton Summie—for your time, efforts, guidance, and patience in helping me get this book into the hands of readers.

To my girlfriends (you know who you are) and to the many women I have met in book clubs, salons, and writing groups through the years.

To Deborah Serra, an extraordinary writer, phenomenal human being, and dear true friend through it all—words are not enough.

To my grandfather, Peter Alexander Zadeik, an epic weaver of tales who taught me that embellishments make a story more interesting for the listener, and to my parents, Peter Alexander Zadeik, Jr., and Esther Behling Zadeik, who showed me the meaning of unconditional love and gave me the opportunity to tell "the most important thing that happened to you today" at dinner each night, providing me with my earliest storytelling venue and an audience that had to listen.

To that audience, my siblings—Phil, Amy, Tricia, and Michael—for supporting and loving me from the very beginning, putting up with my red-light, green-light stories, and being some of my favorite people and best friends. I am so very lucky.

And to my husband, Tom, and children, Olivia and Jack—you are my heart, my joy, and my reason for getting up every day. For always being there. Always. This is for you.

ABOUT THE AUTHOR

Michelle Goane

ANASTASIA ZADEIK is a writer, editor, and narrative nonfiction performer. She lives in San Diego, CA, where she serves as Director of Operations for the San Diego Writers Festival and as a mentor and board member for the literary nonprofit So Say We All. *Blurred Fates* is her first novel.

SELECTED TITLES FROM SHE WRITES PRESS

She Writes Press is an independent publishing company founded to serve women writers everywhere. Visit us at www.shewritespress.com.

A Cup of Redemption by Carole Bumpus. $16.95, 978-1-938314-90-2. Three women, each with their own secrets and shames, seek to make peace with their pasts and carve out new identities for themselves.

After Midnight by Diane Shute-Sepahpour. $16.95, 978-1-63152-913-9. When horse breeder Alix is forced to temporarily swap places with her estranged twin sister—the wife of an English lord—her forgotten past begins to resurface.

Fire & Water by Betsy Graziani Fasbinder. $16.95, 978-1-938314-14-8. Kate Murphy has always played by the rules—but when she meets charismatic artist Jake Bloom, she's forced to navigate the treacherous territory of passionate love, friendship, and family devotion.

Glass Shatters by Michelle Meyers. $16.95, 978-1-63152-018-1. Following the mysterious disappearance of his wife and daughter, scientist Charles Lang goes to desperate lengths to escape his past and reinvent himself.

Shelter of Leaves by Lenore Gay. $16.95, 978-1-63152-101-0. When a series of bomb explosions hit on Memorial Day, Sabine flees Washington DC on foot and eventually finds safety at an abandoned farmhouse with other refugees—but surrounded by chaos, and unable to remember her family or her last name, who can she trust?

Stella Rose by Tammy Flanders Hetrick. $16.95, 978-1-63152-921-4. When her dying best friend asks her to take care of her sixteen-year-old daughter, Abby says yes—but as she grapples with raising a grieving teenager, she realizes she didn't know her best friend as well as she thought she did.